PENGUIN MODERN CLASSICS

The Flood

J. M. G. Le Clézio was born on 13 April 1940 in Nice and was educated at the University College of Nice and at Bristol and London universities. His knowledge of English enabled him to work closely with his translator on his debut novel, *The Interrogation*, which won the Prix Renaudot in 1963. Since then he has written over forty highly acclaimed books and has been translated into thirty-six languages. *The Interrogation* is published by Penguin and three of his early novels are now Penguin Modern Classics: *The Flood*, *Terra Amata* and *Fever*. Le Clézio divides his time between France (Nice, Paris and Brittany), New Mexico and Mauritius. In 2008 he was awarded the Nobel Prize for Literature.

J. M. G. LE CLÉZIO

The Flood

Translated from the French by Peter Green

PENGUIN BOOKS

PENGUIN CLASSICS

Published by the Penguin Group
Penguin Books Ltd, 80 Strand, London WC2R 0RL, England
Penguin Group (USA) Inc., 375 Hudson Street, New York, New York 10014, USA
Penguin Group (Canada), 90 Eglinton Avenue East, Suite 700, Toronto, Ontario, Canada M4P 2Y3
(a division of Pearson Penguin Canada Inc.)
Penguin Ireland, 25 St Stephen's Green, Dublin 2, Ireland
(a division of Penguin Books Ltd)
Penguin Group (Australia), 250 Camberwell Road,
Camberwell, Victoria 3124, Australia (a division of Pearson Australia Group Pty Ltd)
Penguin Books India Pvt Ltd, 11 Community Centre,
Panchsheel Park, New Delhi – 110 017, India
Penguin Group (NZ), 67 Apollo Drive, Rosedale, North Shore 0632, New Zealand
(a division of Pearson New Zealand Ltd)
Penguin Books (South Africa) (Pty) Ltd, 24 Sturdee Avenue, Rosebank, Johannesburg 2196, South Africa

Penguin Books Ltd, Registered Offices: 80 Strand, London WC2R 0RL, England

www.penguin.com

First published as *Le Déluge* by Editions Gallimard 1966
First published in Great Britain by Hamish Hamilton Ltd 1967
Published in Penguin Classics 2008
3

Copyright © J. M. G. Le Clézio 1966
Translation copyright © Peter Green, 1967
All rights reserved

The moral right of the author and translator has been asserted

Printed in England by Clays Ltd, St Ives plc

Except in the United States of America, this book is sold subject
to the condition that it shall not, by way of trade or otherwise, be lent,
re-sold, hired out, or otherwise circulated without the publisher's
prior consent in any form of binding or cover other than that in
which it is published and without a similar condition including this
condition being imposed on the subsequent purchaser

978-0-141-19140-9

www.greenpenguin.co.uk

Penguin Books is committed to a sustainable future
for our business, our readers and our planet.
The book in your hands is made from paper
certified by the Forest Stewardship Council.

AT the beginning there were clouds, and more clouds, heavy, black, blown by intermittent gusts of wind, contained within a ring of mountains on the horizon. Everything began to grow dark, objects took on a regular pattern, lapped scales like thin blades of steel, or chain-mail, that frittered away what little brightness still remained. Other objects, themselves sources of light, began to flicker feebly and unhappily, overwhelmed by the vast proportions of some ill-defined yet imminent happening, made ridiculous by the mere fact of comparison to this enemy (as it were) against whom they had to sally forth and do battle. The movement gradually faltered, not through any loss of intensity or change in approach, but because its impetus was exhausted by the effort to hold up the advance of this freezing universal oblivion—its very stillness imbued with a quality of eternity—now creeping on, and on, biting into the earth, swallowing it inch by inch, infiltrating any manifestation of activity, breaking up the established harmonies of contrast, penetrating to the core of all matter, annihilating the very origins of life itself. Delicate and paper-light, the texture of darkness lay upon every surface, creating a multiplicity of silhouettes, and enhancing the intensity of such brightness as there was to a quite remarkable degree, so that a single point of light, reflected from the broken glass lying along the sidewalk, where the water-truck had crushed it, blazed out for something like a hundred light-years over an area bordering on infinity, and with the fierceness of three or more suns.

Any part of the view—as it might be four hundred square yards of concreted surface, occupied by buildings made with cement and steel girders—now seemed a kind of weird glacial desert—a desert set down on top of the living soil, a tidy, planned desert, at once accommodating and abrasive, and self-contained, that is, equipped with an absolute, all-inclusive scheme of things, in which movement of bicycle + wilderness of streets echoing women's footsteps + trickle of water seeping along a crack in the macadam + railings in sharp perspective + an almost complete absence of loud, shattering noises + fourteen storeys + cold air in frozen blocks like slabs of marble and a flurry of artificial rain smelling of polythene indicated the exact steps that had to be taken, plotted the rules of the inhuman game.

The various elements—all sorted and classified in their card-index universe—rearranged themselves in accordance with this new factor (time of day, atmospheric pressure, degree of humidity and temperature) and quickly produced a terrible, diabolical image, which allowed for every move being played several times over, an infinite number of times. A children's maze, in which all the paths converged on the same spot, opposite the site of the buried treasure, where pirate and crocodile lay in wait together. A strange world, hard and infallible, in which not the tiniest rivulet flowed at random, not a single flower protruded through the protective asphalt, not a tree lived, not a door was opened, not one cigarette fell and was stubbed out, unless it was so willed by that vast, solitary, nameless demiurge who parcelled out all things in the world, set his mark upon them, and bound them into the structure of his formal pattern.

A world in which all objects, every atom could be expressed by the letter A, and every happening and construct, of whatever sort, traced out the formula of the magic square:

$$A \ A \ A \ A$$
$$A \ A \ A \ A$$
$$A \ A \ A \ A$$
$$A \ A \ A \ A$$

—that is to say, in which they kept up a constant process of simplification and purification, until the moment (impossible to describe it) was reached at which event and object, chain and link, were merged in a single phenomenon, A. The moped moved along the section of street between corner X and street-lamp Y, with a fading sound and reflected light glinting out from its hubs. But the moped as such was limited to this particular stretch of street, to the sound it made, to a glitter of light. In a moment its motion would be arrested, perhaps for a thousand years, or alternatively it might repeat, again and again, that quick, rhythmic passage from corner X to street-lamp Y, till the movement itself became the expression of its being. The rain would always go on falling here, the sidewalk would stretch away to the right for all eternity, yet both would be something different, rain and side-walk no longer; there would be no more moped, no more corner, no more street-lamps, either lit or unlit, no more peeling walls, no more sounds of chains or wet tyres, no more bleak, chilly smells or dew-heavy smoke-drift hanging in mid-air; instead there would be a small, peaceful, undisturbed picture, a still-frozen image, dead before it had a chance to achieve immortality, part of a game which was no longer understood. Like pictures with such titles as 'View of Port-Louis and the Pic des Tois-Mamelles', or 'The Crossing of the Beresina', or 'Engraving of the Thames and the Houses of Parliament', and so on. Everything would come to this in the end. Meanwhile the water went on trickling down the gutters, and a whole host of small objects floated this way and that in the puddles along the road. It was the beginning.

Yet this was without importance, because from the moment the game began, the world had ceased to be—and to have been. There was a certain number—a little above the predictable average—of ideal curves and perfect angles. These were the last to fall, since they embodied, over and above such things as 'Imbert and Phelippeau Building' and 'Rue Paganini' and 'War Memorial' and 'Atlantis Cinema', various intellectual concepts—not to mention a number of vague and ill-defined smells, such as those of smoke, or earth, or cooking soup, or even smells *tout court*, adaptable to hundreds of different requirements. In the same way colours, though tagged with a name three-quarters of the time, could conjure up an illusive sense of abstraction. Reds, whites, browns, greens, blues—it was often because of them that the landscape began to split and crack apart.

3

A patch of white, for instance, might constitute the initial fissure; then, as on a sheet of glass or a frozen lake, other fissure-lines would radiate out around this central crack. Starting from the point of white, the break-up would spread and deepen visibly, gradually disintegrating both the object and its context. The sequence produced: white—round—pale light—3 m. 12 cm.—humming and flickering—heat—steel, bronze, smelting—verticality. . . .

Gently the fissure would expand and encroach, so that, viewed in perspective, one object could break up another by a simple process of superimposition. Similar movements were being set up at countless different points, and the mere prolongation of two straight lines, in accordance with roughly geometrical principles, was enough to do the trick. Each fresh viewpoint increased the fragmentation of matter, so that it became an easy matter to achieve the demolition of a twelve-storey apartment block, with 198 windows, in less than sixty seconds. A series of these windows (the light glinting off them took on a violet tinge) would initiate the movement and then repeat it inexhaustibly, so that the ascending progression became generalized upward motion. This spatial development was accompanied by a parallel phenomenon in the time-factor: the extremities of time were looped together, duration bent into a circle, beginning and end merged together, establishing the perfect sphere. Just as the first and the twelfth window were no longer distinguishable, but both subsumed to the same idealized movement of ceasing-to-be and coming-into-being, so the first and the twenty-fourth hour, the first and the sixtieth second, shaken together by the uncertain rhythm of a no longer forward-moving time-sequence, would come and go, achieve and conclude their existence millions of times over, preserved from any progression by some dark hour, by a particular negative second, the retroactive impulse of which—predictable and inevitable as the next tick of a metronome—exemplified a species of mechanical perfection.

This, or something like it, was what must be taking place now at this point on earth, this complex sub-section of the world. It

4

seemed to be decomposing like an animal's cadaver, to all outward appearances intact still, but in reality decaying throughout, tortured and gnawed in all its parts. The walls of houses, the surfaces of the streets, the outlines of apartment blocks, the very air and the noises carried on it—all these, when seen from a distance, had a solid quality about them, reminiscent of bronze or marble; and yet the mere proximity of conscious awareness had a somehow stiffening effect on them, so that they revealed the existence of their own internal rottenness. Under one's scrutiny they swarmed and faded, vanishing darkly behind a veil of clouds and mist. Confusion blurred previously clear outlines, overlaid the colours of down and hair, separated out previously pure elements, broke up the logical order of things, denied the evidence of the senses. Everything was shifting and reverberating simultaneously. There was a sound like the sea, a rumbling stillness, a universal thunderous roar. Mopeds sprouted feathers, men and women were spotted with peacock-eyes, skies took on checkerboard patterns. Hitherto indeterminate colorations formed into patterns of black and white, then regrouped themselves according to their two basic and contrasting characteristics, light against dark. The expression of form was reduced to a schematic minimum—straight line, spiral, angle. Sounds, smells, silhouettes, all hived off into their separate groups, teamed up afresh. Slowly and quietly a kind of vast, meticulous fresco was coming into being, an unchecked, passionless advance by sappers from one redoubt to the next. Anyone overtaken by the freeze-up very quickly cracked and broke apart; his hot and cold elements sloughed off around his feet like a cast skin, and almost at once his naked body could be seen rising from the confusion, sharp and thin as a knife-blade, and setting its mark on the rest of the process, with a series of distorted movements and nervous twitchings that verged on caricature. Then it would take on the semblance of a statue or an engraving; a few bold strokes and there it was, burning like a torch above the world, a world at long last restored to pristine clarity, to the realm of abstract ideas, indescribable in its vividness and beauty, a species of intellectual hell.

Flight was out of the question: each object and being was caught by surprise, in mid-flight. There was an instant when chaos began, a day on which light began to fade and the outlines of every feature were scribbled, as though in charcoal, on a surface more virgin than paper and harder than any stone. All was enmity and watchfulness; the circle closed little by little, it was as though great ramparts were there, growing thicker, moving closer to one another. The universe was being transformed into a room, its windows opened on to other windows. Men's eyes fabricated a kind of impenetrable barbed-wire entanglement. What had previously been free and variable was now locked in a mad immutable pattern. Objects were replaced by sharp, angular figures, trees were transformed into Turkish scimitars, houses into sharp mountain ridges, flowers to jagged, bristling peaks. The four corners of the horizon swung in towards one another, tilting up vertically. It was like being cut off in a fortress, with the drawbridges going up on every side. It was now that the banked up clouds appeared on the scene, now that the first skirmishing movement towards shadow and darkness began. Cut off from the horizon in every direction, the town now writhed round on itself like some mortally stricken rhinoceros. The wind had turned to stone; though it blew still, there was no movement in it. It had become a monument erected to the memory of movement, and its downward-dragging gravity held a dead weight of millions of tons. In one quarter of this shattered town the forces of cold and silence had established themselves. A two-dimensional boulevard, its chaotic movement frozen into stillness, hung poised in mid-flow. Bare trees renewed the sap in their branches for all eternity. Adjacent blocks of flats gaped vacantly into the void, not yet in ruins, but no longer habitable. The windows that opened from those wan walls still grouped themselves in a regular pattern, but their character had changed; now they were nightmare freaks of fancy, a spectacle as sinister and mechanistic as the windows of a train moving past in a station. They hinted at a phenomenon as disturbing as it was powerful; they were dream-figments of an exhausted brain, which had somehow contrived to by-pass the

6

pitfalls of stupor and oblivion: monotonous, blackened, repetitive features of this burnt-out landscape, ubiquitous and eternal.

There was no further relationship between them save in the context of these endlessly forming vertical or horizontal brick courses. All that had been done at other times and in other places was still contained in them. It was *there*, automatically, undeniably, on the façade of this apartment block; it offered a totality of vision, built up from the cumulative sum of various experiences, various likely inferences, which was self-perpetuating and progressively narrowing down its field. From town to town, from porch to porch, from tree to Cadillac, to railings, back-alleys, streets, corners, finally arriving at this vast white regular plane surface, this wall with its twelve storeys, 198 windows, eighteen doors; with its bustling corridors, its elevators (movements downwards, upwards, sideways), its diagonals, zigzags, lozenges, crosses, and the rest of it. This was where the trail had led to, this many-sounding wall (broken murmur of the rising tide, trains whistling in tunnels, tapping of feet on stone steps, hum of traffic, police car sirens, squeal of tyres, whining jet aircraft). It was there, amongst other places, that the great noisy hall, a kind of ghost-stadium, had come into being: a hall in which the loudspeaker, like a collective mouth, had carved out its particular niche.

Later the façade itself had collapsed. The elements of existence had, if that was possible, contracted still further: the world was shrinking in on itself, like a pool of spilt and evaporating petrol, that seems to move upwards towards some point in the sky as its total area diminishes. It had retreated from the outer edges of the building, withdrawn its frontiers until they comprised only a few rows of windows. For a while it had been contained between the eighth and second horizontal rows, and the tenth and the third vertical ones. Then it had retreated still further, slipping along the wall, tearing loose fragments of light and sound as it went. Now it had reached the last window on the third floor, window number thirty-nine. It was here that life had chosen to maintain itself, an intense and blindingly bright life, a star that concentrated within itself all the hundreds and hundreds of square yards which made

7

up the town. On this square of violet-tinted glass the world had formed a sheer, outjutting mountain, endlessly toppling, collapsing, reforming, marking time, gleaming in rainbow iridescence. Here time still moved on, perhaps, in a film-strip of memories, unleashing its rough blows against the glass, fighting its profound and mysterious battle. It was the core of what used to be termed relativity, colours without colour, nameless names, inaudible sounds, transparent and volatile odours. Window number thirty-nine had stripped bare an entire world, leaving its inhabitants dead or naked, uncovering the harsh peaks and reefs, the bones of existence, all around it. Elsewhere all was blanched white: skeleton squares and streets, the fossil remains of men and dogs lay abandoned here and there beneath the scorching sun of awareness. They aged gently, powdered over with dust and sand, like so many huge shells cast up by the sea. Window number thirty-nine in the block—blacker and more concentrated than a child's eye— drew them irresistibly to itself, sparked off their powder-trails of desire. Parched hair-lines converged on its centre like so many luminous rays. The rain drummed down on these bony relics with a soft, caressing hiss; and between each separate drop of water, each sonorous explosion, there sprang up a spinning vortex of wind which redirected the centrifugal elements towards the centre of the window-pane. The earth's scales were hard and insensitive, like those on a fish's sides. Torpor swam in the air; the great cavern of silence extended its vaulted roof still further. Like a loudspeaker in reverse, the window's gullet swallowed up the sum of all noises in the town, and left nothing but tragic calm behind. No one could look steadily at it without flinching: it was a second sun, black and mournful, spreading out its rays of darkness. Within its globe matter fused, boiled, endlessly bubbling over and through itself. Ice had formed at the heart of the volcano's turbulence: the tension on the glass was so strong that the whole earth seemed to tremble because of it, and the slightest thing, one felt, might trigger off the explosion.

All the cold of earth and sky, too, had met and coalesced here. It had erected its wall, and from this flat surface there proceeded sharp rays like splinters of ice, which pierced through flesh and melted in the very centre of the wounds they inflicted. A new sensation, somewhere between sound, smell and light, had thus been conjured up in the heart of matter; its birth had been helped on and influenced by this confused throbbing rhythm, its heart-beat followed a detectable pattern, it glittered and sparkled with all the appearance of life, and seemed to endure for all eternity. It was an odd mixture of toughness and friability, a dead period between two mysterious dangers, religion perhaps. It was an invisible yet familiar halo, a child-like wavy line, something soft and out of a fairy-tale, like the aureoles worn by saints in holy pictures.

At the heart of this disintegration landscape still existed, a blend of memory and illusion. It bore traces of shadow, fragmentary exercises in relief, haloes the colour of which had faded after being washed clean a thousand times, over and over again. It was undulating, cracking up in all directions, a fleeting and unreal image dancing in a cone of light. First there was the street, just as it had always been, a perfect rectilinear figure, bare, frosty, shrunken. The steely hue of the macadam matching that of the sky. Trees tirelessly growing, dense and black against the snowy backdrop of the walls. Beneath the ground their roots stretched as far as their branches, continually exploring, digging between clods of earth, clutching at crumbling soil, seizing fragments of damp life still crawling with worms and decayed matter, letting them run through their fingers like the sea. Close to the fifteenth blackened plane-tree on the right-hand sidewalk steam was rising from a sewer-vent. The sound of empty cigarette packets being crumpled up mingled with that of footsteps crunching over the ground. A broken beer-bottle, lying beside the circular impression left by some ritually deposited dustbin, continued to rehearse every facet and variety of smashed-up ugliness in the world. At the centre of a smell approximating to that of butane, an aircraft inscribed its cross on the squared chart of the sky, making a thousand more, by implication, on each separate square, repeating the same game, for ever playing a winning gambit against itself.

9

Cbjects previously fleeting and transient were now caught photographically on the ground, against the walls, embedded, as it were, in any plane surface. An empty cigarette-packet, thrown down an hour and a half earlier, lay there on the tarred surface in the cold. Now it was no more than a bright blue patch, a sharply defined area in that vast expanse of brown, roughly rectangular, tending towards shapelessness at the corners, its outline finely sketched in as though with a pen. Any unevenness on it had become a shadow, and nothing more. One ran towards the centre, dividing the printed letters on the label; another towards the bottom left-hand corner; and another one, long and regular, lay striped across the right-hand side. No wind, however strong, could whisk this object away now, no rain could besmirch it, no brush could sweep it up and quickly dispose of it in some dustbin, already stuffed with old newspapers and orange-peel. Whatever anyone might do, whatever action might be taken by the old man in blue who would pass that way during the night, would make no difference. If this empty cigarette-packet were to be removed from its apparent position, it would instantaneously re-create itself, just as a playing-card, removed from the pack, reveals another one beneath it.

So it lay there, floating on that damp, ochre-coloured surface. Silence had invaded the world in a series of concentric circles. An ovoid sun shone back in an infinite series of reflections from the plate-glass: everything glittered, a bright whiteness of pain was all around. Something akin to an atonal musical theme—yet detached from its essential substance—scrawled itself in space like a line of writing, a public graffito endlessly repeating erotic or political catch-phrases. Some sharp, fine motif might well have created a pattern in this context. With the help of a brutal, emphatic rhythm, the concept could have advanced to the point of its own destruction, joining the general negation of colour and substance, mingling with the other sensations, moving forward and back in the pure, regular motion of water enclosed in a kettle, visible still by virtue of this seemingly logical succession of speed and inertia, poised now in equilibrium, tracing out a Byzantine-style decorative motif, sketching a helical pattern, a kind of spiral staircase for ever circling round the walls of a tower, replacing the visual image of darkness and light, concentrating more and more in intensity, yet at the same time expanding, merging with infinity, then coming into violent collision with the rampart of glass and polished steel, the mirror of crudeness and hate, till, stopping short with the final bar of the theme-tune, it planted itself in time like a fatal dagger-thrust, at one point and one only, in the criminal outrage of shattered tonality, with one sound uttered once and for ever, a cry quivering arrow-like at the very heart of the target. Distant horror had usurped the atmosphere. Objects recoiled centrifugally one from the other. Colours exploded like bombs and their fragments rose up in fine powdery clouds. Then they suddenly withdrew from the foreground, became thick curtains, swarms of birds or cicadas, and swiftly sank again in stormy tumult. Outlines broke up into hard, downward-leaning pothooks that flickered along the haze in endlessly repeated patterns. They had no more duration than a lightning-flash, but—like lightning— they burnt themselves permanently into the retina. Other substances, less easily identified, were exploding and volatilizing, a momentary flash, then gone: matter conceived of centrifugal and uncompoundable elements, of botched radiations, already destroyed, without essence or identity. An epoch too soon, or too late, metals came together in fusion. All the mute, colourless, non-material matter secreted by the human brain now floated free, purposeless jetsam.

So at the same time as the nexus of forces had gathered on window number thirty-nine, this mushroom-like growth was expanding over the empty cigarette packet. By now it was considerably more than an ordinary swelling; it had achieved something close to the configuration of a volcano, or the deadly folds and creases thrown up by an earthquake. Stealthily, possessed by the memory of that music and rhythm, of the colour blue, of various tastes and odours, tension had blown up an invisible balloon of air; and this heavy, swollen envelope was now encroaching on the centre of the macadam, oscillating over it like a

II

giant bubble, quivering, turning purple, growling with fury. Then, abruptly, it burst, only to reform a little farther on, against the foot of a street-lamp, in the sky, on a balcony, at the top of some church steeple, over a streak of shadow, in the glint of a bicycle hub, at the heart of a chestnut-tree's elusive scent, on the tip of an eyelid, in the belly of a pregnant woman—in any place where it could swell to bursting point, develop its egg, crush the inert flesh, sprawl over the mud, pollute clear colours, trouble the waters of the air, screw up any part of space, however infinitesimal, and blow up the blister which resembled that made by a red-hot iron.

It was as though the whole world had been laid out by way of public entertainment, with the elements dotted about in space like printer's type. There were no more bicycles, no more old cigarette-packets, no more orange-peel. They all lay about *en masse*, just as though they had been tried, condemned, and executed: chill and melancholy objects, mere refuse now, immobilized by death.

At the bottom of the building there hung a kind of frayed blind. Then came a cigarette-end, an empty box, a stained handbill; and another cigarette-end, another empty box, another handbill. They were no longer attached to any living entity, and it was this fact of withdrawal which alone endowed them with some sort of tangible surface. From a sheet of glossy newsprint carrying the photograph of a Pakistani girl, and a continual, endlessly repeated stream of phrases which told the same vague, semi-legendary story (crammed with dates and proper names—Naaz, Pritibala, Mehmood, Dattaram, Ved Madan, Shashi Kapoor, opp. Tooting Bec 19 18 49), some indefinable pattern was beginning to take on shape and substance. In an arbitrary and random sequence words were replacing fragments of reality, and inscribing themselves one below the other on this white placard-like object, the back (it seemed) of some gigantic poster. This done, they remained there, mere senseless signs now, no longer hoping for decipherment. The letters followed one another (sometimes dropping out of place or even disappearing altogether), detached themselves, fell from sight, were gone. Here, caught in the cold beam of reality, was an abstract, illegible poem, which restored the sense of physical immediacy, of direct contact and understanding. All in an atmosphere of calm, absolute calm, unruffled serenity. The mountains had been flattened, the rivers all drunk dry, and the stains on the earth had dried out: all that remained were words, and still more words, a moving column of them, tapped out in a series of minuscule explosions on the white, jerkily advancing paper. They fastened upon it, bare and solitary as nails, dozens of nails.

```
             12th floor
             11th floor
             10th floor              sun
             9th floor
             8th floor
             7th floor
             6th floor
             5th floor
             4th floor
night        3rd floor               p
             2nd floor               p
             1st floor               p
          choice piece               p
gol          cigarette  tzracks!     p
          ooooo    fold               p
aaa                              charabanc
          tssktipptong!
                he he she
                              'Spada'
tree roof apartment block
             ORANGE
                      Imbert and Phelippeau Imbert and
          currant jelly    January February March Apr
             feather pillow
             macadam
```

Chaos stood revealed, disintegration was complete; and yet from this piece of ground, this pile of sterile refuse, the movement was an upward one, a process of ascension. Each object was a source of radiance, and one let oneself be gently borne up on these rays, in the patient expectation that they would take one to some destination. The universe was constructed like an inverted pyramid; each element produced its angle, and the further one moved from the pyramid's base, the greater grew the area comprehended, opening up like some splendid corolla. Every being and object on this surface, whether alive or dead, was a point from which two lines ran skyward, forming a sign shaped like a waterspout, which tore you free from the grasp of actuality, and inspired you to explore the more easily accessible depths.

Down below the town had been flattened: at some points houses and gardens repeated their two-dimensional geometric pattern *ad nauseam*. A layer of pale, silent cotton-wool padded the roofs and walls. Huge square gleaming blocks rested on the ground. Wires prolonged themselves to infinity, guttering was scored in the concrete beside the pavements like spreading roots. A unique and faintly sinister humming note could be heard under these carapaces of stone and steel, strong enough to make the soles of one's shoes vibrate. In secluded corners of the squares, several men were curled up in hand-carts, as thought hibernating. On the esplanade, less than a hundred yards from the river, lay a litter of rotten tomatoes and potato cores: a scene of calm, cold desolation, like a photograph. To the left of the S.E.B.A. yoghourt shop, exposed to wind and rain, a great black dog stood barking fiercely in the middle of a barbed wire enclosure. At noon and seven p.m. (and when there was a war on) a siren screamed from the top of the hill. Perhaps it was the siren that began everything.

One day, 25th January, at half past three in the afternoon, it started up for no apparent reason. At the precise moment when its wailing note first burst upon the air, at the precise moment when it began to sweep round from one concrete structure to the next, growing louder every second, at that absolutely precise moment when everything seemed to be collapsing in total disorder

14

the following incident took place. A young girl on a moped appeared at the corner of the boulevard, between the avenue of chestnut trees and the main entrances to the S.P.A.D.A. store. Her passage down the street coincided exactly with the noise of the siren. She had emerged from the tall clutter of buildings just as the first ululation went up; and she disappeared three hundred yards farther on, swallowed up by another group of office blocks, just as the sound died away into silence once more. What took place between these two points was unbearable. She rode on, sitting very stiff and straight in the saddle of her blue moped, hair drawn back round her childish face, eyes staring straight in front of her. The wheels whirred as she moved, light, transparent. Their hub-caps gleamed, their dirty tyres crunched over the asphalt. Legs bare, knees gripping tightly, the young girl kept going; but already she had lost some part of her own identity. Under the pressure of that unique sound, that blind and strident note, she underwent a metamorphosis. Her body shredded away into scraps, became fine dust, and gradually vanished altogether. Her moped, pierced through by the tension which the vibration-frequencies set up, became mere shrill metal. What took place at this moment, without warning, was something like *the conservative influence of long final i labializing short i into ü.* The young girl continued to advance down the middle of the soaking wet street, her black-and-white body held stiffly forward. The wailing of the siren was (it seemed clear) inside her, and echoing waves of sound burst from her eyes and mouth and nostrils. She was utterly alone, like some mechanical doll, and passed into oblivion at the bottom of the street; some indescribable impulse was urging her towards annihilation. The monolithic masses of the buildings on either side hemmed her in, guided her, traced out the route which, now, there was no escaping. The slightest deviation from it would have stripped away her skin and flesh, ripped out her nails, broken every bone in her body. All that would have remained to commemorate her gesture of rebellion would have been a spatter of blood and hair and brains on the grey surface of the wall.

So, cleaving through the air on her moped, the young girl

advanced towards the end of her journey. A damp film covered her eyes. Her half-parted lips looked as though they were drinking some invisible liquid, and light shone from the glass of her head lamp. This was how she looked as she passed straight through the various barriers and bridges, the multiple layers of sounds and odours, smoke and ice. She rode through them all, supported by the single wire of that harsh, sawing noise, then dwindled away and vanished at the bottom of the street. At the same instant as I, or we, saw this door (as it were) opening for her between two solid blocks of houses, the siren stopped. There was absolute silence. And nothing, *nothing* remained in our minds, not even a living memory. From that day everything began to go bad, rotten. Today I, François Besson, see death everywhere.

From time to time (I may either be up or in bed) I stiffen, and stare out through the window, forehead pressed against the cold glass. Behind the closed shutters I see a long curving street with people walking up and down it. A violet shadow has fallen across the ground; and it is on this shadow that men and women walk, not saying a word, slip away into oblivion and are gone. The glow of the lighted street-lamps and the glitter from the shop-windows are both reflected all around: the shadows retreat reluctantly, like fringes of dark fur. Everywhere twinkling points of light are visible.

They are dead, I know it, no question about that; they are dead because everything external to myself is dead; a faint aura in the semblance of a winding-sheet hangs about their silhouettes as they pass. I feel as though I were casually leafing through some vast periodical that had ceased publication, and that it was on its pages I saw these printed names and faded photographs, the headlines and dates and figures, the blunted rubrics. Buildings and images have now been replaced by a bare and silent cemetery, some ten thousand square yards in extent. I see future generations arriving here. I see funerals and memorial plaques. Today the world is finished. Nothing lives any more. Ecstasy and pain are mere geometrical expressions.

On my feet once more, pausing now in front of a wall, I let all movement stream on past me. I am a survivor from the maelstrom. The foreshortened column of the water-spout has left me here, in front of this wall. Death has not spared me. I too have been caught in the vortex, I have been flesh, colour, space, time. But now the effects of that encounter have receded far from me, revealing— like some dried-up marsh—a quite new composition, no longer dominated by fluctuating moods, anger or desire, but by hard certainties, granulated surfaces, aspects of immortality. The gloss left on a vase by the last lingering traces of dampness, mounds of fine sand that the waves have licked, rough-textured shells eaten away by salt: the sort of shells that murmur like the sea when you put them to your ear, you surely remember the noise they make, that gentle, muted, breathing sound, so close to the rhythm of a city that one's inevitably reminded of the time one was caught in the midday rush-hour, right in the heart of the city, marooned on a traffic-island while cars surged past all around one. You feel that appalling swelling sensation spread through the arteries, flooding your guts like blood spurting through a perforated intestine, wringing your heart with agony; and you let yourself go with it, overwhelmed by the murmurous, humming flow, vanquished, blissful, to the point where your identity is gone, merged in the vortex, senses swooning away. Impossible not to yield, just a little, to despair; and the forces of memory always took advantage of this, subjecting us to those damned childhood sensations of ours, those we shall never recapture again, moments of quiet pleasure and idleness, hints and intimations of the future, the simple patterns we loved so well, warm, secret hiding-places, pockets of air in which the sun and rain mingled, retreats full of wonderful objects, red and gold, delicate creatures like sea-anemones and limpets, dumb, fragile organisms, liquid scents and sensations on the fingers, small white chunky stones, whole universes like a dictionary, you know, the things they call pools of water; and all this returns slowly, trying, in vain, to pierce the surface of the living being, and you know that the whirling vortex which seemed to spring out of nothing, from the void, was in fact ultimate mockery, the meaningless scream of monkey or parrot.

17

This was the fate meted out to each being, hanging over every object. One man lay sprawling in a wicker basket-chair, caught short in the middle of his own private affairs. His hands rested flat along his thighs, just above the knees, and his round back was pressed against the back of the chair. He was beginning to find breathing difficult; every three or four seconds he gave a harsh, rattling cough. He was in the process of dying there, imperceptibly, with no regrets, and quite alone. Outside, beyond the window, the sky was blue. But the concentric circles grew and multiplied; one by one, like so many vultures, they crossed the threshold of this room, where already the smell of death hung in the air.

It was the same along this snow-covered wintry boulevard, and, yes, round about that window, that focal-point of glass, and in the unknown hiding-places scattered through the countryside, middens and iced-over ponds and ash-pits: what still remained? What flame still glowed in the firebox of that stationary locomotive, what whistle went up from its steam-vent? What light shone inside the tinplate storm-lantern? Events were modulated to an infinite variety of frequencies, so that they eluded the eye and continued their business alone, in an unending round of self-induced growth and destruction. There was no longer a woman getting out of a red car at the crossroad and continuing her journey on foot, clumsily patting her hair into place with one hand as she passed a shop-window with the word ASPIRIN inscribed across it in large letters. Instead there was a movement of a soft, slim arm which imprinted itself for ever on the reflecting surface of the glass, and revealed the silhouette of a seeming statue, three bent fingers touching that electric mass of black hair. Facts were flights of stairs down invisible corridors.

Then, in a flash, peace returned to all these places, spreading over hard intractible matter as though guided by a conductor's baton. It did not so much encircle the state of fixity as prolong it, overtracing and completing the outline of the pavement, the sharp, three-dimensional pattern of the cast-iron street-lamps, the circular bandstand in the middle of the public gardens. Other

18

human beings, or animals, very calm and quiet, stood frozen into familiar postures, in their houses, outside doors, beside windows; hands resting on tables, gnawing a bone perhaps, or lips set to a glass. On them, on each and every one of them, fell the fine rain of ashes. They were dying peaceably behind celluloid posters. Their lustreless eyes had taken on a leaden tinge, their substance was draining away drop by drop.

What delicate design, drawn with a fine-pointed pen on the surface of coarse wrapping-paper, what exquisite music—its notes rising into the air like a flight of ravens—what rich savour, constantly generating itself by the catalysis of acids, the regular breakdown of fatty elements, theme and variations played out by alkaloids and carbohydrates, what piercing pain *there*, in the nether belly, would suffice to portray this luminous, rounded, frozen kingdom—this domain of which I formed part, in which I lost myself, floating in some strange fashion on my back, arms crossed, stretched out to my full extent in the middle of this supporting surface, silent and afraid, watching the gods move about their business? An expanse so wide it seemed like infinity, stretching widely to the sharp division of the horizon. An empty page with a line moving blindly over it, a springy motion, up a little, now to the left, still left, left, now right, cutting a pattern on life. Life. Superb, heroic, majestic, hammer-forged and childish, impossible to destroy. So pure and lovely, it looks as though one simple gesture would suffice to blot it out of view. I stretch on my back, and float; black veils and mourning drapes, hollow, cavernous, abyss-like surfaces pass slowly overhead, draw me towards sleep, volatilize my being by the pristine freshness of their ghostly premonitions. Now, perhaps, I am going to die: no more steel then, no more keen and cutting blades of light! But this world is terribly *here*. Everything overlaid with yellow and gold. Below me stretches this vast expanse of stone and stucco, this stark bird's-eye view, a line on an aerial photograph, everything closed and dead—hospitals, mental homes, factories, power stations. The railway tracks are rusted up. But this process of decomposition, having corrupted every species and spared no object in the world, now finds that it may, after all, have achieved nothing. It is possible, in fact—not to go too closely into the matter—that nothing has changed in any way: sounds are as rich and complex as ever, trees still stand where they did, cottages still gleam with corrugated iron and formica flooring. Men and women looked just as smooth and healthy as they had always done. And yet *something* had happened. The threatening presence of some diluvian past hung everywhere in the air, a throat-catching memory. The smell of ill-buried corpses, perhaps, or the dry rottenness of fallen branches.

No point in exaggerating: the concrete and sheet metal were flimsy enough, the tiling a bad joke; I still saw despite them.

Look at it in yet another way. About seven minutes to eleven every noise in the town merged and concentrated like salvoes of gunfire. Here the movement was so well timed that it achieved its own destruction. Under the clear daylight the houses stood in yellow rows. Rain streamed off the rooftops, the gutters gurgled. A strange wind, warm and moist in texture, sent scraps of refuse fluttering against walls and windows. All these little episodes were contained in a hemisphere of grey sky.

So you move away from this centre, at a reduced speed, and climb up in the direction of the near-by hills, mounting worn steps thick with mimosa, going up, up, till your breath begins to come short. Crows circle round the mountain. You cross a silent, macadamized road. Cats, hidden behind flower-pots, watch you go by. Goitrous lizards scurry away beneath heaps of old stones. You still climb on, up flight after flight of steps: nine of them before you reach the summit. You have to cross the road four times. You count sixty-three electric pylons, and about four hundred red-roofed suburban villas, with laurel hedges and orange-trees in the garden. You make out other mountains (which may be on fire) and the floating dome of an observatory. Greet an old woman with blackened hands. Kick through millions of fallen leaves, and ants, and olives. Catch the obscene odour of fig-trees. Then, somewhere high up the mountain, between the eighth and the ninth flight of steps, hidden away to the left of a small artificial square where children play, you come upon a fountain of icy water, issuing from a copper spout embedded in a stone monument. It bears the date 1871. All around it, in wild disorder, are various *graffiti*—J.C.B. 12/4/46, JOJO, HARRISON, 6/10/1960, MIREILLE, LIPOL, LUC, MAINANT, I WAS HERE—D.D., L.R., S., T.A.—M., 25/8/58, REG, 1st AUG. 1961, CASABLANCA, DIDI, 1949, POZSA, 1949, J.B., A.ZIN., HELSINKI 57, VICTOR HUGO, 12/8/1963. The water gushes out in sharp spurts and falls into the bowl of the fountain. You could sit there too, on the edge of the basin where the horse-flies hover, after carving your initials with a knife beside all the others —J.F.B., 9th April 1963—so as to know what's going on. This would constitute the renewal of not-all-that-ancient history: history which had already left its mark on the stone stele above the fountain. For instance: A. and DAISY, 6th July 59.

Albonico—Daisy finds it very hot.
The sun had finally penetrated those thousands of tiny leaves. Later its angle had reached a point where the progressive ovalization of the shadows it cast produced innumerable mouth-like shapes. At present the sun was going down, trembling on the very edge of these triangular leaves, uttering tiny cries as it touched the gravel, glimmering jerkily downwards, yet with a smooth motion, so smooth—The tree in question was a pear; and this pear was cracking under the impact of the day's heat, imperceptibly raising its head again now in the cool, stretching out its dry branches by millimetres, spreading each individual leaf. Like a dorsal fin. The air was almost completely still. Twenty-five yards farther on, under the patio of a villa, between the tomato-patch and the parrot-cage, the red mercury-column of a thermometer was steadily rising past the 80° mark.
Albonico sat under the pear-tree, espadrilled feet resting on the gravel. At that moment, it seems, a droning sound became audible, drilling its way through the atmosphere; and a wilting plant, sapped by the lack of water, bent over yet a

little further. On this famous stretch of gravel one pebble stood out from the rest, because it was tall and pyramidal, whereas all the pebbles surrounding it were short and round —unless the near by splashing of the fountain created an illusion, by shedding a strange lustre on the stone's facets, something midway between a reddish reflection and the sound of the sea. If Albonico had taken the trouble to dig there, with the toe of his espadrille, he would undoubtedly have unearthed an old coin, lost there some months earlier, and now very dirty. Only the cigarette-butts had escaped burial. Daisy pinched the base of her nose between the thumb and first finger of her right hand. Then, with the same hand, she traced out the contours of her full lips, and went back to the desultory perusal of some romantic magazine, *Confidences* or the like. The sun, burning hot and with widely scattered rays, shone on the glossy paper at four separate points. On the left, again, a withered stem quivered, letting fall some pistils, or stamens. A variety of sounds drifted up across the steps, from beyond the edge of the trees, skirting rows of back gardens, re-echoing and dividing. They originated at every point of the landscape—in the Foglia garage, for instance, or the Rosa-Bonheur warehouse. The sound of banging bottles, or a diesel engine, or a dog's bark: all were flattened, made barren by the fierce-thrusting rays of the sun. The tin roof of the garage lay square to the sky's smooth simmering surface. They might have been superimposed layers of sheet aluminium, each serving to reflect the other. Every twenty-four seconds a gong-stroke shuddered through the air, echoing on, blurred by much rubbing and grinding. A very long bundle of piping, lying wired up on the ground, gave back the slow, cadenced stroke of a perspiring man who was banging it with a hammer. Amid the general murmurous fragmentation of sound, the vague humming caused by the heat, these hammer-blows carried some unseen ghostly entity forward, while at the same time thrusting back an equally invisible obstacle, starting oscillations in a cloud.

Every twenty-four seconds, another yard gained; a yard every twenty-four seconds—a sphere dilated a little further, something opaque and nebulous, like a foetus, or magma, and lost itself in the landscape. Dispersed. Or, to be more accurate, a coat of dust settled on everything, caking the dry-stone courses of the wall, thickening the outlines of the pebbles. The very sky, perhaps in an attempt to make its texture more like that of the ground, was hazy with a fine flour-like substance. Winged particles floated on pockets of air, collected in nuclei. No doubt it was the intense heat that, penetrating to the earth's very core, had released these clouds of ash, lifting them, fanning them into airborne motion until they formed a long-lasting envelope round the world. At this point Albonico took the trouble to scrape with the toe of his espadrille, in the precise spot where the old, dirty coin lay, hidden beneath the surface. He found it, picked it up, and showed it to Daisy. It looked very round and ugly, lying there in the hollow of his hand.

'I've just found twenty francs,' he said, 'down on the ground there.'

'A coin, you mean?'

'Strange, don't you think?' he said.

'Someone must have lost it.'

'I wonder.'

Daisy gave it back to him. Then she wiped her earth-stained fingers against the stone wall.

'It must have been there quite a time. It's thick with earth.'

'No—not earth—'

'*What*?' she said.

'No, I mean, *not* earth, not exactly. More a kind of dust, something like ash. Here, I'll clean it up a bit. Tear me off some of your paper—'

He began to clean the twenty-franc piece, very carefully, sitting there close to the sea, facing the fountain, half in the sun, half in shadow. He scraped every tiny corner and recess, using the sharp fingernail of his right-hand index finger,

wrapped up in a scrap of paper. But the metal remained worn
and lustreless, permanently blackened by its contact with the
soil.

Far beyond the world of peace and quietness, far from that
secret paradise where springs gush forth in undisturbed tranquillity, a place of murmuring trees, where each light breeze and
wasp moves as the fancy takes it; far from the rain drumming
down steep roofs and into the gaping maw of the gutters; far
beyond all these scarcely-formulated worlds, this flesh-coloured
beauty, these innumerable swarming crevasses, these mouths for
ever muttering their interminable stories, mingled with breath
smelling of food and soda-water—far away and beyond all this
there seems to be a weight binding your feet and hands, a weight
that tears you away, all trembling and bloody, from any pleasure
in life. It's like a block of marble, high as a house, weighing countless tons, dragging you through the birth-pangs of mortal being.
Before you know it you're off, without knowing where, the freezing cold penetrating every pore in a trice, while you vainly try to
cry out, even to get your breath back; but those grim metallic
shafts pierce through you like the long swift movement of a sword
thrusting into your vitals. There are no set limits to this race: it is
virtually interminable, so that nothing—neither the act of writing,
nor a name (such as T E A P E), nor birth itself could check its
advance. Imperceptibly, during this descending progress, the
world expands: not in depth or surface area, but in *quantity*—the
universe multiplies, colours, elements (both static and alive),
living creatures, all become increasingly divergent. Strange endless scribblings encircle every part of space and make it incomprehensible. It is as though speed of movement, or the sharpness
of the senses, or some such factor, were blowing up reality to the
point where it passed beyond one's grasp. Patches of light, dark
shadows, straight lines, emphatic or lightly sketched shapes, all
simultaneously merge, yet remain distinct. Every object becomes,
at one and the same time, akin to, and different from, every other
object. Then comes a murmurous sound, swelling into wild,

harmonious music, rising from the heart of matter and mingling its mournful vibrations with those of the light. It is, you might say, as though the earth were on the boil, a slow succession of bursting bubbles. The human observer, deceived by his own sensibilities, plunges further into the depths; rhythm and theme catch him in mid-flight, while colour-patterns (ever-changing, ever-destructive) cast a camouflage over him. Voices have a heavy, cavernous boom, are linked every twenty-four seconds to the rhythm of a man hammering away with all his strength on a spark-bright bundle of crazy steel tubing. Somewhere between earth and sky there oscillates a large, flattish object, its surface daubed with blood, apparently made of riveted and interlapping steel plates, sliding to and fro with each compression or expansion of their overall mass, and yet very much all of a piece, easily liftable on some gigantic bar, like a curtain. Then, deeper still, the effect is akin to that other sea one discovers after plunging beneath the surface. The rhythm is slow still, that gong-stroke every twenty-two or twenty-three seconds: but the quality of the sound has changed. It is no longer music, but rather a kind of soft, continuous frictional note, somewhat like falling rain, or the hiss of wet tyres. Sometimes, especially round a gas-flare, or a cigarette-lighter, or even a flash of light off the bodywork of a car, there forms a note so high and shrill as to be quite unbearable; but it never lasts for long. Very soon it splits into two notes, then three, then four, then five, then six. A kind of musical shrubbery has been brought into existence. It grows, spreads, extends its branches, mingles with the other vegetal tissue of sounds about it. After some 2,503 further subdivisions, the shrill note has become no more than a fine, disembodied whisper, the sound of a finger brushing across skin, magnificent to the nth degree, the scarcely audible sound of a hand caressing the dry, powdery texture of some young girl's thigh. Such is the unremitting frictional sound that accompanies these speeded-up movements in the blue of the sky; later, the blue might have been replaced by orange, but now colours, too, are separating off and multiplying—not in a static context, as it might be the white wall of the apartment block, but

25

as part of the universal *va-et-vient*: a subtle and alarming movement, that modifies every least detail of existence, something for
the insect world to imitate. Now time, too, splits up, propagates,
drains and devours itself. The stereoscopic patterns divide: the
higher ones pursue their vertical flight into the void, those
beneath them plunge greedily downwards, are swallowed by
oblivion.

And above this scene of chaos, these ear-dulling noises, it seems
to me that I myself am poised, dreaming, or drifting in chill and
monumental splendour, like some great iceberg, blue depths
glinting, nine-tenths under water, a solid mass of stiff glacial fury.
My ears are filled with words in unknown, inhuman-sounding
languages. The syllables jostle and trip against one another, build
patterns in the void. They are not addressed to any person;
they form a termite-language, their volubility is made up of endless tiny points. Nothing has any further significance. Everywhere
—on the peeling walls and the monumental fountains, across the
doors of dark, stinking retreats, in the station booking-hall, over
millions of virgin pages—there runs that delicate secret writing
which no one can read. Here are set forth facts of immediate
concern and all-too-ghastly reality, which must yet pass unre-
vealed: rather like those frightful accidents, known yet somehow
kept from the mind, which lie so heavy on our consciences. All
measure and restraint have been lost; it seems to me that the
world is in torment, that it bears an incurable wound.

Besson stands rooted to the spot, staring straight in front of
him, unable to see anything but this horror, and looking like some
exotic statue. All unbeknown to himself he has become a fragment
of black wood, a sculptured piece of ebony. His thick lips are
motionless, his neck has stiffened into a knot of old cords. His
limbs are thin and tough, his belly excessively swollen, hard and
distended like that of a pregnant woman. Beneath his belly the
penis is erect, pointed. There are no muscles or veins visible on
the surface of his body: the whole thing is as smooth as a pebble.
At the centre of his belly lies a hole dug with the point of a knife,
enclosing a canal: this is his navel, like the puncture left by a

pistol-shot. Besson's legs are short and bowed; his toes are splayed out in an unpleasant fashion, rather as though, somewhere higher up, he were making the ghost of an obscene gesture. Above all, under the dome of his skull, breaking the frontal curve, are two enormous eyes, two balls of black wood set in black wood, two blind, senseless domes, soft to the finger's touch: such is the persona, the frog-mask, that François Besson has chosen to wear. It is this monstrous weight of sorrow and pity that he allows to drag him down, so that he falls, falls, passing the striated layers of the earth's surface, the sudden reddish explosions of the elements, basic clusters of matter; he falls deeper and faster than a man confronted by a smoking cigarette; yet he knows he will never arrive at any destination. Foreign languages all have their word for hope; but this word sticks in the throat. I am not isolated; I can communicate with you all; but it is bound to be too late. It may be that—caught in this trap, caught in the very midst of life—such languages work their way through me, turn me into a phantom, irresistibly strip me of all the individual characteristics I once possessed. After days of this journey, with nothing left of myself save this vast and vulnerable body, open to every emotional assault, I was expecting some sort of triumphal conclusion to the matter—and in the very midst of a clear and levelled world, I am still taken unawares. I have had scant opportunity to extract myself from my dilemma, since the town I am entering is very like the other one, I am hemmed in by near-identical walls, overwhelmed by the same colours and sounds and desires: time and space have made a complete revolution. On the other side of this liquid mass, on the earth's further face, the darkness—despite the chaos close at hand—has not diminished one jot. It still holds everything in its vice-like grasp, covers each object with its friable skin. On the high level ground to the left of the town, a level area of a few acres contains emblems signifying silence and death. Here everything is rectilinear, comprehensible, and as a result almost joyful; under the vaguely aligned crosses, caught by this species of three-faced mirror, lie no end of curious beings. And it is true enough that, once upon a time, they were alive: vigorously, insolently alive. Now nothing remains of them but an ill-defined oblong of blackish earth, and two white sticks nailed together in an upright position. The burial-grounds of men, dogs, beetles and briars have merged and become one. Perhaps, indeed, the cemetery is a cemetery no longer, but rather a kind of vague terrain extending over the whole earth, a vision, it may be, to superimpose on that of our daily existence, to spread out—everywhere and to all eternity—the soul racked by indecisive respect and terror? The earth is a night-soil dump, very tranquil, very neatly ordered, where the device of these small meticulous crosses allows every being, despite their annihilation, to persist in the shape of black letters inscribed on pine-wood lathes.

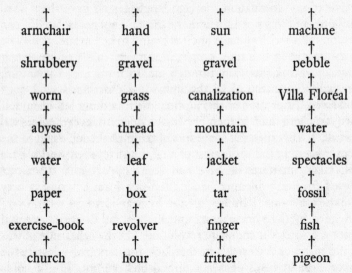

†	†	†	†
armchair	hand	sun	machine
†	†	†	†
shrubbery	gravel	gravel	pebble
†	†	†	†
worm	grass	canalization	Villa Floréal
†	†	†	†
abyss	thread	mountain	water
†	†	†	†
water	leaf	jacket	spectacles
†	†	†	†
paper	box	tar	fossil
†	†	†	†
exercise-book	revolver	finger	fish
†	†	†	†
church	hour	fritter	pigeon

Of necessity, one wandered among these tombs without understanding them; the clouds had piled up thicker and thicker in the sky, and rain was pouring down. The turn events had taken came as a surprise, like a precipice beside some mountain road. From this cemetery, and from each of those symbolic crosses beneath which the world lay at rest, there rose the smell and the sound of death; a little way off the ground the two of them formed a still, sluggish layer of mist. It was like walking backwards through the streets of a totally destroyed town: not so much exploring a maze (since everything was clear-cut and visible) but running the gauntlet of trick mirrors, *trompe-l'oeil* devices, a series of cunning schemes and traps. In this symmetrical pattern there was no room, despite death's presence, for sleep. True, there was a general atmosphere of tranquillity, or seeming tranquillity, to which the bare external shape of things, the austerity of their proportions, contributed something. Perhaps, indeed, this calm was the genuine article, the only kind of peace possible—that bred of violence and despair. Moreover, the memory of a time when things had been quite different—when colours had been firmly blocked in, when landscapes glittered with light, when every place and time had enjoyed a spell of drowsy relaxation at will, and then faded away as though they had been mere chimeras, without any importance—did not now evoke any self-flattering nostalgia. It had merely become unlivable, so that every allusion to the topic opened a door into Hell; the world's elements had undergone such a swarming upheaval that the mere idea of the past could no longer restore them to their previous simplicity. In fact, there was no longer any question of purity or simplicity: both had become inevitable casualties. The thread of life running through them was now slender and elusive: so fine now, in fact, that the merest moment's neglect could have proved fatal. The situation bore some resemblance, perhaps, to that of a giant thousand-year-old tree, so vast and heavy that it seemed, from its appearance, to belong to the mineral rather than the vegetable kingdom. The distance between these two kingdoms was minimal: the merest breath—a botanist's defection, say—would have sufficed to push the tree over the border. Yet, despite appearances, life stirred in it still, though it was hundreds of years since it had last put out fresh branches or new spring leaves, or pushed its roots farther afield. Nevertheless, it continued to exist. Deep beneath its armour, at the very heart of the trunk, a knot, a core of wood still throbbed with life and continued to grow, till its circle was complete and the dry, withered fibres thrust back another tenth of a millimetre. It also bore some resemblance to a flimsy partition, separating two conflicting elements—though without any motive for such an arrangement being found, much less the corroboration afforded by bracketing two opposites together, as it might be air and water, water and stone, fire and air, gold and lead, darkness and light. The line between life and death had by now become so fine that everyone was vaguely expecting it to break at any moment, and let the blue and crimson tides meet in the breech, one mingling with the other, spreading out, rushing on with deep whirling eddies, bearing pebbles and gravel (soon to sink and be lost), ceaselessly driving forward the third, most terrible tidal wave, deeper in hue now, an ominous purple. This ghastly rupture, the one break that could really have fatal consequences, was in fact impossible: the barrier could not be broken down. It existed in analytical terms, could be named, figured out, placed—and yet, and yet, just supposing the situation *did* break loose, not through a brutal fusion of the two elements, but by an inversion which decreed that henceforth all that pertained to life should become dead, and all that had been dead should become life. Supreme illusion, raucous laughter from the Devil, a syllogism that could expand on the sustenance provided by white walls, staccato movements, carefully observed and described expressions, moments of ecstasy that for the time being managed to keep chaos at bay. At all events, symmetry was preserved; the world, so virgin in appearance, had been reduced to a state of utter weakness. In private rooms and public bars, down streets and alleys, numbers of men and women were living through this process of logical contraction. Their various destinies did not run together in confusion: both in the world of the living, and in that of the dead, excitement mounted steadily. There was discussion and gesticulation, or, if you prefer, muscles came into play and bones cracked, some four and a half yards underground. Gradually the truth began to shape itself, composed of noise no less than of silence, of bodies as well as corpses. Far from horizontal—indeed, decidedly animated—truth, disguised as a middle-aged woman, went striding down the middle of the street, hair plastered down

30

by the rain, a somewhat blurred silhouette, hands shoved into the pockets of an indigo mac and held akimbo against her hips. The rain beat down on the ground in its ancient, delicate, well-worn rhythm; the ground reflected the middle-aged lady's figure, and at every step she took towards her unknown destination, it seemed that she could no longer escape from herself. From steep roofs down which the rain of heaven coursed, all eternity watched her pass by; the songs in the bars became one united song, the urgent appeals of the upright and godly merged together, hundreds of voices were uplifted in the cold and the wet, wrapped her about in their rhythmical cocoon, then, finally, dwindled away skyward, among the clouds. And this manifestation of truth was neither sad nor gay: from the moment it had accepted the person of a woman, and had donned that indigo macintosh, and had agreed to walk the street in the rain, above her own pear-shaped reflection, it was as though she had saddled herself with a task for all eternity, something compounded of damp earth, tear-stained fabric, heavy breasts stretching the material of the bodice, weary legs plodding yard by yard down the street. Sighing voices murmured in your ear, telling you which way to go. One fell back into the very heart of existence, rather like a stone plummeting to the bottom of a well.

The town was an extraordinary kind of vortex, in which every movement or collision could be clearly felt by the individual. Like so many points, like so many agonizingly sharp needles, the eyes and hands and necks of other men began to converge on your life. The eyes, the eyes above all, were terrible: ceaselessly stripping, flaying, burning with fury. Millions of eyes opened now, at the corners of the streets, however far distant, and on each leaf of every tree. A rising current of humanity blew like a storm, though in no ascertainable direction. A man, picked at random from the swarming ant-hill of the town's population, wore the hunted and visionary air of some black death's-head spider, swaying under a rain of insecticide. The flow of speech was swelling to Babel pitch; all down the street, between the black trees, near the gutter-gratings, there was a constant echoing reverberation—isolated cries, angry muttering, quick, volatile chatter. Behind drawn blinds, on the second floor of the hospital, one old woman had borne her name—Janine Angèle Erebo—to the end of her allotted span. The blinds were the product of S.I.M.A.C. (Fabrication française), and many other names were involved, such as Hoizai, Serre, Fillipacci, Guigo, Zimmerman, Amerigo.

And, like a spark leaping from point to point, the dominant quality of each character was translated in terms of his name: the women's faces were framed in masses of blue hyacinths, leaving nothing visible save the dark smudges beneath a pair of tired eyes, heavy with sleep, and from time to time dissolving into tears. An eddy in the vortex hid their faces once more, but others appeared in their stead. Behind this impalpable curtain, fine as smoke, such architectural human groupings deployed themselves after the manner of cathedrals: long slender noses, terminating in arched and Gothic eyebrows. Mouths. Parted lips, the indefinable mystery of incisors, their white stained with tartar. Memory of freshness, something verdant and bloody at the same time, the clinging pasty remnants of dentifrice. Or, under the bright glare of a naked electric light-bulb, the criss-cross play of lines and wrinkles. Cheeks hollowed themselves, wisps of hair fell cleanly about one's ears under the razor's edge. Jaws lay in their condyles, square or triangular. One forehead stood out high above the rest, lovely as a domed crag. On its thick-set base were inscribed the individual crow's-foot lines made by frowning eyebrows. All around these faces, these craniums, lay thick darkness, powerful and immutable.

Individuals emerged from nothingness, grouped themselves into cohorts, and the dull crunch of their footsteps began to circle around: here was a future revolution in embryonic form, rage and solitude intermingled, the strength of the future contained in matter. The purposeful will that they had created, which had emerged almost at random from a series of disordered agitations, was now taking over. At the heart of this rainy symphony, at the centre of this obscure and filthy muddiness, one found oneself caught, held, wrenched out of one's own awareness, sidetracked from silence, compelled to follow them, march with them, cry out, speak, live. The attraction was too new and too subtle to be resisted. It was like being seated at the window of your room, at midday, in winter. As the noises increase and colours fade away, as countless different wave-patterns set their mirages quivering beyond the glass, this great gaping hole drains you of your peace and abandons you, naked, shivering, hunched up on the corner of your mattress, overcome by the weight of your no-longer-moving blood-stream. At such a time you must abandon the field of solitary contemplation, the false protection of forgetfulness; you have to sally forth recklessly into the open, determined to explore the outside world in all its aspects, driven on by a mad desire to invade every space and drain every attraction to the dregs. No longer, either, by analytical reason, but by a willing acceptance of the illogical in your reactions to every room and person, each tree, each speck of dust.

As on other occasions, the music carried you away, but you were no longer responsible for it. The combinations of notes were produced somewhere behind you, in a forbidden tabernacle; and farther off, in the shadows, the thematic material fused and soared with the mounting arrow of the melody.

The town was an inexhaustible sea, and its ebb and flow contained harmony. Not the kind of harmony that you or I knew, intelligent comprehension of the links between life and death, for instance, or faith in ultimate limitations, but a literally monstrous harmony, something quite unique, which, being a collective phenomenon, could not be perceived by the solitary individual. It was, so to speak, lucidity returning to darkness after its work of destruction was accomplished. Man set in the world like a grain of sand lying on the earth, and knowing nothing more. Like the planet one inhabited, everything with spherical, magnificently spherical. Perfection was the reigning deity. And if there had not been this constraint, if there had been no mouth to suck your sap, pumping it through your body, impelling it towards that beyond-ness which is called life, without pause or digression, then there

33

would have been nothing at all. At this time, under men's frigid scrutiny, I was full of doubt. Though personally alive, I remained the prisoner of my anxieties; I existed in a kind of permanent time-lag, a staggered relationship between me and myself. My head and limbs were foggy, my reiterated questions always went unanswered: but it did not matter. What really counted was , frozen on the ground of the here-and-now, pinned down and paralysed by decomposition and analysis. The universe of mankind was akin to darkness, verging on corruption. There were fearful desires, followed by inexplicable feelings of disgust. A kind of nervous tremor seemed to invest each concept, making it shake like a packet of gelatine.

Men and women no longer possessed much privacy: they formed a collective mass. And in this barbarous chaos you—you personally —were lost. You were overwhelmed by such an environment; in your naïvety you had thought you could stand aloof. There was a time, long before, when you had, in a sense, placed yourself outside time: you had been that miniature landscape—remember? —that plaque of pale blue and pink mosaic representing the Acropolis. The one patch of light in the centre of a black marble slab. You were, theoretically, the open window—or, better still, the curved and swelling surface, the blister, the bubble of life. You were, perhaps, a central point, or a circle, in any case an irreducible geometric figure, incapable of assimilation. And yet, one day, you were forced to surrender. At first there had been no more than the suspicion, an isolated corner of your solitude, a sense of unhappiness. Then the thing grew and spread, and by the time you understood, it was too late. The trap had been sprung on you. Cynicism, evil-doing, the temptation of weakness—there was nothing left for them to achieve, since you were now a mere victim. You were already nothing but a shifting, mutable halo; you no longer possessed a self to offer. That was how I entered life. Now I know nothing else. Trees have grown up here and there, houses have been built, they have driven tunnels right down to the sea, trimmed and tidied the roads, enlarged the public squares, enclosed the gardens. This is how a district becomes

34

unrecognizable. In any case, as far as I am concerned these woods and houses and gardens may exist for others, but not for me. I no longer even perceive them. I have no new sensations, nor any past to sharpen my taste for them: I am in a state of immanence. There are many who live through this unconscious conflict, without hatred, without beliefs, never piercing the black veil that enshrouds them. One might say that they had lost something, were it not that their condition is very far from that of deprivation; yet somewhere along the line they have had a difficult passage, perhaps failing to stop at some intermediate point when they should have done. It is the power of the unknown, that damaging chain of unresolved analyses, that have (all unbeknown to them) affected their judgment, and left them with a haunting, ever-greater fear of abduction. It is the same process that still gains control of them today, by wearing out, and then simply destroying, all elements of clarity and light; it begins its circuit in hell, where suffering is for all eternity, snuffing them out one by one, but there'll never be an end of them, those myriad lines and wrinkles, darkness in the heart, the soul's abysses, gauze dressings on the wound, death after death, each encompassing a thousand other acts of destruction.

But already events are moving on, with a series of minute changes in every square inch of space, changes that set the whole complex rocking. No doubts, no fears: man, if you like, is gradually dwindling away, moving towards the vegetable condition *en route* for the mineral. The rich, fluctuating body of matter which formerly provided his relaxation now wholly eludes him, flows out of and away from his body without his even being aware of it. Once he possessed a halo of mystery, the product of his collisions with the real world; then a dream, a premonitory vision of ruin and destruction enters the picture, and this man at once becomes united with his true self. The gods are sent packing, the void spins around him, and the earth becomes, in his eyes, a deserted planet, a complex place full of signs and booby-traps. He no longer sees or hears anything; even his sense of touch betrays him. The earth is mist-bound and sterile; towns no longer have any weight—

perhaps they are floating, perhaps this is only an illusion caused by the two gaseous spheres; the sky has penetrated solid matter and blown it up, the whole world is gas and more gas, smoke and cloud; everything here merges and blends. Old distinctions are jettisoned: the horizon smokes over Uranus, and what before was hard and brilliant, rough-diamond-edged, has passed into drops of water, whence it disperses in the air. That is the measure of what this much-buffeted man's power has contrived to accomplish.

He has lost his kingdom, which was one of light and of rocky places. Speed he has relinquished in favour of shadow; the ground he treads now is compact of sounds and odours; a loud yet almost melodious uproar swells and runs all around. The uproar becomes a scarlet torrent, a spate of blood, gushing out interminably before his eyes. The man, being cut off now from his little household gods, cannot remain a homogeneous entity for much longer; he melts and flows, spreading into holes, and his heart, his central kernel, solid and hard and imperturbable as flint, founders gently beneath the furred surface of some brackish tideway. Soon there will be nothing left for him but these things: death, stitching him into its shroud; his wheezing, panting breath; the milky sap seeping drop by drop through each clod of earth; the long pendulum swing of rubbery continental land-masses, drifting over roof-tops all lustrous with boiling magma. This is what the man dreams of. And this dream pierces him to his very bowels, spreads through him like a poison, pulses in his veins, sheds its dust over the delicate membrane of the eye: a fearful dream, since it dwells not merely in his own life, but in the reality beyond time and space.

All this was contained in one single skull, yet remained universally present. What despair, what unimaginable agony it must have brought to all earth's inhabitants—that precise, mind-shattering assemblage of countless howls and screams, rhythmic and assonant, a hymn of joy and of stricken misfortune, a flood of sound that streamed on and on, spreading and extending towards the mist, so that the cliffs re-echoed with the last cries of suicides, yet never overstepping the dimensions of a single object; a controlled outburst, a force turned back on itself and achieving its own destruction, an orgy that aroused and sustained every living creature, a savage breath blown out in an explosive spiral, suddenly offering an insight into the perfect hallucination, and vertigo, and queasiness, and the bottomless pit of the intellect. Then the floor and the walls of the houses and the whole town resumed their original aspect, their embryonic roundness. Men were becoming increasingly solitary and myopic: seen against the vortex they looked no bigger than insects, a sort of warrior-ant. Each bore on his skin the fatal tattoo-mark, the sign of time passing, guttering uselessly away. Under the flesh of their faces, like some sterile seed, there always lurked the same death's-head, with its gaping orbital sockets and anonymous rictus, its worn cheek-bones and converging suture-joints. In the narrow square, together with the weight of the void, that time-honoured landscape, a hard and tangible passion now made itself felt. Each body, every fragment served its purpose: none were ignored or cast down at random. But this did not signify friendly agreement: the force binding mankind one to the other seemed more like some invisible and malevolent spirit. Messages were displayed everywhere: in the form of letters of the alphabet they could be read on walls. First names collided, odd phrases refused to vanish. On the big off-white wall of the factory had been inscribed the legend PARKING FORBIDDEN.

*

The frosted-glass door clicked open from time to time as women passed through it. Or there was this man dressed in blue linen trousers and a nylon shirt, his eyes fixed and staring, only the faintest flicker of awareness discernible in them under the electric light: he was in the middle of a room where heat was dormant, smoking a Gauloise 474 from a half-empty packet with the factory-letter J on it. Farther on, or rather to one side, a young woman was walking down the town's main thoroughfare: her quick, short steps carried her easily forward. Yet her entire body —shoulders, breasts, neck, hips, belly—was quite rigid. For her,

37

too, time scarcely existed; it streamed down in the rain, something ineffable and far away. Stiff in her movements, isolated from the rest, oddly submissive, she seemed weighed down by the burden of endless thousand symbols, figures and memories. So she moved forward, well-rooted in reality, and even had one counted her steps one would have failed to get the better of her. Her gait—which was quite remote from any normal human rhythm, yet made use of her intensely feminine feet—thus presented an odd phenomenon, abrupt and nervous in the extreme; her red leather shoes clipped down on the pavement, spike-heel first, sole afterwards, with a faint flick of loose laces. These footfalls did not have a regular pattern; they simply occurred one after the other, individual and autonomous, an explosive *clack!* against the massive asphalt surface. The ground, as though shaken by their impact, seemed to rise up at each touch of the steel heel-tip and thrust the girl's weight, all 114 lbs of it, forward into her next step. Yet there was nothing could force that tap-tap-tapping into a two-by-two pattern, and their monotonous progress seemed to have no end in sight. It was not an absence of rhythm, exactly: hearts continued to beat approximately ninety-four times a minute, the movements of thigh-muscles were still as usual, respiration remained normal, there was no changing in the blinking pattern of eyelids. But this particular pattern of sound was mechanical. It concealed no form, enclosed no melody. It was a graph-curve that evolved below zero, the discharge of a flood of events that coagulated instantly, like blood. The woman walked on and on, through the hissing rain, and entered the slack-tide area. Its tension penetrated to her vocal chords: her lips parted slightly to form some indistinguishable sound. Her darting eyes gleamed against the reflections of the wet cars, her hands opened, her white unruffled skin shivered at the touch of the wind. Under her woollen dress she was superbly naked, and frozen. Reinforced concrete had poured down her body, moulding every minuscule detail, outlining the snake-curves of her silhouette. She was here, or there, eternally alive, jostled on corners, fashioned by matter to the condition of matter. Solitude and pride were both abandoned at this precise point of life's natural progression: a mass of flesh, a statue both warm and cold, two legs in motion, mud, polished nails, stiff or lustrous hair. She was a black insect with long overcrossing wing-sheaths, a cockroach in the cupboard, a reptile, a night-bird, or, more solitary still, a small pile of domestic garbage: orange-peel protruding from the open mouths of empty cans, while under trickling gutter-water wrapping-paper and the rolled-off tops of sardine-cans lie scattered around, and the smell spreads and drifts, and ashes descend, and a thin layer of grease settles on the sides of these pyramidal heaps; futile as a shroud they stand, waiting for an indifferent dawn to fulfil their destiny at last, through the agency of street-cleaners armed with shovels. This woman, and all these other women, blindly marched on the way they were going; events proceeded in the same fashion everywhere; outside a bar the neon-lights winked day and night. Right above the door, close to the first-floor balconies, two advertising signs had been set up, one sky-blue, the other pink; they announced, respectively, ADELSCHOFFEN and BIERE D'ALSACE. Very low down, on the left of the entrance, glowed the letters P.M.U. [i.e. 'Pari Mutuel Urbain', or 'City Tote Stakes': Trs.]. Between the two a white neon legend proclaiming BAR TABAC winked on and off in five different stages: (1) White lettering with a ring round it; (2) Just the ring; (3) Just the lettering; (4) The lettering flashing on and off three times; (5) Lettering and ring flashing on and off three times together. After this there would be four seconds of darkness, and then the whole cycle would begin afresh. It might go on for hours, days, years: these vague words floating in front of the bar were not subject to any limitations. They were eloquent, they described real and forgotten things: whole towns abandoned to men's devices, huge squares where the cars are all parked diagonally, vast exhibition halls, factories with names like Martini or Maccari and Franco, endless labyrinths of grey streets to which the sun never penetrates, coastlines and valleys, concrete fly-over bridges spanning motorways, airports loud with the roar of jets tearing themselves free from earth's pull, black boulevards where heavy-laden trucks thunder past, wharves smelling of coal-dust and oil, wire-cluttered, loud with the screech and rattle of cranes.

The houses now stand packed close against one another. Their roofs form a continuous, compact surface of red and brown, open to dust and rain: a new sort of regular-patterned floor that calls for a certain crazy extravagance in the user.

Trucks pass down the streets, wheels close to the sidewalk; the sky, heavy with clouds, tilts square to the vertical. The horizon is hemmed in by those volcano-like mountains, with vapour rising on their flanks. In some secret den or underground cave there must be men held prisoner, stifling from confinement. The sidewalk throws up people who have been buried alive, bodies steeped in bituminous deposits, which the worms refuse to eat. Everything has a suffocating air of impenetrability. Down there a hundred children are jostling each other in the dust of a gymnasium.

These were the things one could see, at that moment in time, if one climbed the hill where the cemetery stood. At the top of the gardens there was a landmark-indicator, together with a marble slab on which were inscribed the main references to the area, such as couplets by Byron or Lamartine. This, then, was the moment to lean over the balustrade, and listen to the sound of the artificial waterfall, and look at everything with an avid intensity, as though one were condemned to die immediately afterwards, or at the very least to go blind.

When you got down to it, there could have been no worse setting for love than this town; yet before love could be achieved, there had to be knowledge and understanding, one had to acclimatize oneself to this empty void, this sad mockery of freedom.

If only it were possible, one ought to be left to oneself again, among the stones and trees, the names, the shop-windows, the traffic; among the great close-packed crowd of men and women, among the shouts and smells and passionate emotions. Prepared long since, matured in antechambers charged with thunder and lightning, where the tension had swiftly become more shattering than the face of a god revealed, the atmospheric drama was now gathering to its climax. Now clouds were bursting in their dozens, the sky streamed with water like a plate-glass window. Burning perfumes gathered in clusters, began to revolve about each other like constellations; people caught at the storm's centre hurriedly took shelter in doorways, anxious to avoid being left out in the open. Earth and buildings alike took on a bluish tinge, perilously liable to attract lightning and the plastic elements of water. And the same storm, dry, intangible, began to gather in men's hearts; buildings, to all appearances intact, were collapsing internally of their own accord; every drop that fell from the sky took a small fragment of reality with it briefly tapping out a rhythmic pattern, a vague suggestion of something—conscious awareness, perhaps —before dissolving into nothingness. Very soon these palatial buildings and columns would vanish, leaving nothing but white ruined shells. But what was appalling, unbearable even, was that this process of destruction never reached completion: it went on continually, in every direction, over and over again, but never succeeded in exhausting the resistance of matter. The houses were nothing any longer, yet they still existed; movements, colours, desires—none of them had any further meaning, yet movements, colours and desires continued as before. Men were brute beasts of the void, mindless and bloodless, set in their ways—yet they still *existed*. You could walk down every street, even out into the stony, rain-rich countryside beyond, and nowhere would you discover true solitude, the fulfilment of that haunting passion for the absolute. Nowhere would you find complete silence.

Everywhere you went, you were bound to come up against existence, walls of solidity and life that drove you back like some echo of the birth-agony. It was all a trick with mirrors, reflection upon reflection, as intense as they were pointless. There was nothing in the world that could absorb and destroy you, return you to the indifferent blank expanse of the void; nothing that could be penetrated by the rapier of your frenzy. Wherever your footsteps carried you, the world was a kind of travelling circus, presenting you with a special vision: each object was self-contained, adaptable, and meticulously ringed round with a thin black wiry line. Reality, truth, the power of nature: vast-stretching deathless concepts against which the keen light of understanding and communication bruise themselves for ever. In this organized chaos there was no chance of escape. Four streets converging on a square where the clock in the clock-tower said six o'clock now held this inner reality for ever, stamped with its seal: hundreds of square yards of asphalt and concrete and plaster, rain beading its surface like sweat, right-angled corners on the pavement, gleaming rivulets down the gutters, scars left by winter frost and summer heat, cracks, the chalk marks of old hopscotch games, names, names, names: Salvetti, Geoffret, Milani, Apostello, Caterer, Chez Georges, Chinaware, Port Pharmaceutical Store, Astoria, Dental Surgeon, S.E.V.E., La Trappe de Staouëli, Lanfranchi, Caltex Tyres; Chevrolet 418 DU 02, winter banana, Motta ice-cream, Simon, 84.06.06. Empty spaces that darkness absorbs without effort, long streets lined with plane-trees at regular intervals, their branches bare and leafless, each planted in the pavement and growing up through a sunshaped iron grating. Fountains, concrete and stucco buildings, balconies overgrown with creepers; roofs bristling with aerials, or tilted over as though the sky leaned down more heavily on one side of them, barred windows, shutters open or closed, plywood doors, spy-holes, culverts and gutters. At one point in this rectangular pattern, a little way up on the left, stand two parallelopipeds, an exception to the general rule: it is just a trick of perspective, or are they really like that, two bluish blocks apparently joined at the top and forming a sort of triumphal arch? In fact they are the walls of the XVth Army Corps Barracks, St. Anne's Hospital, and Police Headquarters. These walls are pierced with heavily-barred windows, which look out over the sidewalks, respectively, of the Rue Durante, the Rue Gilli, and the Rue Carnot.

At midday, during the rain, there is a man standing behind each of these windows, hands clutching the bars, staring out into space. You can see about a dozen of them in all, half-hidden by the shadowy background of their cells, tirelessly scrutinizing the bright and grimy world which they cannot reach. At first they are possessed by a violent desire to break through the metal barricade, free themselves in a flash—this, surely, is what freedom means—, embrace this patch of road in all its stunning brightness, so light in comparison with the gloom of their cells it seems the sun must be shining on it. Then the urge fritters away; they seem to retreat before a still stronger barrier, something like a thick sheet of glass, unseen and unexpected, doubtless the phenomenon they call 'reason'; and their eyes relax into stillness again, gaze for days on end at the vision of freshness and brightness outside, never moving, so that in the end their overflowing love makes them cleave to it till they reach the point of oblivion.

In this state of counterfeit reality, this amalgam of atmospheres, equipped with this precise and clearly-outlined relief-map, one still would be hard put to it, at this moment, to tell whether it was raining still or a blazingly sunny day. The moment has been reached when the rectangle becomes progressively more blurred and undulating: other smaller rectangles exist within it, each enfolding its own adventure, human or vegetable. All that remain now are the edges, as though neatly cut out from the soft velvet shadows. At last, with the neat finality of a tunnel unfolding around a car in motion, the patch of white light opens its window on the infinite.

Chapter One

François Besson—François Besson listens to the tape-recorder in his room—The beginning of Anna's story—Paul's departure—Advice from Besson's mother—The vendetta

THIS is the story of François Besson. One might have begun it somewhat earlier, after his meeting with Josette, for instance, or when he had given up his teaching job in the private school, and had come back to live with his parents, in the old dilapidated house near the centre of town. But granted one embarked on it at this later point, then François Besson was lying sprawled out on his bed, amid a disordered tangle of sheets and blankets, towards the end of winter, and, for the moment, not smoking. His eyes were shut. He was no longer asleep, but remained in the same position, fists clenched. The light from the street outside struck the wall of the building opposite; its reflection shone into Besson's room, and stayed there. The yellow-bright chinks between the shutters showed occasional patches of paint.

Besson lay in a bath of colour. When it reached his face, the yellow shaded off into various tones of bistre; it was round his nostrils that he took on the most cadaverous appearance. The light distorted his naturally youthful features, sharpening the jawline, obliterating tones of red and brown, wrinkling the skin around the eyes. Colour, real colour, remained outside, beyond the closed shutters. What stalked the interior of the room was more a species of very soft and subtle reflection, much like the shadow cast on the ceiling by an electric light bulb.

When Besson got up and moved across the room, with measured steps, feet bare and both hands thrust into the pockets of his pyjama jacket, shoulders a little bent, it was like a cloud passing over the moon, or whatever else—street-lamps, headlights, the sky—might be producing that yellow illumination outside. Suddenly he came to himself, forced his eyelids apart and un-gummed his lips. There were dark rings under his eyes, he breathed noisily, and one of his ears was redder than the other, because of the way he had been lying on his pillow for the past hour.

He walked. He set down his bare feet on the cold tiled floor, one after the other, toes crimping as he did so. He only stopped when his nether belly bumped into the table. Then he abruptly tugged open one of its side drawers, and began to search through it, still in semi-darkness. The drawer was crammed with a variety of objects—dirty handkerchiefs, unwashed socks, notebooks, sun-glasses with cracked lenses, razor-blades, a toy pistol, ink-soaked sticks of chalk, postcards, boxes of Italian matches, a packet of miniature cigars labelled 'La Neuva Habana', an assortment of wastepaper and scraps of cardboard, an Air France application form for a post as steward on one of the international lines, a fragment of mirror, an English-French French-English dictionary, the bottom of a Stiegl glass, a magnet, a snapshot of himself taken in a snow-covered London street, a roll of adhesive tape together with a pair of blunt-nosed scissors, passport, cufflinks, a watch-strap with no watch, a key-ring with no keys on it, a toothbrush-tube minus its toothbrush. He did no more than fumble through this detritus, with his right hand, using his left to keep the bottom of the drawer steady. Then he must have become aware of the discomfort of his position: he abandoned the bureau for a moment and went to fetch the one and only chair, a metal one, which stood at the far side of the room. He cleared off the heap of clothes littering it, and brought it slowly across, feet dragging, stubbing his rubbery toes on the tiles.

Walking thus on bare crimped feet, in a kind of uneasy glide, held up by the chair's noiseless bumping over every crack between the tiles, Besson found the going progressively more difficult, with sudden swoops and twists of the body, like some boxer filmed in slow-motion. At every metallic bang on the floor he felt a kind of electric shock surge up his spinal column, through

46

the marrow, dilating each vertebra as it went, spreading little clusters of thread-like matter through both sides of his body. This matter moved in a series of spasms up to his neck, where it formed a vast imbedded knot, a starved and avid glandular growth, round which the electric current spun in a vortex, rotating ever faster, crushing cartilage walls, desperately seeking some way out, fighting to resist invasion by other shock-waves; then hardened, petrified to a point at which it was no more than a kind of hoarse, intensely shrill cry at the bottom of an echoing, shadow-filled cavern, and at last exploded, one final red-and-white set-piece, a kind of floral illumination. Then, without warning, it would disappear, until the next time the chair struck a tile-edge. But meanwhile something else was happening: the last remaining electricity-charged fibres, doubtless in a final flare-up of energy, instead of disintegrating were transformed into fissures, which radiated out from the base of the neck over the entire length of the skull, thus capping Besson's head as though with a hand, an insidious, hurtful hand, each time thrusting its bony fingers a little deeper into bone, flesh and meninges. Besson stopped; he waited there for a few moments, trying to erase the memory from his mind.

As one way of accomplishing this end he began to whistle softly between his teeth. Then he resumed his tangential advance, a consciously preoccupied expression showing on his face. He sat down at the table, placed the drawer on his knees, and began to ransack it once more. But almost at once he stopped, and returned the drawer to its place.

Outside, in the street below, some car was sounding its horn furiously. Besson looked at his watch, which lay on the table beside him, and then at the spirit-lamp for heating coffee, with its little tin saucepan on top. He put out his hand, almost touched the stand of the lamp, changed his mind, and instead picked up a coffee-spoon with his fingertips, planting it upright in the middle of the empty cup, and morosely stirring the mixture of coffee and glued-up sugar. Next he took the ashtray (a proprietory brand) and emptied it into the cup. He pushed the coffee-spoon round until ashes, cigarette-ends, sugar, coffee and matchsticks formed a kind of unified compost.

The sound of the horn interrupted him. He got up, opened a shutter, and looked down. He saw wet pavements, as though it had been raining, and a large number of stationary cars. The air was cold, and the sounds came from some distance off—the other side of the town, probably. It was like being shut at the bottom of an elbow-shaped cave, vaguely conscious, in the distance, of this white, confused mass of sound, light, scent and movement, Besson took it all in for a moment; then, very naturally, (insofar as having one forearm placed on the windowsill, his head resting against the open shutter, and his body bent forward in such a way as to throw weight on the pectoral muscles impelled him to take *some* sort of action), he settled into the pose; he also took a cigarette from the breast-pocket of his pyjama jacket, a box of matches from one side-pocket, and lit up.

When he had finished smoking, he stubbed his cigarette out against the window-sash and flipped it into the street. He remained there a moment longer, staring at the small black mark burnt into the wood, like a tiny extinguished brazier; then he quit his post, closed shutters and window once more, and returned to the middle of the room.

This time he made for a kind of commode, or chest of drawers, which stood in the left-hand corner of the room. On top of this commode stood a tape-recorder. Besson switched it on.

He waited without doing anything further until the greenish control light flickered on, shedding the faintest suspicion of brightness amid the yellowish gloom which had hitherto dominated the place. Then Besson pressed a button, and the spools of the tape-recorder began to revolve at top speed, clattering as they did so. Besson kept one eye on the revolution-counter, spelling out the figures as they flicked past: 145, 140, 135, 130, 125, 120, 115, 110, 105, and so on. When the dial of the counter showed 45, he pressed another button, and the spools stopped. Then he switched over to 'Playback', hesitated a moment, and jabbed his finger down on the starter. Almost instantly the sound of a woman's voice, a young girl's voice pitched to something like F sharp, filled the room. With one swift movement he lay down on the bed and began to listen. At first there was a very soft hissing noise, like the resonances of some long and barely pronounceable word, such as parallelopiped or Ishikawa Goyemon, a sighing note shaped to an H or a J. Then for several seconds there was purring silence again, pullulating with words and gestures. Finally the green light at the far side of the room shivered; someone began to speak and breathe, mouth held close to the microphone, in a most fresh, delicate voice, a living, pulsing body encircling the warm machine. Though her words were barely audible, they seemed to quiver with power. They were murmured, breathed out with a husky catch in the throat, but vastly magnified by the loud-speaker. Now each syllable was a shout, consonants crashed against one another, the least indrawing of breath became a fearful death-rattle. A sort of spurious fury permeated every corner of the room, settling on the furniture and the odds and ends, gathering in each stratum of shadowy air.

. . .'cause I had no idea what to do. I tried writing to him, sent him a letter for Christmas. He'd written me once, a postcard from Coventry, without his name on it or anything. He'd even disguised his handwriting. That was silly of him, he knew very well it couldn't be from anyone else. Even supposing, even supposing he didn't think of that on the spur of the moment, when he printed the letters in capitals and the rest of it, all the same he can't have helped realizing the truth when it came to signing the thing. It was a view of Coventry Cathedral, you know, something like that anyhow, and he'd sketched in a cowboy on top of the photograph, taking pot-shots at the passers-by with a revolver, and on the other side of the card he'd written, in English, *Wish you were here*. And he'd signed it with an imaginary name—scratched it out afterwards, but you could still read it, he couldn't even be bothered to make a proper job of an erasure, and anyway he did it on purpose so that I'd try to decipher it. I looked through a magnifying-glass, and there under the ink-scratches was written John Wallon, or John Warren, something like that. It was so *silly*. If I—

Besson jumped off the bed and stopped the tape-recorder. Then he went through the whole rigmarole over again, except that this time he checked the spool when the dial showed 15. He pressed the button, and turned his head a fraction to one side, as though someone were on the point of entering the room. At the same moment, his eyes concentrated on a particular part of the wall, at the far end of the room. The tape played through in an uneasy silence, with tiny murmurs and whirring sounds from the motor, and the tense, quick note of his breathing. Something oppressive and conspicuous had dropped in on the scene, some single object as solid as a meteorite. The night was stifling, it must be like a tight band round people's temples. The penetrating sound of the girl's voice seemed held back in time for ten or a dozen minutes; and yet the genuine quality of this voice, the echo-presumptive of those preceding remarks, had already filled the whole place, was vibrating in every corner of it, spiralling out towards the kitchen door and the hall, exploring keyholes, sometimes comprehensible, sometimes not, disruptive of all ties, inimical to real life.

It was rather like making the attempt to catch a fragment of wind, entice it through an open window and shut it up in some bare, cube-like room. Or, more closely, like constructing a small cardboard box, lined with mirrors, in order to imprison a ray of light: the lid once shut, the ray of light would go on reflecting *ad infinitum* from one side of the box to the other. After catching it you would keep it a long time, a year, maybe, or even more, and then one evening, one particular evening, when it was dark, you would carry the little box into your room, and there, very gently, you would open it. And you would see the ray of light dart out, piercing through the night like a star, before it vanished into the black veils of darkness, oblivion's pitchy chiffon.

François Besson went back to the bed. First he sat upright on it,

50

keeping his eyes fixed on the traditional point some 22 cms to the left of the map of Europe pinned to the wall; then he let himself slump back, not even supporting himself on his elbows. His head missed the pillow by a good foot and a half, but he paid no attention. He stretched out his legs on the mattress, and avoided looking at the ceiling. Since he had to look at something, he preferred it to be an object which brought to mind the long hours he had spent on his feet during the past few days. He scrutinized his jacket, now suspended on a coat-hanger from the handle of the right-hand window. The winking neon-sign outside, by pure accident, suddenly began (having chosen an absurd reflection-point) to adorn the end of his nose, the cleft in his chin, and the tips of his eyelashes, at regular intervals, with little red patches. Every wink changed the colour-tone of the room by something like the ten-millionth of a degree. Then the girl's voice began again, a hint of a tremor in it, like a guttering match:

François—my dear François. You're going to find all this very silly. It's just the way I felt like talking to you today, I don't know why. How it came about I've no idea, but suddenly I began thinking of you. I was getting bored all alone in my room, and it was raining outside, and I had this attack of 'flu, oh *you* know—Good, you're there at last, h'm? Then yesterday I ran into Lina, and she talked about you. Not directly, oh no, she just happened to bring the subject up in some other connection. She didn't even remember your name, she told me: didn't you ever see her again? That big thin gawky girl who was trying to make a career as an actress, remember? And then she went straight on to something else, so that I didn't have time to think about you then. It was this morning, just as I was getting up, that I began to. I remembered I hadn't even answered your letter, the one you sent two months ago. No, I hadn't forgotten, but every time I meant to reply some snag came up, a visitor, something or other, and I put it off till later. Anyway, I had really made up my mind to get in touch with you, today, or a bit later. I tried to write a letter, but it wasn't any good. The more I thought about the idea, the more difficult I found it. You know, generally letters are no bother to me at all, I mean, I just take a sheet of paper and the thing dictates itself as I write. But with you it was different. I read your letter through again, twice, do you realize? And the more I looked at it, the more it—the more it *scared* me. Really paralysed me, in fact. I mean, it was so well written, and so sincere too, and there was I with absolutely nothing to say. I know it's absolutely ridiculous, but I just didn't dare try to produce something in the same class. That's the truth, I swear it, really it is. There was nothing so extraordinary about your letter, nothing all that *literary*, I mean, but it just, I don't know, it just struck me as *difficult*. I didn't even feel like *trying* to compete with it. In a way it was something that had to remain unique, like a compliment, do you see what I mean? I just couldn't reply, if I had the whole thing would have been spoilt. I thought—well, for a moment I thought the best way out was to send you a very short little note, on a visiting-card, saying something like 'Thank you for your letter'. I'm sure you'd have understood that. Or else I might have sent you a telegram, or come round to see you at your place. Or just done nothing at all. Nothing at all. Because, in the last resort, it was the kind of letter that doesn't need a reply. I believe—But I was afraid you might be cross, and then I had an idea. Why, I told myself, I could tape my reply, and send you the spool. That way you can hear my actual voice. Besides, I can talk as I feel, I don't need to make up any fine phrases, it doesn't *matter*. I really do get the feeling that you're going to listen, that I'm free to say what I like. So I went round to Lina and asked her to lend me her tape-recorder and a clean spool. I didn't tell her why I wanted them. She agreed. Oh, there's just one thing—when you've finished with the spool, she'd like it back. Just send it through the post, her address is 12 Rue de Copernic. That's all.

It's been a long time since I've seen you, so I've got an

excuse for saying I hope all goes well with you. There's a whole heap of news I could tell you about me and the rest of us—but I'm not all that anxious to hold forth to you on *that* particular topic. Well, anyway, I'm still very much the same —going to psychology lectures, and working now and then. I've been doing some painting recently, too. I find it absorbing, but heaven knows if my stuff's any good. For several days now I've been having a red phase. You simply have no idea what an extraordinary colour red is. I never realized till I started using it. I cover vast canvases with red and nothing else. Now I find myself noticing every red object, and you know, there's an awful lot of them around. I've begun collecting them, too. Anything, so long as it's red. I've got bits of material and cardboard boxes and scraps of paper, oh yes and cigarette packets, those Craven A ones, you know. I even keep bits of cotton-wool with blood on them, but the trouble about that is that the blood turns black when it dries. Remember the letters we used to write each other in the old days? Funny the way we invented excuses to send a letter, anything would do. And then we'd post them, very seriously, going home from school, and read them privately in our bedrooms. It was a fine idea for public holidays, or New Year's Day or Easter, or celebrations like 21st September and 5th July. If we wanted to correspond at other times we had to find some special reason. I used to look in the calendar to see which saint's day it was, and then write: My dear François, I'm sending you this note today with all my good wishes on the feast of St. Thingummy or St. Whatsit. I even remember there were occasions on which no saints appeared in the calendar, and then I'd send you good wishes for the Immaculate Conception, or the feast of Christ the King. Remember? But that's all over and done with now. I can't use dodges like that any more. Even with you. Even if I could be certain you'd understand. Even if I was sure you wouldn't tell me I was trying to play arty poetic tricks with past memories. Anyway, my position nowadays is very simple on *that* score—I just can't write any more, not a word. It's—it's a kind of illness. The mere sight of a blank white sheet of paper's enough to depress me half out of my mind. Frankly, it beats me how anyone still manages to go in for writing—novels, poetry, that kind of kick. Because in the last resort it's quite useless. Pure dumb egotism. Plus the urge to expose yourself, let other people gobble you up. Anyway it's so exhausting. Honestly, I just don't get it. I tell you, I can understand people writing letters and postcards better than I can someone settling down to a novel. It serves no purpose, there isn't any truth in it. I mean, you don't make any discoveries or isolate any area of knowledge, you just wallow in illusion. To my way of thinking, it's like an animal manufacturing its own parasites, a shellfish that creates its own seaweed and attaches the stuff, personally, to its carapace. Art. As far as I'm concerned, I've had it. I just don't believe in it any more. You know, when I told Marc Morgenstein that the other day, he just laughed at me. He said it was all nonsense—I wrote far too well, he liked my stuff, and I was crazy to take myself seriously on such a subject. He also told me that art's never existed anyway, people talking about it is the only thing that counts. According to him, *anything* can be reduced to conversation. He also said that when someone had written a piece like 'Imitation Leather'—you know, the story of the housewife who gets an obsessional thing about her trolley-bus— well, that proved they had something to say. And when one's got something to say, sooner or later one always manages to say it. I told him that made no difference— everyone in the world had *something* to say. But he didn't get it. All the same, I really believe it's true. I *do* want to say things, yes, but not in the way I did before. I get the feeling one can express them equally well by—by doing almost anything, going round to the baker's for bread, or having a chat with the concierge. Obviously I don't talk about this to the others. You're no longer in favour. But I don't think it matters. What's the point of being regarded as a person of

54

intelligence? One can get along very well on one's own, don't you agree? What's really needed, I feel, is the ability to detach oneself, stand aside. Anyway as far as I'm concerned it's the end of the road. I can't stomach lies and poetry any longer.

You know, when you get down to it, people like Morgenstein are about the lowest sort of bastards going. I might be sitting in some café, for instance, lost in my own thoughts—I mean, the kind of ideas that run through your mind sometimes when you're on your own, and it's raining, and you get the feeling that—that everything's *stopped*. Then in come these types like Morgenstein, sit down, and begin to talk a lot of highflown guff about God, or Marxism, or that line you've got at the corner of your mouth—*and* about the sort of character you represent in their eyes, all alone like that in a café at two o'clock in the afternoon. It's sure to remind them of some favourite quotation or other, some slop from Racine or Lorca—that kind of thing always gets me so *mad*! Then—as though you hadn't thought about it enough on your own in the café or at home, as though you weren't capable of such a reaction, as though the most you could rise to were silly whims and pseudo-problems—they say things like: Ah yes, I really enjoyed 'Imitation Leather', it reminded me of Conrad, or Kipling. You've got to go on writing, they tell you, you're young: it'll come, you see if it doesn't. It's not so much what they actually say to you at the time—what I can't stand, what really disgusts me, is the thought that when you've left they'll still be at it with some other victim. *They* couldn't care less. They've had their little moment of friendship and private confidences, they've rinsed their mouth out with it and feel quite cock-a-hoop. They're satisfied. The world belongs to them. I know what they make me think of, they make me think of all those half-wits who rush round back-stage after a performance to unload their crappy compliments on the actors. Just *perfect*, darling. I so much admired your performance. Honestly, no kidding, you were just great. You try to hide, but they pursue you into every corner, and the more compliments they shower on you, the more naked and half-witted you feel yourself. This sort of thing's worse than any insult. Oh, I know I've no right to talk about you like this, I mean, I haven't any experience, I only acted once in my life, with Morgenstein's group. When it was over I was *exhausted*, you've just no idea how exhausted I was. I felt like throwing up, I was trembling from head to foot, I wanted to kill everyone in sight. Yet at the same time, isn't it odd, I felt empty, flaccid, incapable of doing another thing. And there were other types who managed to catch hold of my arm, and embrace me, and offer their congratulations, and all that jazz. I mean, it's the same sort of thing if you're a writer, these days. Morgenstein's remarks didn't add up to anything on their own. But before that, you know, when Paul left—no, I'm wrong, it was several days earlier, I think—oh hell, it doesn't matter anyway. Well, this is the honest truth, I damned nearly emptied all my mother's tubes of Gardenal down my throat. I'd just finished a short story about a snail called Albert, pretty pretentious stuff, but at least I believed in it this time. All the same, thinking it over again now I can see I'd picked up all the smart mannerisms, *you* know, bombastic tricks of style, and cute jokes, and crude bits of allegory about self-awareness—and it all had a most unhappy ending, I mean, the snail was cut off from the rest of the world by having the opening in his shell sealed up, just a layer of calcareous matter did the trick, and there was Albert, immobilized. And died. It had amused me to believe in the whole idea, not so much because it might prove a work of genius, or any junk like that—but simply because it was good for a giggle. Well, that wasn't how it turned out. Quite the reverse, in fact. I thought I'd got the thing under control, but I hadn't. That snail really took it out of me. At first I set my-self to love it a little, just a shade more than was normal. I spent whole days correcting and rewriting the story. Each time I gave the snail a different first name, to see which one suited him best. I tried calling him Jules, Baptiste, Jean-Bernard, Mathieu, Antoine, and heaven knows what else. This probably strikes you as childish, and now I come to think of it again, it strikes *me* as childish; but at the time I felt it was terribly important. I felt I'd caught, well, a kind of realism, if you like—realism which went far beyond the bounds of the plain narrative. And that as a result there had to be a special first name for every kind of character. I mean, a snail can't be called anything but Albert, and a goldfish is always Stanislas, and alley-cats *have* to be called Rama. You know the kind of thing. In fact they were the last props, the last underprops I really mean, of my entire, well, my entire hypocritical life, no not that exactly, but—oh *you* know, that sort of sudden realization that your life's one great lie, that you're lurching on through a mass of trick-effects like a damned doll, a puppet with someone else pulling the strings, and the worst thing of all is that throughout you're convinced you're *you*, your real self. You let yourself be manipulated like this, and all the time you're beaming a sunny satisfied smile, you're happy, you imagine you've actually invented something on your own, that you're writing *because that's the way things are*. And all the time someone else is pulling the strings, some mentor is controlling your comings and goings, making you write words on bits of paper, and remember bits of your past, leaving you alone in your room, or on the street, in cafés, cinemas, buses, on the stage—do you understand? He's the one who always leaves you in silent solitude, he's the one who gnaws away at your confidence, who gets you down, little by little, breaks your spirit, an endless process of slow attrition.

That's what really makes me sick. You know, there I was, working on this story of Albert the snail, spending all day pounding my typewriter—and then Paul took off, just walked out on me. I—I told you all about that before, in the park, remember? But I didn't tell you everything. You must have thought me a complete ninny, going overboard for someone like Paul. It's true he's not an interesting sort of character, really, but all the same—I don't know how to explain this—he's got something, there are amusing sides to his personality, and he's so *unpredictable*. One day he'll come home and set about being a sort of caricature drunk, without taking any notice of a word you say for anything up to a quarter of an hour. Or else he'll hurl himself at the typewriter and knock out a surrealist poem. I've known him get back at midnight, turn on the light, and start walking round and round the table like some sort of nut, pretending to be two people at once, answering his own questions. When he's like that, he's fine. Just fine. But he's a bastard, all the same. I didn't realize that at first. I couldn't understand how anyone could spend fifteen minutes making you laugh, and then, the next instant, behave as though you just didn't exist. I thought that under it all Paul must be an unhappy character, full of complexes and the rest of it, who wanted to hide his real personality. I felt that because it's the way I am myself. What struck me as so incredible, though, was that anyone could play the kind of game that seemed to be saying to people, Look, you know I really love you deep down, the way children carry on—and then not give a damn when it came to the crunch. I didn't understand, then, that people like that are really the worst of the lot, because they're so totally self-obsessed. Like Morgenstein. It's true, you know —it never struck me before, but when you get down to it Paul and Morgenstein are two of a kind. Every time they put on a comic act, or look hurt, it's pure eyewash—they're thinking about themselves the whole time, cocking an eye to see if they're catching any applause—they fairly gorge themselves on praise, the conceited creatures. They can't stand being losers, either. Oh I know I sound as though I'm working off some personal grudge against them, that's obvious, but I'll swear to God that's not what really turns me up about them. No, what gets me is that these bastards always come out on top. I'm a sucker, I fall for it every time.

They pretend to be drunk, but they're—they're just making a fool of me really, and even then it doesn't make a damn of difference, I'm happy as Larry, I think they're so good-looking and sensitive and intelligent they just make me melt. That's the way it goes, every time. They're always the winners. Even now. Paul really hurt me, do you realize that? There was I, wasting my time trying to get words down on bits of paper, going round the bend over this nonsense about a snail and its limed-up shell, while all the time he, *he*—God, he just didn't give a fuck about the whole set-up, he knew perfectly well he was going to get out. He used to take off down the street in his new suit, and spend every evening going round the night-clubs—he picked up other girls, too, he—and on top of all this he was just plain bored, and made no secret of it. When he was with me he never said a word, unless he put on his drunk act. I want to tell you what happened the night before he left, though. I was sitting typing at my table—still the story about the snail. I'd made up my mind to start the whole thing again from scratch, changing all the names. I left nothing the same except the verbs. Some time between eleven and midnight he came in. He stared at me a moment without saying a word, narrowing his eyes the way he does when he's looking at something that doesn't interest him. As though he were examining you through the glass wall of an aquarium. I stopped my work and asked him what he wanted. He made no reply, just went on staring at me in that vague way, completely silent. So I started typing again, and just behaved as if he wasn't there. He stayed like that for a moment, not doing anything, and then suddenly he went into one of his routines. This time it was shadow-boxing. He pranced all round the room, weaving and feinting, jabbing away at the curtains and the pillows on my bed. Then he squared up to me and threw phoney punches at my face and stomach. He fell down for an imaginary count and got up again, he groaned and panted, he made *kh! kh!* noises through his nose to represent the sound of fists hitting flesh.

59

After a moment I'd had more than enough of this, and I told him to knock it off and leave me to work in peace. He took no notice, just went on worse than ever. I went out to the kitchen and drank a glass of milk. When I came back I found him sitting on the bed and smoking one of my cigarettes. I said to him: 'Are those cigarettes mine?' and he replied: 'I don't know, probably.' I went back to the table and started typing again. He just went on smoking, and that irritated me, because I couldn't write with him sitting there on the bed. So I stopped again, and asked him (more for something to say than anything else) if he'd go and get me some more cigarettes when those ran out. At this he smirked rather unpleasantly, and got up to leave, glancing at me in that ironic way of his as he did so. His eyes held mine for about three or four seconds. Then he stubbed out his cigarette in the ashtray beside the typewriter. I pretended I didn't give a damn, but the truth is it gave me quite a turn, seeing his arm and hand pass under my nose like that to stub out his cigarette in my ashtray. You—well, you know, it wasn't just his arm as such, or whatever, it was, it was just the heap of odd thoughts that flashed through my mind as he did it, the notion that he could have been my *brother*, for instance, and only being able to see this detached bit of him, just his arm and the beginning of his pullover sleeve, a few inches from my nose. It made me feel queer to think that it could have been *my* arm, that in the beginning—him and me, I mean—it was like being one person.

What I want to say is, I get these weird ideas going through my head the whole time, about me, and Paul, or my father and mother. I can't shake off the feeling that somehow I don't *exist* in the way other people do. Or else I find myself wondering why I'm not Paul, why Paul is the one who's stretching out his arm towards the ashtray. It's just the same with my mother and father. I know it's silly of me, but I can never isolate them as individuals, define them in relationship to myself. What I'm trying to say is, all I manage is the act, the external act, do you see what I mean? And that doesn't, can't, isolate anything, it just reflects back at me like a mirror. Paul was—Look, François, please, I'm not telling you all this just for the fun of it. I want you to understand why—why Paul going made such a difference to me. I think one of these days I really will take that overdose of Gardenal. And I wouldn't want you to think I'd just done it for nothing but messy sentimental reasons. I—look, I think I must be having a kind of nervous breakdown. But there are always thousands of things like that, little hints and details that go over my head. It's true, though, I'd hate you to think it was just maudlin self-pity. It's a matter of general understanding, awareness, do you see? Well, anyway, I'd better finish my story. Paul stood over me like that for a moment, and then he began to leaf through my typescript. I can't stand people going over my stuff when I'm there—I mean, reading a word or two at random on each page. Oh, *now*, obviously, I couldn't care less, people can do what they like with my manuscripts, it's all the same to me. They don't mean anything to me any longer, they might as well be today's newspaper. But at that particular moment it still really drove me crazy. I just sat there waiting till he was through. After a bit he must have got bored with turning pages over, because do you know what he did, he picked one out of all the pile at random, and began read it aloud. When he did *that*—oh, you won't understand, but it was at that moment I really saw what a bastard he was. I mean, he—it wasn't just that he read it as though he didn't give a damn about it, but on top of that, and this is what I found really awful, he read it so *well*, as though he understood every word, in a fine, serious voice, the works. Paul's always had a beautiful speaking voice. He used to talk very loud, to make sure people noticed what a beautiful voice he had. The nerve of it, playing a dirty little trick like that on *me*—and with one of my own manuscripts! You know, he read so wonderfully, that was what got me. He didn't give tuppence for the words, and *still* it was superb. It was, oh I can't explain, like an apple with maggots inside it, do you see what I mean?

So there was Paul reading, and I wanted—oh, I don't know what I wanted, not to cry, but to go really cold, suddenly, as though someone had removed an important, an essential part of my body. I watched his big heavy hands gripping the paper, heard that serious voice as it intoned my words, very relaxed, but with great power and life and individuality, while I—Oh hell, what does it matter, when he'd finished reading he walked out of the door and I haven't seen him since. That isn't quite the whole story, though. You remember he was alone in my room for a moment while I went out to get a glass of milk? Well, in the time it took me to open the fridge, get out a bottle, and have my drink, he managed to search the room and pocket the money I'd hidden in the wardrobe, under a pile of pullovers. There must have been about sixty notes there, and he took the lot. That's why he put on such a performance when I came back—to distract my attention. That was really pretty steep, I thought. I suppose it's how he paid his fare to England or wherever he went.

Afterwards I felt pretty mad because I had no idea what to do. I tried writing to him, sent him a letter for Christmas. He'd written me once, a postcard from Coventry, without his name on it or anything. He'd even disguised his handwriting. That was silly of him, he knew very well it couldn't be from anyone else. Even supposing, even supposing he didn't think of that on the spur of the moment, when he printed the letters in capitals and the rest of it, all the same he can't have helped realizing the truth when it came to signing the thing. It was a view of Coventry Cathedral, you know, something like that anyhow, and he'd sketched in a cowboy on top of the photograph, taking pot-shots at the passers-by with a revolver, and on the other side of the card he'd written, in English, *Wish you were here*. And he'd signed it with an imaginary name— scratched it out afterwards, but you could still read it, he couldn't even be bothered to make a proper job of an erasure,

62

and anyway he did it on purpose so that I'd try to decipher it. I looked through a magnifying-glass, and there under the ink-scratches was written John Wallon, or John Warren, something like that. It was so *silly*. If I could ever—But it's too late now.

There. I've told you. That's what I wanted to talk to you about. When I'm gone, try not to condemn me. I suppose everything I've said still comes under the heading of literature, really: a monologue doesn't qualify as non-fiction, does it? But I'd like you, at least, to believe me, because of the rest of them, my father and mother, my friends, even Paul if somebody tells him about it one day, believe that I didn't do it out of despair, or just for sloppy sentimental reasons, you know what I mean, but simply because there was nothing much else left for me to do. Tomorrow, if I have the courage, I shall take a glass and a carafe of water, and swallow all my mother's little pink tablets. I'm stopping now because the tape's just about finished. *Au revoir*, Anna Mathilde Passeron.

Besson got up and stopped the tape-recorder. Silence suddenly descended on the room again, mingling with the chiaroscuro, so palpable now that it was no longer distinguishable from the areas of shadow. Then it slipped and shifted, moving sideways with an indescribable pendulum-like motion. It penetrated even to Besson's inner self, filling the secret recesses of his mind, stifling thought. Silence began to reverberate through his head and chest, with a sound not unlike the roar of a large cataract. He could feel its breathing, too, a gentle up and down motion. There was no room for anything else, neither sound nor colour: nothing but illimitable silence, here, in the night, amid this surrounding darkness: a silence that clung to every object, a horrible vast chill calm, clammy, tangible, that left you lying flat and helpless on the floor of an empty room, all alone, moving towards death.

For a long time Besson continued to stare at the motionless objects in front of him. He stood and scrutinized them with a gaze of fixed and burning intensity, which neither saw nor made any attempt to comprehend them. The words just spoken had entered his skull, and it was they that now swarmed in the silence. Like so much furniture, like a row of heavy, useless, ornamental vases, they had dragged on, vacant, floating, unattached; and now they were back in their own proper domain, that mute kingdom from which they would never re-emerge. From nothing they came, to nothing they returned. The world of insanity, the filthy sewer-flow of battering words, syllables chopped from distorted human lips, pointless and interminable chatter. And what, truly, was the object of it all, what was it after? To try and hook on somewhere, put out tentacles, infiltrate other people's minds, though with all this they still never achieve personality. Accursed, accursed be the tongues of mankind! Had they never existed, had they not duped humanity century after century, how much happier would life on this earth have been!

After this lengthy contemplation of the deep-shadowed objects before him, Besson went back to his bed. For a moment he gazed up at the ceiling, with the reflected glow from passing cars' head-lights moving across it; then he stretched out on top of the blankets and tried to sleep. But it was not so easy. In the first place, the shadows had begun to move. Then there was music somewhere, a tune which Besson, though he stiffened his resistance till it was rock-hard, still could not help humming under his breath. At first it was an easy, flexible theme that could be followed without any trouble. But soon the parts multiplied, the humming became a regular symphony orchestra, complete with trumpet, clavicord, oboe, flute, violin, cello, harp and cymbals.

When he was tired of sorting out the score and following its variously divergent threads of melody, Besson opened his eyes, sat up on the bed, and waited.

The room was still the same: a large cube with barely visible walls, a grey expanse of floor, closed and white-slatted shutters: a sealed-off, private place, and one that he knew by heart. Sounds from outside drifted up the face of the building and made their way in through the window: familiar, unimportant noises, easily identifiable during their leisurely passage—the whirr of car-tyres on wet macadam, the drone of engines, a motor-cycle put-putting down the street, slowly fading away in the distance. The tap of heels on the pavement, murmuring of voices. A tremendous thunder-clap. Rain-drops pattering on the shutters. All these sounds were pleasurable. One forgot everything—even the fact that one was alive.

The darkness was rich-textured, its black surface shot with bluish glints, grey half-tones, gleams of whiteness. The room was sealed, hermetically sealed, and he, Besson, was inside it. Neither hot nor cold. Time passed smoothly, second by second, impalpable, untouched by chaos.

It was like being in a small and cosy dream, a house of one's own, bought and paid for, surrounded by a big silent garden. A piece of property at Lorgues, two acres of land, umbrella pines, the scent of lavender, with a sweet little stream flowing through it, a five-roomed farmhouse, a well, some cobbles. In fact it was even better than that, because one possessed nothing at all. No, it was enough to be oneself, alone in a closed room, without light, with the sound of rain-drops tapping against the slats of the shutters. Minutes and hours stretch out interminably, their slow passage is sheer delight: actions and thoughts form a sequence of harmonious moments, lucid, exquisitely clear, suspended in continuity. What a good thing, what a *really* good thing it is to have a room of one's own!

With slow movements, François Besson lit another cigarette. The flame of the match, white at first, then yellow, pierced through the darkness in the room. The loose strands of tobacco at the tip of the cigarette writhed and glowed, the paper caught fire. It occurred to Besson that what he would really like was a room lined with mirrors, so as not to miss any detail of what he was about. The match suddenly went out, without his needing to blow it, and all that remained in the darkness was a red glowing hole, close to his face, which got a little deeper each time he inhaled.

After a while Besson got up and began to prowl round the room. He wandered from one piece of furniture to another, peered through the slits in the shutters. As it was cold, he slipped his coat on over his pyjama jacket. Then he sat down on the edge of the bed again. Here he remained for a moment, quite still, contemplating the square mass of the table.

It must have been about half past twelve or one in the morning, because the church clock nearby had only chimed once. Somewhere off in the middle of the town a fire-engine was tearing along, siren screaming. From time to time a rumble of thunder could be heard. But inside the room there was no danger: neither rain nor lightning-flashes could penetrate there, and all remained still. There was no breath of wind. Everything was tranquil and assured; each object had its appointed place, the disposition of surfaces remained constant. You could shut your eyes, and when you opened them again a moment later nothing would have changed.

The whole thing was just right. François Besson sat there inside his calm and minuscule pattern, as though encircled by a frame. It was a very fine pattern, traced with a pen on white paper, where everything was fixed for some sort of eternity; a genuine caricature, too, in which every object—each ashtray, each piece of furniture—had found its precise silhouette recorded. The dado on the wall, with its small scrawled design, ochre against a white ground, had been faithfully reproduced; so had the handle of the door, a green plastic knob, and the key-hole, its wards so cut that it would only take the right key. Then there were the bedclothes, a pair of slippers, two chairs with purple cushions; the double window with its greenish shutters; the map of Europe pinned to the wall, with all those strange names printed against capes and peninsulas: Mandal, Cuxhaven, Penmarc'h, Jamaja, Mechra el Hader, Tomaszów, Ape, Sasovo, Yecla. And at the centre of the pattern, squatting on the edge of his bed, was this caricature of a man, with scrawny limbs and high cheekbones and cropped hair, who sat quite still, staring into space. It gave one an urge to develop the pattern further: to colour it, for instance, or write something in one of those white balloons emerging from people's mouths, such as 'I wonder what I'm doing here', or 'It's good to

66

be indoors at home when the rain's coming down like that outside'.

Besson got up and walked to the right-hand window, pressed his forehead against the cold glass, and looked around. The street was almost deserted. Rain was beating down on its surface, and that of the pavement on either side; a great pool of unwavering light spread round the foot of each street-lamp. All the shops had turned off their illuminated signs except one, where a line of neon still glowed at the bottom of the display-window. Cars sped past with a hiss of tyres. From time to time some stooping, shadowy figure, wrapped in a macintosh, could be seen hurrying along under the lee of the walls. The way the shutter-slats were aligned, Besson was unable to see the sky; but the odds were that it was near-black with perhaps a touch of pink, and the rain coming down from the middle of it, and from heaven knows where before that.

Very slowly, standing there by that icy window with the condensation forming on it, eyes eagerly scrutinizing the peaceful stretch of road where perhaps danger yet lurked, ears alert for the sound of innumerable fine rain-drops falling in unison, while the town beyond pullulated with a thousand sounds and lights, Besson felt a strange sense of intoxication surge up within him. He was *alive*, then, in his body, contained in his own skin, face to face with the world he had designed. Sensations ran together in his various organs, established a cautious foothold there, jostled one another for place, struck up music. A series of deep pulsing vibrations arose from the heart of darkness, out of flatness and obscurity, and then through him, through his conscious body, they became movement, throbbing, powerful movement, measuring time. They mounted straight towards the sky, dominated unknown space, plumbed the abysses of mystery and emptiness. The void, the enormous void, a living, breathing entity, was always *there*, eternally present behind each individual object. It dug out chambers beneath the earth's crust, it forced its way through the stiff metal uprights of the street-lamps, light was carried on it in tiny eddying vibrations. The void was present in glass and bronze and concrete. It had its own colour and shape. And what, finally, enabled you to see the substance of the void was nothing other than this sense of intoxication, which went on growing without anything to support it. Like a bouquet, like some joyous explosion of giant flowers, gleams of light all fusing together in a single mystical efflorescence, life traced its pattern on the face of the night. No ordinary ray of light could ever, ever make you forget the shadows. There had to be this irresistible feeling of intoxication, this joyful sense of being really *there*, for one to comprehend the full reality of the void: to shiver at its chill contact, to perceive the transparence of it, to hear the terrible, heavy roaring sound of silence, bare, skeletal silence with its multiple voices, its tunes that surge and swell and carry you up till you could put out your hand and touch infinity; to intone with it that agonizing song of the years going by you, the actions you perform, the song of all that *is*, that's triumphantly alive, that embodies life with an undying ephemeral glory in such immensity that when you have been dead and rotten for centuries it will still not have reached the first moment of its advent.

Then, when everything had been touched, breathed, seen and heard with minutely detailed attention, Besson went across to the door and switched on the electric light. In a flash the room was filled with yellow radiance, which illuminated every remote corner, made objects stand out from the floor as though by levitation. Besson went back to his table, and sat down. But this time he did not touch anything. He simply rested both elbows on the wooden surfaces, and kept quite still.

Outside, the rain was still falling. There came a steady drumming from the swollen gutters, and another, softer sound, as each separate drop filled up another tiny patch on the exposed white stucco façade, very gently, without seeming to do so. The wind was blowing in sharp gusts, so that loose shutters banged to and fro, and twigs were torn from the trees and came pattering against the windows.

As he sat there Besson felt a numb torpor steal over him, the terrified urge to burrow right down to the bottom of a heap of leaves, and hibernate. He sensed something of what trees experience: sadness and melancholy clutched at his heart, his life seemed to ebb perceptibly. Beyond the ramparts of his room the sky still loomed heavily. Each time he drew breath, a pall of vapour penetrated his lungs, a strange sense of *weathering* descended on him. Was it for *this* that one was alive, was it for *this* that one tried to *think*, at all costs, that one fought to encompass the world by the power of reason? To be an organism scarcely distinguishable from a tree, to have, in the last resort, all these roots, these yellowed and slowly falling leaves? To become stooped and bent, to feel your bones creak, and wear out your ancient wrinkled skin in its long battle with time? To be shovelled away into the ground, held close in its vice-like grip, and achieve oneness with the turning seasons?

At this point someone knocked twice on the door of the room. Besson heard, but made no reply. A few seconds later the summons was repeated: four knocks this time. Besson turned his head towards the door and said: 'Come in.'

A woman entered the room. She was about sixty, and wore a brown dressing-gown with red slippers. Her face was heavy with fatigue, and her grey hair hung loose down her back. Cautiously she took a step or two towards the table.

'Can't you sleep?' she asked.

'No,' Besson said.

The woman sat down on the edge of the bed. She had very large eyes, with brownish rings under them. She smiled, tentatively.

'You ought to go to bed,' she said. 'It's nearly three in the morning.'

Besson made a show of searching for some paper on his table.

'I'm not sleepy,' he said.

'You'll make yourself ill—'

'No, really, I'm not tired.'

The woman looked at the table.

'Are you working?'

'Yes.'

'Tiring yourself out for nothing,' the woman said. 'You'd be better off asleep.'

'Yes, I know,' Besson said. 'But I'm in the middle of sorting out these papers.'

She said nothing for a moment. Besson looked at her hands, and noticed that they were covered with thick bulging veins. Then he glanced up at her face.

'What about you?' he said. 'You're not asleep either.'

'I heard you playing the tape-recorder just now,' the woman said. 'You'll wake your father, you know. You ought to—'

She did not finish the sentence.

'I'm going to bed in a minute,' Besson said. 'I had no idea it was so late.'

'Very nearly three o'clock.'

'I didn't hear the clock strike.'

'What about your watch?'

Besson glanced down at the table. 'Twenty-five to three,' he said. There was another silence.

'Aren't you cold?' the woman said.

'No.'

The woman turned her head a little to one side.

'What a stink of stale tobacco-smoke,' she said. 'Don't you think you ought to cut down your smoking a bit?'

Besson shrugged. 'Yes, maybe,' he said.

'All those cigarettes can't be doing you any good.' She pulled her dressing-gown tighter round her. 'Well, I'm off to bed then,' she said.

Besson began to fiddle with the coffee-spoon.

'Have you been drinking a lot of coffee?' the woman asked.

'No, just one cup.'

'Because *that* isn't going to help you to sleep, you know.'

'Maybe, but it keeps me warm.'

She got up and came towards the table.

'Don't be too long getting to bed,' she said.

'No, of course not, I'll be off in a moment,' Besson said.

'Up every night like this till three o'clock, you'll end by making yourself ill.'

'There's no danger of that, I assure you.'

The woman looked towards the windows. 'My, just look at that rain,' she said.

'Yes,' Besson agreed. 'It's certainly coming down.'

'The end-of-winter rains,' she said, and began to retreat towards the door.

'I'm going back to bed, then,' she said.

'Good,' Besson said.

'Don't sit up like that too long, François.'

'No, I'm going to bed too.'

She hesitated a moment, then said: 'And—and don't go on thinking about . . . all that business, François.'

Silence.

'Do you hear me? Don't go on thinking about—'

'Yes. Yes, I heard you.'

She made a great effort. 'It can't—I mean, it does no *good*, do you see?'

He made no reply.

'You mustn't think about all that business. Go to sleep. Don't think about anything.'

'All right,' Besson said.

'If there's anything you need, just let me know.'

'I don't need anything, thank you.'

She began to go out; and then she turned her puffy face back towards Besson, and the sight pierced him to the heart. Eyes, hands, mouth, grey hair—all carried the same message, of compassion and love. Besson lowered his head and looked away.

'Goodnight, François,' the woman's voice said.

'Goodnight,' said Besson.

'Sleep well,' she said. 'See you tomorrow—' Then she gave a little laugh. 'What am I saying, tomorrow's today, isn't it? I mean, three in the morning—'

'Goodnight.'

'Sleep well.'

71

'Goodnight.'

The door closed behind her.

For a moment Besson remained quite still, as though his mother might have taken it into her head to watch his actions through the key-hole. Then he got up and, an imaginary gun in his hands, began to act out a vendetta within the four walls of his room.

Chapter Two

In the street—The eyes—François Besson visits the first café and reads the paper—The broken glass—François Besson visits the second café and plays the pin-ball machine—Meeting with his brother

THE second day, as soon as the sun was up, François Besson dressed and went out. He walked quickly through the streets, observing the scene around him. The sky was grey, with a faint flush of pink towards the east. On waste lots, and around the buildings, patches of undried mud glistened in the morning light. Crowds of men were on their way to work. They stood queueing for buses on street corners, or hurried along on foot, with bicycles, in cars. Unaccompanied women walked very fast, wearing black or red macintoshes, or, very occasionally, tartan. The mist from the thickest clouds still floated down almost to ground level: drops finer than dust-particles hung suspended between earth and sky, rising and falling, till they finally dissolved on some flat surface, noiselessly, leaving not so much as a small damp halo behind. They melted before they reached the ground, and mingled with the substance of the air. A blanket of mist hung over the town, filled the trees, clung to the skin of those abroad in the streets. Nothing was distinct or clear-cut any longer: outlines blurred and ran into one another, or even vanished altogether, as though wiped out with an eraser.

It was through all this that Besson set out to walk. He passed down two or three avenues lined with bare, leafless trees. He negotiated squares and crossings, streets and alleys. He waited when the lights were red. He skirted roundabouts, back-tracked out of blind alleys, and avoided stretches of dug-up pavement where men were toiling with picks and pneumatic drills. He slapped the flat of his hand against two or three No Entry signs.

73

He bumped into obstacles, right in the middle of the street. From time to time, when he was crossing the street, he would deliberately slow down in order to make cars brake.

When he reached the town centre, he put his hands in his pockets and gazed around him. The air was very fresh, the fine mist was still mizzling down, but taken all in all it was pleasant not to be able to see the sun. All that was visible of it was a pale disc, behind banks of grey moving clouds, no brighter than the moon.

The place gave the impression of being a strategic focal point: buses and cars came streaming in from every direction, and the pavements were crowded. People passed to and fro ceaselessly, as though it had always been like this since the beginning of time. There was not so much as a pocket of silence anywhere.

The dustbins were still standing there in the gutter, crammed to overflowing with tin cans, potato peelings, and apple cores, awaiting the arrival of the big, clattering garbage truck responsible for emptying them. A whole day's life had accumulated in these heaps of refuse: people had bought, eaten, sucked, chewed, and, finally, thrown out.

Already there were men and women walking along loaded down with bags of vegetables and parcels of meat. These were making ready for the following day's garbage—crumpled-up balls of grey paper, the leafy part of leeks, date-stones, stale and blood-patched bones. The dustbins would always be there. At about the same time every evening, people would furtively carry down their stinking bucketfuls, and empty them in one quick, unregretful movement. In this way life was consumed, day after day, without any fuss or difficulty. Fragments of fatty edible matter would flow through the pipes, and tons, mountains of excrement would return to the earth once more.

Outside the shops women in aprons were sluicing down the sidewalk with buckets of soapy water, and sweeping it off with brooms. In one butcher's shop whole young calves were hanging from hooks, all the blood drained out of them, split clean down

74

from chine to rump. The sawdust beneath them was slightly spotted with red, but hardly enough to matter. In box-like refrigerated display-cases dead chickens and rabbits lay lined up, side by side. As he passed by Besson noticed their strangely protruding eyes, and the ridiculous way the stumps of their severed paws stuck up into the air. Inside the shop, with its white tiles, and the legend FAMILY BUTCHER prominently displayed, women were jostling one another to get a better view. Plump hands lifted up hunks of meat, prodding and pinching. Greedy eyes, voracious mouths, dilated nostrils, all hung calculatingly over raw flesh. Behind the counter stood a ruddy-faced man armed with a cleaver, engaged in an unending process of chopping, slicing, and general mutilation. His movements were quick and precise, and he took no notice of the bone-splinters that flew up into his face.

Farther on, there was the smell of hot bread, wafting in waves from an open doorway: that heavy, doughy odour that went straight to one's head, evoking long-forgotten memories. Yellowish smell, rounded smell, faintly burnt, fresh and warm towards the centre, soft, pliable, full of richness: crackling and crisp outside, yet something that melted on the tongue, and gently spread through every tactile fibre in the body. Bread. Hot bread, feathery-light, still coated all over with a fine layer of dust that tasted like uncooked flour.

On the edge of the pavement, outside an empty shop, there stood a group of large brick-red flower-pots with geraniums growing in them. Besson stopped to look at them for a moment. He studied every detail of these unremarkable plants, standing up so straight and stiff in the pebbly earth with which their pots were filled. He observed their flat, somewhat star-shaped leaves, and the rain-drops that lay lightly on them. A faint breath of wind stirred, and the stems quivered, almost imperceptibly. Each geranium stood bolt upright in its pot, held fast by the tenacious soil packed round it.

On one or two of the leaves, that seemed older than the rest, there were marks resembling old healed-over scars, hinting at damage in the past. Despite the drops of water that trickled continuously over the leaves, gathering round the flowers, dropping one by one down the steps to the black humus below, the geraniums nevertheless retained a dry, almost dusty appearance. There was no insect life in the pots, not a single snail nibbling away at a stalk. In each of these tiny potted deserts there was nothing but the geranium itself, nothing but this pale green skeletal shape, with stiff, spiky branches, fixed in its vertical position, expecting nothing: alive but motionless, the grimy surface of each tiny warped leaf turned up towards the light and air and water. It occurred to Besson that he, too, could have very well lived in a flower-pot, feet deep-rooted in the soil, its grainy texture close around him, his body reaching up, still and silent, into the air. Well, perhaps not, after all, it might not be all that enjoyable: really he was lucky to possess two legs and the ability to use them whenever he felt like it.

Away on the horizon, through a gap between two window-studded blocks, stretched the equally immobile mass of the mountains. Suddenly it struck him how lucky he was not to be a mountain, either. Curious. Clouds passing slowly overhead. Arching one's huge rough back, all covered with thickets and ravines, encircling the town. Even a house, when you began to think about it, offered some sort of existence, lapped in peace, the majestic peace of reinforced concrete, calmly watching the ebb and flow of life around one, with an occasional odd tickling sensation as the lift ascended its shaft.

All this was curious, amusing. The thought made him uneasy.

A bald man wrapped up in a black overcoat was coming towards Besson. As he advanced, he turned his head a little to one side and spat in the gutter. It was as though he had spat in Besson's face.

By now the pavement was a mass of violent activity. Besson felt himself caught in a vortex of legs and faces, chaotic movements, bent backs, hands clasping objects. Bodies continually brushed against him, touching his clothes and stirring up tiny little puffs of air. Pallid faces, eyes staring, loomed up over him, then swerved aside at the last moment. There were men standing outside shop doorways, staring into space. Others, esconed in their cars, let their gaze wander through the closed windows. Children threaded their way between the groups of passers-by, screaming and shouting. Horsy women with large busts standing awkwardly outside greengrocers' shops. A nasal sing-song of voices from the counters of the chain-stores. Even as high as the sixth floor, a number of shadowy figures could be seen hanging over balconies in a menacing way, as though to keep watch on the streets below.

Besson let himself go with the movement of the crowd, empty of all desire, conscious of nothing in himself save the mysterious pattern imposed by all these faces and bodies: walking, walking, sometimes close to the walls, sometimes on the edge of the pavement, dodging landaus, skirting round groups of people, walking, walking, ascending a kind of stark spiral staircase that almost certainly led nowhere.

Time passed: nothing changed. One could go on for years in this way, without doing anything. Without ever having anything to do. Without talking or thinking, just walking on, eyes taking it all in, ears cocked, nose alert, skin exposed to every fluctuation of heat and cold, while a sequence of insignificant events announced themselves by means of small discomforts, fleeting sensations, anonymous sounds. There was no limit on the time one could spend thus, an entire lifetime, perhaps, swallowed up amid this debris, wandering through the jungle for an eternity stretching from birth to death. It was easy: one just had to let oneself drift with it.

Besson observed these men and women: and suddenly the truth of what he saw came home to him. These people had no jobs, no family problems, no professions, no names even. They never talked or made love or felt afraid. No, all they did was walk, wandering at random, not knowing where they were going, expressionless, eyes glazed. The entire town was populated by full-time walkers, every day of their lives idled away on these long, complicated, indecisive and utterly futile excursions.

At one street-corner a stern-faced man came out of a tobacconist's shop with a newspaper in his hand. He began to read it as he walked, frowning, occasionally pausing to decipher some phrase more easily. It was a clever performance, but Besson was no longer to be taken in by such tricks. A careful scrutiny revealed what a put-up job the whole thing was. The man did not know how to read; he kept his eyes glued to the same spot in the middle of the page, all the time.

A little farther on, in a glass-walled telephone booth, another man was pretending to make a call. His face was flushed, he looked as though he were choking. His mouth opened and shut as though he were shouting insults at someone. He waved his fist. But as far as Besson was concerned, the man was wasting his time. Quite obviously he had put no money in the box—either that, or else he had dialled a non-existent number.

In one doorway a man with a moustache stood talking to a girl. He was very close to her, and as Besson passed, he took the girl's hand and began to hold it as though it were a detached object. Besson perceived that they were talking, but the murmur of their voices merged into the general clamour, and he could not hear a word. In any case this did not matter, since they had nothing intelligible or necessary to say. They were there by pure chance, speaking words without hearing them, incapable of altering their lives. The days and nights would pass them by in a flash, without their noticing, without their having achieved anything. At a certain moment they would find themselves old. At another, they would be dead.

Besides, everything in sight was just as they were: the walls, the trees, the lined pavement stretching down the street; these houses and their occupants, these apartments with large white stifling rooms and tablefuls of food; the beds smelling of sweat, with their grubby pillows and greying sheets, countless hidden lairs that gave off the odour of humanity. Everything was permeated by a cumulative sense of exhaustion. Movements were reduced to a minimum. In the open spaces life crouched coiled back on itself, nursing its sickness and shame, the wearisome, implacable emptiness within it.

A group of pigeons scattered at Besson's approach. Some

78

fluttered into the roadway, others made as though to take wing, others again really did so. Their small yellow beady eyes turned briefly to observe the silhouette of the man advancing on them.

The sky was now a curious rusty colour. Rain continued to fall patchily, first in one place, then in another. The plane-trees in the squares stood encircled by their own fallen leaves. A few more days, one could easily suppose, and the smell of decay would be everywhere.

As time passed, and Besson walked on, the crowd in the streets became steadily denser. Now, wherever he looked, he could see nothing but legs, bosoms, faces, backsides. There were street-barrows everywhere, piled high with merchandise, and gimlet-eyed women lurking behind them. A constant flow of idlers streamed in and out of the shops. There were unending waves of fat faces, thin faces, long and snub noses, mouths gaping blubber-lipped or shut in a thin tight line; small glinting eyes, sunk in the slack flesh round the eyesockets like black nails. Bodies jostled, arms swung to and fro, hands dangled. Rib-cages rose and fell with an even, regular motion. Throats irritated by cigarette-smoke emitted every kind of grunt, rattle, and cough. The soles of count-less shoes beat at the ground with angry persistence, as though bent on exterminating an army of insects. Hips collided tangen-tially, material rucked and creased across bellies, buttons laboured under a constant strain. The rain drizzled down unendingly on people's faces, mingling with perspiration, thirstily settling in forehead wrinkles or the creases at the corner of the jaw. It soaked into women's perms, trickling through a mass of scented curls, down the back of the neck, finally reaching the bottom of their dresses. It drummed delicately on open umbrellas and the hoods of macintoshes. It made crêpe soles stick to the tar in the road. Nothing escaped it. Everything was moving out and away, yet remained *there*, producing a sense of vertigo.

Men and women swarmed and struggled, never moving from the same spot, attacking, possessing. To be handed over to their mercies in this town was a thankless adventure.

But inside each skull, each little box with its casing of flesh and

79

hair, life could not be denied. They were prisoners, everyone of them, a whole race of tiny invisible imps beginning to stir in their bonds.

It was the eyes that were responsible. They were all the same, damp glazed marbles, horribly mobile in their anchorage of skin and muscle. Black hard points, glinting two by two from all these faces, fixing on you like a polyp's suckers, determined to penetrate, digest, expose. Even objects abandoned against walls—dustbins, bicycles, bits of packing-cases—possessed eyes, all turned permanently and insatiably on the passing show. The houses, each tall grey apartment block, acted as pitiless mirrors. In every direction, from every angle, it was the same silhouette they reflected: a feeble, clumsy figure, walking on purposelessly, unable to get away. Ah, let the day of the blind beasts come, let it come soon, the empire of the ants and moles and larvae! How restful, then, to burrow peacefully in the mire, knowing nothing, expecting to know nothing, through the sweet opaque darkness, calm, blissful, never-ending!

At the bottom of the street there stood a newspaper kiosk, its coloured shape rising bright amid the grey slabs of paving-stone and the moving tide of humanity. For Besson it appeared some sort of refuge. Feverishly he began to tack towards it through the busy crowd, taking care not to incur angry looks or get himself jostled as he proceeded. He could see the kiosk from some way off, with its conical roof and countless gaily-coloured notices in blue or yellow or red. These bright patches shone out above the heads of the crowd, yet there was nothing aggressive about them: they caught the eye like headlights, each sending out its appeal. Around them it was cold, with dampness in the air. They alone remained pure and dazzling, they irradiated the heat of the vanished sun, they were stars. To reach them was a lengthy business. Besson had to push his way past helpless old women, children, dogs. But this did not bother him. His eyes, raised a little above the heads of the crowd, saw nothing but this polychrome peak, this glowing tower with its ever-larger writings and medley of colours.

At last Besson got to the kiosk. He came close, put out a hand, touched it. In front of him, behind a window, large numbers of papers were pinned up on display: illustrated periodicals, magazines, photographic journals, weekly reviews. Look where he would, everything was written, painted, set down in print. Besson drank it all in, intoxicated, unable to take his eyes away, listening to the steady tramp of footsteps behind his back.

On the cover of one magazine there was a blonde woman, her smile revealing dazzlingly white teeth. Her lips were red, her eyes pale blue, the skin on her neck and shoulders as smooth as silk. She went on smiling like this, without seeing anyone, as though enclosed in some tiny cabin where the weather was always perfect. Beside her, similarly framed in a periodical, was another woman who wore an identical smile. Her hair was black this time, but her huge deep eyes had been tinted a most odd colour, green and violet together, and so transparent that it looked as though one could pass through her physically, like penetrating a smoke-screen and remain on the far side of her enclave, in a kind of paradise.

All the rest of the display-window was the same. Left and right, top and bottom, there was nothing to be seen but women's faces, women's bodies, bright and supple figures—sometimes naked, clad only in their own pink and satiny skins, sometimes wearing exotic dresses full of gold and purple, their folds merging and overlapping, forming great blocks of shading that threw the rest into high relief. And everywhere the same kind of face staring out from the paper, ablaze with freshness and youth: rich deep hair, a tawny mane cascading down over the neck, a blonde fringe concealing the eyes, jet-black curls and tresses, luxuriantly alive, blue-tinted waterfalls in which countless captive points of light glittered. Smooth foreheads, arching eyebrows, fine retroussé noses, full lips parted to reveal a row of seven pearly white teeth—or sometimes set in a smile which produced two oval dimples at each corner of the mouth. Ripe breasts, fixed in a pose of tranquil uplift, sweetly curving necks and shoulders, arms and legs, dimple-soft navels, cheeks almost invisible against the light, or hidden altogether behind faint shadowy graining. And the

81

eyes: so enormous, tranquilly displaying the classic almond-shaped outline, edged by feather-thick lashes: unfathomable eyes, with changing colours, liquid precious stones that brought to life endless minuscule universes, shut in and self-contained, full of echoes, changing facets where one could lose oneself completely in the magical fluctuations of hope and despair.

There was nothing ephemeral about these faces; these bodies held no illusion. Their printed substance would hold the same pose for ever, or very nearly. Some might moulder at the bottom of a drawer, or be used to line a dustbin; but at least one of them would survive, in all her vivid, flashy beauty, to testify how enjoyable life on earth had been at the time. These women would never grow old. Despite the passing years, their skulls would retain the mask of flesh that covered them; their parted lips would continue to smile, hopeful for kisses, revealing the same row of seven pearly, undecaying teeth; their multicoloured eyes would gaze through the glass for ever, without pity or irony or malice, at the world of those who deluded themselves they were alive. Love unbounded shone in their expression, an abundance of love for the entire world.

Besson strolled round the kiosk. Behind the second window there were foreign newspapers and one or two pornographic magazines. The third was devoted to children's comics, mostly of the strip-cartoon variety. Besson stared at these little mannekins dressed up as cowboys. One of them, a great hulking fellow with a black scarf tied round his neck, had a white balloon issuing from his mouth which proclaimed: 'Hey, kids, look—Apache tracks, still fresh! I'll bet it's Walking Stick and his band again! Let's make tracks for Fort Elmer!' The fourth window was crammed with a collection of miscellaneous periodicals, and had a hole in it. Through the hole Besson could just see the head of an old woman. She looked at him and said: 'Yes? What d'you want?'

'I—er—' Besson stammered.

And bought a paper.

It was with a certain sense of regret that he left the kiosk, and walked on down the street, the paper under his arm. He passed a

long row of shops, and saw that the crowd was still pressing c.
up against the display windows, just as before. Besson felt a kin
of numb fatigue stealing over him. It was important not to meet
other people's eyes, and to ensure this meant walking either with
one's back bent, looking at the ground, or else very upright, eyes
on the far horizon. But this couldn't go on for ever.

The rain began to come down a little harder: it was getting cold.
Traffic continued unabated. Walking like this, Besson was afraid
he might reach the outskirts: after all, it was not all that big a town.
If he just walked straight on for long enough the houses would
begin to thin out, gardens would give way to waste lots, and the
pavement would vanish altogether. Suddenly, without realizing
it, one would be in the countryside, brushing through grass,
losing one's way on sharp, stony paths. To avoid the risk of
reaching the town-limits, Besson decided to walk round and
round the same block.

During each of his first three circuits he took shelter for a little
under the awning of a radio repair shop to get himself warm.
Occasionally he lit a cigarette and stopped to smoke it in some
doorway or garage entrance. On his fifth time round he began to
worry in case people recognized him. At this point he crossed the
street and went into a café.

It was a large café, lined with mirrors. Customers, both men
and women, filled nearly every table in the place. The air was loud
with canned background music. Besson settled himself in a corner,
near the door to the lavatories. Then he opened out his paper at
the page which contained most printed matter, in order to avoid
having to move more than was necessary. It was the small-ad
page. He read:

WANTED: Young girl as family help. Maret, 34 Boulevard
Lamartine.

ENGLISH FAMILY seeks maid general duties, knowledge
cooking. Ring 381.541.

WANTED: Part-time pastrycook, apprentice pastrycook.
Blés d'Or, Rue du Pontin.

Mechanic qualified panel-beater/sprayer. Cana-
lefort.

L CENTRE seeks laboratory assistants (male or
undertake night duty on roster system. Box 2126.
D: Jobbing workers ferro-concrete erection. Box 800.

YOLANDE'S DOLLS LTD seeks needlewomen dressmakers
dolls' clothes. 4 Rue Gauthier.

The next ad was in English:

STENOGRAPHER WANTED 1-2 days week, knowledge English-
French, for U.S. sales organization's Monte Carlo office.
Reply with photo, salary requirements, past positions held,
date available for interviews and commencing work. Write
Box 2581.

WANTED: General maid, fond of children, non-resident,
meals found. Mme Tomasi, 1 Rue du Ray.

ROOM AND KITCHEN offered in villa, plus wages, to childless
couple in return normal hours housework, husband req'd
spend hour or two weekly gardening. Bourgoin, 20 Avenue
des Bosquets. Tel. 88.65.42.

And so on. When Besson had finished reading both pages of ads
he raised his head and looked about him. The waiters were
hurrying to and fro between the tables: it was a long room, and by
some accident they had failed to notice Besson sitting there behind
his paper. But at any moment now they might look and see that
he had not ordered anything. They would march up to him with
that inquisitorial air, and demand, loudly: 'What's yours, sir?'

In order to forestall such an occurrence, Besson got up,
collected an empty glass from a neighbouring table, and put it in
front of him. But he did not go on reading his paper. Instead he
let it slide gently to the floor, and put his feet on it.

The glass was a tall one, and still streaked with the remains of
some foaming, yellowish liquid: beer, probably. A little ash had
stuck to the rim. The man who had been drinking from it had
probably gesticulated excitedly while still holding a cigarette.
There the glass sat, on an expanse of canary-coloured formica,

enthroned in solitary splendour, patched with its delicate lacing of foam. Besson stared intently at this transparent cylindrical object, and the patterns on it, lit by unwinking reflections from the neon strip-lighting. It was a glass like any other glass, no doubt, the hasty product of some factory which turned them out by the million, all identical. Yet to look at it was an intolerably moving experience. It was an object, a *thing*, nothing more, a superb and basic object which stood there on the table like a tower, unseeing, never grating on the senses, with no desire to find utterance in speech. It was so lovely and so tranquil that one would have liked it to stand there for all eternity, without anyone touching it, dirtying it, or breaking it. Men had no idea of what they were doing when they placed such objects on a bare table. It never occurred to them that they were setting beautiful deadly traps, ready to close on anyone who beheld them in all their dazzling presumption. They had no idea that for people such as François Besson, so desperately in need of immobility and silence, they and their transparent objects were, quite simply, flinging wide the gates of hell. But how could they have known it? People like them, with their nervous hands and voluble tongues and impatient twitching limbs, could never have let themselves become so hypnotized by the sight—at once soothing and terrible—of one empty glass standing in the middle of a yellow table.

More time passed. Besson continued to stare at the glass, without moving a muscle. At first he had decided to make a complete study of it, until he knew it by heart. Then he saw that the glass continually changed its shape. It became more elongated. It swelled out like a soap bubble, then shrank back to its former size. It sharpened to a point, it turned upside-down, or assumed the shape of a square. Besson realized that he would never be able to *know* it; he had to content himself with looking at it, seeing it afresh every moment, in a never-wearying progression. The yellow texture of the table. The yellow. *The glass*. The foam. Tiny bursting bubbles. Its shape at the top, and at the bottom. The reflection of the light on its right-hand side. A tiny mirror-image of the street on the left. Its vertical line. The polished, rounded

85

rim. An endlessly turning circle—now, and now, over and over again. Top, bottom, middle. Right, left, up, down. The yellow surface of the table.

This was true reality: something inexhaustible, never-failing. No words or ideas, no sensation even, could fully express it. For the glass was *there*, it had escaped time and memory. It was action, action that caught the spectator's eye, multiple and simultaneous action which passed endlessly into itself without ever emerging. Triumph. Triumph.

But to see it was not enough; one had to touch it as well. It was essential to run one's fingers over that cold, slippery, cylindrical surface, to grasp it, touch it to every exposed part of oneself, if one really intended to *know* it. Besson's hand inched forward hesitantly across the table. His fingers touched the transparent surface, but too late; the glass tilted, rolled, and then—for no very comprehensible reason—disappeared into space. There came a terrible crash. Besson did not look, but he knew the glass was broken. The knowledge caused him distress, but perhaps it was better this way: such beauty, such immensity had nearly turned his wits.

A man in a white jacket came across, looked on the ground, and said: '*De profundis*, eh?'

'I didn't do it on purpose,' Besson said, in a hoarsely protesting voice.

The man began to laugh. 'Here, don't look so cut up—these things will happen—'

Besson said: 'How much do I owe you?'

'Nothing,' the waiter said cheerfully. 'Have this one on the house. I'll just get a brush and dustpan and sweep the bits up. Broken glass can be dangerous.'

But Besson persisted, almost angrily: 'Look, please, I want to pay for it. I really insist on paying for it—'

He put a few coins on the table, then went out without looking back. A little farther on, across the road, there was another café, with big open doors. Besson walked through them into the bar. It was a sort of white-walled corridor, fitted with strip-lighting. At

86

the far end of it, lined up against the wall, were half a dozen illuminated pin-tables. Besson made towards them.

With some curiosity he studied these boxes, perched there on their tall legs, and the various signs written under each glass top. All the pin-tables were free except the end one, where a young boy, not more than ten or eleven, was busy playing. Beside him stood a man in his thirties, quite obviously his father, watching every move.

The boy played with a kind of obsessional frenzy, hands gripping the sides of the table or pushing the button to bring down the balls. There he sat, squarely balanced on his chair, mouth tight shut, frowning in concentration, a small, nervous, absorbed child, pulling the metal striker back each time as hard as he possibly could, watching every move of the ball as it blipped off the bumpers, totting up the figures as they flashed on the illuminated screen. Besson had never seen a pin-table player like him before. The balls pursued their labyrinthine course, blipping against one rubber bumper after another, shooting out with explosive violence. From time to time they rolled back down to the bottom of the table, whereupon the boy, with one neat, precise movement, would send them straight back to the top again. The man, who stood leaning over him on his right, watched all this in silence. The figures went up and up, multiplied rapidly. After the first shot the scoreboard indicated 1,300. A kind of sharp report resounded from inside the machine. The boy took no notice of it. He continued to play non-stop, never tiring, a serious, almost tragic expression on his face: fierce, stubborn, the implacable determination of a grown man. The total increased steadily: 1,600, 1,800, 2,000. Further sharp bangs could be heard from the machine's innards, accompanied by various metallic clankings and rattlings. The boy's forehead was finely pearled with sweat, and nervous shudders flickered along his legs in time with the electric motor. He grasped the table with his thin arms and shook it in all directions, or banged it with the flat of his hand. Face bent over the glass, he stared, fascinated, into the heart of this minuscule labyrinth, eyes following the ball's erratic progress, calculating,

87

working out the best route for it to follow, then sticking to it with fierce possessiveness.

Besson went a little closer. It seemed to him that the pin-table and the boy perched on his chair were a single entity, a strange and barbaric mechanism, something full of violence and noise and flashing lights. Heart pounding, he followed the little metal ball's progress, noting the way it blipped off obstacles, spinning and turning, clacking against the trap-gates, with tiny flashes of blue electricity that ran right through his body, touched every nerve-centre. He flinched back. He had been wounded. The idea left him exultant.

When the last ball vanished into its hole, with a machine-gun-like rattle, the entire table lit up in a splendid variety of colours. The scoreboard indicated a total of 9,999.

The boy pulled himself away from the machine. He was very pale; his face was worn, almost elderly, and agleam with un-healthy sweat. The man helped him down from his chair and said: 'Well done. That's thirty-two goes you had.'

The boy wiped his hands on his shorts.

'But I still missed it twice, you know,' he said. 'I mean, that second ball, I wanted to shift it over to the right and get it on target, because at that moment the score was 400 up. Well, *that* was all right, but then I calculated wrong, and it banged the bumper and came back straight down out of play—you saw it, didn't you? I just couldn't get it back. You must have seen. Straight bang through, right in the middle. I wanted to bounce it back, but I was afraid I might tilt the table too much—'

'Yes, I know,' the man said. 'But you did pretty well on the last ball.'

'Not too bad, I'll give you that. Three times on the 100, and once on the 500.'

'Well, you got the highest possible score, didn't you?'

'Yes, but it took five balls to do it. What about the time I hit the jackpot in two?'

The boy walked off towards the door. The man caught him up and they left the café together. Besson glanced briefly at the doorway through which they had disappeared. He saw a narrow section of pale grey street, with fine rain needling down over it.

Then Besson turned his attention back to the machine. It still seemed to be quivering all over from the bangings and other movements it had endured. It was transparent, metallic, coloured like a jellyfish. On its upright panel various numbers were inscribed: 0–9 999–32. Between the figures was a woman in a bikini, her pink body lit up by the lights, dancing in the middle of a circus arena. To the right of her some uniformed men were cracking their whips at a group of lions. On her left there were two elephants in fancy-dress, a seal juggling a ball, and a trapeze artist swinging on his wire. Almost wherever one looked there was some sort of inscription in red letters—JOLLY BUMPER, CIRCUS GIRL, Score, BINGO, REPLAY, Archibald Swanson, Salem, Massachusetts, and GAME OVER (*Tilt*).

Beneath the flat glass surface stretched the pin-table's tiny world: alleys with red light-bulbs under which was written, in English, 'Score 10 when red light is on'; mushrooms of every variety and colour—yellow, red, red and pastel green; little spring-mounted white gates, made of metal, that opened and sprang back. Lower down, amid other yellow and green objects, there was a small enclosure with a white wheel, marked off in numbers, at its centre. Two blue lights glowed in front of the wheel, and between them ran a curious line of figures, something like this:

500

400

300

200

100

90

80

70

60

50

40

Lower still, the playing-surface of the table ran down to a funnel, with little articulated claws curving back from either side of its mouth. This was the point at which the ball dropped out of sight. After being hurled so fiercely into the midst of all these quivering obstacles, after blipping off the red bumpers, zigzagging from side to side, circling and bouncing downwards a dozen, perhaps a hundred times, then shooting all the way back to the top again, in a flash, when it closed the electric contact and set off all those spasmodic rattling and ringing noises, those machine-gun-like reports, while up on the indicator, beside the bikini-girl's face, the crazy figures flashed on and off so fast you hardly had time to see them, 306, 307, 308, 309, 310, 311, 321, 331, 341, 342, 343, 344, 345, 355, 356, 357, 358, 458, 468, 469; after hurtling down against the revolving wheel like a bullet, and being tossed about for a moment or two in incoherent mechanical motion; after a desperate struggle against the fate that lay in wait for it in every trap-gate and knob, it finally had no option but to roll into this black hole, cross the threshold of death, sink into the belly of the machine, all aglint with points of reflected light, drop home to its rest, an echoing retreat permeated by a most curious smell, as though something had been scorched there.

When Besson had finished playing, he left the bar and walked on down the street for a little. People in cars were laughing and talking, very much absorbed in their own affairs. A woman and a young girl had stopped outside the window of a shoe-shop. They were standing arm in arm, and Besson could hear the sound of their high-pitched voices. Somewhere, hidden behind the clouds, an aircraft was droning over the town. The sound of its four engines seemed, disquietingly, to come from all sides at once. There were puddles of dirty water in the road, and the cars' tyres left visible tracks after passing through them. Besson stopped at the edge of the pavement and waited for a trolley-bus.

When the vehicle appeared, he signalled it with his hand, then clambered up the iron steps and stood holding one of the leather straps. When he had bought his ticket he made his way to the front of the bus and found a seat beside a large fat woman. Either on account of the rain, or the time of day, the bus was crowded. Most of the passengers were elderly, unattractive women, with sagging faces and pouches under their eyes. Their bodies gave off a rank smell, garlicky and goatish, except for two or three men, who smelt more of stale tobacco. Besson let himself go with the jolting of the vehicle, listening to the smooth continuous roar of the motor, and the squeegeeing sound made by the double windscreen-wipers. He looked at the back of the driver, whose shoulders were pulling his coat out of shape. It was very warm. Almost enough to make one fall asleep. Besson thought how pleasant it would be to have a trolley-bus of one's own and drive it around the streets of the town like this. From time to time, when he felt like it, he might pull up at the kerbside and let people get aboard. He wouldn't have the time to get bored, he thought. He wouldn't talk to anyone, but he'd be able to feel it when his human cargo was shaken up over the bumpy bits, and that would suffice him.

At a certain moment a young man made his way up the aisle and sat down facing Besson. He was a tallish person, extremely thin, with long hanging arms and a rounded back. As he moved he uttered little incoherent cries, and his monkey-like face, with its protruding ears and flat nose, was constantly twitching. His whole feeble frame seemed convulsed by a variety of tics, and a sickening smell exuded gently all around him.

He sat like this for a moment; then his head turned towards Besson, and his crazy, deep-sunk eyes gleamed strangely. Besson stared uncomprehendingly at the hideous, grimacing face opposite him; but very soon fear began to stir in him, an ignoble fear, set up by those pin-hard, accusatory eyes. And then recollection dawned in his mind: as though brought back from a forgotten time hundreds of centuries ago, that flat and imbecile mask glued itself to his own features, took the mould and impression of them

91

with the viscous fidelity of a latex squeeze. Through the eyesockets pierced in this crazy face Besson himself now looked out at the world. Through those wide nostrils, enlarged by constant nose-picking, he began to draw his own breath. Through that mouth, through the skin that was encrusted with sweat and filth so that garments clung to it like mummy-bands; through that fuzzy, nit-infested hair, that bowed and broken skeleton of a body, those senile, trembling limbs, those thighs stained with patches of dried urine—through all these things Besson began to live again. He had found him at last. This doltish, repugnant caricature was his brother. Aboard this stifling, smooth-running trolley-bus, here on these worn imitation leather seats, he had met the person he had tried in vain to forget. His brother, his beloved brother, born of the same mother as himself, now sitting in front of him looking like some crazy ape, haloed with stinking squalor, the prisoner of his own stupid, shrunken body, racked by tics and miserable pains. In a burst of tender compassion Besson leaned forward to say something to the young man. But at this the creature turned pale, his eyes bulged, his whole face—apart from the rictus round the mouth, which nothing could efface—became distorted with terror. Then, uttering a strange shrill cry, he leapt to his feet and ran clumsily down the aisle to the rear of the bus. Besson had to get out at the next stop. As he walked through the chilly streets he had plenty of leisure to think up the excuses he would make for the people who had been expecting him all day.

Chapter Three

ON the third day, François Besson had a date with this woman called Josette, at six o'clock, on the corner by the Prisunic. He got there a little early, and waited standing by the kerbside, smoking a cigarette. It was just dark, and the street-lamps were shining out, sharp and clear-cut points of light. The crowd were still swarming inexhaustibly down the street: not one day's respite, not an hour's rest. Even on Sundays and public holidays, they were still there, out in the street, moving to and fro, idling, ogling, picking up and purchasing goods. In the evening they went to the cinema, came out of cafés, banged car doors. In the morning they went to work, queued in pork-butchers' shops, or stood gossiping on doorsteps. No, they never rested, never stopped moving.

But only a few yards above the ground it was utterly deserted. The houses reared their tall silent façades, and there was nothing in the air save empty solitude. The trolley-bus wires crossed and recrossed continually, but nothing *happened*. The walls, the branches of the trees, the cowls of the street-lamps, roof-tops interspersed with garrets—it was all so still and quiet that no one could have deduced what a crawling ant-hill existed down below. The same thing applied underground. Beneath that carapace of tarred asphalt, hammered by marching feet, worn away by tyres, the desert began again: an immense, pitch-black, softly opaque desert, with every ten years or so a gravelly rattle—stopped almost before it had begun—as a mass of fine, close-packed scree shifted its position, after which things returned to that state of boundless mineral inactivity which represented the world's true dominion.

The rain slanted down evenly, on him and in front of him, descending from the sky at a dizzy speed. Besson looked up and tried to make out the point at which it formed into drops. But in that great blanked-out hollow there was nothing, not a star, not so much as the winking navigation lights of an aircraft, no fixed or moving point on which his eye could fasten and use as a marker. Nothing but the void, opaque and unfathomable, glowing with faint reflections from the lights of the town, suspended like some delicate rose-pink dome over the darkness.

There was something frightening about these endless drops that descended from nowhere, pattering on the ground and on one's upturned face. Only a very little change in these tiny tear-like drops, and they would become a lethal weapon. Supposing, for instance, that they all joined together before they reached the earth: then this solid wall of water would thunder down in a single solid mass and engulf the world in a flash.

And perhaps, after all, that would have been a preferable alternative. The present danger was more frightening, because nothing could stop it. One by one these small drops fell, pitting the earth's surface, without violence and without pity. Their minuscule darts struck home everywhere, drilling, sapping, boring, rotting away the substance of things. Granules of stone were rubbed loose, wooden surfaces lost their rough texture, iron plates were hollowed out, imperceptibly but inexorably, by the needling tattoo of countless million raindrops. Not even men's head or faces were exempt. The tiny painless blows beat on their skin, the minuscule bruises increased and spread, turned into open suppurating wounds, edged with gangrenous mould. And still the rain fell, as though it would never stop—cold, diamond-hard, with a muffled hammering note that was somehow highly disturbing. It was horrible to be made the victim of erosion in this way. You couldn't escape the rain, sooner or later it would find you out, its fine slanting needles would brush your skin like a file, reduce it to minute fragments, devour it, dissolve it utterly, without rhyme or reason; it would never let up until you became mere impalpable dust in its own watery domain. The only solution would have been

94

to live in some cut-and-dried region where the sun blazed down continually, bury oneself deep in baking pebbles, and dry out one's whole body, like damp brushwood.

About ten minutes past six a bus ran into the back of a car. Within seconds a crowd had gathered in the road. Shadowy figures gesticulated, and cars began to sound their horns. Besson observed the incident with detached curiosity. He left the pavement and went over to the stationary vehicles. The back of the car was in a bad way: the metal surface had ripped and crumpled like paper. The bus-driver had his face a few inches from that of the car's owner, and was shouting at him, but there was such a loud hubbub going on all around that his insults remained inaudible. The other man, wrapped up in his raincoat, was shouting too, though not so energetically. Presently he made as though to go. He walked to the door of his car, but just as he was getting into the driver's seat he changed his mind, came back to the bus-driver, and began shouting at him again. From time to time he would fumble in his raincoat pockets, as though about to produce some documents, or a handkerchief, but he never took anything out.

A tight ring of spectators had gathered round them: fat women wearing head-scarves, dogs on leads, men with cigarettes dangling from their mouths. Besson mingled discreetly with the crowd, listening to their random remarks.

'Just look at that—proper mess, eh?'

'It's the bus's fault. They never look where they're going—'

'Too true, they just press on regardless. *They* don't care, it's not them who have to foot the bill—'

'All the same, the other fellow did brake a bit sharply—'

'Seen what's left of the boot?'

'My, doesn't he look cross, eh?'

'Look, seems to me he's punctured one back tyre, too.'

'It's always the same at this crossing. Some sort of accident every day. Yesterday there was a cyclist knocked down by a truck here. Every day something happens here. Every bloody day.'

'Well, if that bus-driver was in a hurry, he certainly got his come-uppance.'

95

'They all drive like madmen—'

'And they all just bash through regardless, and devil take the hindmost.'

'Did you see how many deaths there were on the motorway last Thursday? Twenty-seven. *Twenty-seven.*'

'Buses ought to have a special road all to themselves, don't you think?'

'They ought to have one-way streets everywhere, that's what they ought to do.'

'They always rely on the insurance companies to cough up when they have an accident. It's true, I'm telling you. Why should *they* care?'

'Hey, Momma, come and see the accident!'

'Stupid pinheads—'

'I agree, madam; I absolutely agree—'

'Henri! Did you see the fellow's face? Just like a chimpanzee—'

A quarter of an hour later the whole incident might never have happened. The crowd had dispersed, together with the traffic-jam. There were no more blowings of horns, no more gesticulations or insults. The only sign that something had really happened was a scatter of broken glass in the roadway. Besson stood there by the kerb, staring at this glittering relic, now being methodically washed down by the rain.

A moment later Josette pulled up in her car and hooted at him. Besson walked round to the other side of the vehicle and got in beside her. She let in the clutch and the car moved off.

'You're late,' Besson said.

She did not so much as glance at her watch. 'Not all that much. Were you waiting in the rain?'

'Yes'

'Why didn't you take shelter?'

'I was afraid you might miss me.'

She trod on the brake sharply. 'Did you see that? He ran across right under my wheels—'

Besson lit a cigarette and looked around for the ashtray. She pressed a button.

'There you are. What filthy weather.'

'It certainly could be warmer,' Besson said.

'Did you get my letter?'

'Yes, this morning.'

'I very nearly didn't come. I'm supposed to work till seven, normally.'

'It was you who wanted to see me, though.'

'I know, but I was wondering, after—after the other day—'

Besson stared at a group of pedestrians standing on the edge of the pavement. The man had a black umbrella and was wearing a very long overcoat. The two women were watching the approaching car.

'It was more than a week since we'd seen each other,' said Josette. 'I thought you'd come round. When I realized you weren't coming, I made up my mind, and sent you that letter. I—it just can't go on like this.'

Besson made no reply. He looked at the girl beside him, a rapid glance first of all, just long enough to see her profile, with its sharply outlined nose, overlaid now by shadows and reflections; then a lingering, detailed scrutiny, that took in every square inch of flesh, each curve and angle of face and body, the black hair drawn back in a chignon, the pony-tail hanging down in two pluming curves.

She stiffened. 'What's the matter?' she asked.

'Nothing,' Besson said. 'I was just looking at you—'

'Oh stop playing the fool. I was hoping—I was hoping we'd be able to have a serious discussion. Once and for all. I'll park the car somewhere—'

She turned off into a side-street. Both hands gripping the black plastic-sheathed steering-wheel, the upper part of her body leaning to the left, eyes alert, mouth firmly shut, feet pressed on the pedals, she threw all her strength into controlling the moving weight of the car.

'If you see a place, tell me,' she said.

'Look, there—'

She braked, then drove on.

'That won't do, it's the entrance to a garage.'

Besson relaxed against the upholstery. The engine purred steadily, now and then increasing in volume. The windscreen-wipers moved to and fro together, and at every jolt the seats creaked under them.

'How's the car going?' Besson asked. 'All right?'

'Not too badly,' said Josette. 'Not now I've had the valves reground.'

'What sort of speed can you get out of it?'

'Well, you know me, I'm a bit scared of driving fast. But when I'm on a good straight road I step it up.'

'How much do you do?'

'Oh, it depends—'

'No, I mean, what's the most you've ever done?'

'I don't know—eighty, eighty-five, something like that.' She turned and looked at Besson. 'You're pale, you know,' she said. 'You—well, frankly, you look tired out. You haven't a job now, though, have you?'

'No,' Besson said. 'I'm doing nothing just now.'

A traffic-light shone red ahead of them. The car drew to a halt at the crossing, and a crowd of shadowy figures hurried across. The seconds passed insistently. It was as though the cessation of movement had suddenly revealed their existence, concentrated now on the circular red light, unwinking, like an eye. The girl sat beside him, hands resting on the wheel, not saying a word. Besson watched her, saw her face react, become gently drawn into the scene outside. With her contained, withdrawn body, her made-up eyelids, the pins and ribbons supporting her hair, she was pal-pably present, *there*, prepared to fight and to win. Besson made an effort to shake off the torpor that was stealing over him, to make conversation.

He said: 'I saw an accident just now, while I was waiting for you outside the Prisunic. A bus ran into the back of a car.'

'Was it serious?'

'Yes—well, not too bad, actually. The car had its boot smashed in, but the bus wasn't damaged. I don't quite know how it happened—I suppose the driver of the car braked a bit too sharply, and the other chap didn't have time to react. Unless the car backed into the bus, of course. Anyway, they started slanging each other in the middle of the street, and a crowd gathered. But the police didn't even bother to come and see what was going on.'

The light changed to amber, then to green. The girl's arms moved, her hands busied themselves with shifting gear, turning the black ring of the wheel, flipping down the indicator-lever. The idling engine roared into life, and the car moved forward, as though on rails. Far off in the night, above the roof-tops, came a flash of lightning, white tinged with pink, momentarily revealing heavy-piled clouds. While Josette talked, Besson kept his ear cocked for the inevitable sound of thunder. But whether because of the distance, or the rain, he heard nothing.

'. . . or never. Do you understand, François? It's true, you know you've been different for some time now. I can't really understand why. I'd like to have a serious talk about the whole situation—don't you think we should?'

Besson stubbed out his cigarette in the ashtray beside the dash-board.

'If you like,' he said. 'But you're wrong when you say I've changed. It's not me that's changed, it's the things around me. I honestly think—' He broke off, then said: 'Look, we can't have this kind of discussion while we're driving round town.'

'I know,' Josette said. 'I'm looking for somewhere to park. I've got to go to the post-office and send off a money-order first, anyway. After that, if you like, we can go and park somewhere quiet, out of town. Up on the hill, for instance.'

'All right.'

Finally she pulled up in a space reserved for taxis. As she was backing her bumper hit the front of another car.

'I'm only going to leave it here a minute,' she said. 'Just long enough to send this money-order. You coming, or staying here?'

'I might as well come,' Besson said.

'All right then, close the window your side.'

They got out of the car. It was hard to tear oneself away from that imitation-leather seat, especially when it was so cold outside. Besson thrust his hands into his pockets, and the two of them walked off together.

The post-office was warm, well-lit, and crowded. Besson sat on a bench and watched Josette while she queued. Behind the counters a number of girls in sky-blue uniform were writing or telephoning. In the main hall there was an interminable ebb and flow of feet over the flagged floor, men's, women's, walking, standing, coming in, going out. The walls were painted a dirty white, and shone with the bright glow from the electric light bulbs. This was a temple dedicated to work, where time was, as it were, abolished through total mechanization, divided into infinite particles by the rattle of typewriters and dull thud of franking-stamps.

Alone in one corner, an old woman, accompanied by her dog, stood facing the wall, searching through a directory for some name or other. The dog, a long-haired bitch, had its head down and was sniffing at a grey patch on the floor. Besson felt an impulse to follow their example. He moved slowly across to the wall-desk, and with back bent and nose deep in the pages of the massive volume, he spelt out these magical and fortuitously juxtaposed names:

Sébestien
Séchard
Sechardi
Ségur
Senon
Sepia
Setton-Prince
Shave
Simon
Simon
Simon
Simonetti

There was certainly no lack of names: they packed every page from top to bottom, and behind them, behind these curt, spiky rows of letters, lurked human beings, full of movement and death, young or old faces, lives as self-contained as so many glass balls. They existed, they lived here on earth, they had names and surnames and addresses, jobs which they performed conscientiously or with indifference, wives, children, friends. No doubts, no self-correction. Hermetic and impenetrable, they remained the people who one cannot know and dare not laugh at. These thick, worn volumes, with their dog-eared pages, each blackened by the touch of innumerable sweaty fingers, served as a kind of bible for them the living. This was their stern and factual saga, the tale of their adventures reduced to one simple sign, a sort of small cross made with a ball-point pen that marked them out as something hard and inflexible amid the muddy flux of existence. If one were to read them all like that, name after name, without emotion or hatred, one would possess them all, incapsulated within oneself, possess the very core and essence of their lives, make them close neighbours. They would no longer be able to get away from you, perpetually escape to their unknown hide-outs.

'Looking up something?' Josette asked. Besson raised his head.

'Yes—no—that is, I was just looking.'

They walked out of the post-office together.

'Did you send your money-order?' Besson enquired.

'Yes. Why do you ask?'

'Oh, I don't know. Have you anything else to do?'

She opened the car door. 'No,' she said.

Inside the air was warm and sluggish. The closed windows muffled any noise from the street. They could hear rain pattering on the roof overhead.

*

The car climbed steadily towards the top of the hill, headlights full on, negotiating hairpin bends and passing through shadowy stretches of woodland. From time to time houses showed up by the roadside, great black masses pierced by a single yellow window. The hill was a vast outcrop of rock and trees, a deeper black than the night. It dominated the town, rearing up beyond the flatness of sea and plain in all the might of its great arched ridge, so full and solid that it might bave heen a living creature. Riddled with wells, a bristling mass of shrub and undergrowth, it loomed up through the night like some gigantic stray animal, with its steep scree-covered slopes, its patches of waste ground, its scored, deep-cut water-channels, bare and arid, rain streaming softly down its flanks, dust-particles frittering away, quivering on its foundations. Here one climbed towards stillness, past streets winding or stepped, all lights out now, a slow ascent to that flat summit—not a tree, not even a ruined house—whence all other sounds had been banished by the wind, skirting invisible obstacles fissures, abandoned tracks, masses of rock half broken away from the soil but still hanging at a crazy angle; passing deep pools of water, compact bubbles of darkness, the rain dancing on their surface like bullets. More private property, barbed-wire fences, but nothing behind them save faint fluttering mystery, a kind of cloud, wisps of drifting mist. Crumbling chateaux, hidden cathedrals, floating towers. Then the road came out on the cliffs above the sea, and the bright red point of a lighthouse beacon became visible, drilling at regular intervals through the flux of the elements. Everything seemed to hinge around this light, according to its own metallic rhythm, as though each wink of that red beam, glimpsed through the curtains of rain and darkness, advanced the march of time, of knowledge, promised days of intense sunlight, a hard bare landscape stripped back to the bone by brightness and heat. The hill was rising still, its road stretching away ribbon-like between knolls and hollows. There were straggling bushes with a dense, rounded mass of foliage, pressed down now by sheer weight of water, and weird stunted plants with wide-spaced branches. Ruined walls, boundary-fences, and sometimes other blurred shapes which belonged to no recognizable order of things, but simply sprang up out of the darkness in a casual fashion that was both graceful and somehow alarming. Phantoms propped against each other, not people, not houses, but small dingy figures, decrepit possessions, stake-fences, skeletons planted in the earth and undulating fluidly as one glimpsed them going by, perhaps animated from within by some mysterious respiratory movement.

Higher still the hill was hollowed out towards its summit like the crater of a volcano. The road ran its lonely course ringed in by a circle of rocks, through strata of chilly air. The darkness was total—not a glimmer of light anywhere, not even a solitary street-lamp from which to take one's bearings. The ground was invisible, it merged with the shadows, and the trees seemed to float above it. Besson found himself plunging into this empty blackness on foot, half paralysed by fear, struggling forward through the mud, not able to recognize anything, eyes searching the void, feet clumsily sliding on loose shale, frightened stiff by the darkness and the power it contained. Onward now across the vast shifting plateau, searching for the right path, walking into gusts of icy wind blown from the uttermost ends of the world, whistling razor-sharp over the hillside. Down now among silo-like rock-formations, endless wells with no walls, no bottom, no entrance. Down, down, falling maybe. The rain seemed to bounce back off the ground, shoot vertically skywards. Or perhaps everything was gone—no more sky, no more rocks, no more hill, nothing. Nothing but this vast fluid emptiness, this impalpable void, in which sombre patches of colour continued to spread and multiply.

Then, suddenly, as though seen from a parapet, the whole city appeared below, a shimmering carpet of light, so far below that it was as though it no longer had any real existence. There it lay, vivid and resplendent, a pool of brightness rippling on the earth's surface, with its myriad windows, its pin-bright street-lamps and twinkle of crawling headlights, all exposed in the cold and the stillness; exquisite, remote, a vision so magnified and transmuted that one felt one had never seen anything remotely comparable to it.

Behind Besson a voice suddenly called: 'François! François! Where are you?' And a moment later: 'Hi, François! *Fran-çois!*'

It was a strange feeling of apprehension which made Besson

turn back. His clothes sodden through, he made his way—more by luck than judgment—to the point in the middle of the hollow where the car had stopped. He saw the dumpy lines of its body-work, and the girl still sitting inside it. He was aware of himself moving forward towards the centre of the basin, and with a stab of delight he saw that it was no longer black but white all over, with the radiant whiteness of hoar-frost, a dazzling landscape of snow and marble where silence grew and spread with the wind. He got back into the car.

'Where were you?' Josette asked. 'What were you doing?'

'Nothing—over there,' Besson muttered. 'Come on, let's get moving.'

When she started the engine the headlights came on, and the two converging shafts of yellow light picked out the shadowy figure of a man crouching beside a bush. Two peeping-tom eyes glinted for a brief moment, and then the man made off across country. Besson, watching him go, felt how much he, too, would have loved to be free just then, able to observe other people when they came up here to make love, secretly, in this milky nocturnal landscape.

Chapter Four

François Besson watches the sleeping woman—He sketches the map of her body—The noise—A chained mongrel in a garden prowls round in the rain—Conversation with the blind paper-seller—In which we are concerned with a person who lived in a barrel

ON the fourth day François Besson awoke fairly early. He found himself lying in a double bed, with a comfortable box-mattress and brand-new sheets. The pillow, where his head was not actually resting on it, felt cold, and the whole place gave off a damp and disagreeable atmosphere, heavy with the smell of stale breathing. Through the slats of the shutters a pale half-light filtered into the room. The ceiling above the bed was flat, almost colourless, and there was no electric light cord. It looked as though there was no one else apart from himself in this room: nothing but a pale ceiling suspended in space, a vast and plain-like expanse stretching further than the eye could reach.

Then, suddenly, in the cold grey depths of the room, Besson heard a noise approaching: a slow, soft, powerful sound, that sprang from nowhere, travelling from the furthest bounds of silence beyond sleep, a rasping, saw-like note, light, regular, unemphatic, seemingly produced by some mechanical task that called for great persistence and effort. Besson listened carefully, and almost at once identified it as the breathing of a woman— Josette—who was stretched out in bed beside him. The deep, even note rose and faded peacefully in the still air: Besson lay and listened to it without turning his head.

It began with a tiny, almost inaudible whistling sound, which gradually swelled to a crescendo, growing rougher as it did so, then dwindled away once more: there followed a kind of raucous gasp, and the sound repeated itself (no doubt in the opposite direction), tenuous at first, then rising, a solemn droning descant, to dwindle and sink once more, this time into complete silence. For a fraction of a second silence would reign in the room, and reach up to blanket the greenish surface of the ceiling. Then the sound would repeat itself as before, powerful and inescapable, with a hoarse, musical edge to it that penetrated every last square inch of air in the dimly-lit apartment.

For some time Besson simply listened to the sound without doing anything. Then he set himself to breathe in the same cadence rhythm, imitating every detail with perfect accuracy. It was not an easy task. Sometimes the noise stopped abruptly, for no apparent reason. When the rhythmic sequence began again, it was prefaced by a long, unhappy sigh. There were occasions, too, when the noise mysteriously quickened its tempo, so that it turned into a kind of panting. It interspersed with shrill and broken little cries that emerged all blurred and unrecognizable, and were quite impossible to imitate.

Other sounds likewise reached the room, a slow, monotonous procession that drifted in through the slatted shutters and rose up until they plastered themselves against the wide and dismal surface of the ceiling. Hooting of car-horns, vehicles back-firing, the clatter of iron shutters being raised somewhere along the street. A faint, mournful, sibilance, impossible to pin down, compounded of tyres on wet asphalt, water pouring from gutters, the hiss of air-brakes. All this went on more or less non-stop, without a break, merging with the repetitive rhythm of Josette's breathing, the fresh damp air, the grey light outside. Easy enough to stay like this for a long while, ears and senses alert, without moving or thinking. So François Besson continued to lie in bed, eyes wide open and fixed on the ceiling above him.

At length he turned on his side and scrutinized the horizontal outline of the sleeping girl. She was entirely hidden under the bed-clothes, and nothing could be seen of her apart from a tangle of black hair on the pillow. Strands of it had straggled loose, and lay there quite motionless, like so much sodden seaweed.

Besson sat up in bed. The alarm-clock on the bedside table

beside Josette told him it was a quarter to eight. The noises outside in the street suddenly intensified. Cars began to tear past in a kind of frenzy, and there came the unmistakable sound of someone sweeping the sidewalk. Besson reached over Josette's recumbent body and took a packet of cigarettes from the bedside table. He found a box of matches in the drawer. With tidy, careful movements he lit a cigarette and began to smoke. Then he realized he had no ashtray. He leaned across to the bedside table again, but this time drew a blank: after which he settled back where he had previously been, and made no further attempt to move. Smoke and cold air plumed out of his nostrils simultaneously. The smoke drifted gently ceilingwards, forming two thin columns, each of a different colour. That which came directly from the cigarette spiralled up in fluctuating bluish rings: that which emerged from his mouth or nostrils spread like a patch of dull grey fog. Besson watched the two columns of smoke for a moment. About a yard short of the ceiling they dissolved in the air of their own accord, without it being possible to determine exactly how this vanishing trick was brought about.

When Besson had finished his cigarette, he stubbed it out on the floor, beneath the bed, tucked the tab-end away out of sight, and blew on the tiny pile of ash to disperse it. An odd scorching smell hung in air for a moment, then everything returned to normal.

Slowly Besson turned towards the girl's body, lying there so still under the bed-clothes, and studied this mountain range, with its folds and patches of shadow, its harsh hollows and spurs, its ridges and traverses. He watched the white sheet rise and fall with a regular, peaceful motion, disturbing one or two folds as it did so. Indefatigably, exuding a sort of confident energy that nothing could upset, the silhouetted figure continued to swell and sink, never jerking, very gently, like the sea rising and falling in a narrow inlet, with that dull booming sound compounded of wind and water, simultaneously alive and dead. It was indeed an extraordinary spectacle, and anyone might have stayed there, like François Besson, resting on one elbow, simply in order to enjoy it: to stare in fascination at the rising and falling of this white sheet in the chill prison that was a bedroom half lit by morning light.

The black hair visible above the sheet was spread out in a star-shaped mass, rather like an ink-blot on absorbent blotting-paper.

With infinite precaution Besson grasped the edge of the sheet and gave it a tug. Little by little more hair appeared, some of it lying in curls. The sheet edged down a little further. A warm and sickening smell rose from under the clothes. Then the forehead came into view, followed by the entire face and neck. The head was asleep, upturned towards the ceiling, resting on the white bulk of the pillow. On that pale brow, where the hair had been flattened down, there was no trace of any wrinkles. Her skin was taut, almost transparent, so much did sleep rob it of life. The double arch of her eyebrows lay peacefully above closed eyes, and a bluish-grey shadow marked the line of the orbital sockets. Her nose, straight and fine, barely quivered at the very edge of the nostrils. There was no flush on her cheeks, and through her half-open mouth, above the slightly receding chin, the upper incisors were visible, gleaming white against lips that were nearly as white themselves. The head lay there, quite motionless, as though weighing like a stone on the stuff of the pillow. Small, neat, rounded, it looked like the head of a casualty on a stretcher: a head, so to speak, that had been surgically separated from the rest the body, and through which the respiratory process operated as though it began somewhere quite different: a mask, perhaps, a plaster mask without any life of its own, not formed from bone and flesh, that neither slept nor dreamed, and was incapable of smiling. A sad, impenetrable death's-head, all apertures closed, with some vague and woolly matter gradually crumbling away inside it; embalmed, wreathed in orange-blossom, the face of a saint, all the blood drained out of it, a smooth ivory ball lying balanced on the rough, crumpled sheets.

François Besson stared at this woman's unknown face, and a feeling of doubt and uneasiness crept over him. He wanted to find out more about this calm, nostalgia-ridden case-history, this body now presented for his inspection in a deep-freeze compartment at the morgue. He wanted to learn this woman's true nature and identity, to see how this alabastrine head fitted on to its body—always supposing there *was* a body. Gently, without making a sound, he drew the sheet right down. There on the bed, all covering now gone, head and naked body lay stretched out, still breathing.

The upper part of the torso, against which the breasts showed even whiter than the rest, rose and fell deeply, in a long, slow movement. When the rib-cage sank back, for about a second the heart-beat was visible on the skin covering the midriff. So the body was alive, beyond any doubt, preserved its internal heat, had air and gases passing through it, secreted smells, breathed through minuscule pores. These legs with their heavy thighs, these full hips, the sexual cleft, the long, rounded arms, the worn hands, clenched into fists—surely all these possessed life? Yet this pale, naked flesh, this woman, was nevertheless acting out a comedy of death, with Besson as spectator. The whole thing had been laid on for his benefit—the inert limbs, the bony vertebrae that seemed about to break through the skin; all for him, this slack and flaccid body, its head—a wretched ball too heavy for the neck to sustain it—lolling back as though on the point of breaking off completely. He had to look at her for a long time, with every ounce of concentration he could muster. Half gagging, tears of shame in his eyes, he knew he must scrutinize this embodiment of abomination and indulgence down to the smallest detail. He had to pay, yes, *pay* for his life: and the woman, rejected and miserable, must exact her own retribution. He had to bend down over her, listen to her powerful, mysterious breathing, hear the air rasp hoarse as a bellows beneath those white breasts, feel the warm odorous exhalations gather above her dilated nostrils, *there*, inside this room, while outside, beyond the barrier of the shutters, people trudged down the damp street, to and fro.

With a kind of glum intensity he bent over the outstretched body and began to examine it. He studied every square inch of pale flesh, each separate hair, each brownish line scored across the skin, every mole and pimple. Then he made what might be called a mental map of it all, to ensure that he never forgot what he had seen. When he had taken in every visible detail, he got out of bed, leaving the girl's body as it was, exposed to the cold air. When Besson left the apartment she was still lying there on the stripped bed, still breathing, utterly alone, ghastly in her pallor, deep in that heavy sleep, as though after some act of profanation.

*

Besson walked along the street just as he had done on the previous days, between groups of pedestrians and passing cars. It was Saturday, or Sunday perhaps, and a great deal of activity was going on. The rain had almost completely stopped, leaving large muddy puddles everywhere, so opaque they reflected nothing. People had rolled up their umbrellas, and the windscreen-wipers were enjoying a rest. Wind-blown clouds scudded across the sky, high above the roof-tops, and from time to time the pale disc of the sun glided into sight from behind them.

Besson passed a church where some kind of funeral procession was assembling. Then he walked down towards the sea, and came out on a square jam-packed with stationary vehicles. A removal van had broken down, and as a result all the traffic had ground to a halt in the adjacent streets. Besson found himself caught up in a dense crowd, and did not even attempt to extricate himself from it. He simply let himself go with the tide. When he had reached a point near the sidewalk someone asked him what was going on.

'I have no idea,' Besson said.

'An accident, most likely,' the man remarked. He was a short person with a cloth cap and a cigarette stuck in the corner of his mouth. Then a movement of the crowd separated them.

It was at this point that the noise made itself heard over the square. It began in the far distance, with one or two warning signals. The roar of engines seemed to increase in volume, and from somewhere only a few hundred yards away there came an incomprehensible explosion. Besson shrank back against the wall, mustering all his strength in preparation for the approaching din. He felt it steadily mounting as it got nearer, like a hurricane. The shining cars that blocked every corner of the square had all begun to sound their horns by now: the separate notes merged in a single ear-shattering cacophony. Deep and shrill simultaneously, vibrating in the bass register at ground-level while drilling shrilly through the upper air, like a jet engine, the sound-waves surged outwards, bouncing off the surrounding buildings, until they filled every last cubic inch of empty space. Beneath their metal coverings rows of engines were revving up, and the sound of their exhausts swelled and intensified, echoing all around. Human voices were drowned by this collective uproar, faces grimaced inaudibly: it was as though the entire world had become deaf, or dumb, or perhaps both at once.

The phantom aircraft seemed to remain over the square for an interminable period, shifting on from cloud to cloud with sluggish reluctance. Its thunderous racket blasted the whole district, formed an invisible cone which pressed down on every exposed surface, kept the whole maelstrom of sound shut in, as though a lid had been clapped over it. In the space of a few seconds the scene had changed from normality to nightmare, had become a vast, congested, frozen expanse, an area littered with steel or stone objects and quiveringly racked by this all-pervasive, agonizing din. Individual noises no longer existed, there was only a kind of solid vortex pressed continually against one's ear-drums, forcing them inwards. People themselves seemed temporarily bereft of movement; they stood there in the street staring blindly at nothing, held captive by the blast of sound passing over them. The uproar was anchored to the earth's central core, whirled round and round with its motion through space. It had permeated every reflection, each source of light. It had its own individual smell, you could touch it. It was a stony matrix that lay like a dead weight on your chest, made your heart palpitate. It hurt your eyes to watch the way it beat down in the light, a grey and white sound that exploded on the pavements and in the sky like some vast snowfield. Outlines and colours abruptly melted, ran, realigned themselves. Cars floated airborne above the asphalt, and the windows of every building were ablaze together. When the intensity of the noise rose to 135 decibels, or thereabouts, Besson felt as though he were about to vanish down some deep hole.

Slowly, with a vast effort, he managed to raise his hands as far as his ears, and held them there for a moment. The din tried to penetrate his very skin, humming and vibrating like a swarm of wasps. But when Besson at last removed his hands, the awful din had vanished, leaving only the normal abundance of sharp-edged, delicate, individual sounds. Colours had gone back to something very like normal, and people were beginning to move along the sidewalks once more. Cars moved off one behind the other, haloed with hot, shimmering exhaust fumes. The jet air-craft was no longer audible.

François Besson moved away from the vicinity of the square with one or two unimportant lesions in the cells of his nervous system. He was on the look-out for some narrow, shabby back-street, and found himself hugging the wall as close as he could while he walked. He was a little jumpy at the moment, and the slightest unexpected noise—a motor-cycle back-firing round the corner, for instance—was liable to make his heart beat faster. Without making it obvious, he began to concentrate minutely on avoiding contact, keeping objects at arm's length.

In this manner he walked back up towards the town centre, not paying overmuch attention to where he was going. Men hurried past him, wrapped up to the chin in damp overcoats. He met young women, old women, the occasional beauty, all their faces cruel and expressionless under the make-up they wore. He walked by electrical repair shops, bookshops, furniture stores, chemists and florists. He saw what looked like shell-holes in the pavement, and machines pumping out the drains. He passed stretches of wall with vast posters plastered all over them. One of these showed an orange the size of a car, cut in two, with a drop of juice forming on its yellow pulp, and a monstrously vast baby's head, that must have covered several square yards, with its fat pink cheeks and bald skull and bubble nose, and two big black eyes shiny as metal balls, with the juicy inside of the orange reflected in them. Lower down, under the picture, there was written, in bold lettering: AN ORANGE IS WORTH ITS WEIGHT IN GOLD FOR GOOD HEALTH. The houses across the way were flanked by rows of tall wooden fences, now much dilapidated, and small gardens chock-a-block with mud and rubbish. Clumps of irises sprouted amid a litter of grey stones: water dripped down on leaves and old piled-up packing-cases.

Life had strictly limited horizons here: the rest of the world remained an unknown quantity. In one of these abandoned gardens, beneath blank, empty windows, a mongrel was going round and round on his chain, while the rain drizzled down on him. He no longer even bothered to bark. It occurred to Besson that he too might have shut himself up in the middle of some waste lot, beside an old wooden shack, and gone prowling round the same ancient slate-coloured prison, occasionally glancing at the pitch-black sky, with neither hopes nor expectations.

As he passed by a recessed doorway Besson noticed an old man sheltering under it, with a pile of newspapers beside him, and sitting very still. He was not all that old, in fact: perhaps sixty at the outside. But there was a broken, defeated look about his face and posture. He sat on a folding camp-stool, with the pile of papers close to him, waiting, waiting, his head leaning back against the door-jamb. People came and went on the pavement in front of him, but he never called out to them. He might have been deaf and dumb; he just sat there, huddled in a lumber-jacket, its collar turned up over his ears. He wore a sou'wester, and his eyes were hidden behind thick tinted glasses.

Besson paused to look closer at him, and realized that he was blind. Then he went across into the doorway and bought a paper. The blind man counted out his change competently enough, feeling the coins with his fingertips.

'You can't be very warm there,' Besson said.

Without so much as a nod by way of greeting the man said: 'It's all right.' He had a strong, somewhat nasal voice.

Besson said: 'Filthy weather, isn't it?'

'It's raining, all right,' the man said. 'We'll have floods before it's through.'

'Think so?'

'I don't think, I know,' the man told him. Then, gesturing with his hand, he added: 'Besides, just listen. Hear that noise? It's the flood building up.'

Besson strained both ears, without success.

'I can't hear anything,' he said.

'Try again. Listen carefully. There's a sort of dull rumbling, down there, underground.'

'With all these cars passing I can't hear a thing.'

'That's because you aren't used to it. But it *does* make a noise. It's all the small water-channels in town rising. If they go on like that for another week, we'll be flooded out.'

'You really think so?'

'I'm telling you. Here, shove your ear down against the pavement, you'll hear it then.'

Besson knelt down and rested his head on the concrete surface. At once he caught the muffled, vibrating roar of the swollen water-channels. It was a most disturbing sound.

'You're right,' he said. 'There *is* a noise down there.'

'It's the beginning of the flood.'

For a moment neither of them said anything. Besson watched the man's face. He had heavy, sanguine features, and an absolutely impassive expression. Not even his wrinkles stirred. Round his dark glasses, close to the eye-sockets, were several curious scars. They had a whitish, puffy appearance.

'Have you—have you been doing this for long?' Besson asked.

'Doing what?'

'Well I mean, selling papers.'

'Oh, the papers. Four years and more now, yes.'

'What did you do before that?'

'Oh, I've had a go at everything. I've sold National Lottery tickets, and done odd jobs. But I prefer papers. They pay better, and you don't need to keep shouting.'

'Do a lot of people buy papers?'

'Heavens, yes, indeed they do. But the Lottery, now, that's something else again. There were days when it was all right, and others when I didn't sell a single ticket.'

'Just a matter of luck, h'm?'

'Well, sure. What d'you expect with the Lottery?'

'But—but what do you *think* about, sitting there like that all day?'

The man coughed.

'Oh, I've got plenty to occupy me. You'd be surprised how quickly the time passes. I think about whatever I please, or sometimes I'll listen to the radio. I've got a little transistor set in my pocket. Here, have a look.'

The man brought out a small black and red object. He turned a knob, and music blared out of it. He held the set against his ear for two or three seconds, then switched it off and shoved it back in the pocket of his lumber-jacket.

'I'm very fond of music,' he said. 'And there are always people who enjoy a bit of a chat when they buy their paper. Sometimes my wife comes and keeps me company. I count my takings, too. It all helps.'

'All the same, there must be days when you get fed up with the whole business.'

'Well, yes, when it gets really cold I'd rather be at home. But if I stayed away too often, someone'd pinch my beat.'

'Is it hard to get one?'

'Too true it's hard. First you have to get a permit. They don't go handing them out to just anyone. And that's not all, either. After you've wangled your permit you have to buy yourself a beat. Costs the earth, I don't mind telling you. When I've had enough of the game I'll sell my beat to someone else. The only trouble is, if you're away, some other bastard always moves in.'

'Suppose you're sick?'

'That's just a risk you have to take. But most times it's another regular, see? They're not the sort to set themselves up in a corner without knowing who it belongs to.'

'Doesn't it ever happen?'

'Sure, it happens, but not often. Besides, it's nearly always a tramp or a beggar. They go looking for trouble. Luckily for us, we've all got permits, so we just whistle up a cop and get our beat back.'

'And you say you've been here four years?'

'You mean on this beat?'

'That's right.'

'No, no, only a year here so far. It's a good beat, this one. People pass by on their way to the station, so trade's pretty brisk. No, before this I was further down-town. I sold up there and took over this place. But I had to fight for it. At the beginning we had those wide Paris newsboys here, a regular gang of them. You know the ones, they all wear blue blouses and peaked caps. Get in everywhere nowadays, they do. They've got those sort of small mobile kiosks, and just sit by them all day long. Well, they soon saw I'd got myself a good beat, and they tried to intimidate me. But I wasn't having any, I stood firm. I may be blind but I've got my head screwed on the right way. Got the best of them in the end, too, put the union boys on to them, and after that they left me alone. But it was pretty tough. They're young, they can hold down jobs—why don't they let the old folks be? If there was anything else I could do I shouldn't stay here long, I promise you.'

'And is it a long time since—I mean, that you've been, well, like that?'

'Like that? Oh, my eyes, you mean.'

'Yes.'

'Oh, it happened ten, fifteen years ago.'

'How?'

'At work. A petroleum explosion. But that's all old history now. The doctors told me they'd try to save at least the one eye. Had three operations, but it didn't come off.'

'What did it do to you?'

'How d'you mean, what did it do to me?'

'I mean what effect did it have on you, not being able to see any more, and all that?'

The man reflected for a moment.

116

'Well, it shook me all right, that's true enough, But you soon get used to it, you know. It's pretty good hell at first, I don't mind admitting—you bump into everything, and hurt yourself, and you're always scared of falling. But you get acclimatized soon enough. You know, when you get down to it, being blind isn't so very different from waking up during a power cut. You sort yourself out fast enough, it doesn't take long to get organized. It's all right in your own home. But outside on the street—' He broke off.

'On the street, yes?'

'Yes, well, on the street it's quite a different matter. I don't mind admitting, I'm not too fond of having to get back home by myself, even now. I'm always scared that there'll be some manhole left open on the pavement, and I'll tumble down it. But if I'm with my wife, then it's all right, I'm not frightened.'

'And you—you don't regret not being able to see—'

'See what?'

'No, I meant, do you ever regret not being able to see any more, period?'

'Well, I don't know, there's got to be a good reason for wanting to, hasn't there? Of course, when I hear a pretty young girl go by, there are times when it gets me down a bit—but there aren't all that many things that are worth the trouble, indeed there aren't.'

A middle-aged woman came up and bought a paper. The man felt the coin and dropped it, with a clink of metal, into an old tin can beside him. Then he resumed his motionless vigil, head held very straight, hands thrust into the pockets of his lumberjacket.

'What's your name?' Besson asked.

'Bayard,' the man said, and then, after a momentary hesitation: 'What's yours?'

'Besson,' said Besson.

There was another silence. Besson fished a packet of cigarettes out of his jacket pocket.

'Do you smoke?' he asked.

'Are they dark tobacco?'

'Yes.'

'Then I'd be very glad of one.'

Besson held out the packet: the man's hand reached up, groped, found the cigarette-packet and clutched hold of it. The fingers of his other hand fumbled in the aperture and extracted a cigarette.

'I'll light it for you,' Besson said.

'No, give me the matches.'

The man struck a match, and held the flame under the tip of the cigarette.

'I prefer to do that for myself,' he said. He blew out a cloud of smoke, and returned cigarettes and matches to Besson.

'It must be difficult,' Besson said.

'What? Lighting a cigarette?'

'Not just that—everything. The slightest action. Even the slightest action must be difficult when you can't see what you're doing.' Besson lit his own cigarette.

'All right,' the man went on, 'eyes are useful things, I'll give you that. But you can get along without them. There's a whole heap of things people should be able to do blindfold. I find out where objects are by touching them. I only need to come up against any obstacle twice, and after that I've got it taped. I know where it is, and what sort of thing it is. I don't forget it. Living in darkness sharpens your memory, and that's the truth.'

'Don't you have a stick, for walking?'

'Yes, in the street. But today I know my wife's coming for me in an hour's time, so—no need of the stick.'

'How do you tell the time?'

'Oh, that's easy. Look.' He held out his wrist. 'You see? I had a watch specially fitted up. My own idea. They've removed the glass and replaced it with a hinged lid. When I want to know the time, I just lift the lid and touch the hands. Good idea, don't you think?'

'Very much so.'

'I used not to have a watch at first. It was so annoying. I had to ask people the time when they bought a paper. Or else I turned on the radio, and made a guess at it from the programme that was on at the time. But the watch is far more reliable.'

'And it—it doesn't worry you not being able to tell when it's night?'

The man inhaled. 'When it's night?'

'Yes. It's all the same to you. You never know whether it's night or day.'

'That's true enough, I've no way of telling. But I don't bother about it. To begin with, my wife knows even if I don't. She always tells me what the weather's like, if it's sunny or overcast. But I don't really care all that much, come to think of it. When I get home in the evening I'm tired. I go to bed and sleep. I wake up when it's morning. So in the last resort it makes no difference to me whether it's day or night.'

'And you—'

'Actually, the thing I honestly miss most is not being able to watch the telly. My wife watches in the evening, and I listen. But there are times when I'd really like to see what's going on.'

'Do you have any children?'

'Yes, I've got two children, both boys. They're married now, so I don't see them all that often. They're working. I miss reading the paper rather, too—funny thing, me selling them, isn't it? My wife reads me all the news after lunch, but it's not the same thing.'

'Have you never tried learning Braille?'

'You mean the set-up with all those raised dots?'

'That's it.'

'No. They tried to teach me in hospital. Too damned complicated.'

'Yes. It must be complicated.'

'Besides, the papers they do that way aren't the interesting ones.'

A car went by, very fast, its engine roaring. The blind man jerked a thumb after it and said: 'Hey, that was a Lancia. I know the sound of its engine. Right?'

'I don't know,' Besson said. 'It was a red car—'

'Low-slung?'

'Yes.'

'It was a Lancia, I know it was. I can recognize them all now. Just from the sound of their engines.'

'Do you practise spotting them?'

'All day long. I very seldom make a mistake.'

He flipped the ash off his cigarette on to the pavement.

'I listen all day long,' he said. 'That's how I find things out. Look, I bet I can tell you all about yourself, just from your voice.'

'Really?'

'That's right, just by listening to you talk. I can tell you how old you are. Twenty-six, I'd say. Well?'

'Twenty-seven,' said Besson.

'Fair enough, twenty-seven. You're tall and thin, and you've got black hair.'

'Absolutely right.'

'You don't do any kind of manual labour, that's for sure. Yet you have a loud voice. You must be a lawyer or a teacher, something like that. Am I wrong?'

'I'm a student,' Besson said. 'But you're right, I have been a teacher.'

'You see? It's easy. I listen to people talking, and work out what they're like just for the fun of it.'

Besson glanced at a group of people approaching them on the pavement.

'I can go a bit further, too,' the blind man said. 'You're not married, are you? If you were, you wouldn't waste your time chatting me up like this.'

'Quite true,' Besson said.

The man began to laugh. 'I enjoy trying to work out what people are like,' he said. 'It's all there in the voice. They don't know how much their voices give them away.'

'You're a philosopher,' Besson said.

At this the blind man gave another laugh. '*Me?* Well, I don't know, maybe you're right. I haven't read any of those old books, though—'

'It isn't worth while reading them, you know,' Besson said.

'I'd have liked to have an education. But my parents couldn't afford it. I had to go out to work as soon as I could.'

'Education isn't worth all that much.'

The man pondered this for a moment. 'You shouldn't say that. It's not true, you know—education *is* worth something. It's good to acquire knowledge. I wish I could have done it.'

'What would you like to have known?'

'Oh, everything. The lot. How to write well, and figure, and think properly. That's what I'd have liked. But the thing I really wanted was to be a doctor. Understand how to heal people, find out all about drugs, know all the diseases. That's what I'd have found really interesting. Doctors are good people. Well, not all of them, I know that, but some of them are really decent. When I had my operations, the doctor who looked after me explained the whole business. Of course, I didn't understand some bits of it. But it interested me just the same. And the doctor saw I was interested, that's why he told me all about it.'

'You remind me of someone,' Besson said.

'Oh yes?' said the blind man, 'and who might that be?'

'A man who lived a long time ago. He was rather like you.'

'What did he do?'

'Nothing, really. He was a philosopher. He lived in a barrel and listened to what was going on around him.'

'Was he a writer?'

'No, not even that. He just sat there all day in his barrel, and learnt a whole heap of things. He lived at Corinth, in Greece, a long time ago. He spent his time observing life, and he didn't give a damn for anything or anybody. He went around barefoot, and slept where he felt like it, in doorways, or even in his barrel. One day he saw a child drinking from cupped hands at a fountain. He said to himself: "The child's right. He's taught me I've still got something which serves no useful purpose." So then he broke his bowl.'

'He must have been a queer sort of fellow,' said the blind man. 'Surely he was a bit cracked, though?'

'Yes, and another time he heard a philosopher saying that man was an animal with two feet and no feathers. So he took a chicken, and plucked all its feathers, and threw it down in front of the philosopher, saying: "Look, there's your man for you!" '

'Bravo,' said the blind man. 'That's the sort of stuff to give 'em. But I bet the other man didn't appreciate the joke.'

'I must say I'd be surprised if he had.' Besson stubbed out his cigarette on the sole of his shoe. 'I have to be going now,' he added.

The blind man flicked his butt-end into the road. 'Come back one of these days,' he said. 'You can tell me more about this character who lived in a barrel. It sounds as though it might be amusing.'

'I'll be back,' Besson promised. 'See you.'

'Goodbye, then,' the man said.

'Goodbye,' said Besson.

Besson emerged from the doorway and took a few steps down the pavement. Then he turned back for a moment and gazed at the hunched-up figure sitting there in the shadows, with the pile of newspapers and the tin can full of coins beside him. He sat quite motionless, hands thrust in the pockets of his lumberjacket. Beneath the blue rainproof cap the face with its pointless lines was in repose, and reflections glinted from those large, opaque, impenetrable glasses. It was true, of course: this was the way he had to live, squatting on a section of pavement that was his unquestioned property, a section of property that he had bought. People might pass to and fro all day long, but he remained *at home*, in his own place. He had nothing to fear from the hubbub around him, or from people staring at him. His quest was over. He could settle down in his little retreat, his private, well-protected hiding-place; and there, quite unhurriedly, he would begin to play that lengthy game which can only be observed inside one's own head.

Chapter Five

Besson at work—The games—What one sees from a window—The story of Black Oradi—How François Besson triumphed over gravity

ON the fifth day, Besson remained in his room. He sat at his table, not thinking of anything, having previously hung a placard from the outer doorhandle on which he had written, with a red ball-point pen: WORKING PLEASE DO NOT DISTURB. Then he began to examine his surroundings, in front of him and on either side. It was about three in the afternoon. Through the curtainless windows he could see the house opposite, a dirty grey building with its own lace-curtained windows, and a segment of dull, neutral-coloured sky, in which not a single bird could be seen.

The light came straight into the room, without making any shadows. Besides the drumming of the rain, various other odd noises were audible: whimperings, dull thuds, creaks, whirrs, whistles. Men's voices, the screams of children. Bottles rattling in crates. Heavy bangs above the ceiling or under the floor. Scraping and shuddering noises of unidentifiable origin, a pebble rattling down noisily in some area, windows vibrating as a truck passed by. Susurrus of tyres. Water gurgling down the gutter, the pistol-shot banging of front doors, a self-starter coughing into life. All this was normal, absolutely normal, a rich and confused medley of sound ebbing and flowing like a pendulum. Time passed softly and easily with these noises to help it. It was rather like being asleep.

Nothing in particular happened. Out of the street or secluded behind closed doors the little sounds continued, never suggesting anything but the existence of life—life in miniature, tittuping along, nibbling at the edges of things, consumed by a vague itch yet unable to let go properly.

123

Above Besson's head the ceiling stretched motionless, a sure fixed point, and in the cube of bright air below it an unlit electric light bulb hung on its cord. The walls of the room were just *there*, they took no action. They were quite content to be walls, good solid walls and nothing more. Yet there could be little doubt that a constant process of attrition was at work on them, crumbling away their substance, sending out clouds of white dust from them. Damp got under the yellow wallpaper and quietly worked it loose from its paste, millimetre by millimetre. Everything looked so strong and permanent, yet it was a virtual certainty that in two or three hundred years there would be no surviving trace of this room. There would just be an old hollow ruin, looking as though it had been eaten away by cancer, in the middle of a thorny, overgrown waste lot.

But for the present the room was peaceful enough, with hardly anything happening in it. Besson sat there for a while, elbows resting on the table. He carefully scrutinized each separate object, down to the last sheet of scribbled manuscript. He took in the penknife, its blade still open, and the box containing 50 drawing-pins, and the bottoms of paper cups, and the keys, and the empty inkwell. Periodicals lay about everywhere, with crumpled pages and minus their covers. A schematic swan swimming on a match-box. Besson read everything, in an unhurried, almost hypnotic manner. Everything he looked at was strange, all the words printed on the white pages seemed full of trickery and illusion. On the left-hand corner of the table, beside a stub-crowded ashtray, a dictionary lay open at page 383. Besson began to read the catch-words, softly at first, then progressively louder and louder:

Helium
Helix
Hellene
Hellenic
Helleniser
Hellenism

Hellenist
Helminth
Helvetian (m. or f.)
Helvetian (adj.)
*Hem!
Hemacyte
Hematite
Hematocele
Hematopoeisis
Hematosis

After this he leant forward and picked up a paper. He unfolded it slowly, found the Amusement Page, and then spread it out on the table. The big sheet of newsprint left smudges on his fingers. It was covered with a number of strange drawings, with captions written underneath them. Here, enclosed in their black frames, were men wearing white tunics, armed with spears and shields, or inscrutable women, draped in décolleté robes, their faces heavily made-up and their long tresses studded with outsize jewels. At the top of the page, above the drawings, was written:

The Empress of the Desert: Zenobia of Palmyra

There were other strip-cartoons running across the same page, showing bald men in space-suits shooting other men with death-ray guns. Underneath these, again, was a group of men and women standing in a sun-lounge, with lots of big windows. Two of them had white clouds billowing from their mouths, with the following legends written on them:

'That's great, Steve. You take Thompson in the Bentley. Sir Bernard and I will stay here and wait for instructions from the boss.'
'O.K. We'll go as far as Stevenage on the main road. That's forty miles from here. By the way, what about the man watching the house?'

125

At the bottom of the page there were also various games and riddles and one or two jokes, this kind of thing:

'I'm a real paragon,' a man wrote in his private diary. 'I don't drink. I don't smoke. I don't go to the theatre or the cinema, and I'm unswervingly faithful to my wife. I never so much as look at another woman. I go to bed every evening at eight o'clock, and get up and go to work at dawn. Every Sunday I attend church. But it's all going to be very different once I get out of jail. . . .'

When Besson had finished looking at all the pictures, and had read every caption, he took out his ball-point pen and did the crossword. He studied the clues for a moment, then began filling in the empty squares. Three across was 'Signifies proximity'; Besson wrote 'Here'. 'Close pair' produced 'Tights'. 'All the clues there if you follow them' suggested 'Thriller'. Ten across was 'Spy with the field variety?': Besson filled in 'Glasses'. 'Mutual absorption' turned out to be 'Osmosis'. Thirteen across, 'Roussel had them all dancing right through his party', defeated him.[1] 'La Fontaine made one for the nymphs of Vaux'—'Elegy'. He turned from Across to Down. 'Completely effaced' must be 'Erased', while 'Accustomed to a new way of life' was 'Acclimatized'. Four down, 'bare horror', produced 'Stark', but 'Scarcely more than skin and bone' he left blank. 'Saurians from tropical America' were 'Iguanas'. Thirteen down, 'Arab water-hole', was 'Oasis'. 'A hundred down here in Paris produces Roman dual': Besson wrote 'ii'. Nine down, 'Money's the surest one', turned out to be 'Investment'. 'Sometimes broken in conversation' was 'Thread'.

Besson passed a good half-hour in this way. Then he got up and walked across to the right-hand window. It was a large window, taller than it was wide, with eight panes of glass mounted in a brown wooden framework. The fourth pane up was cracked from top to bottom. The sixth vibrated very faintly. Besson looked out through the third at the houses and street, the passing scene

[1] Presumably a reference to the ballet *Le Festin de l'Araignée*, by the French composer Albert Roussel (1869-1937) [Trs].

before him. Through the fine drizzle tiny figures, old and young, men and women, were hurrying to and fro. Cars slid to a stop at the cross-roads, changed gear, moved off again. From time to time someone would sound his horn, a sharp and generally brief blaring note which produced no echo. It was a familiar and superficially peaceful scene. Yet all the same there was something disturbing about it. To be high up in this apartment block offered security of a kind, but not for ever. The tide of activity gradually surrounded you, cut you off without your noticing it. Its clamorous, eddying flow constantly wore away the walls of the building, rubbing off fragments of plaster, tiny bits of stone, loose flakes of ochre-coloured paint. These men skulking along the sidewalks were not as inoffensive as they looked. Their lowered heads concealed murderous thoughts, and it would take very little—a revolution, for instance, a simple upsurge of mob fury—to bring them out. They would advance like a horde of voracious ants, and gather in crowds under the windows, shouting and waving their fists, screaming for blood. They would surge up every stairway, break down all the doors, and strike without mercy, again and again, great razorish slashes, till finally each head fell free from its body, the neck one red and gaping wound, the life-blood ebbing away.

Best not to think about such things, best to see no further than the surface appearance of reality, to play with it continually like a set of knuckle-bones. Obstinately Besson set himself to count the cars passing by outside. He took a sheet of paper and a ball-point pen. A few minutes later he had produced the following list:

Citroën	14	Fiat	9
Renault	51	Alfa-Romeo	1
Dauphine	29	Volkswagen	1
4 CV	12	Ford	1
R4, R8	10	Porsche	1
Peugeot (403, 404)	25	Dodge Dart	1
Panhard	5	Volvo	1
Simca	6	Unidentified makes	3

People still crowded along the sidewalks behind one another. From his high eyrie François Besson watched them attentively, forehead pressed to the window. He saw young women dressed in red and black macintoshes, some bare-headed, others wearing scarves or hats. There were men in their forties, smoking as they walked. There were old men, and soldiers in uniform, and middle-aged women with children, or dogs, who dithered a long time on the edge of the pavement before crossing the road. Besson saw groups of little girls on their way to or from school, satchels slung over their shoulders, always jostling each other and squealing. He saw a man in a dark grey overcoat who stared at all the women passing by. He saw dawdlers and hurriers, cripples, polio cases, one-legged men on crutches. Some walked with a brisk, decisive step, others slouched; one or two turned their toes in. He saw them all, tiny manikins stretched out in insect-like columns, tight-packed, wedged against one another, timid, ridiculous, anonymous creatures—it made one feel sick to look at them. These were the people who owned the town, who had jobs and professions, who thought a little, who spent all their time swarming through this labyrinthine gallery-ridden termite-hill of theirs. Life here belonged to them. They had taken possession of this territory and become its exclusive occupants. None of them ever gave up. None of them ever renounced his shadowy status as a living creature, none of them ever simply stepped out of his clothes and his skin, and quietly melted away on the tarred asphalt. Such an idea never occurred to them. They were strong, incorruptible. Amazingly strong.

With a twinge of regret Besson sensed that from now on he would not be able to look at them all that often. He opened the window, and took a deep breath of cold, rain-damp air. For a little longer he continued to watch the wet street below, with its endless stream of mauve and green cars (more figures for his list) and all the women in loud raincoats, heels tapping a frenzied tattoo along the pavement. Then he drew the shutters to, and carefully closed them. He walked back to the middle of the darkened room, hesitated a moment, then went over to the door, pressed the light-switch, and watched brightness instantly spring out from the bulb.

The light hung directly above the table. Besson stood facing it for a moment; then he sat down in the chair and stared at the litter of papers spread out in front of him. The sheet of newspaper he had been looking at now lay close to one corner of the table: Besson gently dropped it on the floor. The entire working surface was cluttered up with scribbled sheets of manuscript, letters half-sticking out of their envelopes. Everything was in a chaotic muddle, but the muddle possessed a small confused life of its own, that kept whispering endless confidences in one's ear. It made one want to send messages everywhere, all over the world, postcards with 'kind regards' written in the space reserved for correspondence—just 'kind regards', nothing more. It made one want to write stories, odd and trivial stories with the names of places or people, and dialogue, and inverted commas and exclamation-marks and question-marks and dashes. It made one want to doodle little patterns on a scratch-pad, crosses and spirals and circles. Or to play soldiers, sketching a mountain range at the bottom of the page, and putting in rows of little men with guns—white heads on the left, black on the right. A flag and a colour-bearer in each camp, too, that was essential. Then you made them shoot at each other, by tracing a long black line from the muzzle of the gun, which would curve over and down into the enemy's camp. One for the whites and one for the blacks. After that you counted up the corpses to decide which side had won.

Besson took a sheet of paper and began to write. Slowly and hesitantly at first he traced each letter, one after the other, watching his pothooks marching forward all by themselves (well, almost by themselves) across the paper, navy blue on white. He took great care over capitals; he dotted every i and crossed every t. After a moment or so he began to go faster. He forgot the jerky motions of his hurrying hand, he no longer noticed each loop and flourish in the words he set down. He plunged into the act of writing like a landscape, without any conscious goal, never slackening speed. He saw whole phrases pour out of his pen, filing

129

swiftly to the right like tiny animals. He heard the soft abrasive squeak of the hurrying nib, and the regular rub of his hand against the paper, What a strange phenomenon it was, this meticulous scribbling which—little by little, line by line—filled the entire sheet, besmirching it with a whole private system of strokes and and loops, this strange object marching on of its own volition, how, no one could tell, forward, always forward, describing, erasing, pointing the flow of time. There was something alarming about it, it was quite capable of pulling a fast one on you, saying things off its own bat, things you had no idea of. It was language in isolation, a kind of Braille alphabet in which each sign or group of points had stolen something from the substance of life and was preserving it in minuscule form. Like an obscene wall-inscription, a thumbing of the nose against the ineffable weight of eternity. Or perhaps more like some magical formula, some highly complex and specific spell which, if pronounced correctly, can bring about ignoble metamorphoses, trigger off strange chemical reactions, turn children into toads, moonbeams into emeralds, sunlight into rubies.

On the sheet of paper Besson wrote:

'Cavalcade.
Venenom.
Leaf
Sclor   Bergue—Wiggins Teape Papers.

I am writing. I am writing that I am writing. I am writing that I am writing that I am writing. I am writing that I am writing that I am writing that I am writing.

I am looking at my watch. I am very fond of my watch. I would not like to lose it. I would not like anyone to steal it. I have already damaged it once: I forgot to take it off in the bath. I had to take it round to the watch-mender for cleaning and oiling. It has a beautiful white metal dial, with tiny strokes instead of figures. Right at the top, where the hands indicate noon or midnight, there are two strokes instead of one. Near the centre of the dial is written, in English: JUNGHANS. Shockproof. Anti-magnetic.

Waterproof. Made in Germany. There are two hands, the shorter one pointing towards the stroke which represents 4, the larger one vertically aligned downwards, covering the stroke at 6. So this is the time my watch tells me it is: half past four. Oh, and there's another indicator, a very long fine needle, which sweeps round the dial with a vibrating motion. It's really a very fine watch. I would hate to break it. I am glad it belongs to me. It has a nice pigskin strap, and a bright metal buckle. The glass has been a bit scratched on the outside, ever since I banged my wrist against the school wall. It was a present from my mother, two years ago. For my birthday. When I put it close to my ear I can hear its tiny heart beating away, tick-tick-tick, never stopping. It's nice to have a watch of your own. Wherever I go people can ask me the time, and I can look at my watch and say "A quarter to two", or "Half past seven", or "Three minutes to twelve", or whatever it may happen to be.'

A little lower Besson wrote: 'This ball-point dribbles.' Then he pushed the sheet of paper aside, and taking up the ball-point again began to scribble words wherever he could, feverishly covering scraps of paper and cardboard, the bottoms of paper cups, match-boxes, all picked up at random, with such words as 'Messenger', 'Vander Beke', 'Cruelty', 'Lang', 'Urhell', 'Matton', 'Zailer', 'Physics', 'Dallas', 'Nail', 'Jerrycan'. Finally pressing, as hard as he could, he inscribed a very long word on the wooden surface of the table: 'Angersonysbonagugehlbouduyrouehavleffavyi'.

After this he ceased all practical activity. There were several photographs lying on the table, and he picked them up. The glossy, grey-tinted slips of pasteboard showed various carefully posed girls, and some dull, depressing landscape shots. One or two were of Besson himself, wearing dark glasses in summer, or posed against a wintry snowbound garden.

Then, at the very bottom of an open drawer, beside a tattered pornographic magazine, Besson came upon a little exercise book, its pages yellowed with age and covered with childish handwriting. On the cover there was a pencil drawing of an engine with five funnels being driven by a man wearing a tarboosh. Above this picture, in capital letters, was the legend: BLACK ORADI.

Besson opened the notebook and began to read. It was not an easy business, since the words had been written in pencil, and after twenty years were badly blurred. The speillng, too, left much to be desired, and many of the sentences needed to be read two or three times before their meaning became clear. But it was an interesting task, and Besson, poring over the faded manuscript, set about it with unhurried deliberation.

Chapter One.

Black Oradi lef the monf 1940 the day of his birfday. He wated seven days, the bote was called the Condé. He stade at sea 31 days then he saw he had gon too far on the sea. He told the captin he wanted to go back but he woudnt, finaly he arived in America. The captin thort he was in Africa or azia 1947. He spent three days in azia, the next day he lef for Corsica, the captin still thort he was in Africa, but Oradi said it wasn't true, first because in Africa there were black peple like him and also because there was the Bush which went on and on for ever. Then the captin began to stamer when he tarked, he said er ah um, Oradi said you shood tark mor clearly or else wate and think what to say before you say it and not swollo yore words. So just you stop it mister captin, and stop splutering like that.—How dare you tark to me like that when Im the captin.—You just had to say what you wanted to say, without that I cant understand anything—Pooey on you said the captin be off with you to yore cabin if youve got one.—But look I know joly well this is Corsica.—You dont know anything, youll never be realy brany.—What do you mean Im a police officer myself.—Ah well policemen arnt brany.

Chapter Two The Sinking

Three days later Oradi was on the hi seas. For four days he saw an enormus moving mass. He didnt know what it was,

132

he never said anything to anyone because he was afraid they woud be cross with him. But all the same he was dying to tark about it. One day he said he had seen an enormus moving mass. I believe it is a wale sir. But plese dont tell anyone or theyll kill it. Sudenly the enormus mass hurld itself at the ship. The ship put on full speed. But the wale gave the ship a big wack with its tale at the stern. The ship began to dance about up front then it went down at thr stern and all the water came in. The captin and Oradi were furius. They got out the harpoon. But as the harpoon was heavy it almost got dragd away, luckily the captin manneged to hold onto it otherwise he would have been pulld down in the sea and eten by the wale. The wale thort it was a fly or a bird, it thrashd the water with its tale and upset the bote altogether. Then the captain became quite mad with rage, since the bote was loded with stores and catl, and the casks were bobing about all over the sea. Each animal climed on a cask (a barrel for putting oil in) and made a little jump and got rite inside the barel. As for the captin, the captin had got into the enormus barel usd to fil the others. But no mater the mane thing was that it was emty with nothing inside, and Oradi swam holding on to the captin's barel from behind. The captin kept shouting in a stern (curt) voise Come on now find somthing hollo to get in.

Chapter Three The Swop

They arrivd the monf July 1947. They stade at sea six days then they took another bote a saling bote this time. The bote could not put out it was bloing grate guns and they coud not leve harbor. There was in the crew (1) the first mate Jean Bestieau age 45 (2) the new hand Yves Randort age 37 (3) the captin Jean Brideau age 83 (4) the wet cooper Bastien-Grade age 94 (5) the cook Jean luc Troncor age 39 (6) the doctor François Cablot age 33. You are too old mister Grade you will have to retire! I am going to give you this little note this will show you you are retiring.—Oh thank you very much mister Brideau!—Just a minit mister, ah the way these drores stick, got it now, heres a safty pin, kindly do it up for me will you.—How can I, this safty pin of yors is very hard. —If you like I will try to find another, but Im not shore if I have one.—No please dont do that.—There we are its in now. —Thank you!—Hey cabin boy dont go down in the hold thats where the cooper is. No hes not hes here you can see him. Dont ask him anything hes retird. Go and find a replasement. The cabin-boy took the lader and let it down on the key and he saw two men saying to each other We'll get a job as cooper on a bote Ill go and catch them said the cabin-boy. Dont just tark and get nowhere he told them come on follo me up the lader, come and see the captin. The captin said I cant do with two of you, one will have to be cooper and the other do watch duty. No! they said Yes! he said No! they said. Come on you, he said, youll be cooper. What about me then! You'll do watch duty! Why said the man but mister Brideau went off without saying anything.

Chapter Fore the Pirat

The other man said ah I've a good idea what about becoming a pirat. Ill kill the steersman and steer the bote onto a reef and make it sink its a new bote. He huried downstares. Then he bort a super sord and sheeld and came up agane, he went over to the steersman and cut of his hed. Oradi was angry. He said Why did you kill that man? Shut up you mad fool because hes a pirat thats why. Oradi saw the bote was beginning to fill with water. Then he ran of. The bandit larfd. Oradi told the captin that water was poring into the bote the captin was astonishd and arsd him why. Sudenly the captin and Oradi were throne against the servants dore the dore burst open and they saw the servant drowning in the water.

The bote began to sink under the water very sloly.

Help shouted the captin, rescue, Oradi, my first mate my cook my doctor my cooper, help! The negroes this being south Africa got into there canoes and rescued them. The bandit made for the shore and hid in a hole. The captin got out of his canoe and went to the beach for a swim. He saw the bandit pulling a rock down on top of him so no one shoud see him. The captin lookd at him and left him to get on with it. He took off his clothes and put them down beside him. He had to go a long way to swim because the tide was rite out. While he was gon the bandit took his clothes. He undresd and lef his own clothes ther insted. Then he dresd in those belonging to the captin.

When the captin came back he coud see neither his clothes nor Oradi. His eyes bugd out of his hed when insted of his own fine clothes he saw a pile of red and green stripd rags, zounds said the captin he has taken my clothes! Luckily he cort site of Oradi holding the bandit and shouting Help Help! Then the captin ran as fast as he coud and cort the pirat and demanded his clothes back, Here they are then the pirat sed.—And what have you don with the steersman? —I kild him. —Your going to com along with me, then.— What for, sed the pirat.—Youll see . . . He laffed and laffed. He was sure theyd kill him. Im going to put you in prisn! To prisn with the fellow! Keep a tite hold on him Oradi!— But why?—You never ask why. Go on, hold him tite, if you dont hold him hell get away. Im going to tie him up, put your hand there.—Here?—No not there, on the not Im tying, there, now dont move. Oh, youve made me let the not slip loose. Now Im going to get into this handcart with the bandit and youre going to push it.

Oradi took to his heels because the bandit was running after him. The bandit threw a stone at him wich landed in the mud and stuck ther, he cort his foot on it and stumbeld and overturnd the cart and Oradi straind both his legs. The captin cort the pirat agen, he came back and saw Oradi lying on the ground. He said to the bandit Im going to take you to north Africa and drown you. He tide him up firmly to a tree and went off to find his fore black frends like Oradi. He said to them, cut me some long bamboos and make too holes in them. Then you must thred twisted stror thro the holes so we can put Oradi on it.—B-but, but, said all the negroes at once, straw, straw, thats going to brake!—If you plat it strong it wont. The fore set to work. They took fore nales, stuck them in the bamboo and threded the stror. They put Oradi on it and lifted him up saying oop-ah, oop-ah. They carid him as far as a rest house and here they put him down on a bed made of iron and wood. He had to stay in bed six days.

Chapter Five Rescue and Sinking

Three days later they ran into the Clafte which was a bote very like the Gland Duke which was there bote, the too botes met near America, the Clafte rose up and fell back so hevily this time that the wave past over her. But not only had the Gland Duke sunk too and the litle rescue botes were bobing about but the Grelon which was a German submarine was sinking the canoes one by one, there were at least twenty of them. This took place at $15°$. The submarine missd first time and dived back to the bottom to recharge. Then Oradi grabd his chance and tride to jump into the comander's bote. He misd his footing and fell in the water, luckily he mannagd to hang on to the side of the canoe. The captin pulld him out and brort him back, he took a nale and hamered it thro too compresd air tanks. The Grelon's bows came at them. Oradi and the captin rode as hard as they coud. He shouted to the comander ahoy there ahoy were going to be sunk by the Grelot! Quick! He ran out the rope lader and said clime up quick!—Yes but get the lader a bit closer, thats right.—The Grelot's rite into your canoe!— So what let it sink, Oradi and I are out of it.—But dont you think—Dont we think what?—Well um ah—The hell with you were coming up. The comander went away and let go the windlas.—Come back quick the windlas is running out well be drownd in the bottom of the sea. Before the comander coud get back to the side all the rope lader had run out of the windlas. He called the cabin-boy and lots more of the crew to wind it up again, there were at lest eiteen of them counting the captin but seventeen without him.

The captin and Oradi made noises like glug glug, shouting Hel glug slurp, glelp, glug. You coud here the tackle creking and hel glug helslurp noises. The captin said what a row there making, yes shouted all the others at once. Oradi climed up again, phew he said and took sevral deep breths, in out in out phew. The captin and Oradi went back to the Clafte. Whats this sir havnt I got a cabin?—Im sorry no Ill give you a tent its all Ive got, all the cabins are full including mine.—What about a table and chares?—Im sory there all taken.—In that case what can we do?—You can sleep on a mat and sit on cushons.—Will they be properly stuffd?— Yes with kapok.—But itll all come out!—Not if there properly sone up.—Come on then get this canvas redy and quick about it.—What for?—You mene you dont know?— No I havnt the fogiest.—To make the tent.—And the cushons.—Wate a moment wile I look for them.—Sir!—Yes what is it?—May I take one of these cushons?—Yes take as many as you like.—Eight then?—More if you want.—What I reckon is Ill take eight for them.—Go on then take them.— Here they are. Now if I look in this corner Ill find some more canvas. Too bad if theres scorpions lerking there. Whats this it feels like an armchare when I tuch it its cold, dont bother looking there it isnt anything interesting. Oh but look here whats this underneath when I lift it up, this wite contrap-shun, lets try a bit futher down, all right, why its a super icebox that shoud fix them. Oops, thats got it clere, keep it rite way up its got some bred and wine and a glas inside it. Bang, thud, now weve got it standing on its legs.—Lets sit down said the captin theres sure to be somthing good inside now Ill open it ooh ah its wine just look at this lovely wine.

At midday Oradi went to the ships cook and said in Inglish Im hungri.—Eh whats that? The captin hurrid in and said to the cook dont you understand.—No.—Well in that case you cant understand inglish.—No I dont.—He says hes hungri.—All rite said the cook if your hungri Ill give you a cat.—What, to eat?—Eh, no, just to show frendly. Oradi went off furius.

Saying Goodbye

Oradi said goodbye to his friends and went abord the Triglant. The siren blew and they left, Oradi lowerd a canoe into the sea with himself in it, he made a runing bowline and tied the canoe to the bote. He stade at sea 29 days. And when he got to north Africa he told them all his advenchers.

When he had finished reading, Besson dropped the small yellowing exercise-book back on the table, amid a muddle of papers and old pencil-stubs. Then his gaze lost itself in the soft shadows that filled the room, and he began to dream a whole series of minuscule adventures. Without stirring a muscle, in a mood close to tender compassion, he sat and watched every object rise and move in unison, miraculously freed from their ancient lethargy. The furniture acquired the texture of rubber, or marshmallow, and melted slowly across the floor. Grass sprouted, green and fresh, the walls silently contracted, sheets of paper covered themselves with signs and symbols. Fabrics blossomed in a flash with strange incongruous flowers, their tremulous petals spreading across the material like so many blots. An imperceptible breeze passed through the room, blowing the curtains out horizontally. Everything was floating, in suspension. At peace with himself now, all fear gone, having passed far beyond the roads that lead to life or death, François Besson similarly surrendered himself to the wind, let it bear him up and away. He felt the wings of the elements caress and sustain him. The earth in this moment was no longer viscous, no longer needed to engulf beasts and men. Its voracious belly was full to satiety. A few more hours, a few more years perhaps, and it might be possible to break loose from it like this, easily, without effort or suffering, one jump with feet together— So that day, having conquered the force of gravity, Besson spent a long time as he floated in air observing the reddish surface of the floor, seeing it swim up towards him, swollen and angry as an incoming tide.

Chapter Six

Meeting with the redheaded woman—Besson tells her fortune—Brief discussion with a child of four and a half called Lucas—A respectable man—How François Besson and the redheaded woman found themselves lying on the linoleum floor of the kitchen—Another night

ON the sixth day François Besson met the redheaded woman. She was a tall girl, five foot eight or thereabouts, pale-complexioned, and her great brown eyes had dark smudges under them. Her figure, and the absence of lines on her face, suggested an age somewhere between twenty-five and thirty, though she could have been younger—or, indeed, older. She was sitting in the bar where Besson had gone to have a beer, staring into space, doing nothing. When Besson sat down next to her she gave him one quick glance and looked away again. Besson lit a cigarette and began to talk to her. She answered him easily and calmly, just as though they had been sharing a compartment on a train journey. Besson offered her a cigarette: she took it with her left hand, and two silver bracelets jangled together on her arm as she did so. She smoked in an unhurried fashion, occasionally flicking her ash over the edge of the table, since the ashtray (an advertising handout) was stuffed with sugar-lump wrapping-papers. It also contained a long drinking-straw made out of pink plastic, bent into three and bearing traces of lipstick at one end. There was an endless stream of people in and out of the bar, all talking, laughing, downing their drinks. The waiters shouted their orders right across the room— 'One pint of draught beer!' 'Two espressos and a plate of ham!'

The chair opposite Besson and the redheaded woman was occupied by an old lady wrapped up in a woollen shawl, who sat there knitting busily. Besson felt pleased at having found someone like the redheaded woman to talk to in this bar. It filled him with confidence, he was the equal of all these other people around him. He was no longer on his own, he had become the hero of an adventure. At last something was going to happen, though exactly what he had no idea. But just how this encounter would turn out did not matter: the point was that it had a future, of one sort or another. One might endeavour to predict it, sitting there over one's beer, playing with the underside of the paper cup, casting a curious eye over one's fellow-customers—but an hour later the whole thing was quite liable to be over. The redheaded woman would get up, smile, shake hands, and say: 'That was nice. Goodbye for now. See you some time.' Or maybe they would leave the bar together, and he would walk her as far as her bus-stop. One could even try to guess her name. Maybe it was Catherine. Catherine Roussel. Or Irene Kendall. Or Vera Inson. Age: twenty-eight. Occupation: laboratory assistant. Born in Casablanca, Morocco. Mother's first name: Eléonore.

Besson said: 'What's your name?'

'Marthe,' said the redheaded woman.

'Marthe what?'

'Marthe Janin.'

'How old are you?'

'Twenty-five,' she told him.

Besson watched a man and woman pass by their table. Then he went on with his interrogation.

'Profession?'

'Come again?' Martha said.

'I mean, do you have a job?'

'Oh, I see. No, I don't have a job. Why are you asking me all these questions?'

'No particular reason. Where were you born?'

'Here,' the woman said. 'What are you up to? Want to tell my fortune?'

'Maybe,' Besson said. The hardest question still remained to be asked. He preferred to prepare the ground for it in advance.

'Do you live with your parents?'

'No,' said Marthe, and quickly added: 'Just with my son.'

142

Instantly Besson backed his hunch on the boy's first name: it would be Patrick.

'What's he called?' he asked.

'Who, my son?'

'Yes.'

'Lucas.'

Besson stubbed out his cigarette in the overflowing ashtray. Finally he said: 'And what about your mother?'

She stared at him in surprise.

'What?'

'I mean, what's *she* called?'

'Do you really need to know that?' she said.

'It's essential if I'm going to tell your fortune,' Besson said.

She grinned. 'My mother's dead,' she told him. 'But she had the same name as me, Marthe. There.'

Besson relaxed for a moment. He sat staring into his glass of beer without saying anything. The woman touched his arm.

'Well? I'm waiting.'

'What for?'

'My fortune, of course. Don't tell me you've forgotten already?'

'Ah yes, your fortune,' Besson said. 'I'll tell you it now. You're a very delicate person. You suffer from rheumatism and asthma. But this also implies great sensitivity. You're afraid of hurting people, and you hate tactlessness in others. You prefer summer to winter, and your favourite landscape has a lot of water and woodland in it. You're very nervy. When you were a child you must have had a bad fall from the top of a staircase. Your favourite colour is burnt topaz. You often have dreams about horses, and you write up a private diary every night. Be on your guard—you run quite a risk of dying by the hand of a murderer.'

'Very funny,' said Marthe. 'You've certainly got a vivid imagination. But you're wrong about one thing: my favourite colour's verdigris.'

'Anyone can make a mistake,' Besson said, and took a good pull at his beer. The young woman's cigarette joined Besson's in the brimming ashtray. Paper began to smoulder, giving off an acrid

143

smell. She coughed, and poured a few drops of coffee into the ashtray to douse the fire before it got going.

'My turn now,' she said. 'What's *your* name?'

'Paul,' said Besson. 'Paul Thisse.'

'How old are you?'

'Twenty-seven.'

'Do you have a job?'

'Not at present, no. I'm a student.'

'Do you live by yourself?'

'That depends,' Besson said. 'At the moment I'm living with my parents.'

'What are their names?'

'My father's called Georges, and my mother Gioia. She's Italian.'

'Have you any brothers or sisters?'

'No.'

She reflected for a moment.

'All right, then,' she said finally. 'You're intelligent, and rather timid. You're inclined to be nervy too, I should say. You find it hard to make up your mind, and you don't like people laughing at you. You had a very happy childhood, but now you're scared of turning out a failure. You're afraid of death, too. No, wait, I haven't finished. The woman in your life will be called Thérèse. You'll marry her and have lots of children. But before that happens you'll pass through some great ordeal which will cause you much suffering. You will have an accident. You'll be very ill. But fortunately everything will turn out all right in the end. There. Will that do you?'

'Fine,' Besson said. 'But you haven't told me my favourite colour.'

'The colour of the sun,' said the redheaded woman.

They went on talking like this for over an hour. All the time people kept entering and leaving the café, and the old lady in her woollen shawl never once stopped knitting. From time to time someone would put a coin in the jukebox, and the room would be flooded with music—loud, monotonous, coarse-rhythmed.

Besson asked the redheaded woman endless questions about herself and her family. He found out that she was not married. Her son was four and a half. She had been ill a few months ago. She wrote poetry. She had taken the examination for a librarian's diploma, and was waiting for the results. When she had saved enough money, she was going to buy a small car, probably a Fiat. Her father was in business in Paris. She had few friends, and very seldom came out to the café. Besson told her things about himself, too. He said he had nearly got married several months before, but that in the end it just hadn't worked out. He was in the process of breaking off with his fiancée. One day soon he would write her a letter, or maybe call her up on the phone, and tell her what he really felt about her. He had taught history and geography in a private school, but had given this job up some while back. He had no real idea what he was going to do now.

The young woman listened to all this with great composure, her eyes fixed on the polished nails of her right hand. Besson noticed that she wore a heavy gold ring on her ring-finger, with the initials J.S. engraved on it. This was probably the name of her son's father, Besson thought. Jacques Salles. Or Jean Servat. Unless it happened to be Jerome Sanguinetti.

They smoked another cigarette together. Then the girl got up and went across to the toilet. Besson watched her move over the floor of the bar, holding herself very erect, hips swivelling a little under her beige jersey dress. By the time she got back Besson had paid both bills. They left the café and walked off together through the fine drizzle. After they had gone a few yards the young woman turned to Besson and began to say goodbye.

With some embarrassment Besson said: 'I haven't anything much to do right now—maybe I could walk a bit further with you?'

She hesitated. 'The thing is, I have to go and fetch my son from his nursery school.'

'That's all right,' Besson said. 'I'd like to meet your son.'

They moved off again together, side by side, one couple in a multitude of men and women threading their way through the

145

streets of the town, past endless rows of shops. Fine rain drizzled down on to their faces out of a black sky, and the drops were instantly absorbed by their skin, without trickling. They fell on their hair and foreheads and noses, sometimes even dropping through their parted lips. This rain was soft and cold, all of a piece with the wind and air and odours all around them. Cars swished by in the roadway, spattering their legs as they passed. Besson suddenly felt as though he were on a boat, or walking along a beach. With quiet persistence the falling water went about its tack of dissolution. Everything gleamed damply. Even the lights were misty and humid: the naked bulbs that contained each spark of electricity looked like grotesque globes of moisture.

The redheaded woman walked on beside Besson, wrapped in her blue raincoat, legs and hips moving briskly. Her leather hand-bag swung from curled fingers; she advanced as though she had a motor hidden somewhere inside her body. Her face looked straight ahead down the pavement, eyes very much alert, though half-hidden by drooping eyelids and lashes, mouth open to breathe, a regular palpitation fluttering her throat. Lower down the move-ment became clearly visible: her shoulders followed the rhythmic swing of her arms, her backbone oscillated to and fro, while from time to time her torso would bend either forwards, or—with an abrupt, twisting gesture—to the left or the right. The overall impression was of a powerful, smooth-running machine, work-ing at full pressure. From its birth onwards this body had been taught the gestures and rhythms of life. These clumsy arms and crazy legs, these heavy hips—all had been permeated by some mysterious and subtle substance which now controlled them. From a mere mass of flesh and bone there had been created a woman.

Besson walked beside her, not saying a word; yet already it was as though he had been caught in the wash of some big steamer. Without even knowing it, she had taken him in tow. It was she who elbowed through the crowd, and followed a safe course down the middle of the pavement. Yet perhaps, at the deepest level, she *was* aware of it. It must be stamped all over her body, on every square inch of bare skin, on the moon of each separate fingernail. She was the dividing-line between life and death, a kind of figurehead that bore the distinguishing mark of humankind blazoned plainly across it. Her impassive and wellnigh immobile features, set like a mask above those thrusting shoulders, proclaimed to the anonymous, obscure and hostile mass of townsfolk that she was blazing a trail for humanity. Without either fear or hatred, simply in the awareness of her own unquestioned rights, she asserted her claim to a place among the rest; and they understood this instantly, making way for her as she approached, opening a small postern gate in their defensive ramparts to let this one small congeneric atom slip through. Sheltered by the mere proximity of the redheaded woman, François Besson advanced without fear. Eyes might stare at him now if they chose: they would not penetrate beyond the surface. The human territory he was traversing had become *his* domain also. He could take shelter and sleep in the houses, or drink with easy nonchalance in the cafés. He could book himself a room in any hotel. He could walk through the public squares or stare at the goods in shop windows, just as he pleased. It was a wonderful feeling not to be alone any longer.

When they reached the door of the nursery school, Besson let the girl go in alone. At this point he was so buoyed up by her presence that he found himself able to stand there motionless on the kerb, smoking a cigarette and watching the passers-by.

After a few minutes the redheaded woman returned, leading a redheaded little boy by the hand. When the child saw Besson, he scowled. Marthe pushed him forward. 'He's a bit shy,' she said. 'Say hullo to the gentleman, Lucas.'

Besson bent solemnly down and shook hands with the little boy. His small hand felt cold and crinkly, like a monkey's paw.

Then all three of them set off the way they had come, Marthe holding Lucas's hand and Besson walking beside them. They made their way through a good many streets, at an easy, unhurried pace. The girl talked to her son and Besson in turn. At one point the little redheaded boy said he wanted a chocolate ice, and Besson bought ices for all of them. They walked on, licking their ices as they went, making occasional little jokes. It was all very peaceful and harmless; it could have gone on like this for days, even weeks. It was like strolling down a long warm beach towards the sea, with a fresh breeze blowing in your face; or, again, like wandering round a fair, without a thought in one's head, gazing at the shooting galleries and the merry-go-rounds, inhaling the resinous odour of pralines and toffee-apples. A little further on they met a group of little girls and boys, and Lucas stopped to stare at them. Besson heard what the children were saying: it was an argument to decide, yes or no, whether there were any Indians in this part of the world. At another point the girl decided to go into a shop and buy herself a girdle. She left the little boy with Besson and vanished, saying: 'Won't be a second—'

After a moment Besson followed her into the shop, bringing the child with him, and watched her look through an assortment of elastic girdles. He released the little boy's hand to light a cigarette: when he finished, the child's hand crept back into his, quite naturally, as a matter of course.

Besson looked at him and said: 'What's your name?'

'Lucas', said the little boy.

'How old are you?'

'Four and a half.'

'And where do you live?'

Silence.

'Come on, tell me where you live—'

'Don't know.'

'You mean you don't know where your house is?'

'Over there. . . .'

'Or that one there, maybe?'

But the child turned his gaze somewhere else, and that was the end of the conversation.

When the girl had bought her girdle, they set off along the sidewalk again: but this time the little redhaired boy held Besson's hand.

Later, about nine or ten o'clock, after dinner, when Lucas was asleep in his own room, Besson and Marthe still sat talking in the kitchen. Here, more or less, is what they said to one another.

'He takes after you,' Besson said.

'Lucas? He's got my hair, yes. But in every other way he's the image of his father.'

'Doesn't he ever ask where he is?'

'Where who is? His father?'

'Yes.'

'No, I told him his father was dead. That way he doesn't ask any questions.'

'What does he do?'

'Him? Oh, he's a lawyer. Pretty well-known locally, too.' She began to shred the cigarette she was holding, rolling it between the thumb and index finger of her left hand.

'I'm not sorry I broke up,' she said. 'Not even for Lucas's sake.'

'Why?'

'Oh—he was a really seductive type, *you* know, everything a woman could want. All the same, he was just a plain stinker. I never had the guts to cut loose from him, though. In the end *he* ditched *me*. Bit of luck, I suppose.'

'He—he ditched you when you became—when you had your child?'

She shook her head. 'No, not then. It happened about a year ago. Oh, he used to go out with every woman he met. He'd set me up in a bedsitter with—with Lucas. He used to come and visit me every evening. But I never saw him during the day. And yet he was really fond of his son. Used to play with him, all that sort of thing. Brought him toys. Which didn't stop him being a plain bastard. Money, that was the only thing that mattered as far as he was concerned, money, money. He wanted to make more and more, all the time. He lashed it all out, too. To make people admire him. He liked being admired, it gave him a kick. Trouble was, I didn't admire him enough, to his way of thinking. I didn't flatter him. That's what he couldn't take about me, I reckon.'

'Why didn't you get married?'

She shrugged.

149

'Was it he who didn't want to?'

'Oh, at the beginning he was all for it. But that didn't tell me anything. He wanted to marry me because of the kid. There mustn't be any scandal. Besides, he'd have liked to get Lucas to himself—his son, you know, to do what he liked with. Then after a while we got used to not being married. It wouldn't have made any difference as far as I was concerned.'

Besson said: 'Basically, he sounds the jealous sort to me.'

'Yes, maybe. But I'm still not sorry it ended.'

'Are you so sure?'

She did not answer. Besson began to fiddle with his coffee-spoon, twisting it round on the green oilcloth.

'Everything he did, he did for his son,' Marthe said. 'He wouldn't lift his little finger to help me. But his son was another matter. Besides—It's a bit embarrassing to admit it, but—well, he's still supporting me. Every month, ever since we broke up, he's sent me a money-order. So I can bring up his son. Funny, isn't it?'

'Decent of him.'

'*Decent*?' She gave a bitter laugh. 'Why d'you suppose he's doing it? He's scared. He's afraid of gossip. Don't you see it? He's—well, he's a very respectable citizen. He's afraid of what people might say. He feels a certain responsibility for his son. He's fallen out with his wife—mistress, if you like. All right. But he still sees to his son's upbringing. He's a good father, I'll admit it. And he doesn't act that way purely out of self-interest. It comes naturally. That's the way he is. He's respectable. He has responsibilities. It really is funny. All right by me, though—the cash certainly comes in handy.'

'You should have refused to accept it.'

'Yes, I know. I ought to have sent his money-orders straight back to him. I did, the first time. But I wasn't having any luck finding a job. It's tough getting work when you really need it. Then, the next month, he sent more money. After all, I thought, what odds does it make? He can't buy me back this way.'

'You ease his conscience for him.'

'Well, fine. But that one'd have a good conscience anyhow. Besides, I'm no heroine, I'm telling you.'

Besson was silent for a moment or two. He sat there, hands resting on the oilcloth, rounded back hunched into the tubular metal chair, staring at the dirty plates and half-filled glasses of water that still littered the left-hand side of the table. The electric light beat harshly down on them, and the brightness reflected from each object pierced through his eyes to the inmost recesses of his mind, or body. A sense of fatigue, a drowsy stupor began to steal over him. He felt himself drifting far away from the immediate situation—the remains of supper, this bright-walled kitchen, this table, the harsh gleam of unwashed dishes. Yet the redheaded girl sitting opposite him was so close that he could almost fancy he had her in his arms, was clasping her roughly to him, a mere object.

He said: 'I want to hear about your father. Tell me what he does, what kind of man he is.'

She smiled. 'He's just an ordinary sort of man, like anyone else.'

'What's his name?'

'Louis.'

'How old is he?'

'I've no idea. He must be a bit over sixty. Sixty-two, I think.'

'What does he look like? Describe him to me.'

This time she laughed quite openly. 'What does he look like? Wait a moment, let's think. He's tall, and grey-haired. He's got very pale eyes, but that's a symptom of old age—every time I see him I'm astonished by the colour of his eyes. They're translucent, grey-blue, touches of green as well. Oh, and he's got lines there, on each cheek. And another vertical one between his eyebrows. Maybe he's got rather too strong a nose, but I think he's very handsome. No, really, it's true, for his age he looks pretty good.'

'What's his character like? All right?'

'Some people would say No. Some people would call him very bad-tempered. But he's always been terribly gentle with me. He let me do just as I liked.'

'Then why don't you live with him?'

'Oh, I don't know. I couldn't before, because—well, because of *him*. And now I've got used to living here. But maybe I'll go back to him one of these days. I just don't know.' She eyed him with some curiosity, and added: 'Now what about you? Tell me about *your* father.'

'He's a very reasonable sort of man,' Besson said, simply. 'I suppose you'd call him a disciplinarian, but I'm very fond of him. He's got his fads, but then so has every—'

'And your mother?'

Besson hesitated. 'My mother? She's my mother, that's all. What else is there to say about her?'

'Don't you like her?'

'I love her to distraction, I loathe her guts, I despise her, I believe in her. She's—well, *she's my mother*, don't you understand?'

'You live with your parents, and you—'

'Yes, I know. You're right. But it's only a temporary arrangement. As soon as I get a new job I'll rent a bedsitter somewhere in town. Unless *you* felt like offering me bed and board.'

She looked at him quite seriously. 'Why not?' she said. She began to trace a pattern on the oilcloth with her nail, in a mechanical fashion. Besson saw that she drew a series of parallel lines, and then filled the spaces between with them crosses.

'Maybe it would teach *him* a lesson,' she added, as an afterthought.

Besson said: 'He wouldn't send you any more money-orders.'

'Don't be so sure. He'd be rather proud of a situation like that. He'd look as though he was thinking: *Well, there you are you see, what a woman—but my son's my son, regardless. Let her do what she likes, it won't make any difference.*'

'Anyway, you can't stop yourself thinking about him, can you?'

She looked at him, her eyes still serious: but this time there was something almost tragic about her expression. 'No,' she said, 'it's true. I can't. Let's talk about something else.'

They went on chatting, with intervals of silence, still sitting at the kitchen table, arms on the green oilcloth. At one point she got up to go to the toilet, and Besson heard the solemn sound of flushing water. Then she came back and made some more coffee. Besson watched her moving close beside him. Her tawny hair was tousled; there were dark smudges under her eyes, and a strange light gleamed in the pupils, something akin to impatience. Her fine, slender hands moved nervously, with glints of yellow reflected light flashing off the ring marked J.S. From one unidentifiable source—perhaps the neon strip-lighting that flickered in the middle of the ceiling—a halo of quivering, palpable radiance had descended on her, permeating every last inch of her body, electrifying her hair and nails, the outline of her face, each movement of her fingers. Harsh light sparked continually from the fuzzed woollen surface of her beige dress, as though it were a second skin. Every element in her was dry and clearcut. Neither hot nor cold: electric. Faintly, as in a dream, Besson heard her voice speaking. It was different now, it had become fierce and raucous. Without rising from his chair he took the hand with the golden ring gleaming on it, and drew it towards him. The rest of her body followed easily, it was like pulling a go-cart. It hung poised and motionless for a moment, at the point of balance: then, suddenly, they slid down together, dropping softly and easily on to the linoleum flooring, where the harsh light was reflected like the sky in a pool of water. Before he plunged into the abyss Besson heard the voice whispering, close to his ear yet at the same time immeasurably distant: 'We mustn't ... No, don't ... Mustn't ...'

'My name isn't Paul Thisse,' Besson said. 'My name is François —François Besson—'

But it was already too late. She did not hear him. So Besson entered the sphere of action, alone amid a gigantic rosette of expanding hieroglyphs, all of which bore the same identical message.

*

During this time night had fallen over the town. Darkness had covered the high relief of the buildings and the deep crevasse-like

153

streets. Wrapped in silence, the ruins rose straight into a sky where clouds scudded invisibly past. The sea had become opaque, impenetrable, with the hardness of a vast polished steel ball, so that the earth could no longer slip softly by along the strand which divided them. Street-lamps glowed steadily amid a halo of mosquitoes and butterflies. Far away, over the roof-tops, the beam from a lighthouse intermittently slashed through the curtain of rain and darkness. The night was teeming, black, rich with the smell of smoke and momentary glimmers of light. Nothing could break down its barriers. Occasionally something would happen— a car travelling slowly through the streets, a bat flitting after a swarm of insects. But such moments did not last. The blind, heavy mass, like a tide of jam or molasses, would close over these brief points of action and at once obliterate them. One was caught in the trap, and nothing one could do would get one out of it. This whole sector of the earth was wrapped in the same vertiginous and glacial abyss, was held captive by its static immensity. No landmarks, no lights, no scintillating warmth: nothing but the dryness and barren expanse of the desert, crystalline hardness, opaque transparency, the diamond quality of utter nothingness, the void.

What difference did it make if there were a few patches of moisture here and there, one or two small warm humid droplets? They would not last long. Soon, too soon, they would be absorbed by that gigantic ever-thirsty mouth, always sucking, consuming. Minuscule sparks were born in the darkness, and floated swiftly away into space, so swiftly that they might have been mere illusions. What mattered, the only reality, was this eternal blackness, this silence, this unfathomable and all-engulfing infinity. Blackness. Blackness. An ocean of boundless shadows, where invisible waves surged to and fro from one edge of eternity to the other; an ocean activated by a slow, constant ground-swell; the great black flag ceaselessly covering all moving objects with its folds, gathering in and appropriating everything. An indescribable flux, the breathing of some never-to be-recognized giant. In the space of one-tenth of a second he could consume everything, so greedy was

154

he for living sustenance. Water, fire, rocks, pale stars and red stars, disintegrating suns, delayed explosions and torrents of lava —all this he would devour without ever being satisfied. Time, the dimension of attrition, was made out of these elements. Seconds, seconds—grains of salt falling gently on top of one another. Whole years of honey, fat centuries dissolved magically in floods of acid. Nothing remained. Nothing here was left in peace any longer. Meals chased one another interminably, the process of digestion never reached an end. And in this expanse of darkness there was no more measure or proportion. Continents, whole galaxies were as grains of dust. High and low merged indistinguishably into one another: circles and angles, parallel straight lines and spirals, colours, distances, weights—all these, even when you examined them closely, were reduced to tiny identical points. Things that had been really hard-textured, like concrete or marble floors, opened up under the pressure of foreign bodies and engulfed them gently, like a quicksand. Everything had been reduced to a common, formalized identity, and the world might just as well have been nothing but a page of writing.

The blackness of the night, blackness fallen from the uttermost depths of the empty heavens, had descended on earth, and was implementing the true reign of matter: sleep, chill non-being, mastery over death. Under its sway days and months had fallen silent, had increased their numbers in darkness, and now there was nothing left to cover the minuscule activities of life but this profound eternity, its dull and constant sound-waves expanding all around, ecstatically unfolding its sumptuous petals of dying light and mingled colours, to reveal, at last, the face of darkness.

Night had spread its substance evenly over the town. Out in the streets the cold air stirred from time to time, and blew along the rows of closed shutters. Bright white or red holes in the darkness, near the bottom of buildings, formed words such as: CAFE CINEMA BAR PIZZA MOTEL. Pigeons slept in corners of ledges, each with its head tucked under its left wing. There was also, running through the middle of the town, a river, its wide bed choked with stones and thorns. The night had poured into this channel, and now it was a mere carbonaceous crevasse that looked as though it went right through to the centre of the earth. The sound of its waters rose up with the mist, and it was a noise of blackness and terror. Not far from the sea a bridge, with three still arches, spanned the river. Cars sped over the damp macadam, each with two red, mistily shimmering stars of light behind it. Far away to the north the mountains blended with the vast yawning gap of the sky. And in the country, not to mention along the boulevards, countless trees were sleeping where they stood.

They were not the only sleepers. Men and women slept too, inside their little private castles, lying on their flat beds, in numbers past counting—many millions, probably, stretched out stiff and chill, eyes turned up, breathing lightly. Jacques Vargoz, for instance. Or Sophie Murnau. Noëlle Haudiquet. Hott Ben Amar. Infinity had descended upon them, and they were gently breathing it in without knowing it. They were savouring the calm of eternal being, and their bodies were sliding perilously on the slippery slope of peace. Tomorrow, perhaps, when the feverish day began its course once more, some of them would remain prisoners of the night, and never wake again. Children, curled up in their cots, would begin to dream of monsters. One of them, torn abruptly awake for no particular reason, open eyes trying vainly to brush away the veils of darkness, began to scream, all by himself, drilling his red point of life in the heart of the void, making an act of creation, standing up against the flatness and emptiness, taking chisel and hammer and carving into that vast indifferent wall the words that liberated him: I AM ALIVE I AM ALIVE I AM ALIVE.

Chapter Seven

*François Besson watches the sun rise—The vegetable market—
Besson looks at the river-bed—Brief discussion with the man with
the cigarette-stub—Besson packs his bag—The adventures of Texas
Jack: Episode 26: The fight against Rattlesnake the Indian*

ON the seventh day, the rain more or less stopped. Besson had not
slept at all. Very early in the morning, before first light, he left the
flat. The redheaded girl and the little boy were still asleep. He
went into a truck-drivers' café and had a hot espresso to keep out
the cold. Down the far end of the bar, near the door to the W.C.,
was a very old man, all covered with wrinkles, and dead drunk. A
group of three or four men, plus a woman who looked like a
tramp, were standing by the counter, talking, laughing, shouting,
singing. Suddenly a corpulent, elderly man began a row with a
bearded youngster, and after a preliminary barrage of insults,
began to beat him over the head with both hands. The
bearded one backed away, holding up his arms to protect himself.
A general brawl ensued, and while it was going on the young man
slipped out of the bar. Besson waited a few minutes, until things
had quietened down again. Then he walked out and sat down on a
bench facing the sea.

It was here that he saw the sun come up, very slowly, behind a
mountainous rampart of clouds. At first, for an hour or more,
there was the gradual retreat of darkness, as that great black vertical plane ceased, little by little, to be a hole, a nothingness, and
objects began to fill it, one after the other, materializing imperceptibly, blocking in the void. The horizon became visible towards
the east, a stretch of coastline, the surface of the sea. Far out from
shore the white glint of the wave-crests became increasingly
visible. Then, as the growing light continued to dilute that inky

expanse, the water became progressively dirtier, its surface showed up harsh and wrinkled. The various points of light— yellow from the street-lamps, red from the light-house beacons— lost their former blinding intensity. Deep patches of shadow, till now so impenetrable and terrifying, gradually shrank in on themselves, retreated, like pools of water drying in the sun. Above the sea the clouds suddenly swam into view, rising palely from the darkness like troops of elephants or buffaloes. Minute by minute their outlines acquired more solidity and depth. Great balls of cottonwool hung motionless in the vault of heaven, and through their ragged edges shone glimpses of clear sky, midway between pink and grey, empty, limitless. With ebbing strength the night swung westward, in retreat now, so that more and more objects which had been limed in its viscous blackness were released, almost without one noticing. The blackness lost its intensity, became merely sombre, then grey; paler still now, the colour of milk, then skim-milk, till even this pallor began to fade, retreated beyond the visible limits of whiteness. It was as though the earth, stripped of the membrane that rendered it invisible, had nevertheless not, as yet, recovered its pigmentation, and was floating between these two violent extremes, undecided, ghostly-pale, almost non-existent. On the opposite side of the horizon, above the town and the mountains, there was a sort of dark funnel-shaped gulf into which the shadows were slowly absorbed.

After a while the landscape emerged in every detail, but still lit by that unearthly pallor. Then the true light began to appear. It climbed the sky like rose-tinted smoke, with the majestic movements of some great bird taking flight, a great pear-shaped mass that slowly spread out above the clouds. Everything, on land and sea alike, began to glitter as though dusted with thousands of tiny nacreous crystals. The concrete surface of the pavement, the balustrade, the pebbles on the beach, the troughs of the waves, the windows of houses and the topmost branches of trees—all lit up in a moment, and glowed peacefully, each with its delicate crust of pink icing-sugar.

The boundaries of the sky receded further and further: everything seemed to expand, grow deeper, stretch out into vast and distant perspectives. Like a desert. For a quarter of an hour or so everything was tinged with pink. Then, one by one, the other colours returned—on chunks of scrap-metal, on rocks, in the middle of cloud-formations, at the bottom of clumps of grass. Shoe-polish brown, mahogany, straw-yellow, periwinkle blue, mauves, blacks, mouse-grey, Veronese green. Imperceptibly, as the minutes passed, these variegated dots of colour began to glow and expand. Pink was still the dominant motif, but a close scrutiny revealed the presence of these other colours, all jostling and struggling for precedence, streaming out in wild confusion. For a little while earth sky and sea resembled a gigantic confectioner's counter. Then the sun came up over the horizon, transforming the landscape from sweetshop to abattoir.

Behind a blood-red cloud, and haloed with garish radiance, the sun's disc slowly swung up: Besson did not actually see it, but he could sense the circular shape, and felt the first rays of direct light strike home on his eyelids. The brightness spread swiftly over the earth's visible surface, flushing the last shadow-bound objects from their hiding places: match-ends lying on the pavement, scratches in the paintwork of the iron balustrade, folds in clothes, hairs on the back of the hand, the reticulating branches of shrubs, the skeletal nerve-pattern on dead leaves. Though still hidden behind a curtain of mist, the sun was none the less *there*, huge and terrifying, pursuing its solitary course through a sea of radiant air. All darkness had vanished now. Despite the occasional fitful breeze, a kind of warmth began to disseminate itself everywhere, spreading over the earth and penetrating the substance of things.

Eyes wide open, Besson gazed at the area dominated by the sun: it was like an abyss, a silent maelstrom sunk into the heavens. Everything, absolutely everything moved centripetally towards it: even the mind, with its caravans of thoughts and ideas, was irresistibly attracted by this dazzling focal point. To struggle against it was out of the question: you had no time to put up any defence, before you knew what had happened you were its slave.

Down, down you went, deaf to all sounds, quite helpless, caught on the earth's lift-platform, sinking to some unknown destination, while behind its screen of scarlet clouds that colourless sphere mounted royally towards the zenith.

Little by little, as the sun gradually detached itself from the barrier of the horizon, each large patch of red was reabsorbed, gave place to the ordinary light of day. Blues became permanent, orange and yellow elements darkened, and one by one the sparks of reflected light went out till they were all gone. Finally, these colour-changes more or less came to a halt, except for the brief occasional appearance of violet and purple streaks drifting over the sea, or when some cloud parted asunder and a great cone of yellow light gleamed through the torn gap, its base picking out a chain of mountains, its whole length laced with rainbow spume and a scribble of slanting rain.

By now there were plenty of people hurrying along the pavement behind Besson. The town was waking up. Men's footsteps clacked noisily past, then faded in the distance. There was a muted hum of car-engines, and seagulls swooped overhead, with their shrill *yap-yap-yap*. At one point all the street-lamps were suddenly extinguished but this made no difference to the general picture. The rows of blue star-points went out, one after the other, till the entire town was visible, solid, opaque, an integral part of the day now beginning.

Besson lit a cigarette at this point, and then set off through the back streets, away from the sea. In a leisurely fashion he began to make his way up towards the centre of town again. In one corner by a shop he came on an automatic vending machine. He put in a coin, pressed a button, and got a small waxed-paper cup full of scalding coffee, which he drank in two or three mouthfuls.

Further on, he passed a big covered-in square, where the market was held. Besson walked in down the nearest alley, and let himself drift with the general movement of the crowd. On either side were stalls laden with crates of fruit and vegetables, and at each a big fat woman, greasy hair tied up under a headscarf, bawling her wares at the top of her voice. Despite the early hour, the place was a hive of activity. People kept elbowing each other aside, shoving through the crowd, shouting interruptions. From every corner of the market came the stallkeepers' unremitting sales-talk, and the tinkle of coins being dropped into tin mugs. Bare, fat, heavily muscled arms plunged into the crates, shovelling up runner beans, potatoes, endives, tomatoes, peppers. Oranges sat each in their little nest of crumpled paper, apples tumbled down on top of one another, their green skins often marked with big rotten bruises. Over everything there hung a faint yet rich odour of earth, leaves, pulp, juice. About a yard and a half off the ground every smell, whether from vegetables or fruit, merged into one indistinguishable whole, a composite smell that permeated the entire place. Through all this movement and bustle Besson advanced like an automaton. Several times fat women stallkeepers, standing behind their piles of merchandise, hailed him in high screeching tones, like so many squawking chickens: 'Lovely potatoes, lovely potatoes, this way, this way . . .' 'Come on, mister, try the runners, fresh this morning . . .' 'Fine apples, specially picked, beautiful apples, fresh every one of 'em, two hundred the kilo, lovely fresh apples . . .' 'Come on now, walk up, walk up, walk up. . . .'

Down the alleys between the stalls the crowd ebbed and flowed, wandered in all directions, trampling over old cabbage leaves and scraps of newspaper. Old men with string bags stood examining the vegetables or counting through the wads of filthy notes in their wallets. Women went to and fro dragging children after them by one hand, or stopped, stooping down, to cram their purchases into their shopping-bags. A pregnant girl in a flowered maternity smock wandered slowly along the row of stalls: she had dirty frizzed-out hair that the wind perpetually blew forward into her face. A little further on was a group of men in berets, sitting on upturned empty crates, smoking and gossiping. From time to time, in some corner of the alley, a mangy mongrel could be seen licking its paws. Large numbers of ragged old down-and-outs, backs bent, went round picking up the rotten vegetables that had been thrown out of the crates, and greedily stuffing them into their gunny-sacks. There was one very ancient and very dignified-looking little man, with a slightly nervous air, who tittuped along in front of the stalls, from time to time snatching a potato or pear with a quick, clumsy gesture, and instantly popping it away into his sack. When he saw Besson watching him, he turned his head away, more nervous than ever, and began to stare up at the roof of the market with a kind of terrified and angry determination. He remained in this pose for several seconds, not budging an inch, and then resumed his peregrination past the stalls, with a comic air of would-be unconcern.

Besson walked from one end of the covered market to the other. After he was out in the street again—and despite the fresh air and busy traffic—the sickening smell of early vegetables and fruit pursued him for a long way.

Later, much later, when the whole town was awake, Besson walked round to his parents' house. On the way he met someone he had known previously, when he was working at the private school. They stopped and chatted for a moment on the kerb. Besson would have liked to continue the conversation for much longer, since this he found an admirable way of passing the time; but the other person was apparently in a hurry, and after exchanging a few banalities they parted.

A little further on, while crossing a square, Besson caught sight of the river. It was quite a large river, that ran in a straight line through the centre of the town, passing beneath a series of bridges and esplanades. The closer he got to the riverside *quais*, the louder grew that dull monotonous roar he could hear, with increased volume and more deeply resonant note. It was like haze made audible: what in fact produced it was water rasping over wide-spreading the shingle bottom. A vivid sound, this, alive with gurgles and ripples and a booming undertone which hinted at reserves of power; a sound that mingled with the general hubbub in the streets and flowed down unceasingly toward the sea. Besson was intrigued by the noise; he walked over to the railing and took a good look at the river.

He saw a single unbroken stretch of water, flowing between

162

rampart-like banks. On both sides, to left and right, there was a kind of stony embankment, overgrown with weeds and bushes. Such was the course the water followed in its long journey from the hinterland, bearing with it the cargo of driftwood and silt it had eroded from various mountain-sides *en route*. In the centre of the channel the river flowed deep, and was a beautiful dark blue, scored lengthwise with fine ripple-marks: it moved swiftly, with a soft, muted roar, and one got the impression that this was all the river there was, this bankless stream flowing down to its outfall, this heavy, swollen, full-blown effluence. Hardly an eddy to be seen. Only this lane of water gliding past, level and unbroken, except where the bridge-caissons divided its flow each ringed with a small collar of foam.

On either side of this central current the river was a dirty greenish colour, seething over pebble-ridges and round fallen tree-trunks. Beyond lay the shore, reduced to a narrow line of shingle on the right-hand side of the river, but spreading out to form a wide ripple-marked expanse on the left. Further off still, above the *quais*, were rows of houses, with leprous, peeling walls and loose ends of string dangling from their balconies. Below the houses several sewer-mouths were visible, round black holes slowly dripping their contents on to the river-bed. Between these piles of waste-matter, where rats and mongrels were always nosing around, the water lay in stagnant puddles, the sky reflected from its surface.

Besson scrutinized every detail of this scene with the greatest care. His eye travelled right along the line the river took through the town, on to the valley which, century after century, it had slowly hollowed in that hard, mountainous landscape. He noted all the colours floating on the surface of the water, each tiny cats-paw of wind, every tuft of grass being carried down, slowly or at speed, by the current; the various mounds of shingle, the gravel strand with its border of sticky yellow foam, the shell-craters hollowed out by successive flood-tides, and now filled with rain-water. He listened to the sound the waters made as they plunged through the hollow bowl of the valley: a powerful, solemn note, a

163

deep and colossal organ-boom. He also heard the rhythmic chuckling of its eddies and whirlpools, the curious hissing note, *pchchchchch*, produced by hundreds of small cascades falling one on the other. He travelled over this cold, deserted no-man's-land, with its myriad reflections, as though the balustrade on which he was leaning had been the bridge of a ship. He scrutinized every cranny, each damp black hole, each hollow with its layer of rotting detritus, the piles of polished pebbles, dulled under their layers of dust. He could smell the depressing acrid-smoke odour given off by long-dead fires, and his nostrils also picked up the powerful, subtle, carrion stench (it might have been wafted from the decaying corpse of a giant lizard) which the sewerage outflow spread abroad. The wind was blowing in the same direction as the natural flow of the river, and vanished somewhere out to sea. Here all movement was a retreat, a flight from the point of source, a continual downstream progress where all individual elements merged in a loud, abrasive, roaring confluence that sounded, weirdly, like some squadron for ever at the gallop.

He ought to stop here for a while too, he thought, build himself a hut of damp driftwood, with an old packing-case to sit on, and just wait until he was left all by himself with only the running water for company. Here, in this desert at the very heart of the town, surrounded by invisible men leaning over the various bridges, he would pass all his time just watching the river, learning to love it, till he felt its presence in every movement he made, however slight, as though it were some living creature.

Higher upstream, near the outskirts of the town, there stood on the river-bed a crane, two or three tractors, some bulldozers, and a cement-mixing machine. Besson could even make out the shapes of various men by the water's edge, all busily occupied. He turned to a loafer who was leaning on the balustrade close by him, and said: 'What's going on down there?'

The man removed a damp cigarette-end from his mouth and said: 'It's the bridge. They're building the bridge.'

'Oh yes?' Besson said. 'Many thanks.'

The man put the cigarette-end back in his mouth.

By now it was not far off midday, and Besson set off once more in the direction of his parents' house. When he rang the bell it was his father who answered the door. Besson had to explain his actions, and this involved a certain amount of lying: he said he was going to stay with friends for a few days, and had come to collect his things. He got out a blue canvas beach-bag, and packed it with his electric razor, his toothbrush, a raincoat, a clean shirt, and two or three other unimportant objects. This done, he said goodbye to his father, and walked out into the street again. His mother was out shopping in the neighbourhood, but he did not wait for her. Instead he made a bee-line for the redheaded woman's apartment.

On the way he bought an illustrated comic for the little boy. He got there in time for lunch. The girl didn't ask too many questions and when the meal was over, she let Besson lie down on the bed and have a siesta. He spent the rest of the day reading the little boy the story in the comic. It was all about a cowboy called Texas Jack, who was such a dead shot with a revolver that he could knock nails into a plank from ten paces. His enemy was a man called Hobbes, who owned several ranches, and had raised a posse of gunmen to settle Texas Jack's hash. He had even hired the services of an Indian half-breed called Rattlesnake, whose speciality was throwing little knives poisoned with rattler's venom. During the night Rattlesnake got into the house where Texas Jack was sleeping, but he mistook the bedroom and was on the point of killing another cowboy. Texas Jack caught him just before he could throw his knives. Rattlesnake had left them lying on a table, blade turned towards him. Texas Jack fired: the bullet struck one of the knives on the handle, and sent it flying straight at Rattlesnake's throat. The Indian died instantly. Then there was a shooting-match with Hobbes's posse, and finally the villain himself was taken prisoner and handed over to the sheriff.

For the following week, the comic announced another episode in the adventures of Texas Jack: this one was called 'Death in Gold Nugget Valley.'

Chapter Eight

*The storm—The wind—François Besson and Marthe talk together—
What might have been the beginning of love—A walk through a
hurricane—The sea—How to become immortal—The pattern of a
lightning-flash*

ON the eighth day a storm blew up over the town. The wind had
come from the east. After travelling across the sea all night, it
reached the houses and the riverside early that morning. It burst
furiously on all these stone and concrete canyons, smashing
against the façades of buildings, bending the trees, driving down
on the ground in whirling eddies of dust, whipping up the breakers
so that they surged high along the line of the groins. Invisible
ramparts of air were set in violent motion, with a long sinister
wailing sound that filled the chimney flues. Clouds stretched out
across the sky, shredded into wisps, acquired long off-white tails
reaching from one horizon to the other. Doors began to creak
softly; and on each closed shutter or pane of glass there was a
feeling of *pressure*, as though some gigantic panting beast were out
there on the other side, pushing and grinding at it with vicious
tentacles. All along those worn, crumbling walls, loose bits of
stucco tore free and plunged groundwards into the street, falling
very fast, leaving a thin trail of dust behind them. Scraps of paper,
leaves from the plane-trees, odd bits of material would go spinning
into the air, as high as the upper storeys of the surrounding houses
then fall back, then whirl aloft once more, as though they had
suddenly gone mad. Various objects were blown off roofs and
balconies. Sudden whirling columns of air formed at street inter-
sections, weird raging maelstroms that—revolving round a still
point at their base—hollowed out deep craters in the lifeless dust.
At the very centre of these inverted vortices was a point of

concentrated nothingness, which moved with great precision, thrusting its single upturned eye down over the surface of the earth. Through the wind's steady whistling the whole town resounded with a series of cracks and bangs and underground rumblings. When the storm was right over the town, the wind began to launch its assault on the houses. Regularly, several times a minute, an airy avalanche would roar down against walls and windows, in an effort to penetrate, to breach the defences. It did not last long, but each time it happened—after a second or so of lowering silence—it felt as though every vertical object were shuddering and cracking up. Even the thickest walls, great blocks of ferro-concrete, roofs, colonnades and all, would quiver in unison under this violent onslaught. Gaping holes, swollen with liquid gas, opened their mouths wide. The corridors of the streets, every gap and crack, yawned open for a brief moment, while there surged into them, torrent upon torrent, this bestial *thing* that had come from so far to be their conqueror. From time to time, between one squall and the next, a flight of pigeons would take off and vanish in the mazy back-streets, fleeing the invisible enemy, searching desperately for any hiding-place—under the guttering, beside a balcony, in the lee of some thick bushy tree, where these lethal attacks could no longer find them. People, too, were trying to escape. They were running along the pavement, sodden clothes plastered to their bodies, hair all anyhow, eyes red from the dust that had blown into them. They would take shelter for a moment in doorways, wait till the gust died down, and then stagger on their way, struggling clumsily against the heavy pressure of the atmosphere. Slowly, far above them, a jet aircraft forced its way through the wind. Women's skirts lifted like wings, giving fleeting glimpses of pale, lardy thighs.

For more than an hour Besson stayed in the room, listening, while the storm rose to its climax. He saw the sky clear, close in, and then lighten again, enough to let the sun's rays struggle through. He heard the wind smash against the walls like a battering-ram, again and again, the whining, slamming rumpus of its impact. Outside even the daylight now seemed unsure of itself: it wavered intermittently, sometimes becoming so dim and overcast that one felt the flame had finally gone out altogether. But then it would pick up again, suddenly blaze out more brightly than before, flooding walls and pavements with sheets of light against which the shadows stood out black and intense.

It was comfortable up there in the room; one felt truly sheltered and protected, it might have been a ship's cabin. The air was tranquil here, nothing stirred, no fear of stifling. The flies were all asleep, upside-down, clustering on the light-bulb or hanging from the tulle curtains.

Besson stretched out on the bed. In the kitchen the redheaded girl was busy ironing, a green apron tied round her waist. Occasionally she, too, cocked an ear at the noise the wind was making against the windows. Finally she turned on her transistor radio, and the flat was flooded with music—a cinema organ recital that floated in the air, nasal, monotonous, vulgar, sometimes rising in a run of excruciating trills, then falling back, a blurred mess of sound, only to repeat the pattern once more: endless wearisome reiterations, a kind of recurrent stutter that swathed you from head to foot, paralysed not only your movements but also your speech, your very though-processes, and finally toppled you into a kind of shallow black hole, quite helpless.

Besson heard the music right through to the end. When it stopped there was the sound of a woman's voice, talking fast and volubly, but the radio was too far away for Besson to make out what she was saying. When the voice ceased, there was silence for four or five seconds, broken only by the crackle of static. Then came more music, but swing this time, and a woman singing to its accompaniment. The song had a slow, muted tempo, occasionally rising to a harsh crescendo, sometimes lingering softly on one word, sustaining the note. Besson tried to catch what the singer was saying, but the most he picked up were single words or mere broken syllables: ' . . . me . . .', ' . . . I . . . flowers . . . ow . . . ers . . .', ' . . . told me . . .', ' . . . you knew . . .', ' . . . me . . . or people . . .' ' . . . ated . . .', ' . . . fi-i-ire . . .'

The song ended with a most curious sound, a sort of low-pitched throaty buzz that vibrated in the air for a long time, together with the accompaniment, and then stopped, abruptly. There followed another three or four seconds of crackling silence, and then the same voice as before began to speak again, very fast, telling an incomprehensible story in its unknown tongue. What it actually said was more or less as follows: 'Listen, ladies, don't worry about wind and rain and seasonal inclemencies of that sort, you can tame them, yes, you can make them your best friends, the most reliable aids to your beauty, if you just know how to get the better of them, these furious elements will freshen up your complexion, put a bright sparkle in your eye, fill you with *joie de vivre*, but if on the other hand you don't take them seriously you'll wish you had afterwards, they'll dry up your skin and ruin your delicate complexion and give you premature wrinkles, in fact they'll treat you as enemies, they'll be absolutely pitiless, so get the better of this severe cold and wind and rain, ladies, learn to preserve your beauty just as you preserve your health and happiness, and to achieve this, make a rule of using Pollen Face Cream every morning, Pollen, exclusively manufactured by Boyer-Vidal, which will keep the proper quota of moisture in your skin all day, Pollen, the face cream for every occasion! Good shopping, ladies!'

Besson stayed where he was for some time, listening to the voice from the little white-and-gold plastic box. If his watch was right, it was half past three; but the clock that stood on the refrigerator, in the kitchen, made the time nearer four o'clock.

A little later the redheaded girl came in, and they talked for a while.

'It's funny,' she said. 'I've sort of got used to seeing—to seeing you around.' She used the familiar *tu*, and the word came out with embarrassed hesitancy.

'What do you mean, seeing me around?' Besson asked.

'Well, here. I mean to say, you've become a feature of the landscape, haven't you?'

Besson tried to make a joke of it, but felt depressed despite himself.

'That's serious,' he said.

The girl fumbled in her apron pocket and fished a cigarette out of a new packet.

'Got any matches?' she asked.

Besson offered her his box. As she took it, she grasped Besson's hand at the same moment, then let it go again. Her hair was tousled, and its flaming red texture seemed to be reflected in her face. Even her eyes had a red glint about them, under the fine sweep of her gleaming lashes. She smoked her cigarette, watching Besson all the time.

'You're not in the least like him,' she said. 'He was always chattering, always on the move, couldn't keep still for a second. Whereas you—well, honestly, I've never seen a more inert character.'

'Oh, I can move, all right,' Besson said.

'You? Why, you spend all day stretched out on that bed.'

'It isn't true. I go out a lot. I take plenty of walks.'

'You don't do a job of work, though. You don't want to—'

'Oh, I've done that, too. When I was a teacher. Off I'd go to school, day in day out, and rattle off the same stuff to a classroom full of idiots—'

'Did they rag you?'

'No, not really. At first I made a real effort and kept them under control. Afterwards I let them do whatever they liked. They used to read the comics. Some of them even smoked—those at the back of the class, anyway—and drank bottles of Coca-Cola. But they didn't make any noise. I told them one day. Do whatever you like, but I'm not having any noise. I had a book to read, you see. I told them, if I hear so much as a whisper, I'll paste the stuffing out of you. That was about it. I spent my period reading, and when I heard the bell, I just got up and went.'

'You weren't a good teacher.'

'I was, you know. My lessons were fine. I prepared them very carefully. But the kids just weren't interested.'

'Were they all like that?'

'No, of course not. There were two or three—at first they used to stay and ask me questions, after class. But I soon sent them packing and, they got bored. In the end they got to be just like the others.'

'And what—'

'There was one who did interest me, though. A boy called David. He showed me his poems, once. He was an unhealthy kid, with a lot of lines on his face for his age. He really *was* different from the rest of them. He wrote the weirdest poems, all about the story of the Creation. There was a character in them called Elleüs, if I remember rightly. It was all very much in the mythical tradition, but not bad stuff by any means. I don't know what became of him afterwards.'

'What about the others? Did they just play along?'

'Three-quarters of them, sure. But I didn't bother. It was their look-out. Luckily, in the end, the Head got wind of what was going on. He dropped in on the class one day, unannounced. Some of the boys were smoking, and others reading their comics. He slaughtered the lot of them—and I got the sack, on the spot. That's all there is to tell about it.'

The redheaded girl giggled. 'I'd love to have been there,' she said.

Outside the wind was blowing more fiercely than ever, howling down the street, wrenching loose everything in sight. In the middle of the room, on the bed, Besson and Marthe felt as though they were in a railway carriage, travelling at full speed, and drawn by an invisible engine.

The redheaded girl said: 'That's funny. Do you know, just about the same thing happened to me, too. I used to work in the Post Office, you know. I managed to get a job as a telephone operator. Just part-time, in the afternoon. While I was working I left Lucas in a children's nursery. I did the job any old how, no kidding, just hit or miss. And no one noticed a bloody thing. I had to make up my own mind that I'd got to get out—if I hadn't I'd be there still. But after it was finished I felt so damned depressed. Told myself I was a failure, that there wasn't a single thing in life I was capable of doing, all that jazz.'

She paused, and rubbed the bridge of her nose with her fore-finger.

'Well, maybe in the last resort it's not all that important any-way,' she said.

'Maybe not,' said Besson.

She hesitated a moment, and then, her eyes on the ash-laden tip of her cigarette, added: 'The really important thing is to be happy.'

When Besson made no answer to this, she said: 'What about you? Are *you* happy?'

He tried to answer the question seriously.

'That depends,' he said. 'Sometimes I'm happy, yes. Sometimes not. But it isn't all that important.'

'Yes, it *is* important. Just when do you feel happy?' She looked straight at him as she spoke.

'I'm not sure,' Besson said. 'It all depends. One fellow I used to know said that if you wanted to be happy, all you needed was a system.'

'A system?'

'Yes, you know—religious faith, Marxism, anything you like so long as it's got a system behind it.'

'But being happy's a simpler matter than that, surely?'

'Or more complicated. Maybe it's having a real grasp of what you're about—I mean, you're in a car, and you *know* you're in a car.' He too used the familiar *tu*.

She said nothing for a moment, as though digesting this idea—or perhaps as though she had not understood it.

'But don't you think it's easy to know what you're doing?' she asked him. 'Surely it's easy?'

'No,' Besson said. 'But sometimes it happens.'

Her great deep liquid eyes gazed at him as though they would penetrate to the very depths of his soul. Besson felt a wave of shame surge up within him. In a somewhat lower voice she went on: 'When *I'm* happy I know about it all right. But I never manage to work out why. I'm never happy when I'm alone, though. You can see that, can't you? Well, at this moment, for instance, But I can't figure out the reason—' She paused, then added, nervously: 'Maybe, it's well, because—because of you—'

'You're wrong,' Besson said.

'Maybe,' Marthe conceded.

But it was too late: her white face moved forward towards him, and as it approached—like a tragic mask, pierced by these two dark and heavy-lashed eyes—he felt as though it were an abyss yawning dizzily before him, a void, an emptiness that he could never fill. He tried to forget the eyes, but the head with its mass of tumbled hair settled on his chest, and he had to put his hands behind it, round the nape of the neck. He could feel the warm skin that lay over the vertebrae, and a little lower down a mole or beauty-spot. Her hands were clutching the material of his shirt, on either side of his ribs, fingers crooked and dug in, as though to claw the flesh. And the regular sound of her all-too-human breathing filled his ears, forcing him to breathe too, to be alive, to show awareness.

Then she raised her head, bent it backwards, let the daylight illuminate it—the tremulous, breathing mouth, the fine-bridged nose, pale cheeks flushed with pink, each tiny line and wrinkle, every spot, the fine down along the jaw-line, the pores in her skin that were like thousands of minuscule windows through which the air came and went. Her great staring eyes blurred, became patches of brown mist, floated towards one another, suddenly merged in the middle of her forehead, forming a moist circle within the unfocused framework of the mask, a circle charged with violence and humiliation and hope. Furiously he plunged into it, no longer hearing the fragmentary words that reached him, calling him by name; plummeted down into the troubled waters of dissension and unhappiness, let them close above his head.

*

A little while later François Besson found himself out in the street again, all alone in the midst of the hurricane. Fighting against the wind all the way, he went down through the town, street after street, till he reached the sea. The pavements were more or less deserted, and those few people he did meet looked like ghostly silhouettes: they could be seen struggling across the road at an intersection, or hugging the wall as they advanced, harrassed and wind-tossed fugitives, their clothes blown every which way, scarcely able to breathe. A litter of plaster and bits of wood and loose scraps of corrugated iron sheeting testified to the route the hurricane had taken. Besson followed this trail, leaning now forwards, now backwards, hair standing on end, raincoat flattened against his legs, the wind whipping round overhead. But he no longer took any heed of his surroundings: the shop-windows and mirrors, far from becoming dimmer, more opaque, had taken on an extra dimension of brightness, so much so, indeed, that it was as though reality were contained in them. No more stopping to contemplate the images, whether beautiful or hideous, that they presented: anyone who did so would be struck motionless, frozen, maybe turned into a pillar of salt.

One had to keep alert, too. All over town objects came raining down out of the sky: there was danger everywhere. People were liable to get hit on the head by tiles, or chimney-pots, or even by shutters that had been wrenched off their hinges. Besson kept close in against the wall, hands thrust into the pockets of his raincoat, collar turned up around his neck. The cars passing him in the road were travelling at reduced speed: some had their headlights switched on, others were using their windscreen-wipers. Café doors were shut, and many shop blinds had been ripped to ribbons. Whole newspapers went looping along the streets; 'No Entry' signs rattled themselves loose from their brackets. Refuse went skittering along beside the gutter, across muddy puddles, took off for some unknown destination.

It had not required much to sow the seeds of panic in the town. There had been a sudden, but quite peaceful, displacement of air. That was all. Just a little air in motion. But this air was hard and solid. It slammed into houses with the speed of an express train. It blew in violent gusts along the tarred surface of the roads, made skylights tremble, shook window-panes loose.

With considerable effort Besson made his way towards the sea-front. It was from this direction that the storm was coming. Already he could hear a low malevolent roar, a confusion of sounds that blended with the sheets of spray now being flung up behind the last row of houses, and spreading across the sky over the roof-tops like a great invisible curtain. Besson walked through one square in which the trees would bend over, cracking and splitting, then suddenly whip upright again with a great rustle of leaves. At one intersection he passed there was a crazy spiral of dust whirling round. A little further on, he reached the street which gave directly on to the front, and the wind took him slap in the face, like the wind of a big gun being fired. Besson stopped in astonish-ment, and felt a sort of ghostly hand thrusting his head back, trying to push its fingers into his mouth and nostrils. In order to recover his breath, he was forced to turn his back on the wind for a few seconds; this done, he set off down the narrow corridor-like street once more. At the further end of it, like a mirage, hung the pink and black cloud-patterns of the sky, veiled now by flying spindrift. He tacked from one sidewalk to the other, always moving slantwise, his right hand protecting his eyes. He travelled the hundred yards which separated him from the front without once looking up, his eyes fixed on his feet as they stumbled over the ground. At last he reached the end of the street, and the panoramic spectacle of the sea stood revealed before him.

The impact was total and instantaneous. As the wind slammed against his body, forcing him backwards, he saw the whole of that vast heaving expanse, mile upon mile of it, heard the continuous howling of the storm. From the mist-enshrouded horizon waves came rolling in one behind the other, surging, dipping, flecked with white crests that the wind scythed away as they moved, roaring on till they reached the high bastion of the promenade, then soaring up for the last time, up, up, hanging there briefly as though frozen, so that you could see the great hollow underside of the comber, gunmetal grey, glinting with wisps of straw, then falling in one swift movement, with a bang like a lid being slammed home. Each breaker began to rise far out in the bay, and came closer, closer, its muted thunder shaking the earth's foundations as it moved, till it reached that point of the shore where Besson now stood: then the spray would rise vertically into the sky like a geyser, there would be that noise like a giant casserole being shut, and the spray would form a grey, powdery column that the air blew apart into shreds driving it towards the houses, fanning it out into quicksilver branches, dwindling now, stems, slivers, blades of grass, glittering yet lustreless strands of hair, threads of silver and silk that melted in the gusty air and, as they whipped along, let fall a few big, dirty drops of moisture, which evaporated as soon as they hit the ground.

After each wave broke, Besson's hair and skin and clothes were drenched with spindrift. Tiny globules of spray were blown into his mouth as he breathed, so that he tasted salt and smelt the pungent odour of iodine. For a moment he remained like this, buffeted by the wind, taking an occasional step forward or back, struggling to maintain his balance. The town seemed quite dead. Black clouds scudded over it, heavy, charged with electricity, now and then emitting a great flash of pale sheet-lightning, which sent shadows and colours dancing across the storm-tossed front, as though a great conflagration had broken out on the further horizon.

The promenade was completely deserted. No cars ventured along the road because of the waves bursting over it. The shutters in the houses were closed and barred.

Sometimes a wave would rise up higher than the rest, and it looked as though the swollen waters were trying to regain possession of their ancient domain. Pebbles were scooped up from the beach and sent flying across the pavements or against the foot of the wall. One of them, about the size of an egg, came rolling in front of Besson. He stooped and picked it up, and tried to throw it back into that heaving mountainous mass of water, but the wind caught it in mid-flight and flung it back again. A sudden panic swept over Besson. He wondered whether he ought not get away from there, beat a retreat inland, seek refuge on some mountain-top. But he was determined to see more of what was going on.

He struggled down to the shore, and painfully made his way along it, stumbling through puddles of dirty sea-water, drenched with bursts of spray, twisting his ankles on stones. At the far end of the beach there was a causeway, protected by breakwaters. Besson made his way towards it.

In order to get on to the causeway, he had to climb over a barricade with a notice that read: OUT OF BOUNDS: TRESPASSERS WILL BE PROSECUTED. The causeway ran a long way out into the sea. At its far end there stood a lighthouse, and a flagpole with a red flag flying from it. Panting from the wind, which took his breath away, sodden by bursts of spray, Besson began to walk along the causeway, clinging to the iron handrail. Here the sea was divided into two parts. On the right the great waves came piling in on top of one another, burst against the foot of the wall; on the left lay the harbour entrance. The water here was black, its surface churned up by long eddies that spread out like oil-slicks.

Danger threatened on all sides; the sea writhed into countless voracious mouths, here, there, horrible fascinating mouths that came mooing up at you. There would be a sudden upsurge of water, and the mouth would rise rapidly towards the level of the causeway. For a moment it would hang there, only a few inches away, opening and closing its toothless gums, so that behind that slobbering curtain of spray you could see the black tunnel of its throat. It reached up towards the living flesh, imploringly, with its long tonsils and palpitating gullet and eager belly: it resembled the huge liquid eye of some big carnivore, struggling to reach up further, but struggling in vain. The waves could no longer sustain it, and it would fall back in a burst of fury, break up on the groyne with a thunderous report that left the causeway's stone foundations quivering for some time afterwards. The iron guide-rail shuddered under Besson's hand, and this shuddering sensation passed up his arm into every part of his body, troubling the waters, dredging up silt off the bottom, rapidly opening and closing the feed-valves of depression. Then the healing cloud rose right overhead in the sky, the angry breathing of the frustrated elements was all around him. Besson leaned back and for several long seconds let the chill rain drive down on his face and clothes, which absorbed it hungrily. Then, refreshed by this break he broke into a run.

When he was about half-way to the lighthouse, he came upon a kind of shelter built as a protection against the wind. He stopped there a moment to rest and smoke a cigarette. But the packet had got damp, and the tobacco burnt badly; Besson needed at least fifteen matches to smoke one cigarette right through.

Here in the shelter he had his back to the sea. He heard the noise of the storm behind him, but he himself was facing the town. In the distance, outside the harbour, he could dimly see the old crumbling houses, squared up against the wind, not budging, letting the gusts buffet their vertical façades. Grey, pink-tinged clouds of spume, whipping up off the waves, drifted across in front of their walls and gave them the appearance of retreating. But they did not retreat one inch. They stayed exactly where they were, closed in, four-square to the elements, a chiaroscuro of deep black and the palest grey, like a line of rocks that had tumbled down from the mountainside centuries before. The storm was moving down the valley now: trees bent groundwards, and now and then with a sharp crack, a branch would break. Fields of grass were flattened in every direction, and across the curving hills there was a motion as of some giant hand, stroking their surface to and fro in a kind of caress. Further still, right on the horizon, at the most distant point from the source of the storm, the mountains reared their violet-tinged bastion against the clouds. Sometimes there would be a flash of bluish light above one of the peaks, but no thunder was audible afterwards. The whole landscape was dim, pitch-dark, crazy, and the bowl of the wind had blotted out all other sounds.

When he had finished looking at the pink-flushed sea-front and the rounded hills and the rampart of mountains behind them, Besson abandoned his shelter and began to advance along the causeway again. Progress became more and more difficult the further out into the sea one got. Worst of all, the handrail stopped before the lighthouse, and Besson was reduced to crawling along the causeway on all fours. At one point the water seemed to gather itself, the sea sank back, withdrew so far that the rocks on the sea-bottom, with their clustering limpets, were exposed to view. For a second or so there was nothing but this huge sinister well, this boiling vortex at the foot of the causeway. Then in a flash the hole filled up, and a great column of water soared shuddering into the air. When it began to topple above the sea-wall, Besson flung himself down flat and held his breath. The vast liquid mass came hissing down on him, with such force that it poured across into the harbour basin. As soon as the water had ebbed away again, Besson got up and began to run in the direction of the lighthouse. He reached it at last, and took shelter behind the tall stone bastion on which it stood.

He remained there some minutes, an hour perhaps, in the midst of the hurricane, unconscious of the cold, not noticing that his clothes were soaked through with sea-water. All around him, to left and right, straight ahead, even under his feet, the wild spectacle continued. The waves mouthed and slapped against the jetty, with a drawn-out, clinging, wetly explosive sound. Clouds of spray rose and mingled in the air, daylight acquired rainbow tints. The long black headlands stretching out on either side seemed to cleave through the water like surfaced submarines. Warring gusts tore and ripped at each other, made strange thin noises like sea-gulls or crying children. On the horizon sea and sky blurred together in a welter of spray, cloud, and bright heaving hollows of water. Sometimes the sun appeared for a moment or two, suddenly exposed through some rent in the middle of the dense cloud-base, and yellow rays would slant down on the surface of the waves. At times, again, strange and baffling shadows (or what looked like shadows) formed under the swell, as though some vast creature were swimming along on the bottom. Harsh and incandescent blue patches, like streams of marine lava, would suddenly appear.

The movement of these masses of water was constant and indefatigable. Under the transparent grey skin, with its endless rising and falling rhythm, heavy triangular shapes were in constant movement, leaving lines of bubbles, swift straight eddies, the occasional branching, fibrous vortex boiling round on its own axis. Above, the swooping, gusty air thrust down on this grey and opaque surface with the full force of its atmospheric pressure, carved out hollows, sculpted undulating valleys and mountain ridges and volcanoes and angry, belching sulphur-springs. It was like a dance in which everything joined, even the fish and the waving seaweed in the shadowy depths below, a dance that moved each mass of green and clouded slime, swung it softly but firmly to and fro with the rest. This music, mingled with the wind's shrill whine, marked out a rhythm for the sea's overall sequence of movements. First there came a deep, deep indrawing as of breath, when the water shrank back into itself, emptying the rock-pools, cascading and gurgling down, pouring back on its own substance. Then came the counter-wave, surging back against the sea-wall, trying to breach it, then in its panic-stricken flight creating a loud, choppy crest of water from the two liquid masses in opposition. After this there would be a brief silence while the sea grew still and collected its strength, followed by the muted roar of unleashed energy, the rush and hiss of moving water, a sort of *tchchchchchchchch*, steadily increasing in volume, a harsh, rasping note that echoed round the surging curve of the wave. Finally the sound made by this climatic discharge underwent a swift transformation, reverberating and swelling into a long, solemn roll of thunder, though by now the waves were so huge that even this remained almost inaudible. A vast *chchchbrooooom!*, a thunderous explosion made solid and palpable, a majestic circle, a rampart of stone and spray that rose slowly skywards and floated amid the wind, slowing down everything around it, checking time's pendulum, making the world, for one brief moment, an abode of giants.

Standing there behind the lighthouse, his eyes fixed on the sea. Besson felt himself possessed by this rhythm—the rhythm of eternity, or something very like it. His mind vanished utterly, was lost amid the dance of the waves: it was as though the wind had entered into him, blowing straight through the open windows of his body. Each fresh assault by the waves took shape simultaneously in the very depths of his being, making him stiffen, filling him with an agony of hatred. The violence of these great liquid masses, ton upon ton of water, possessed him completely, and as each wave broke a complementary explosion took place somewhere inside his chest, metamorphosing him into a kind of human bomb. When he was fully attuned to the rhythm of wind and sea, when he was one with it, standing four-square against the assaults of the elements, yet at the same time vibrating with their own exultation, like a rock, or some old black slimy ring-bolt, covered with wrack and barnacles, then he began to breathe. Slowly, surely, he breathed in harmony with them. His lungs filled with the same air as the wave imbibed, leaning on the cloud-swollen horizon, accumulating the same vast burden of violence and determination. His breast expanded magnificently to contain it all, stretched almost to bursting point, he was taller and broader than a mountain. Then the intake of breath ended, and for a moment the elemental forces hung poised in equilibrium. But at the mysterious signal from that whole wide expanse of sea, the unknown signal with so strong and regular a rhythm that he no longer even heard it, the sluice-gates opened and another great mass of water hurled itself at the obstacle in its way—at the town, too, and at those vast gawping crowds—while a sound like a great gong-stroke spread rippling out to the four corners of the horizon, a sun of sheer sound, its rays swimming far above the earth, creating universal panic, leaving all inconsequential objects scattered face downwards.

Like some point of blind intensity, there was created, at the very heart of the uproar, a zone of calm and silence in which, for some few seconds, everything was destroyed, annihilated. But the curse never ran out, the cycle of respiration began all over again, just as before, without haste or exhaustion. Besson felt that in some way he was entering upon eternity. To avoid death was a simple matter: all one needed to do was to breathe in this special way, long slow powerful breaths that followed the rhythm of the sea.

To join the waves in their struggle against the earth's bastions, against scurrying, hurrying mankind, whose tiny hearts always raced madly, like a shrewmouse's.

Soon one's whole body would begin to follow this respiratory rhythm. The skin would turn cold and colourless, like water, and blood would pulse slowy through one's veins, streaky, bubbling, saline, ebbing and flowing in the circulatory system according to the same soft rhythm, flux and reflux. Soon thoughts would no longer roam freely through one's mind, but simply float there *in situ*, captive and unchanging, like sea-anemones, for ever digesting the minute scraps of matter around them: inexhaustible thoughts, without verbal form, bereft of desire, thoughts that all conveyed an identical message, though just what this was it was impossible to know for certain. 'Light and shadow', perhaps, or 'singing singing', or even 'God'.

Eyes would no longer see, nor ears hear; the skin would no longer react to cold or sunlight, nor the stomach be conscious of hunger. All that would exist would be the inner self, the inner self that contained the heaving sea, the wind in its courses, the scudding clouds; the inner self that was absorbed in its proper task of respiration. Every organ would breathe in unison—heart, intestines, private parts, brain, throat, even down to the cells of the skin and each individual granule of bone. The body would inflate itself and breathe out in time with the natural scene around it, endlessly, like some gigantic lung. Here was the secret of eternal life: respiration. Breathe, never stop breathing, breathe in harmony with the rest of creation, breathe in the sea, breathe in the heart of the living rock, in the nimbus of clouds, in the midst of that black void where the galaxies wheel through space. Breathe according to the *rhythm of truth*.

*

The minutes passed, and at last the wind fell. The sky was now completely covered with thick cloud. Darkness was falling on the shadowy town, filling the streets through which Besson walked. Silence had returned, and the sidewalks were crowded once more.

through brightly-lit shop windows various displays of goods caught the eye—fabrics, furniture, decorated pastries. Besson stopped a moment at a window behind which there stood two mechanical birds, done up in green and red plush respectively, both bobbing up and down, clacking their beaks, with much frenzied flappings of wings. Behind the birds was a girl in an armchair, smoking a cigarette and staring in front of her with vacant, heavily made-up eyes.

A little further on, as he was passing a public park, Besson heard the leaves begin to rustle in the trees. A breath of wind stirred the branches, and the first drops of rain started to fall, plopping heavily on the asphalt. Then, high above the town, the black clouds suddenly exploded, and water came slamming down with a noise like a thunderclap. Besson ran across and took shelter in a doorway, and stood watching the avalanche descend. The rain fell at a very slight angle, in thick straight voluted lines, as though the sky were a vast colander.

The gutters soon overflowed on to the sidewalks, washing away masses of dead leaves and bits of paper. Water from the roof-tops came crashing down through every drain-pipe. The whole town was built on a slope, and the water went streaming over concrete and asphalt and tiling as though drawn towards a great hole somewhere near the bottom. Moisture dripped from every object in sight: the impression it gave was not so much that it had dropped out of the sky, as that it was there already, embodied in all matter, and had been given some magic order to distil itself. It came bursting out of everything—leaves, posters on hoardings, cracks in the pavement, manhole covers, even from people's skins. It was like sweat, the kind of sweat that comes streaming through every dilated pore when one's running a high temperature; an endless flow, from the fountain gush to the slow trickle, drop by pearly drop, pitting all its soft and pliant strength against the hard element of stone, the air's impenetrability.

Above the line of trees in the park Besson could see the still dark sky. The roofs of the houses round the square stood out very pale against it, and the television aerials gleamed as though coated with silver paint.

Sounds still existed, but they were no longer clear-cut: the downpour had cast a halo about them, they shone in a brief and murmurous aureole before being drowned and snuffed out. Besson breathed in the odour of damp earth through the covering layers of bitumen. He could also smell the current of fresh air coming down from the upper atmosphere, laden with ozone. He strained his ears to catch any echo, from behind the rampart-like rows of houses, of the river's roar as it rose higher and higher, milk-coloured now, washing down clouds of earth and turf in its spate. He even opened his mouth to catch and taste the flavour of the rain.

But, most striking of all, at this precise moment—without any visible hint of how the effect was produced, there came a bright triple crack in the expanse of jet-black cloud, stretching half-way across the sky, from zenith to horizon. Clear-cut, unmoving, as though traced with a crayon, a pattern of branching veins, this sudden phenomenon broke through the obscurity with such pure unwavering brightness, so intense and snow-white a degree of incandescence that it almost ceased to be light. It hung there, its three-timed fork branching down towards the earth, shattering the sky, carved upon the firmament, like some gigantic root, and at that moment nothing else existed: the sky and horizon, the surface of the town, seas and rivers—all vanished in an instant, shattered into a thousand fragments, were enveloped in darkness. Nothing remained but this vast and silent testament to the presence of electrical power, this divine and blinding emblem of whiteness, beauty, peace; the great unmoving design that had annihilated all else, in whose light years and centuries of effort and striving would find illumination, would be impregnated with violence, penetrated by happiness. Cold and incandescence here blended in a single flashlight crack, one scored line of brightness that had photographed the entire world.

When this moment was over—a second that felt like infinity—the thunderclap followed. It rumbled, hesitated, then crashed

185

down over Besson, making the very earth tremble. The rain now began to flow more freely, flooding the street with its beneficent tide: it was rather like the sensation of opening a door wide to let some fresh air into a firelit room—or warmth into a cold one.

Chapter Nine

*François Besson runs away—Do Indians kill wolves?—The ogre—
People watch the big yellow dog dying—Description of rabies—
François Besson burns his papers—In the canyons of the town—A
missed meal—The sphere of water without water*

ON the ninth day François Besson decided to leave Marthe's
house. There were several reasons for this:

(1) He was getting fond of the girl.
(2) He was tired.
(3) He wanted to see what was going on elsewhere.
(4) The bed was uncomfortable.
(5) The girl had bad breath and sometimes smelt of perspiration.
(6) Time was passing, and he had to act fast.

In the morning he waited till Marthe had gone out to do the
shopping, and then got his things together. The little boy, still in
his dressing gown, was playing with some toy cars on the floor of
the kitchen. After a while he got up and came over to Besson, who
was just putting his razor into the beach-bag.
'Where are you going?' he said.
'Out,' Besson told him.
'What for?'
'Oh, nothing,' said Besson.
'What do you mean, nothing?' the boy said. Then he went
and fetched one of the toy cars, and began to push it round
Besson's feet, making *broo-o-m-broom* noises to simulate a car's
engine.
Besson put the last of his belongings in the beach-bag. The
little boy came back again and scrutinized him with black, un-
wavering eyes.

'Where are you going to, then?' he repeated.

'Outside,' said Besson.

'Going for a walk?'

'Yes,' Besson said. He strapped on his wristwatch and went to comb his hair. When he returned to pick up his bag the little red-haired boy was carefully staging an accident between two of the cars.

'What are you up to?' Besson asked him.

'This one's a Peugeot,' the boy explained, 'and this other one here's a Citroën. It's going very fast, so the driver of the Peugeot doesn't see it. Now watch what happens.'

The little blue vehicle was travelling flat out across the kitchen floor; proportionately to its scaled-down size it must have been doing the equivalent of something like three hundred miles an hour. Then the other car appeared, coming in from the right. This one was bright red. It curved round the table-leg and cut right across the first car's path. There was no time for anyone to brake: they crashed into each other with appalling violence, and both vehicles were hurled across the plastic-tiled floor, bouncing and somersaulting over and over, until at last they came to rest on their backs. If there had been any passengers on board they would have been killed on the spot. Next, the fire-engine came out of a corner at the other end of the kitchen. Zig-zagging over its imaginary highway, siren going full blast, it made flat out for the scene of the accident, stopping at each wrecked car to extinguish the fire before it could get under way. Then, after picking up the dead and wounded, it returned the way it had come, sounding its siren louder than ever. When it was back in its corner, two breakdown trucks drove across to the scene of the accident. When they got there they hooked up the two crashed cars by their bumpers and towed them away across the kitchen.

Besson still had a few minutes to spare before he left. He sat down and lit a cigarette, letting the little boy blow out the flame for him.

'What's your name?' Besson asked.

The little red-haired boy made no reply.

188

'Go on, what's your name?' Besson said again.

'Lucas,' said the little boy.

'Lucas what?'

'Lucas . . .'

'And you live here, right?'

'Yes. . . .'

'And how old are you?'

No answer.

'You mean you've *forgotten*? You know how to count, anyway, don't you? Go on, you know how to count, surely?'

The child wavered on his short podgy legs. He had a heavy head, with high forehead and a very bright pair of eyes under his red hair. His mouth was half-open, and two incisors were just visible, resting against the top of his lower lip. He was wearing a blue bathrobe, check trousers and floral-pattern slippers.

Besson bent down towards him and said: 'Come on—try a bit of counting with me. One, two, three—'

'Four—'

'Five, six—'

'Eight . . . eleven . . . fourteen—'

'No, no! Six, seven, eight, nine . . . You go on from there.'

'M'm. . . . Ten—'

'Well done, that's right—'

'M'm. . . . Fourteen. . . .'

'No not, fourteen, you said that just now.'

'Six. . . .'

'No, not six. . . . Eleven, twelve, thirteen. . . .'

'Fourteen—'

'What's after that?'

'I don't know,' the little red-haired boy said, and began to play with one of his cars again. Besson watched him crawling across the linoleum floor, and for a moment felt the urge to take him along too, have him as a companion wherever he went. He might even teach the kid something, just exactly what he wasn't sure, but maybe, one day, he'd be able to teach him something really useful, like pilfering from shop-counters, or how to swim really fast. But it occurred to him that he'd soon have the police on his tail, with charges of child-abduction.

'Why don't you get in your little cars and drive them?' Besson asked.

The child looked up and puzzled over this for a moment.

'But they're too small for me,' he said. 'Look—'

He held the toy car in front of his face.

'Would you like a bigger car?'

'I'd like a truck,' the little boy said. 'A big truck like that one.'

'Where would you go in it?'

'I'd take it to school. And I'd take Mama for drives round the garden in it.'

Besson flicked his cigarette-ash on the ground.

'When you're a big boy,' he said.

'That's right,' said the little boy. 'When I'm eight. But—but why *aren't* I eight?'

'Because you're four and a half,' Besson said.

'When I'm asleep at night I see lots of things,' the little boy said. 'Wolves, whole forests full of wolves. And Indians.'

'Do the Indians kill the wolves?'

'No, they can't, they're not big enough. But when *I'm* grown up I'll take a stick and I'll kill the wolves, I'll, I'll poke my stick into their eyes, that's what I'll do. There was one wolf wanted to eat me, but I said to him, no, wolf, don't eat me, because—because I'm going to kill you. And he got terrible cross, and caught hold of my throat. So I grabbed a knife and slit him up the middle, right into two halves.'

'What happened then?'

'Then the wolf locked me in a dark room, and kept me there.'

'Were you afraid of the dark?'

'Oh yes, I was afraid, and then when it was light I jumped out of the window.'

'Ever seen the Big Bad Wolf?'

'Oh, I see him sometimes at night—he's got a big stick and he goes through the forest with all the foxes. But I run away and he can't catch me.'

'Why can't he catch you?'

'Because I met an ogre who put me up in the top of a tree. The Big Bad Wolf couldn't climb the tree because the ogre was protecting me.'

'Didn't the ogre try and eat you?'

'Oh no, he was a nice ogre. He never ate little children. He was a kind good ogre.'

'What did he look like?'

'Big, ever so big, with black legs and white hands and face.'

'What about his nose?'

'White'.

'And his hair?'

'Blue. No, bluey-green.'

'Bluey-green?'

'Yes.'

'And his eyes?'

'Yellow.'

'So he was a handsome ogre, eh?'

'Yes, he was. And I went on running for ages and ages.'

'And what did the Big Bad Wolf do?'

'The Big Bad Wolf tried to catch me, so I took a big stone and smashed his head in.'

'Suppose he'd eaten you?'

'Then I'd have cut open his tummy and got out.'

'And why doesn't the chicken you eat cut open *your* tummy?'

'Because he's dead.'

'And you're not dead, eh?'

'Course not.'

'Well, suppose the Big Bad Wolf ate you, would you be dead then?'

'Yes, but I can't die yet, I'm too small, otherwise I'd grow up in a flash, just like that.'

'And why aren't you a chicken, do you suppose?'

'Well, if I *was* a chicken, I'd run off and hide in the forest.'

Besson stubbed out his cigarette in the ashtray.

'At school,' the boy went on, 'there's a little boy called Michel, and he's got a dog called Paddy.'

'What about it?'

'When it's dark, that dog, I mean, it looks just like a wolf.'

Besson said: 'What are you going to do when you grow up?'

'When I was big I joined the army and got killed, twice.'

'What about after you came to life again?'

'I flew off in an aeroplane, very fast, and the plane went up in sky where you can't see it, very high, *normously* high. I nearly fell out. After that I swam through the sea to an island.'

'What was this island called?'

'*I* don't know. It didn't have any name, that's what.'

'It didn't have any name?'

'Then I ate too much chocolate and got a tummy-ache and threw up.'

'Do you know how to write?'

'Oh yes, I can write—I know how to read, too.'

'What sort of thing can you read?'

'Well, the paper—'

'What's in the paper, then?'

'Stories about animals—bear stories and giraffe stories and gazelle stories and dromedary stories and elephant stories—'

'And duckbilled platypi?'

'Yes. . . .'

'And hooded cassowaries?'

'Yes. . . . And tigers and lions and panthers. . . .'

'Microbes, too?'

'Yes, and lions and giraffes. . . .'

'And diplodoci and megatheria and labyrinthosauri. . . .'

'Yes, and tigers and lions—'

Besson sat looking at the child for a little after this, holding his gaze, absorbing and memorizing the soft lines of his face, the way his skull was ridged, those black eyes of his that possessed no depth of their own, simply reflected the external world. He studied his way of sitting and moving, which still had no real connection with that childish body, yet already displayed the mysterious consistency of action which characterizes any individual personality. At the end of this scrutiny Besson decided to go. He picked up the beach-bag, put on his raincoat, and said to the little red-haired boy: 'Right, I'm off now. You be a good boy and play with your cars. When Mummy comes home tell her I've gone, and I don't know when I'll be back. Got that?'

'Yes,' said the little boy.

Besson opened the door and walked down the stairs.

*

Outside the weather had more or less cleared up. The sky was still overcast, but the ground had dried, and a cold wind blew intermittently down the streets. Besson walked on, swinging his beach-bag, and keeping away from the main thoroughfares, where there were too many people. Without consciously intending to do so, he found himself making for the river.

Here the *quais* were lined with tumbledown shacks where the rag-and-bone men lived. Besson stopped at a snack-bar to eat a sandwich and drink a glass of lemonade. Beside him was a soldier, munching his way through two hunks of stale bread with sliced sausage between them. When he had finished his lemonade and sandwich, Besson paid and went over to the water's edge, where he stood with his elbows resting on the balustrade. The river flowed swiftly past below him, in torrential and muddy spate; a smell of decaying vegetable matter rose from it. A little way upstream, the workers on the site were moving busily to and fro behind a rampart of stones. The cranes and bulldozers were not in use, and near the scaffolding Besson could see smoke rising from a brazier.

He strolled on up the *quais* until he came level with the building site. Then he stopped again and took a good look at what was going on. There were about a dozen workers, dressed in filthy old clothes, moving about over the pebble-ridges with shovels and buckets. Some were digging holes in the sand, others stood

193

watching them and smoking. All this looked somewhat disorganized, and was probably quite useless; yet Besson found himself suddenly wanting to do as they did, to labour bent over a shovel, not understanding what he was doing, asking no questions, simply doing his share of the mysterious work which would end one day in a new ferro-concrete bridge. A few moments later a tramp trudged slowly across the site, dragging a sack stuffed full of old papers. No one paid the slightest attention to him, and he slouched on into the bushes, following the swollen line of the river round until he vanished behind a fence, perhaps into the mouth of a sewer outlet. It was an odd sort of desert world to find in the middle of this tough, overcrowded town; a kind of minuscule savannah which, after nightfall, became the hunting-ground of rats and stray dogs.

It was also a little frightening. It stood for depressing things like solitude, misery, or old age. The town, confronted with this frozen, refuse-strewn channel, and the muddy stream running through it, pressed in on it with the full weight of its disapproval, the concentrated violence of its window-studded walls. As he leaned on the balustrade Besson realized that he was exactly on the demarcation-line, the frontier. It cost him quite an effort to drag himself away and return to the centre of town.

Shortly afterwards, as he was crossing at an intersection, he noticed the crowd. He went over to find out what was happening, but at first could see nothing out of the ordinary. People had gathered along the sidewalk, all craning and staring in the same direction. It was only when he got right up to the thing they were looking at that he realized what was going on. Stretched out in the conduit beside the gutter lay a big yellow dog, obviously dying. It lay on its back with its head in the drainage course and its paws up in the air; it was panting away, open-mouthed, and so loudly that the painful rasp of each breath it drew was quite audible. Only a few yards away stood this group of men and women, quite still, just watching. Some others felt a certain ashamed embarrassment, and either stopped a good way further on, peering over their shoulders, or else lurked behind parked cars. Others again, who were driving past in their own vehicles, would slow down as they went by the spot where the dog lay dying. Besson took all this in very rapidly as he walked, shuddering, past the death-scene himself.

He saw the creature's prostrate body, already very nearly the colour of bitumen, its stiffened paws still feebly quivering. He saw the long head, sunk in the filth of the gutter, and trying to breathe the sluggish air. There were no traces of blood on the dog's lacklustre coat, but the effect was even more unpleasant: the skin hung slack and shapeless, like a half-empty sack. And in front of him stood these motionless, silent people. As he made his way to the edge of the pavement, Besson was suddenly hit by the ugly visual image this body presented, lying there sprawled on the ground, wrong side up, still choking for breath. Two glazed and mud-flecked eyes stared into empty space, and the curled tail hung down over the kerbside. Then from that gaping throat, which the air could no longer penetrate, there burst—mingled with dust and slobber—a faint, hoarse, plaintive cry that broke the silence hanging over the intersection. But this sound did not last long. The body continued to heave and pant, in the throes of the death agony now, and Besson moved swiftly away without turning back. He was not really moved, and yet for a long while afterwards, as he walked through the noise and bustle of the street, he could not forget one single detail of that tableau—the weirdly still body of the dying yellow dog, alone at his intersection, and the faces of the people watching.

For a few brief moments he even felt something resembling a tragic recollection of sickness and death: the clutching hand of the unknown, of grim inevitability. No, perhaps rather a sense of remorse and uneasiness, sprung from the hidden origins of his life, and now surging up inside him, spreading along the network of his veins, passing through nerves and muscles, an obscure pain, a kind of spasm, burning, refining, making each individual cell a watchful and malevolent eye. It was like some fatal epidemic, bringing stark terror, frantic hatred, pangs of conscience, and leading to a terrible, ineluctable *dénouement*: plague, nervous leprosy, *l'Ainhum*, *le Goundou*, *le Kala-Azar*, or indeed rabies:

Under normal conditions rabies develops very fast, and the patient therefore will suffer certain psychological symptoms at an early stage of the disease. He tends to exhibit signs of anxiety and melancholia, and to be obsessed by strange premonitions. Sleep becomes impossible for him. Very soon areas of numbness and irritation, together with an itching sensation, develop locally around the wound, which appears soft and swollen. Sometimes the first symptom of which the patient complains is a strange feeling in the throat, coupled with a sense of constriction in the windpipe.

The mental symptoms can be merely hysterical, and in many cases the disease first manifests itself after some psychological shock. Instances arise in which fear or terror can be regarded as genuine symptoms of this complaint. But generally speaking the most frequent initial indication is a rise in temperature. These symptoms may last for several days before the disease declares its true nature, but normally they last between twenty-four and forty-eight hours. Hydrophobia, the main symptom, is dominant in a majority of cases: this is caused by intensely painful spasms which occur in the deglutitive [swallowing] and respiratory organs whenever the patient attempts to eat or drink.

The pain produced by these spasms is such that in all likelihood for sheer intensity it exceeds all other forms of human suffering. This is why the smell, sight, or even sound of water or other liquids will suffice to bring on a crisis. When an effort is made to imbibe even a tiny quantity of liquid, it is instantly rejected, with a violent spasm of the throat and larynx. One characteristic symptom is the hypersensitive state of the nervous cells to external stimulants. A draught or breeze can produce convulsions: the reflexes of the skin and tendons become exaggerated, and the respiratory spasms of the thoracic muscles do not respond to tracheotomy. Solid nourishment can more easily be absorbed than fluids.

Once the disease is past the incubatory period it progresses rapidly. In many cases there tend to be periods of apparent improvement, which might lead one to believe a cure to have taken place, or, alternatively, to doubt the original diagnosis. The patient's mind is in most cases exceptionally lucid, and he will give intelligent answers to any questions he is asked; but then his voice becomes inaudible and his speech incomprehensible. Certain phases of hyper-excitement may reach the level of actual insanity. The patient will smash and destroy everything within reach, although attacks on living persons are very rare. Sexual excitement, accompanied by priapism, is a common symptom. The voice becomes hoarse; the strange sounds produced during major spasms are what gave rise to the popular belief that 'anyone with rabies barks like a dog'.

The spasms and convulsions become increasingly frequent, until the patient passes into a state of paralysis from which death results. The muscles that have been strained to the very limits of endurance now relax; the patient's features lose that rictus of ultimate agony and terror they previously wore, and become quite expressionless. There is usually an excessive secretion of saliva, which the patient is incapable of controlling. Finally, respiration becomes irregular and weak, and after a while stops altogether. Before death there is a rise in temperature. Sugar and acetone are normally found in the urine. When the patient passes into a state of paralysis, his pupils dilate. . . .

Afterwards François Besson returned once more to his parents' house. When he rang the bell they had just sat down at table. They talked for a moment over the plates of steaming food, and Besson said he had one or two more things to collect from his room.

The room itself, he found, had been carefully tidied since his departure. There was a new bedspread, with small red and green patterns running across it. The floor had been swept and polished, the ashtrays emptied and washed.

Besson placed the drawer of his table on the floor and began to burn the papers in it one by one. He held each of them by one end, lit a match beneath them, and dropped them into a large glass ashtray. In this way he burnt everything: it took him the best part of the afternoon. Poems, love-letters, end-of-the-affair letters, handbills, lecture-notes on geography and Latin, algebra problems, sketches of naked women, photographs, vaccination certificates, all the accumulated scribblings and confessions of many years. Not all the papers burnt in the same way. Some flared up and were gone in a flash, giving off a quick wave of heat as they did so. Others went on crackling for quite a time as the match-flame licked up at them; these ones burnt slowly, with a great deal of smoke. The fire crept up these white squares of flimsy, obliterating the handwriting, twisting up the lines of the sketches, bright red patches spreading, slowly guttering out in a black and acrid cloud. The pages torn from pornographic magazines were thick, glossy sheets, which never burnt through properly, so that an irregular bite, ringed with sooty foam, would appear in the middle of some lissom beauty's body. To keep the flames alight you had to supply extra fuel underneath—say a handful of light, scented airmail letters. Sheets of onion-skin paper went black in a second, but on the fossil and all-too-fragile page thus produced you could still see little serpentine lines of lettering against the black cindered background. The flames devoured everything, without distinction or regret, wrinkling up fine parchment, melting glossy surfaces, volatilizing celluloid; and from the tiny brazier there rose a spiral of hot smoke, in which thoughts and acts were reduced to mere ephemeral grey particles floating on the air.

Each time the ashtray was full Besson emptied it out on the floor. Then he patiently began to fill it again, burning sheet after sheet of paper. In order to economize on matches, he watched for the moment when the fire was about to go out, and then presented the guttering flame with a fresh victim.

Soon the air was thick with stinking, acrid fumes that left Besson's throat sore. Tiny fragments floated up to the ceiling and then eddied down again, settling on his hair and hands and clothes. But Besson did not open the window. Bent over the ashtray (which was conveniently placed on the floor) he feverishly gathered fresh piles of paper as fuel for the red and yellow flames. The glass walls of the ashtray were now covered with a kind of orange glue, where the fire touched them, and round the rim blue tongues of heat flickered from tiny piles of soot.

Sweat was beginning to run down Besson's face and off his hands; the fire blazed up, sank, blazed up again, sank once more; the baking hot air scorched his eyeballs, the smoke deposited its stinging cinders in his throat. Now and then a spurt of flame came up and burnt his fingers, but it was as though he felt nothing. He went on fuelling his bonfire, reducing all the papers in his room to malodorous ashes. There was nothing worth saving, nothing worth reading. Every item belonged in this crazy holocaust, in the popping, crackling, flaring eddies of red-hot flame, shot through with spurts of green, in the warmth and light and fanaticism of those greedy tongues of fire dancing over the floor. Besson no longer even bothered to empty the ashtray now; papers rolled blazing across the room, setting fire to others as they went. Besson threw on whole packets at a time, and the fire grew in size, sending up a high corona of flame. The smoke thickened into a sticky black consistency, rose in a single column that only began to spread out somewhere near the ceiling. Unable now to make out anything in this dim fog except the outline of the burning mass, Besson began to throw papers and books into the heart of the flames. Novels, dictionaries, travel-books, philosophical treatises—all vanished into that living gullet, which consumed them instantly.

By the time that Besson's parents—alerted by the unmistakable crackling roar of the fire—came rushing into his room, flames were already licking over the bedclothes and up the wallpaper. There were shouts of alarm, footsteps hurrying across the floor. At this point Besson picked up his beach-bag and went, without one backward glance. In order to shake off the effects of that blinding heat, though, he had to sit down for a bit on a park bench, and smoke a cigarette.

*

When evening came, François Besson strolled through the canyon-like streets of the town. He saw men and women walking along the pavement, in couples, and gangs of children playing war games. Everyone was busy, they all had a warm, comfortable lodging to bury themselves in for the night. In each cell of those vast apartment blocks some heavy-bosomed housewife would be preparing the evening meal, and the brightly-lit kitchens would be redolent of leek-and-potato soup, fish-fries, apple fritters, a peaceful domestic aroma. People smiled as they passed one another: sometimes they called out a greeting, and when they talked it was in very loud voices. But none of this was for Besson. He walked on in silence, and passers-by either stared very hard at him, eyes narrowed, or else gave him a furtive glance and looked away again. Workmen and builders' labourers stood about in the bars, drinking glasses of beer, eyes fixed on the television set quacking away in its corner. From somewhere a long way off came the faint sound of church bells ringing. Shop-windows began to light up, one after the other, and the neon signs embarked on their endless, endlessly repeated, flashing messages. Above one travel agency words flickered along a broad strip dotted with electric light bulbs. Besson read: STOP PRESS NEWS PLANE CRASH AT TEL-AVIV EIGHTEEN DEAD. A little further on he saw some pigeons perched on the letters of a neon-sign, just under the roof-guttering, waddling about and warming their feet. Beyond them he came on an old man leaning against the wall, playing 'Mon ami Pierrot' on a tin whistle, with an upturned hat at his feet. Behind the glass of a display case there were photographs of babies and small kneeling girls. Their mouths gaped open in fixed smiles, their eyes shone as though wax-polished. Everywhere men had left their mark: house-doors, window-sills, side-walk, sky and trees, dogs' backs, rusty iron street-signs—all bore their names and addresses. Nowhere could one get away from them. These vertical mountains, all honeycombed with rectangular holes, were full of spying eyes, mouths that gossiped when they weren't eating, well-washed skin, well-combed hair, bitten fingernails, bodies swathed in wool or nylon. No other landscape had ever existed remotely like this one: such a limited area had never contained so many impenetrable cavities, so many defiles and moraines. No mountain could be as high as these buildings, no valley as deep and narrow as the streets outside them. Some fearful force had carved out these contours, it had taken a hideous and incomparable explosion of violence to erect these monuments, drain the soil, level out the rough places, crush the rocks, plan, dig, manipulate the elements, organize space, and make the little streams run meekly obedient to the will of authority. The houses had their roots dug deep into the rock, and clung to this conquered territory with a kind of ferocious hatred.

Besson walked humbly through these streets in which he had no part, moving aside to let the victors have free passage—the round-shouldered women, the crop-haired children, the men on their way home from work. When he wanted to cross the street he waited until there was a gap in the traffic, no more rubber tyres hissing past. He ducked his head and hunched himself defensively against the assaults of lights and noises and frantic scrambling movement. Lights winked on and off everywhere, at the summits of steel pylons, in the streets, out at sea: red and yellow points riveted into place, then wiped out, replaced by others. It was like being shut under a gigantic lid, made of lead and resting firmly on the ground, a lid that pressed down with its whole weight on one's skin and eardrums and diaphragm and neck. The cold air had become a kind of liquid substance; people were mostly staying indoors now. Very soon Besson had to stop through sheer fatigue. It was completely dark now, and indeed time for dinner. With the money he had left Besson decided to go and eat in the self-service restaurant.

Sitting at a black table with smears of sauce on it, opposite a fat and ugly old woman whose small mean eyes watched his every move, Besson did his best to swallow some food. On his tray he had collected the following: a plate of sliced tomatoes with chopped parsley on them, an egg mayonnaise, a dish containing one portion of roast chicken (leg) and fried potatoes, a glass of water, a yoghourt, three sachets of granulated sugar, a hunk of stale bread, knife, fork, soup-spoon, coffee-spoon, a thin paper napkin with *Bon Appétit!* or some such legend inscribed on it, and a piece of paper which read:

ROYAL SELF–SERVICE RESTAURANT

*80

*120

*550

*80

*15

*20

*==865

Besson tried to swallow the tomatoes and cut up the chicken. But the food was hostile, it slid about on the plate, refused to be chewed or swallowed. Water dribbled over his chin when he drank, as though some joker had drilled a hole in the glass. The egg slipped about in its mayonnaise, and the chicken wouldn't keep still either. It was all somehow quite repulsive—ill-cooked flesh, dead roots, a taste of earth, perhaps even of excrement. Besson attempted to chew this stuff. He swallowed lumps of dry meat and slices of egg-white that smelt of sulphur. He dribbled, struggled, messed up his hands and clothes, dropped first his knife then his spoon. Eating, it seemed, was impossible. And on top of everything else there was the old woman, taking in every detail of his defeat with an ironic eye. Besson abandoned solid food and set about the yoghourt. But this turned out very little better. He managed to get the little spoon to his mouth, but the viscous substance acquired a life of its own: it tried to get away from him, it ran under his tongue, slipped past the barrier of the uvula, came back down his nasal passages. Bent over the pot of yoghourt, in a mere simulacrum of the nutritional process, Besson felt as though he were a small child again. The hard stare of the old woman and the inscrutable faces of other diners scattered through the restaurant all showed him his own reflection, as clearly as so many mirrors: a tenuous, cloudy object, curled up on itself, a phantom, or a foetus still covered with glaireous matter, something that scarcely belonged to the human species.

So there it was, the group rejected him spontaneously, like any freak. Having robbed him of his most intimate thoughts and actions, they were now about to strip him of his body, too, and condemn him to the void. This was the message to be read on the sneering faces around him, the thick hands so competent at dismembering roast chicken, the mouths with their rows of sharp teeth that could chew, salivate, reduce to pulp, the coiled and deep-hidden organs that wanted to transform everything into scarlet blood, its regular pulsing flow pricking out under the skin like millions of tiny needles.

What he had to do now was to fight back, with all his strength: get out of this glittering morgue, to begin with, plunge right into the frozen depths of darkness and seek help there. Walk along the deserted boulevards under a mist of rain, in the grey light of the street-lamps; drink water from a public fountain, gaze up avidly at the invisible sky; then, after smoking a cigarette, stretch out on a bench under the most thickly-leafed tree in some public square, and wait. Then fall asleep, extinguish at one stroke all the lights that burnt in the chamber of one's imagination—if need be smash the hot bulb hanging like a drop of fire at the end of its plaited cord—and plunge, tremulous with hope, into the heart of solitude, the solitude of the unknown.

Stretched out on his bench, head against unyielding wood, eyes wide open, Besson gazed up at the darkness. The branches of a laurel-tree spread their complex architecture over him, hung motionless in the cold air. Everything was dim, sombre. Sounds from the neighbouring streets had an odd muffled quality, that enveloped them like a shadow. There were no insects, no spiders even: the world had the kind of still, fixed quality one might expect inside a marble mausoleum. The night's vast presence loomed above the earth, a vaulted and windowless dome. Its whole weight bore down on these minuscule creatures called men who set themselves up against it, yet it did not crush them. This gigantic floating roofage, more opaque than the sea itself, seemed to comprehend, even to love them. It too, no doubt, possessed a rhythm: not the rhythm of breathing, or heart-beats, but a heavy pendular swing that came and went in silence, permeated with non-presence, vibrant with vacancy, eternal and majestic music that only the infinite could have produced. All stars and planets, suns and nebulae were contained in it; the galaxies nestled in its bosom and were rocked to its measure. Delicate and ethereal, yet full of latent violence, the black dome embraced them all, revolved smoothly on its own axis, for ever turning, turning. This sphere of water without water, so ductile and glacial in motion, advancing and then—its thousands of silver-bellied fishes all atwinkle—retreating little by little upon itself, was prayer, was thought, was life itself. Shadow falling on shadow, a veil of blackness for ever spread and for ever opening, an intermittent umbrella, only vanishing in order to deploy new schemes and offshoots, a smooth dark cloud arching across the universe, for ever drawing up into itself, through a chill vortex, the substance of happiness and unhappiness; alert, uncluttered, watchful, drawing men one by one into the peace of its womb; night, the Great Mother.

Chapter Ten

François Besson experiences hunger, thirst, and loneliness—The smell of bread—The woman kneeling in the church—François Besson submits himself to God—His confession—The organs—How Besson learnt the beggar's trade—The terrible look of the old woman who wished she could die

ON the tenth day, François Besson experienced hunger, thirst, and loneliness. The town was now a crazy maelstrom of hubbub and movement: he was jostled, banged to and fro like a ball, all but crushed to death. Four times he just missed being run down by cars and the walls of the houses leaned in towards him, as though about to collapse in a mountain of white dust and cockroaches. Every time he passed an old corner or alley-way, he would sidle into it and squat there for a while. But the feet continued their endless progress up and down the pavement, beating out a retreat on its surface. They were everywhere, like moving columns, or rather pistons, tapping the ground in regular time, rowing time, the paths they followed bristling with dangers and obstructions. The soles of their shoes resounded on the hard flat ground, and the staccato noise thus produced—first the dull thud of the heel stamping down, then the creak and scrape as the foot flattened out —could be heard far away down the street, growing louder, louder, till it was like a military march-past. The din would reach Besson, dislodge him from his place of concealment, march over his stomach, and then dwindle until it was lost in silence—an even more menacing effect. Footsteps, footsteps, nothing but footsteps, from left to right, from right to left, in one unceasing flow.

There were the cars, too, like great carnivores on the prowl: each one had a man in it, and bad luck to anyone who got in their way. A monstrous indifference had spread over the world, a sort of coldness that penetrated solid objects, that had permeated tree-trunks and car wheels and the pattern of the paving-stones that was painted over paint-work, mixed in with concrete, melted into spectacle-frames, riveted in steel girders.

On the big hoardings, where the posters were wrinkling now from a mixture of paste and rain, was a line of red-cheeked women, displaying cruel-looking rows of teeth, smiling with pale and cannibal mouths, while their dark eyes, capped by moustache-like sets of eyelashes, resembled so many giant hairy-legged spiders. Another advertisement showed a naked woman standing, half in shadow, beside a refrigerator, and the exaggerated curves of her body had a strangely obscene quality, as though she were a female of some quite different species in disguise.

At the back of one opalescent shop window were several wax dummies, frozen in all-too-human postures: Besson stopped and stared at these paralysed bodies, the crossed legs with their generous display of thigh, the hands that possessed such long, tapering fingers, the bosoms straining at the dresses that covered them, the bald heads masked by nylon wigs of various colours—blonde, auburn, raven, rose-pink. He felt a sudden desire to live with these imitation women as though they were the only real ones. He wanted to lie down on the white pebbles of those artificial 'beaches' at the back of shop windows, and stretch out under the blazing 'sunlight' of an arc-lamp. Here he could build himself a hut, amid the unstirring, luxuriant pot-plants, and abandon himself to these bright, shimmering colours, in a quiet, peaceful, prefabricated universe where silence was symbolized by a Veronese-green cloth of some plastic material, this closed-in cube redolent of such pervasive odours as those of moth-balls and powerful cheap scent. Perhaps he would choose a woman, too: say the one with green eyes and long blonde hair, who sat there, slightly askew, on a collapsible metal chair, smoking a dead cigarette, the black material of her draped dress revealing small patches of bare flesh, that ranged in colour from ochre to pale pink. Or perhaps the one who lay stretched out face downwards in the middle of

206

the paper lawn, exposing her skin (already tanned the colour of milk chocolate) to the arc-lamp's rays. Then there was the red-haired girl, who stood there, frozen in mid-step, smiling gently, her two dark-blue eyes, fringed with thick black lashes, staring out through the window. He would have liked them all. He would have spent hours caressing these tall, clean-limbed, elegant creatures, sliding their dresses off those rounded shoulders very carefully so as not to disarrange their wigs, or knock off a hand or foot. That's what I'd like to do, he thought.

But outside, under that leaden sky, there was no chance of peace or relaxation. An army of legs continued to advance down the sidewalk, and the human bodies above them gave off odd flashes of brightness, fierce metallic reflections. Each individual had his armour. Hands glinted as they swung at the extremity of each arm; eyes shone with snow-white scleras, teeth sparkled, noses glowed, hair gleamed greasily, belt-buckles gave off little slivers of light. It was as though the sun had really come down on earth, or else had suddenly melted, behind that curtain of cotton-wool clouds, infusing the rain-drops with a shower of tinfoil and gold. The frozen air was as still and tangible as a sheet of plate-glass.

Towards midday Besson felt the first pangs of hunger. He had eaten nothing since the previous evening, and had spent his last remaining coins on a packet of cigarettes and a box of matches. All around him a faint smell of cooking filtered out through the closed windows of the houses he passed. People were having lunch now. Whether at home or in a restaurant, everyone was sitting down to a heaped plateful of food, was working through slices of savoury meat, potatoes, salad, spoonfuls of spinach purée. Food was slipping smoothly down countless oesophagi, a succession of saliva-lubricated little balls. Blood went surging round the stomach, jaws champed steadily.

After the earlier hubbub and bustle, from noon on the streets gradually began to empty. Life became more and more centred on the kitchen, with its clatter of cutlery and casseroles. There was a somnolent feeling in the air now, reminiscent of an afternoon siesta. Even the animals had vanished. They were either raiding the garbage-cans in people's back yards, or else prowling around the family dinner-table, jaws wide open, eyes bright with anticipation.

Behind them they had left this grey deserted wilderness, over which the wind still blew fitfully. The streets seemed endless, the sidewalks were bare. The invisible tide had ebbed far out, uncovering a flat expanse of silt. People and things had withdrawn into themselves, to savour, each in their private retreat, the aroma of cooking food. Outside in the gardens, very stiff and upright in the black soil, the trees were feeding too. From the bottommost layers of humus they sucked up the soft elemental stuff of life and digested it. Phosphates dissolved slowly between their roots, and the sap, their life-blood, with the colour of milk and the taste of sugar, spread out and up till it reached the topmost branches.

Besson felt this torpor stealing over him, and tried to resist it for a moment. He stood quite still on the corner of an intersection, and tried to imagine himself giving a sumptuous banquet. He set out a dazzling table decorated with dishes of pheasants in aspic and *poulet à l'estragon*. Over their delectable flesh he poured golden wines and rich, thick sauces that spread out in iridescent splendour, like a peacock's tail. He then destroyed the table and everything on it. But this was not enough. The streets and pavements around him were still deserted. Down those long, glabrous vistas, as though traced in the dust by a finger, or daubed with mud, the letters F O O D appeared, a depressing message that nothing could obliterate. As soon as people finished their meals, and the cats curled up beside the garbage-cans and fell asleep, this maleficent sign would vanish of itself. But for the moment it was still there. This was the time of day when people should not be out of doors; those who ventured into the streets would encounter the magic word, and then the winged shadow of that vast exodus would hover over them too, like a vulture.

Besson walked down one street in which the drains were up. The working-site was deserted except for a pile of shovels and pick-axes, and a yellow machine that smelt of oil and combustion, and was now cooling off in the sharp air.

Cars stood parked nose to tail along the kerb; their mock-leather seat-cushions still bore the impression of those who had been sitting in them. It was like night-time, except that even the ghosts were missing.

Outside a bakery, the smell of warm bread and cake brought Besson up short; it passed into his body with the breath he drew, and conjured up a veritable tide of saliva and digestive juices. When it reached his stomach, and stuck there, it became pure agony, turning, spreading, hardening into a sharp cross. Besson went over to the window and looked inside. The bread was there, long loaves packed upright in a big basket, their honey-coloured surface exposed for all to see, still hot from the oven, swag-bellied, dusted with flour, scarred and knobbly, that delicious and potent odour steaming gently off them. Inside the crust the bread was springy, delicate, soft, warm, permeated with millions of tiny bubbles. Its golden surface was so richly yellow that all the fire's brightness, all the heat of the oven still seemed to live in it: it shone like the skin of a fruit. It lent itself to covetous urges by camouflaging the silken folds, crisp and melting at once, both crusty and feather-soft, of a slice from the cut loaf. It wafted the aroma of its bounty in waves to the four corners of the earth; its virginal, sculptured quality drew one gently towards it, and as gently mastered one. Besson felt himself melting, flowing imperceptibly into the heart of the loaf, as though the direction of the odour had been reversed to bring its victim back to its secret lair. He plunged head first into the middle of the warm capsule, swimming, gulping down great mouthfuls of the nourishment that none thought to deny him. He felt the thick, palpable smell of hunger, the taste of flour and yeast course through his limbs like molten stone. Now the odour filled the whole sky: the streets of the town, the roof-tops, clouds, tarred asphalt on the pavement, the bodywork of cars, all had become bread, rich full-bodied loaves, a fresh and foam-light mountain of crumb and crust, crust that one breaks with a sign of the cross over the laden table and its heavy baskets of fruit, bread that opens in whiteness and love to admit the light blessing from heaven, and yields to the holy spirit come down to dwell in it.

Besson stood there a long while lost in contemplation of the bread. After this he no longer felt any hunger or thirst. Round him the signs slowly dwindled and vanished. People began to emerge from their houses again, and cars drove away, accelerating fiercely. Pigeons came fluttering down on the sidewalk, and began to waddle round in circles, uttering short liquid cooing notes.

Some time later, well on in the afternoon, Besson came out on a large square surrounded by red-brick houses. There was a parking lot in the middle of the square and, large numbers of leafless plane-trees dotted about it. Besson crossed the road and made for the church. It was a high, rather ugly building, with a Greek-style portico supported by marble columns, above which was carved the inscription: MARIA SINE LABE CONCEPTA ORA PRO NOBIS. Towards the back of the building there rose a square bell-tower, with a clock at the top of it. The clock-face was white, and had Roman numerals round the dial. The short hand pointed to a spot just past the IV, while the long one was coming up for VI. When the long hand reached the VI there was a single dull chime from the tower; the note floated away over the roof-tops like a layer of fog. Two birds flew up and zigzagged away one behind the other. Besson heard this gong-stroke echoing faintly over the square for some time afterwards: the filaments of its metallic vibrations fixed themselves in his head like a souvenir.

The dial of the clock gleamed there high on the tower like a kind of moon. Eventually he tore his eyes away from it, walked up the front steps, pushed through an old brown swing door, and found himself inside the church.

The change in atmosphere was instantaneous. Throughout the vast and shadowy nave, empty now, and up in the deep, grotto-like vaulting silence reigned, the atmosphere had a dim grey profundity about it. Fine near-transparent clouds drifted slowly round the walls, dissolving into wisps, moving above the varnished pews, spreading across the stained-glass windows. Besson caught the terrifying smell of incense, and for a moment, because of something that stirred inside him, he thought his hunger had come back. But it was not hunger. There was no name one could put to the unfamiliar feeling of distress that surged to and fro between these dank walls, that set a bell tolling, on and on, echoing away deep into the earth, telling the beads for the dead, there was nothing about it that could be known or expressed. It was the fear induced by footsteps advancing over the hollow-echoing flagstones, it was the crushing weight of the vaulted roof overhead, pressing down with ton upon ton of stone, it was the power of everything obscure and ominous, of terror made into a dwelling-place. Shuddering, Besson advanced down the nave. On either side the rows of empty pews faded into semi-darkness. Great pillars soared up like tree-trunks, and lost themselves in the pearly white and foliated radiance of the vaulting. At the end of the nave, moving towards him as he moved towards it, was the pyramidal outline of the altar, glittering in candle-light.

Besson took a few more steps down the centre of the church; then he stopped, sat down in a pew, and listened to the silence. The bustle of the streets could not penetrate these stony ramparts. And yet it was not really silence: there was too rich and dense a quality about it. Rising amid the floating particles of incense, sliding through the shadows like a thief in the night, there came a muted yet resonant murmur, a continual hum like the roar of a distant waterfall, vibrating in the ground underfoot. It was exactly as though some terrifying full-dress quarrel had taken place inside the church just a few seconds before Besson entered it, and what remained now was the mere memory of the shock-waves, the last fading tremors, the atmospheric disturbances that follow any seismic upheaval. Though silence had replaced the previous deafening uproar, it was still quivering, muttering under its breath, filling dark nooks and corners with whispered blasphemies and stifled oaths and obscene phrases.

Besson glanced around him, and, for the first time since he had walked in, saw that there were other human beings with him in the church. A number of old women, gathered round the pillars because they were near the radiators, sat mumbling incomprehensible prayers; some of them wore large black headscarves which completely hid their faces and hair, and were on their knees at the *prie-dieu*, quite still. Their bodies, swathed in black dresses and old coats, bent forward; their heads were bowed towards the ground. In the side aisles one or two old crones were lighting candles before the images, with slow, meticulous gestures.

Not far from Besson, in the same row of pews but half-hidden by shadow, a woman was sitting, and Besson examined her attentively. She was, he saw, about sixty years of age, with grey, almost white hair tied up in a mauve headscarf. Her dress was mauve too, but of a somewhat darker tone than one ordinarily saw. Her rounded back was pressed against the seat behind her; her legs, swollen by varicose veins, were set squarely on the ground; her hands lay clasped in her lap. She sat thus, staring straight ahead of her, not moving her lips. Besson could just make out her pale, deeply lined face, with its strong nose; beneath the eye there was a dark stain, as though she had been crying and mascara had run down with the tears. These brown smudges came very low, following the line of the cheek-bone, and her eyelids seemed to be a curious purplish colour, as though someone had given her a couple of shiners. She remained absolutely immobile, looking almost translucent in the gloom; all that could be seen of her now were the pale patches denoting face, neck and hands. She moved once only, to push away a strand of hair that had fallen over her forehead. She simply looked straight ahead of her with those dark-ringed eyes, indifferent to anything going on around, as though into a mirror. Besson tried to deduce, from the direction of her gaze, just what she was looking at. Her eyes were focused a little above the horizontal, he decided. If one prolonged this line of vision it came out at the top of the altar, against a kind of gilded ornament in the shape of a double palm-leaf. There was nothing above or below it. Both the Cross and the altar-piece were away to one side, where she could not see them. The Tabernacle stood to the right of her, and it seemed clear enough that it too stood beyond her range of vision. Then what was the explanation? Why did she sit there staring at this piece of decoration, with its vague resemblance to a double palm-leaf, as though it were a mountain of gold? What was it about this piece of stucco moulding that attracted her?

After some time the woman rose to her feet, picked up a handbag, and walked along the row to the aisle, her gentle, melancholy face an expressionless blank. As she passed Besson her eyes met his, and he felt his heart beat faster. Then they slipped away again, brown aureole and all, not really looking at anything, like two smooth drops of dark water in the middle of that white face.

Then Besson turned back towards the luminous hole shining at the far end of the church, and let the fear rise up in him. He breathed in the saffron-scented air, and listened to the silence throbbing around him. He was inside a boat now. On every side a wide expanse of ocean pressed against its stone hull, so that it groaned gently. A slight rolling motion rocked the marble pillars, and made the vaulting move up and down. Chandeliers swung from right to left, with a clash of crystal pendants, and on countless candles the tiny point flickered perilously. The hum of the great ship's engines was counterpointed by Besson's heart-beats, thudding in his chest and on either side of his head. Under the smooth wooden pews the floor stretched away, a vast bare grey expanse, feebly reflecting both daylight and lamplight, a lake that had frozen over. The great flagstones lay snugly side by side, so granite-hard, so peaceful, that one wanted to climb right up into the roof and then hurl oneself into empty space, come smashing down on this platitude, arms outspread in the form of a cross, to founder in a mess of blood and pulped-up flesh and bone.

Or perhaps one was imprisoned in the belly of a whale, still alive, and free to move around inside one's living captor. Piping and cavities, rucks and folds of oozy wall—these suddenly began to multiply as one watched. Clustering glands sprang from its side, pink-and-green garlands swimming in gall and shadow. Soon one would be digested. The burning lava flow would come spurting through minuscule holes in the middle of each wall, and overwhelm one. Then the frenzied dance would begin, hurling its cramps and spasms from one end of the empty sac to the other. Beyond this activated corridor came the point of final absorption: swallowed up in gold and tinkling crystal, sucked out at one stroke by this gaudy cupping-glass, one would disappear into the void.

This was it, in fact: the building had a driving urge to engulf you. You couldn't run away, you couldn't shout or make a fight of it. The cold stone weighed down on you with its millions of years, the deathless gold mocked you with the laughter of madness. It was like being a fly, trapped in that abominable flower which slowly closes its clawed and curving petals over its victims; and the perfume that issued from those hidden mouths spread like some deadly poison. Marble, amber, rubies, incense, porphyry, all were ready to hook you.

The universe had been swallowed up. Streets, cars, cafés, sky and sun, trees, pigeons—nothing of this now remained. The world had suddenly become a cavern, an underground cathedral full of huge stalactites, a concrete air-raid shelter.

Besson knew he had to act fast. He knelt on the wooden kneeler and bowed his head. He tried to say a prayer, but the words would not come any more. Then, while vaulting and walls and floor danced in fury about him, he closed his eyes and submitted himself to God.

When the danger had passed, he got up again. A sudden vast tiredness came over him, as though he had just finished an all-night train journey. He left the pew and walked down the side aisle. The black-clad women were still there, silently moving their lips. Near a painted statue of John the Baptist administering baptism, a grey-clad figure knelt, head in hands. A little further on, close to a big candelabra with half a dozen wax tapers burning in it, a group of three or four women sat waiting. Besson joined them, and took his place in the queue. He looked at the candles burning on the tray of the candelabra; the wax had run down all of them, producing the most curious excrescences. At the top of each little column, attached to the wick like a banner, was a little tongue of yellow light, burning with stubborn persistence, more ephemeral and tragic than the life of a butterfly.

Other women arrived and sat down beside Besson, taking the places of those who had gone. Finally one of them turned to him and whispered: 'It's your turn.'

Besson hesitated. Then he got up and walked across to the little black box of the confessional. He pulled the purple velvet curtain aside, and knelt down. After a few seconds there was the sound of a panel being slid open, and a little light filtered through the grille. 'Pray,' a voice whispered in his ear.

Besson listened to the lengthy muttering that followed, spoken in a breathy whisper that filled the confessional. When it was over the voice told him to say Amen.

'Amen,' said Besson.

'When was your last confession, my son?'

Besson reflected for a moment.

'It was—I think it was sixteen years ago. Fifteen or sixteen years.'

There was a brief silence.

'Why did you go so long without confessing?'

'I don't know, I—I lost my faith.'

'What sins have you committed, my son?'

Besson hesitated again.

'Almost all of them,' he said.

'Will you list them, please?' said the voice, patiently.

'It may take a long time,' Besson said.

'That's all right,' said the voice. 'We're in no hurry. What are your sins?'

'I have lied,' Besson said. 'I have been a habitual liar. I have stolen. I have blasphemed. I have had evil thoughts. And—and I have committed degrading acts. . . . I have—I have been egotistical, covetous, full of envy. I have taken pleasure in spreading harm around me. . . . I have doubted the existence of God, and of His bounty. I have been indifferent to Him. I have sworn. I have taken advantage of others for my own profit. I have been idle, and self-indulgent. I have refused to help others, to aid those who might have need of me. . . . I have scorned the poor. I have been luxurious, and full of pride, and on many occasions excessively angry. I have struck my mother. I have felt hatred for my father. I have entertained thoughts of murder, and planned criminal projects. I have committed the sin of vanity, and of complacency in vice. I have refused to follow good advice. . . . I have prayed to the Devil. I have been dishonest. I have failed to keep my promises. I have squandered other people's money. I have desired evil things, I have longed for war. I have been a libertine. I have shown lack of respect towards my parents and relations. I have killed animals.'

'Is that all?' the voice asked.

'No,' Besson said, 'no, it isn't. I have also been coarse in my behaviour. I have fallen into the sin of despair. I have rejected love. I have been cowardly, and have made insulting statements about the Church. I have—I have thought of suicide. I have felt arrogant contempt for others, and I have never loved my neighbour. I have been cruel. I have been malicious.'

'Is that all, my son?' the voice said again.

Besson reflected for a moment.

'No,' he said, 'I have committed many other sins.'

'What are they?'

'I have been impatient, ill-tempered, and unfaithful. I have committed the sin of gluttony. I have laughed at other people's misfortunes. I have never been charitable. I have been unclean both in thought and deed, and I have shown lack of respect both for my own body and for the woman's. I have committed acts of filthiness. I have soiled what was pure.'

'What else?'

'I have blasphemed on many occasions. I have said that God is dead.'

'Is that all?'

'I—I have cheated in my work. I have cheated during examinations. I have been unjust. I have refused to work. I have taken pleasure in hurting other people's feelings. I have worshipped money and beauty. I have worshipped violence. I have uttered slanders. I have transgressed against God. I have loved sinfulness.'

For a few seconds there was silence in the confessional. Besson could hear the sound of regular breathing. As he stared into darkness, his nose picked up the faint odour of box-wood. Then he bent forward to the grille once more and whispered: 'I have tried to find out too much. I believed—' He hesitated. 'I have forgotten what truth is. I have forgotten—'

'Forgetfulness is not a sin,' the voice said.

'I forgot through mere sloth. Because it suited me to forget.'

'Is that all, my son?' murmured the voice.

'I have insulted Our Lady. I have said that Jesus was a man like other men.' Besson paused a moment, thinking. 'I have failed to perform my religious duties. And this I have done deliberately, as an insult. I have not said my prayers. I have disbelieved in the life everlasting.'

'What else?'

'I can't remember anything more now. But there's plenty. I have been indifferent. And I've committed all my sins not once, but a hundred times, a thousand times, as often as possible. When temptation came, instead of thrusting it aside, I would plunge into sin, and snap my fingers at my conscience. I have ceased to be a believer. I have said—' He paused again. 'I have forgotten everything, even the sins themselves. I have been cynical and indifferent. I have thought of nothing but pleasure, my own physical pleasure.'

'Have you been happy?' the voice asked.

Besson's reply was embarrassed, almost inaudible. 'No,' he whispered.

There was a cough from the other side of the grille; and Besson suddenly realized that it was an old man's voice. Its blend of firmness and gentleness bore the weight of the years: it was a voice that had to be heard and reckoned with. It had, surely, already embarked on the road that led to death, and its murmured utterances were all darkened by this shadow, this sense of decline.

It belonged to a physically frail man, with rounded shoulders and pale grey eyes, faded now after much use. Besson longed to catch a glimpse of him, however fleeting. He pressed his face right against the holes in the grille, and tried to make out his features. But it was so dim that all he could see was a vague shadowy silhouette, and the sharp glint of gold-rimmed spectacles.

When the voice reached him again it was tremulous, as though a breath of wind had blown on it.

'Are you sorry you committed these sins?' it asked.

'I don't know,' Besson said.

'Are you sorry, now, that you committed these sins?' the voice repeated patiently.

'Sometimes, yes,' Besson said. 'Some of them.'

'Which ones?'

'Pride. And the lies, and the blasphemies—'

'Repeat after me: Eternal God, Thou art all good, and deserving of all my love—'

Hesitantly Besson whispered: 'Eternal God—Thou art all good—and deserving of all my love—'

'May you find peace,' said the voice.

Besson was touched by the simplicity of these words. He said: 'You are good—'

But the voice began to whisper, in a kind of fury: 'No, no, I am *not* good—never say that. God alone is good. God alone can judge. I am not here to judge you or to understand you, but to give you help. Only to give you help.'

He paused for a moment, then in a calmer voice murmured: 'You will find peace, my son.'

'What must I do?' Besson asked.

'Turn towards God,' the voice said. 'Learn to see Him. Love His works. His beauty is everywhere; it is that you must admire. It is that which will give you rest and peace.' He broke off for a moment. 'God's creatures speak for themselves,' he went on. 'They will show you that life is an eternal principle. Death is no more than a change in the appearances.'

'And what about animals?' Besson asked.

'God has chosen men,' the voice said slowly. 'Men have not chosen God.'

'Why do I not have faith?'

'You have faith,' the voice whispered. 'But you do not know it.'

Besson shrank into himself at this. Then the voice broke silence once more. 'You must humble yourself, my son,' it said, 'Humble yourself both in body and spirit. Renounce idle things. Kill your pride.'

The words came in groups, punctuated by that somewhat sibilant breathing. Besson let them enter him like so many tiny darts aimed at the nervous centres.

'Do you not realize that intelligence is of no use to you? You judge people and events, and think you have understood them. But you have not understood them at all, because you do not love them. Learn to question your own achievements. Feel a little self-doubt. As you did today, or else you wouldn't be here. Realize that you're not alone. Your sufferings are shared by the rest of mankind, and God is well aware of them. You are going to change your way of life. You will renounce your pursuit of self and prostrate yourself before Our Lord. It is a hard decision; but this is the price you must pay for peace of mind.'

'It *is* a hard decision,' Besson said.

'Humble yourself. Humble yourself, and be contrite.'

'What if I have no faith?'

'What do you know about it?' the voice said. 'Do not be presumptuous. Perhaps God had chosen you.'

'Then why—why does He not manifest Himself?'

'He manifests Himself. But you do not know how to see Him.'

'Yet He knows—'

'You are free within His will. Your life belongs to you. But you are free within the will of God.'

'You mean it's an illusion, then?'

'No. This is no illusion, but truth. Beyond you there exists a plane of reality which no one will ever be able to comprehend, but in which you nevertheless have your place. You are inside the circle, yes: but you are free there. If you bow to His will, if you submit yourself, then you will be free. Otherwise you will remain a slave to yourself. Root out pride from you, since pride is the prisonhouse of evil. Become as a child again. Learn anew that you are only one of God's creatures.'

There was a last period of silence, broken only by tiny creaking sounds in the wooden structure of the confessional. Besson listened to the breathing from beyond the grille: it wheezed a little, probably because of a blocked nasal passage. Then the voice continued, in a more solemn tone: 'I am going to give you absolution. While I pray I want you to repeat, several times: O my God, I am heartily sorry for having offended Thee, and I detest all my sins, because they offend Thee, my God, who art all good and deserving of all my love.'

The voice began to murmur behind the grille, and Besson, kneeling alone before the wooden partition, repeated in a low gabble: 'O my God, I am heartily sorry for having offended Thee, and I detest all my sins, because they offend Thee, my God, who art all good and deserving of all my love. O my God, I am heartily sorry for having offended Thee, and I detest all my sins, because they offend Thee, my God, who art all good and deserving of all my love. O my God, I am heartily sorry for having offended Thee, and I detest all my sins, because they offend Thee, my God, who art all good and deserving of all my love. O my God, I am heartily sorry for having offended Thee, and I detest all my sins, because they offend Thee, my God, who art all good and deserving of all my love. O my God . . . heartily sorry . . . having offended Thee . . . who art all good . . . all my love . . . detest all my sins because they offend thee . . . O my God . . . O my God . . . sorry . . . all good . . . all my love . . . sins . . . sins . . . offend Thee . . . my God . . . all good . . . deserving of all . . . sin . . . good . . . my love . . . good . . . O my God . . . O my God . . . all good . . . all my love . . . all my love . . .'

'Go in peace,' said the voice.

As Besson was walking back down the church towards the exit a sudden burst of organ music crashed out, and began to echo round the marbled walls. Besson stopped for a moment to listen to the crystal clear flow of notes from far above him, notes that rippled down into the very depths of one's soul, flooding eyes and throat with their clear, pure water, each individual drop hanging fixed and motionless like a minuscule diamond. Then the notes descended from the heights, became a 'cello, a woman's voice, stirring words that yet said nothing, that wove in and out, unbroken by any interruption, till at last, inexorably, the music plunged down and was lost in some deep subterranean abyss, and the thunderous climax sounded so deep and solemn, so slow, so full of terrifying cavernous echoes, that it seemed on the brink of fading into total silence. Overwhelmed by this great chord—so agonizingly held at the lowest limit of the human ear's capacity to receive it—and bowed down beneath the organ's vast and unleashed power, Besson once more, for the last time, muttered those magic words of repentance and oblivion: '. . . O my God . . . who art all good and deserving of all my love . . . all my love . . . because they offend Thee . . . all my sins . . .'

Then he pushed open the leather-bound wooden door, and went out into the street.

*

By way of penance, François Besson decided to do a stint as a beggar. He strolled through the town at random for a while, to find himself a suitable corner. He examined several different sites, but none of them really satisfied him. If they were not too dry, they were too rain-sodden. Either they had not enough light, or else far too much. Here the pavement was on the slope, and would be uncomfortable to sit on; there the potential pitch was right by a bus-stop. Another was too near a police-station. In one place there was somebody already installed, an old upturned hat in front of him, displaying his empty eye-socket.

Finally Besson found a corner that he liked. It was on a very busy street, with wide sidewalks, and rows of smart shops and expensive cafés. At widely-spaced intervals, on either side of the street, leafless chestnut trees rose from their protective metal cages, the mouths of which resembled radiant suns. Cars drove by, or stood parked at the kerbside. Everything shone and glittered, and the gleam of the neon signs and the streets-lamp was reflected on the tarred asphalt, with clear-cut, clean patterns of light, as though they had been washed down.

Besson settled himself on the pavement and leaned back against the wall. He put the beach-bag down beside him. Then he sat watching the crowds go by. It got dark very quickly. People became dim shadows, suddenly illuminated by the white light streaming out of cinemas and bars. Women walked along swivelling their hips, tripping on high-heeled shoes. The eyes up there in those white, mask-like faces were dull and vacant: they gave a quick glance at Besson, then moved away with indifference. The incessant flurry of footsteps made the ground vibrate, a sound both witless and somehow menacing, like a mass exodus of rats. Besson curled his legs up under him and tried to ignore it. But this proved impossible: the vibration passed right through him, like an electric current, and set him shivering. He found himself wishing he could melt into the roughcast wall behind him, shrink back into the core of all the plaster and rubble, flatten himself, become a mere membrane, a pale splash on the reddish distemper.

The crowd swam past, swag-bellied, a crazy fish opening and shutting its mouth. Faces, faces, faces—weakness and cruelty, glances from under heavy half-closed lids, thick lips opening to reveal decayed teeth, greasy hair slicked down with sour sweat, the smell of tallow, the smell of wet feet, dirt under the fingernails, more faces, degenerate faces, swollen and murderous, the sort that might have come out of hell to gibber round your skylight, yes, *there*, pale grey shadows, all in step, men, women, children, fat and thin, young and old, bald, bearded, lame, short-sighted, sexless—oh, what *slugs* they are, what jellyfish, what wretched uncivilized clowns! Here they come, waves of them, rolling and dribbling up to my window, their cheeks all a-bounce and a-quiver, materializing out of the darkness, crouching there in great heaped-up masses, then suddenly, frighteningly, springing up like so many huge elongated black rags, gliding through the air to usurp my domain: the terror of the Tongs, moaning sirens, like some

222

black and muted nightmare of life after death these ranks of human jelly come pressing and fluttering at the glass. They keep peering at me, besmirching me with their eyes, endlessly, pale ghastly creatures, cruel glances, snickers of laughter. My body is emptied like a trussed chicken's, the looks and the laughter run through it, draw blood.

Now Besson leaned forward a little, and with hand outstretched towards the shadows flitting by, began to intone, in a whining monotonous voice: 'Kind sir, kind lady. . . . Not a bite of food for two days. . . . Kind sir, kind lady . . . please spare a copper. . . . Not a bite of food for two days. . . .'

To his great surprise, several figures detached themselves from the crowd, one after another, and put a coin in the palm of his upturned hand. He kept the money there, and thanked each donor; but the shadows flitted away without saying saying a word, and vanished in the distance.

In this way he soon acquired his own special section of pavement, a kind of invisible circle with him at its centre, and a protective empty space around him. Groups of men or old women would approach, and then make a detour, giving him quick curious glances, then looking away again, attention wandering. Little by little, as time went on, Besson began to learn his new trade. It was simple enough, but required a certain amount of tact. You had to huddle up at the foot of the wall, letting your legs and the bottom part of your body sprawl like a heap of dirty rags. When a group of people passed by, you had to be careful not to scare them off: this meant keeping quite still, so that you were not mistaken for a drunk, or someone who had been taken ill. Watch the feet passing by, keep your eyes fixed on the ground. When people were just coming abreast of you, you lifted your head and looked at them with a mildly worried expression, that could not be interpreted as containing either hatred or cupidity; at which point, with a firm, decisive gesture, you stretched out your hand towards theirs, and softly—yet with as clear an articulation as possible—muttered the words 'Nothing to eat'. Then you followed their movement with your hand, as though merely asking for someone to help you up.

223

The most important thing was not to shout insults at those who went past without giving you anything, but just to let your arm drop very slowly, in a discouraged fashion. Often people would be stung by remorse and come back to make you some contribution. You also had to be careful when deciding who you were going to ask: women were the best bets, especially when on their way to a restaurant or the cinema, and escorted by a man. Children accompanied by their parents were also pretty good customers more often than not, though you had to take care not to scare them, or look them straight in the eye. They would come forward hesitantly, pushed on by their mothers, thrust their coin into Besson's hand, and run off. But as they fled they would look back over their shoulder, with those proud, nervous, inquisitorial eyes they all had. Besson also had to keep glancing up and down the street the whole time, ready to take off if a policeman appeared.

Two or three times people stopped to take a good look at him. The first of these was a man of about fifty, with a crew-cut, and wearing a navy-blue gabardine raincoat. He strolled past Besson a couple of times, then lingered on the kerbside, pretending to watch the cars go by. But his eyes kept glancing towards Besson: there was a very odd glint in them.

Then there was the very old woman who came limping up the street on a cane, step by step, till she at last drew abreast of Bessson, her puffy face thrust forward with the laborious effect she was making. Besson heard her quick, shallow breathing, interspersed with the occasional groan; then he caught sight of her legs, dragging along over the black asphalt like two granite pillars, both of them covered with huge varicose veins and bandaged ulcers. The cane tapped along the pavement to the right of her legs: it had a rubber tip. She advanced slowly, shoulders and buttocks working, a heavy, massive figure whose every step pressed into the ground and left the mark of her suffering there; heaving the solid burden of her body forward, on and on, panting, groaning, coughing, eyes fixed, eyelids snapping, mouth open, dirty strands of grey hair streaming down loose on either side of her forehead.

When the old woman drew level with Besson, she stopped, turned her head very slowly, gave him a terrible look, and began to mutter incomprehensible noises: '*Bé*,' she mumbled, '*Hé* . . . *Mana* . . . *Bé.* . . .' And it was as though no one on earth would ever, from now on, be able to die. It was a kind of boundless malediction, projected through the broken utterance of this creature standing beside him, a piteous cry of outrage that shattered the silence of the street with its longing for death, for peace at the last. She stood there in front of Besson like a statue sculpted in grease, heavy-faced, mouth open, eyelids snapping continuously. Without a word or gesture she still contrived to demand, to implore, using instead her bloated bosom and deformed legs, her aged hands, her sparse, straggling hair, her hunched and dirt-encrusted back. Like a sick rhinoceros, she was looking around her for the instrument of her own destruction. She wanted to see the darts, she was impatient to find some strong enemy lying in wait for her, ready to floor her with a single blow and then—ah, ecstasy—choke the life out of her. But no such saviour appeared. The sharpened weapons remained hidden behind the arras, and the air continued to flow into her lungs, without interruption. This was why she gave Besson that terrible look: it was, quite simply, an appeal for someone to kill her. But did death really exist? Was it not a mere legend, an abominable legend created specially for her, to give her hope, to make her bear her affliction with patience, and accept the agony she suffered? There was nothing, on the face of it, to stop someone chopping her to pieces. She would have collapsed on the ground, bleeding sparsely and with difficulty. Even if one were to carve her limb from limb, and decapitated her, there and then, in the gutter, life would still persist in her; no eternal repose would descend on *her* body.

To be cursed by an old woman who wanted to die was something Besson could not stand for long. He got up, grabbed his beach-bag, and rushed off down the street without looking back.

Later, he went and had a meal at the Soupe Populaire. Here, in a bare room illuminated by the livid glow of strip neon lighting,

the down-and-outs stood eating at a clean, sterilized counter.
The menu had been pinned on the wall:

> Soup
> Boiled Beef and Carrots
> Bread and Cheese
> Fruit

Besson ate quickly, standing between an old man in a threadbare
suit and a bearded tramp with a large wen on the back of his neck.
Nobody said a word. Men and women bent over their plates,
toothless jaws working rapidly. The ultra-white light gleamed on
polished zinc and plastic, making the filth and ugliness of this
human flotsam stand out all the more by comparison. A strange
mixed odour of stew and disinfectant floated in the chilly, silent
air. The bare room reeked of shame and embarrassment.

When he had finished eating, Besson left the canteen and walked
through the night smoking a cigarette. It was his last packet.
When that was gone he would have to pick up tab-ends from the
pavement, or else smoke rolled-up newspaper, which has a foul,
acrid, sugary stench while burning.

He climbed down some steps to the river-bed, near the caissons
of the new bridge, and spent some little while hunting round for a
snug corner where he could sleep, without being too much
exposed to the icy wind that was set to blow steadily all night.

Chapter Eleven

The river flows along its channel through the heart of the town—
François Besson does hard labour—The story of Siljelcoviva—Mass
attack by nocturnal enemies—François Besson kills an unknown
person—A walk through the dark tunnel under the town esplanade

On the eleventh day, François Besson went down to the river
bed and found himself a hiding-place from which he could watch
the construction team at work on the bridge. The caissons had
already been sunk in mid-stream, and now sprouted metal
structures which a man was banging away at with a hammer, as hard
as he could. Under the greenish-grey sky, and the continual rain
—now a downpour, now a misty drizzle—the site looked rather
like a gigantic shell-hole blown in the middle of the river-bed.
A little further down, not far from the next bridge (where Besson
had concealed himself) a bulldozer went juddering along, pushing
up walls of stones in front of it to stop the water overflowing its
channel. A multiplicity of sounds spread clear through the frosty
air, accompanied by a whiff of rotting sewerage and heaps of old
leaves: the river's muted roar, a gravel-screech of shifting stones,
the tapping hammer, the high snarl of labouring engines, men's
voices shouting insults at one another.

On either side of the river-bed—now divided in two by its
temporary dam—the black mass of the town was visible, all its
roofs agleam. A few curious bystanders had gathered on the *quais*,
and were leaning over the balustrade to watch the free circus
below. Further downstream there was a third bridge, with five
arches, that ran right under the town: the swift-flowing stream
disappeared into the three central black holes, leaving the outer
two empty.

There was a great variety of colour, too; but all so low—laid on

227

at ground level, as it were—that it was really better not to try and look at it. Such dirty, depressing colours, too, spreading slowly over one another, like spilt paint, mingling with the sounds and smells, shifting across the silt, drifting slowly over the water, dispersed and suspended in air, the better to force themselves past your defences and bend you to their will. Hideous yellows, the yellow of urine or dead skin. Pinks, creams, indeterminate greens and greys, all tracing their own paths and channels. The pebbles were hard, occasionally broken in two or ground into a mess of half-buried rubble. The arches of the bridge overhead were covered with moss, and all around lay an anonymous litter of tin cans, slowly turning into rust. The rain had penetrated everywhere, permeating every object, making things porous, soft, friable. A light yet sluggish mist rose silently from the ground, and seemed to follow the downstream flow of the river, a few yards above its surface. From all sides there came the gurgle of falling water, and every crack in the walls dripped continually. It was like being in an underground lavatory, where the constant passage of dirty, disinfectant-laden water produces all those blue encrusted cracks in the enamel. Endlessly scoured and washed, this surface, worn by the passage of liquids, new by dint of being old, slippery with layers of grease and soap, a non-stop exhibition of superfoaming detergent.

This was where one lived now, in the long channel down which life's waste products flowed. Whether as tears, or sweat, or urine, water ran continually from the earth's body, and passed away in the direction of that vast septic tank the sea: an essential process, part of the cycle of truth, along with the boiling, writhing movement of organic matter reacting against salt, clouds surging up the sky and letting their delicate pink and grey veils be blown down the corridors of the wind, and then the fall of million upon million separate droplets, returning to the earth once more, filling as many tiny expectant mouths to overflowing, bringing them refreshment, satisfaction. Such a process had its own rhythm, allied with that of day and night, but longer and more terrible: less independent, too, since water never ceased to pass in and out

228

of this porous globe that was the world. Mud breathed damply, sewers poured down to their outflow, streams joined up, mountain rills ran till exhausted; and here, down the middle of its great triangular crevasse, the river flowed on, without interruption or obstacle, muttering day in day out with the same unchanging nasal voice, like an aircraft in the sky, pouring into its own fountain-basin the water which could never run dry, water everlasting, water softly turning its colourless magic wheel, coiled feminine body that would never cease from parturition.

To attain freedom would have needed whole centuries of dryness. Little by little the desert ought to replace earth's liquid element. Raped oases, forests suddenly burnt up under a rain of napalm, mountains hardened by savage frosts and standing alone in the night, gleaming sheer through the darkness like dagger blades.

Then one would have had this bright peace, solitude and calm outstretched like a petrified corpse in the hot-and-cold air. Fine-grained sand would have blown across the sharp upper edges of the rocks; nothing would remain, in the way of vegetation, except sharp-spiked cactus and aloes.

Besson smoked a cigarette he had picked up at the foot of the wall. Lurking behind the bushes (which were stuffed full of old bits of paper) he watched the group of workmen go about their task. They were all young, most of them raggedly dressed Arabs. They went to and fro across the shingle carrying spades and buckets, for all the world as though they were going to make sand-pies. Beneath their hats or caps their faces were grim, bearded, thick with dust, They all had strongly marked lines at each corner of the mouth, and their eyes were very-deep-set. A little apart from them stood a big red-faced man in a leather jerkin, barking out sharp orders.

Besson hesitated for a moment. Then he picked up his beach-bag and walked across to the site. When he reached the working area the labourers glanced at him quickly and turned away again. The big red-faced man called out to him: 'What d'you want, then?'

'Have you got a job I could do?' Besson asked.

The foreman looked him up and down for a moment.

'Yes,' he said, 'if you know how to handle a shovel.'

'Could I start in right away?'

The big man came closer, tugging a notebook out of his pocket.

'Hold on,' he said. 'You got a work permit?'

'No.' said Besson.

'What are you? Yugoslav? German?'

'No.'

'Italian, then?'

'No,' said Besson, 'I'm French.'

The man removed a cigarette-stub from his mouth and ground it out under one heel.

'Fine,' he said. 'That's all right, then. What's your name?'

'Besson,' said Besson.

The man took a pencil and wrote the name down in his note-book. Then he checked the time by his gold wristwatch and wrote that down too. Then he jerked his thumb at a great heap of mixed sand and pebbles.

'Go and get yourself a shovel, over there by the diggers. You can help separate out the sand. You've clocked in at half past ten. O.K. then, get cracking.'

So there on the river-bed Besson began to dig up the sand, rhythmically driving his shovel into the resistent mass, then lifting it over a kind of mechanical sieve. Through one narrow orifice the machine disgorged the sand it had taken in, while the pebbles and heavy gravel were channelled into another, rather larger one. Without exchanging a word, or even looking at one another, backs slightly stooped, the workmen went about their various tasks—pushing wheelbarrows across to the caissons, crunching over the shingle, mixing concrete, burrowing into the sandhills with rasping shovels, swarming up scaffolding, screwing bolts through iron bars. The foreman kept up a ceaseless flow of orders in that powerful voice of his, with hoarse shouts such as 'Come on now, move yourself!' or 'You over there—you asleep or something?' or 'Faster, you lot! Faster than that!'

The site was a minuscule centre of action in the midst of the river, rather like a cluster of ants on a scrap of meat: here hope, and despair, and the individual will were all annihilated. Everything was clear-cut, translucent; everything had its measure and its appointed end. Time was the face of a chronometer, space a surveyor's instrument.

Here in the centre of the town, surrounded by fluctuating noises and vague movements, here in this deserted ragion life was a tough business. All elements were hostile. The surface of the sandhills rasped and tore at your hands, gave you twisted ankles, made the back of your head ring with the noise of a hammer driving nails home one after another. This was the way you had to set about digging, with fury and hatred. Make sparks fly from pickaxe or shovel as you banged them against some buried rock. Trample down rotten branches, dead weeds, a tangled mess of detritus. Keep your eyes fixed on the stubbon soil, and conquer the sheer weight of inertia by one quick upwards jerk of your loins. Make the dust fly far and wide, fling it high int he air, scatter it on the wind, while the machine's chattering mouth gobbles up gravel by the hundredweight, chews and disposes of it between those iron jaws. Earth and men merged indistinguishably, became the same substance, mere mud, a dead weight of mud dragging at your arms and peeling off shovel or mattock with a heavy squelching sound. It was the mud, now, which nursed ignoble schemes, planned acts of degradation, wet spreading mud, a lake of grey and malevolent shingle, sneering, provocative—or, sometimes weeping damply in the folds of its old and whorish skin. It had ideas, it was covered with words or symbols, penetrated by feelings. Men, women, children, animals too—dogs and their fleas, cats, birds, horses led to the slaughterhouse, lions imprisoned in their cages, mice with their necks broken by snap-back traps, flies caught on fly-papers, swatted mosquitoes, spiders and cockchafers, boiling lobsters, dumb fish dying with mouths agape and bolting eyes, red ants drowned in latrines, slaughtered eland and bison, tortoises, dodos, kiwis—all of them were there, now, in the sands and gravels, they had been resuscitated on the face of the earth. There was no end to the killing and maiming of them, pale insubstantial ghosts though they were: one cut them off from the world just like that, with shovel or mattock, a single thrust of arms and loins sent them into the steel maw which ground them to powder.

What had to be defeated, then, was the cruelty of horizontal surfaces. Shoulders hunched, Besson dug away at the sandhill as though bent on creating a new mountain. He would have liked to tilt up the earth's surface and turn it into a towering, insurmountable rampart. The shovel moved to and fro almost of its own volition, and under his clothes sweat and dust mingled. The noise of the hole being dug sang in his ears, and suddenly he felt as though he was going to reach the centre of the world. Through this cavern, created by frenzy, look, the lava comes surging up, swells, blasts out into the air like some gigantic scarlet mushroom. Over the town and the nearby hills there falls a soft, unending rain of fire, soothing as glass, and with it returns that great silence which should never have left the world; life, thus abruptly cut short, has at last ceased to disfigure the high beauty of matter. All it needed was one workman on a river spit, armed with an old battered shovel, to release the soaring pyrotechnical splendours of truth.

*

François Besson worked all day. The gang was made up as follows:

Foreman: Candéla.

Mechanics: Miraulac, Zediaf, Douski.

Air-hammer operators: Panelli, Andréa, Wurth, Van Woow.

Welder: Karl Schultz.

Labourers: Abdul Karim, Mamadou Badia, Cimpeanu, Siljelcoviva, Ocijek, Sedov, Miroslav Kocejve, Oberti, Machan, Haddar, Guenès, Besson, Mohamed Amar, Omar Khelifa, Said Labri.

Bulldozer operators: Dietrich (absent), Lanfranchi.

Exhaustion came slowly: it seemed to rise from the ground and pass into one's arms. Hour by hour the weight of dust accumulated on the toiling gang seemed heavier, and the men hacking away at their stony sandhills could no longer doubt that this time, at least, they would have to admit defeat. At half past twelve, without saying a word, they downed tools and gathered in the lee of the caissons to eat. Besson shared their meal: he got a hunk of bread and a slice of garlicky sausage, and drank two or three mouthfuls of red wine from the bottle they passed round. Then he wiped his mouth with the back of his filthy hand and smoked a cigarette given him by Siljelcoviva, the Yugoslav. He cracked a few jokes, and joined with the others in making rude remarks about the foreman, who had gone off to have his lunch in a bar on the *quai*. The wind began to rise and one of the men got up and lit the brazier. He poured a little petrol on the charcoal, and put a match to it. The others gathered in a circle around the fire, and sat there smoking and rubbing their hands.

A black dog that looked as though it had the mange began to prowl round the group in quest of food. Sedov, Machan, and Schultz, the German, shied stones at it. The dog jumped out of the way, but refused to move on: it stood there, not budging an inch, just out of range of the stones, yellow eyes fixed on the men and their brazier.

Siljelcoviva, who was sitting beside Besson, began to tell Oberti the story of his life. He had decided to leave Yugoslavia when he was eighteen, and had crossed the Adriatic in a row-boat, together with a friend of his. They had set out from Korcula, and spent three days and nights at sea before reaching the coast of Italy. After that they had spent five years wandering around picking up work where they could. But money was hard to earn, so they had started stealing from cars. Then one evening when they were breaking into a villa near Rome the police arrived. Siljelcoviva had been keeping a look-out in the garden, and he managed to get away. But his friend had been caught. Siljelcoviva was forced to make tracks back up north, and succeeded in crossing the frontier over the mountains. He had no idea what had become of his friend. The friend's name was Michael, and he was a bit older

233

than Siljelcoviva. It stood to reason they were after him too, though. If he could find a way to do it, he'd get on a boat for America, and—

At this point the foreman came back, and work was resumed. The afternoon passed like the morning, so slowly that Besson felt he had been there for years. The day wore on little by little; the river continued to flow.

About six o'clock work stopped. The men stacked tools and went off to wash their hands in the river. Some of them combed their hair in little pocket mirrors, smoked a cigarette, chatted a bit. Then they filed past the foreman, each collecting some notes and two or three coins. The sky was overcast, and beyond the *quais* the lights of the town glittered through a fine mist. Soon the workmen trooped off, in groups of two or three, up the steps that led into town.

Now the old lifeless atmosphere settled back amid the debris of the construction site, and other sounds became aubidle once more: the peaceful gurgle of moving water, the distant roar of breakers on the ebbing tide. The air got chillier, shadows spread and thickened in every hollow. Night odours began to stir abroad, the lingering smell of dead vegetation and humus.

*

Some while later, when night lay black on the river-bed, Besson went over and sat himself down by the half-finished bridge. He had a pile of shingle under him, and his back was propped against the cold stonework of the caisson. Then he stared straight ahead of him, trying to make out what was happening in the darkness. Humidity was coming down from the valley in waves, but it had no shape, and made no sound. The town floated, as though in air, like an illuminated Zeppelin, with vast and inky abysses taking shape everywheie below it. The river's flow, too, was audible but invisible. Its moving mass advanced in poised and solitary power, at the heart of darkness, like an escalator held between the twin ramps of the *quais*. Pebble-ridges, bushes, bulldozers, old planking, sand-bars—all had vanished. Objects were successively captured by blackness, kept fading away. Besson tried to make them reappear by dint of imagination, but they never remained the same. Their ghost-shapes became subtly inflated and distorted, wavered as though through several layers of murky water. Pale handkerchiefs fluttered in the wind, then disappeared—where, no one could tell. Contorted silhouettes rose up, so near that it seemed possible to put out one's hand and touch them, yet at the same time so distant that the mere sight of them turned one dizzy.

Besson's arms and legs were trembling with fatigue. He leaned back against the stone bastion and closed his eyes. For a while he remained thus, quite motionless, breathing regularly. He may have fallen asleep. Then, abruptly, he was roused from his torpid state by the sound of footsteps. There came a heavy crackling noise from the bushes: he could hear it quite distinctly. The footsteps advanced slowly, dislodging small pebbles, breaking dry twigs, bending damp ones, squelching over the sand. They stopped for a few seconds, so that the muted rumble of falling water could be heard once more; then, with some hesitation, they began again, on tip-toe, shoes squeaking, the ground beneath them crackling like so much straw.

Besson sat up uneasily and peered this way and that through the darkness. But whichever way he turned, left, right, behind, in front of him, visibility remained nil. It was impossible to tell where the footsteps were coming from. Sometimes they seemed almost on top of Besson, and he could hear the sound of breathing quite clearly. Sometimes, though, they reached him blurred by distance, and it was hard to be sure whether they were footsteps or ordinary river noises. Besson held his breath to listen the better. But he could no longer detect anything: the silence and the roar of water were so intense that all other noises faded before them, as though overlaid by the long wail of a train-whistle, screaming through the night.

Soon, however, the number of noises began to increase. There was the faint dragging sound produced by some sort of soft creature as it crept over the ground, scuffing grains of sand aside with its mandibles. Tiny popping reports could be heard on all sides, like seed-pods bursting. Pebbles were suddenly dislodged, setting off small inexplicable avalanches. Now and then, right beside Besson's ear, there would come the precise abrasive scratching noise of some rodent, the silken rustle of a spider scuttling by. Bats were abroad too, swooping and fluttering just overhead like wisps of burning paper. Winged creatures of some sort—with black shiny bodies, almost certainly—went buzzing past, a few yards above the ground. Worms wriggled through topsoil, snakes uncoiled in the grass. In front of Besson, advancing like an army to the attack, came every variety of parasite: fleas, ticks, lice, bugs, hopping from pebble to pebble, blind, but guided by the smell of blood, prickly-bodied, velvety feelers groping for flesh, suckers and probosces already stirring in antici-pation on those microscopic heads. And like some gigantic moth with the death's-head pattern on its back, a vampire bat now began to fly around, in wide circles, fluttering its hairless wings with a soft, near-inaudible sound that was, nevertheless, full of horror and menace.

Besson stiffened, eyes wide open, ready to defend himself. By now tiny feet had begun to alight on him momentarily, and he could feel wings—lighter than the breath of air from a fan—brush across his face. Insects were beginning to crawl up his legs, searching between the hairs for a good spot to gorge themselves. Little pricking points jabbed at his forehead, his cheeks, even underneath his clothes, making him shudder at the contact. The eggs were laid in his bloodstream, and the tainted fluid spread beneath the skin, raising swellings at each point of contact. This, called for preventive action. Besson rubbed his hand across his face, ran his fingers through his hair, slapped at his trouser-legs and scratched himself wherever he could reach—under the arm-pits, on the stomach, at the back of the neck. But it was useless: the more he scratched himself, the more numerous his invisible assailants became. By now every noise had assumed tangible form: they descended on him *en masse*, whining and humming, covering him from head to foot with the whirr of their wing-cases, busy crunching jaws, hoarse breathing. They stung, tickled, licked, punctured. They slipped their darts into the warm white tender flesh and sucked the fresh blood which only such night-time victims yield.

The sound of footsteps grew closer, more threatening: now they were moving round the caisson against which Besson leant, pressing heavily on the damp earth. Besson could hear feet crunching over shingle, one behind the other, and brittle twigs snapping like bones. There was no mistaking the sound. The animal must have sensed that a man was there by the bridge: it prowled with slow deliberation, gradually cornering its victim. Besson tried to picture the black silhouette now only a few yards away from him, back arched, watching him with phosphorescent eyes. It was a wolf, perhaps, or some wild beast with pricked-up ears and quivering nostrils. His jaws would be salivating, and his throat alive with tiny suppressed growls that he emitted, despite himself, out of sheer greed. Cruelty was a natural element on this lithe shadowy beast, and his slack chops doubtless revealed rows of well-aligned teeth, all knife-hard and knife-sharp. The footsteps advanced, circled round, again and again, unwearyingly, till Besson's head was whirling. Hatred had closed its ring about him: someone had decided that he must die. Heart pounding, his whole body sweating despite the icy air, Besson stepped out in pursuit of this noisy trail-blazer. For a few seconds the crackling noises stopped again. The darkness became more terrifying: Besson braced himself for the assault, expecting to be pinned down, as in a straightjacket, by some dark, violent creature, all teeth and claws. But nothing happened. Then the danger seemed to lose its intensity in the darkness, carrying back years and years of life, melting its obstructive hazard of agony and crime into a huge and distant cloud. Besson half convinced himself he was out of the wood.

But he was wrong. Suddenly the footsteps began again, over the pebbles, and Besson realized it was a man walking. A heavy, awkward, still-invisible shadow, weaving along beside the river on two uncertain legs. The crunch of his feet on the shingle sounded louder as he passed under the arch of the bridge. Like a giant, and wrapped in soot-black rags, the man lurched forward at random over hillocks and holes, tripping over tin cans, shattering mouldy old crates to pieces, twisting his ankles on rotten branches, crunching through carpets of dead leaves, skidding on silt and shingle, floundering in mud-holes—and keeping this up, yard after yard, in the exact direction of the caisson where Besson was sitting. He moved blindly, like a tank, face thrust forward, mouth open, breathing with difficulty. His wheezing, panting efforts were all too audible now, and so were the flapping and rubbing noises his various garments made. The atmosphere was filled with his strong, gamey smell, the smell of a man with unwashed feet and pocketfuls of stubbed-out old dog-ends, a nauseating mixed aroma of stale wine-dregs and perspiration. A dark black shape, slinking through the shadows like a deeper shadow himself, frizzy hair blowing in the wind, he still kept coming on, and on. His eyes gleamed snow-bright in his smoke-grimed face, and his teeth were bared in a glinting lopsided grin. Here he came, hands outstretched, without knife or gun or anything capable of piercing a man's lungs, skewering his throat. Here he came, neither from in front nor from behind, but from all sides at once, with that curious bearing which suggested a victim hell-bent on revenge, feeling his way gently during lulls in the invisible wind, pushing his halo of fear before him. He was not a person one could forget. He dragged his feet forward over the uneven ground, an innocent stripped of his crimes, offering the fat of his belly and the gristle in his face to any unknown pigsticker's spear. He had no real strength, and his dim silhouette remained nameless. Yet he was approaching, making straight for Besson, without pity, almost with indifference. In the night of nothingness, here in this god-forsaken corner of the world, he was still *trying*. His will held. He did his best. He was still blazing a noisy trail in pursuit of his ignoble purpose; he had not been sufficiently chastised. The whip had humiliated him in vain. Though his neck had been clipped by the iron collar, and passers-by had spat in his nameless face, it had all gone for nothing. He refused to understand. He still had to go on putting one foot in front of the other, even though this led him, slowly, step by step, to further punishment. Sins and vices were not enough for him, the cold grey desert of the day had not taught him all he needed to know. His water-swollen feet and varicose legs had not yet had their full ration of pain. Still he came on. He was very close now, and Besson could almost feel the regular waft of his breath against his, Besson's, face. He loomed horribly out of the dark abyss behind the bridge, still moving straight for his target as though along some cold, taut wire, like a tramcar on its rails, with all lights extinguished. As Besson listened to the crunching sound of his footsteps, each individual tread seemed to last longer and longer, as though the foot were about a yard long. Every two seconds or so there came the noise of shingle and pebbles being crushed down, an alarming *crrrk*, *crrrrk*, *crrrrk* that went right through Besson's head. The sky, the surface of the river, the bridges, the twinkling lights of the town floating buoyantly in mid-air—all were subsumed in this vast human silhouette, its black garments outspread like the wings of an albratross.

'Who goes there?' Besson shouted, and again: 'Who goes there?' But his voice was strangulated, not loud enough even to raise an echo.

Then he stood up, back still pressed against the caisson, to face the enemy. He waited, while the minutes ticked away: they might as well have been hours. Heart thudding, eyes hot, vision starred with bright diatomic patterns, legs and arms turning to water, he stood there watching for the monster to materialize. The head would appear first, perhaps, very pale, and floating, as though a detached entity, between two layers of mist. Or maybe the hands, all twenty fingers outstretched, tipped by dirty grey nails. He counted the steps under his breath: two, three, four, five, six, seven, eight, nine, ten. Eleven. Twelve. Thirteen, fourteen, fifteen, sixteen. Seventeen. Eighteen. Nineteen, twenty, twenty-one. Twenty-two. Twenty-three. Twenty-four, twenty-five, twenty-six, twenty-seven. Twenty-eight, twenty nine . . . Thirty, thirty-one. Thirty-two, thirty-three. Thirty-four. Suddenly he felt as though an icy fist had grasped the back of his neck. His heart stopped beating, and a long shudder ran through his body. He put up a hand and tried to free himself, but his hand met only empty space. He half turned, and looked: nothing. He stretched out his arm to its full extent. Still nothing. Then his fear hardened into anger. He stopped listening to the sound of the footsteps, and began to mutter throatily, things like: 'I'll get you—you're there somewhere—I know it, I know it, I'm going to get you—see if I don't get you!'

Muscles tensed, he gathered himself to spring. His hand scrabbled on the ground, got hold of a big sharp stone, grasped it tight. The crunching footsteps were right on top of him now. Three more yards. Two more—Suddenly, like water gurgling in the pipe under the taps, a voice began to whisper in his ear: a voice, a breathy babble, a terrible humming sound, inarticulate, yet the very essence of life, worming its way into the very centre of his brain, seeking a hiding-place. This gabble of meaningless words reached him in the same instant as the man's physical self, and it was as though one had suddenly passed into a vacuum-chamber. The man loomed out of the night in front of Besson, as though to swallow him up, a vast swaying mass all hung about with rags.

Besson gave a strangulated cry, hurled himself forward in blind fury, and struck. The edged stone in his fist hit something soft and slightly resilient. He struck again. The black silhouette slowly crumpled up and collapsed on the shingle, with a tiny moan and a rustle of clothing. Besson crouched over the body, raining blows on its prostrate limbs, his arm bouncing back each time he struck. He went on pounding away until the stone hit a softer part, slipped out of his hand, and went rolling across the ground. Then he got up and looked down at his feet. He saw there was something lying there, but no one could have said what it was. It made a kind of dark hump on the river-bed. The clothes were spread over it like an old coverlet, and from underneath there trickled little rivulets of some thick black tar-like liquid, which vanished in the gaps between the pebbles.

Everything was absolutely still again. Besson picked up his

beach-bag and walked off along the line of the river. He no longer felt any desire to sleep. He stopped for a moment and looked at the lighted windows above the *quai*, and the blue haloes of light from the street-lamps. Then he plunged into the long tunnel that ran under the town. He cou¹ ¹ hear the sharp, resonant sound of people's footsteps on the vaulting overhead, and the susurrus of car-tyres moving to and fro. He could also hear the echoes of his own tread rebombinating against the walls, and smell the deathly odour, that lay hidden at the heart of darkness. He plunged forward through this closed cylinder, where no daylight ever penetrated, his whole body exposed and in agony, like a small scrap of reason and common sense afloat on the bitter ocean of folly.

At one point he passed a secondary gallery, at the bottom of which four or five tramps had installed themselves. They had lit a fire, using old broken boxes for fuel, and were now either asleep or drinking: not a word passed between them. Besson hid behind a pillar and watched them for a moment. Then he made a detour, and continued his walk alongside the big central sewer, through which the river flowed with a noise like thunder. Ten minutes later he came out on the far side of town, facing the sea.

Chapter Twelve

In the public toilets—François Besson goes on a journey—Walking and looking about one—The earth seen from a dirigible balloon—The breath of eternity—A bird circling alone in the sky—Conversation between two children on the beach: a matter of monks and candlesticks—Between past and future—How François Besson became blind by staring at the sun

ON the twelfth day, François Besson began by going to the public toilets for a wash and a shave. He found himself in a big old strong-smelling room, with very clean walls and floor and ceiling, all covered with white porcelain tiles. On the left-hand side, close to the entrance, was an old woman sitting on a stool, and immersed in a paper. In front of her was a table, on which stood a little bowl with a few low-denomination coins in it. The first wall was occupied by a row of wash-basins with mirrors above them. The second was empty, the third had the urinals along it, and the fourth was accounted for by six closed toilets, of which five were marked 'Free' and one 'Engaged'. Men came and went without saying a word. They washed their hands in the basins, combed their hair in the mirrors, dried themselves on the roller-towels. Others urinated facing the wall, pressed into the hollows of the bright white porcelain stalls, only half protected by the shallow divisions between them. They did not look at each other, apart from two or three who flashed quick furtive glances at their neighbours. Some stood at the mirrors and blew their noses, with a loud trumpeting sound, after, which they would stride out briskly, tossing a small coin into the bowl on the old woman's table as they passed, with a tinkle of falling metal.

Besson shaved himself in very leisurely fashion. First he plugged in his electric razor, and the motor began to buzz. Then he ran the razor up and down his cheeks, very slowly, listening to the rasp of the rotary blades as they sliced through the stubble. In some places his beard was tougher than in others, and he had to go over the patch four or five times, giving an involuntary grimace when a hair was pulled out or a pimple removed. His face looked much thinner in the mirror, and the electric light shone directly on his dark eyes, so that they had a bright gleam in them. Daylight only just struggled through to this underground region, and light-bulbs glittered along the walls like so many drops of water. Besson held this buzzing, slightly rounded object in his right hand. He was much attached to his electric razor; he would have hated to lose or break it. Inside that plastic shell the motor revolved at great speed, while the tiny helical blades shaved through endless stubble, flush with the skin, setting up their minute and cushioning current of warm air. The motor was very smooth and efficient: it vibrated smoothly against hand and cheek, nothing more, with a noise that sounded as though it could go on for ever. Holding it was like travelling in an aircraft, drawn effortlessly through the air by four droning engines, sitting safely inside a metal fuselage and watching the patchwork earth slide by far below.

At one point there was the sound of flushing water from the toilet marked 'Engaged'. Besson, watching in the mirror above the basin, saw the toilet-door open, and a tall, powerfully built man come out. He was, Besson noticed, going a little bald on top. He stopped for a moment to button his overcoat. He had a rosy complexion and a sharp, aquiline nose. His deep-set eyes twinkled with vigour and affability. He picked up a brief-case and hurried out, whistling as he went. The rattle of a coin in the bowl accompanied his departure.

When he had finished shaving, Besson put his razor away in a red case, and put the case in the beach-bag. Then he washed his hands and sluiced his face with cold water and combed his hair. He also swallowed two or three mouthfuls of water, which smelt of disinfectant.

He hoped he might get out of the public toilets without paying,

244

but when he drew level with the table the old woman looked up and stared at him over the top of her paper, and Besson was forced to put a coin in the bowl.

Outside, the streets of the town were bustling with life, and the sky was an unbroken blue. Besson counted the money which the foreman had given him, and walked off in the direction of the bus-station. He was going to take a little trip, he decided; he was going to get out of this hellish town, where the houses just sat and sat for ever on the tarred asphalt. Besides, he ran the risk of meeting people he had known—his parents, Marthe and the little red-haired boy, Josette, Bayard, Siljelcoviva, even the police, who were liable to slap a murder charge on him.

When he got to the station he found about a dozen buses there, standing by the kerbside, or manoeuvring slowly into their parking-space. People were waiting in queues, behind various rusty signboards set up at the top of poles. Most of these carried very curious combinations of words and figures, such as:

9 A PESSICART	LAS PLANAS
108 FABRON	10 12
6 ISOLA	ROQUESTERON
AEROPORT	
SAVONA–GENOA	B 444

People elbowed their way through the waiting crowds. Old women sat on the benches with baskets on their knees, and children ran about in all directions, screaming shrilly. From time to time a bus would open its doors, and the crowd would surge in, pushing and jostling. The engine would start up under the mud-encrusted bonnet, and keep ticking over, its every vibration transmitted shudderingly to bodywork and windows. Crates and cases were being loaded on the roof-racks, and men in dark blue uniform, with stained caps pushed to the backs of their heads, stood smoking on the kerbside or shouting at each other. An Arab wandered round trying to sell carpets. A little man with a brown moustache and a tray of confectionery balanced on his head threaded his way through the crowd, singing:

245

'It's me who makes 'em and sells 'em, by golly,
But it's my wife who blows all the lolly . . .'

Newspaper kiosks displayed their motley wares, klaxons sounded, petrol fumes rose in the air, trafficators winked on and off. This was the place of departure, the centre from which people fled the town. The routes to every different destination converged here in this dusty square, mile upon mile of baking or muddy asphalt winding its solitary way through the empty countryside. From here people took off for foreign towns, for unknown territories covered with sprouting jungles of olive and vine. They encountered deserts striped in red and green, great savannahs, hazy oases, gorges running through deep faults in the mountains. They were journeying towards hunger and thirst, and mystery, and fear. Each of them had dressed up for the occasion, and buckled the straps round his luggage, and packed a cold meal to take along—not forgetting a bottle of wine. Besson wandered among the groups at random, soaking himself in this atmosphere, this smell of departure. Little by little uneasiness began to creep up inside him, accompanied by something much resembling hope.

Finally he picked a bus, and joined the queue of passengers waiting to board it. Nothing happened for a few moments; then the doors creaked open, and people began to file inside. It was a splendid white coach, almost brand-new, with anti-glare windows and strips of chromium-plated steel that glinted in the sunlight. The engine was already running, vibrating rhythmically, so that everything which could be made to judder did so. Besson was among the last passengers aboard; he walked down the aisle, head bent, looking for somewhere to sit down. There was a vacant seat near the back, and he dropped into it without looking any further. Then he put his beach-bag between his knees, and sat there, waiting. Beside him, pressed against the window, was a young girl, conversing in gestures with her fiancé, who had stayed outside on the sidewalk. She was so close to the glass that her breath made semi-circles of condensation on it, and her eyes never left the man below, whose head barely came level with the window. She

246

kept waving to him. Once or twice she stood up and put her mouth to some aperture at the top of the window. 'Mind you write to me,' she called out. 'Lots and lots!' She even tried to get her arm through the gap so as to touch the man's hand, but merely succeeded in skinning her knuckles. Then she sat down again and exhibited the scratch through the window, waving her left hand. The man outside lit a cigarette to keep himself in countenance. He was a skinny boy with a crew-cut and a brand-new blue suit.

A few seconds later the bus moved off, manoeuvring slowly out of the bus-station, sounding its horn to clear a path through the crowd. The passengers sank back in their pullman seats and clung to the metal hand-grips. Every jolt bounced their bodies up and down; the vibrations of the engine set their jaws and the fleshy parts of their arms quivering. They drove through the town with the main traffic stream. Up in front, on a higher seat than the rest, sat the driver, turning the wheel this way and that, thrusting his feet down on the pedals, shifting the gear-levers: you could hear the insulated growl of the engine responding to his directions. The cylinders fired smoothly in sequence, and every now and then there came the mysterious sound of compressed air escaping, rather like a sneeze. The lights at the crossroads changed to yellow, then to red. The bus braked to a standstill, and every head jerked backwards. These jolts and vibrations made the passengers look a little ridiculous. Bodies swayed slackly in their seats, passive victims now, manipulated in unison by each plunge or check of the wheels. A jay-walker crossed the road right in front of the bus, and everyone swayed, as though to underline the incident. All down the aisle conversation had broken out. Women wrapped up in thick woolly coats were talking about the weather—would it rain or clear up? One was discussing the ulcer on her leg. Men pointed out houses, or cars. A soldier was trying to make conversation with a plain young girl who said not a word back.

Gradually the bus worked its way out of town, taking a very, straight road that ran along the coast beside the sea. The wind blew strongly here: grass began to appear between houses, and

247

trees became more frequent. The sun shone over the horizon, and the road was hard. Through the window Besson watched the landscape slip past, very fast in the foreground, then more slowly, till the distant scene appeared motionless, even perhaps shifting in the opposite direction. There were waste lots enclosed by wooden fences, with four or five wrecked cars inside them. There were mounds and hillocks and rows of bungalows, each with its watch-dog. There were brand-new white-painted apartment blocks, with endless empty balconies patterning their façades. There were gypsy caravans, and roofs bristling with television aerials, and telegraph poles, and washing-lines hung with women's underwear. There were kitchen-gardens and clumps of rose-bushes or rhododendrons and sheds and rusty abandoned bicycles and parked trucks and cemeteries and blue-and-white filling stations. There was a high brick wall with the words U.S. GO HOME painted on it in white, and a grocer's shop, and a café with several indistinct characters just emerging from it. There were more villas with shutters closed or open as the case might be, and children playing at cops and robbers. There was a church with a pointed steeple and a clock that had gone wrong and showed the time as twelve noon, or midnight. There was a naval dockyard and a general repair shop and a half-built apartment block beside the road, rising amid a curious scaffolding of planks and sticks. Two policemen who had parked their motorcycles and were taking somebody's name and address. A woman with a goitre, looking on at them. An airfield, a hairdresser's shop, and a restaurant with candles on the tables and its name written up in big red letters: LA FOURCHETTE. A group of five palm trees. More waste lots, fields lying fallow, patches of earth and rubble in which the flint sparkled like ground glass. And all these things were in continual motion, streaming back horizontally past the windows of the bus, merging and blurring, receding in a growing complexity of lines and angles. A long way off, behind the moving foreground of houses and tree-trunks, the hills floated, blue and magnified. On the other side of the road the sea's surface revolved round its own axis, like a record. And somewhere ahead of them

248

their destination was vaguely taking shape. Mountains rose up, headlands stretched out into the water, and one small light cloud hung motionless in the sky .

François Besson watched the landscape with eager curiosity. Through every window in the bus he could see it unrolling past them at a great rate, producing the oddest inverted reflections in the polished metal framework of each seat. The vehicle drove straight ahead, very smoothly on the whole, cleaving a path through the transparent air. They were caught in the still centre of movement, of advance without self-propulsion. What they had here was a small section of earth gliding across the earth, not in order to conquer anything at all, but simply floating on the level asphalt with four whirring tyres, cruising, drawn into the void, climbing hills, coming down faster the other side, skimming along on a straight flat road.

Sometimes the bus would stop by the roadside, generally beside a clump of houses; people would get up and leave the vehicle, and others would take their places. People stared at the newcomers for a moment or two, made fun of them in whispers, and then forgot them.

The conductor had by now worked his way down to Besson.

'Terminus, please,' Besson said, holding out a note.

The man counted out several coins, gave them to Besson, and turned the handle on his ticket-machine. With a *ping!* a little piece of paper emerged from the slot, and the conductor put it in Besson's hand. 'Next, please,' he called.

'Les Mimosas', said the girl in the next seat, and the same process was repeated.

On his scrap of yellowish paper Besson read:

    108576329   Route: A
    F   oo   325
        1012   3
            Thank you

He put the ticket in his raincoat pocket, and watched the conductor making his way along the central aisle. He was a man of about forty, with a heavy lined face and rounded shoulders. From time to time he would stoop down and peer through the window, and then whistle to the driver, who stopped the bus. When he whistled again, the bus would move off again, engine labouring.

It occurred to Besson that being the driver or conductor of a bus was by no means a bad job. You walked up and down inside this long metal tube, and turned the little handle which cut off so much paper a time. When you had collected all the fares you went up front and sat by the driver and kept a vague eye on the grey ribbon of road endlessly unwinding in front of you. Or else you were the driver, esconced in that little cabin-like enclosure of anti-glare glass, turning the steering-wheel, following the contours of the landscape. You pulled up at the halts, then let in your clutch and moved off again. You changed gear, first, second, third, fourth, down to third, up to fourth again. You braked violently to annoy the passengers. You could keep up a grumbling commentary the whole time on drivers who overtook you or pedestrians crossing the road, this sort of thing: 'Well, get on with it, then— Jesus, will you just look at that! What the hell d'you think I was signalling for? Yes, *you*, want your face bashed in, then? Move yourself, you half-wit! And what about that clod on the island, is he going to cross or isn't he? Come *on*, you stupid bugger, you clapped-out thing you—' And so on. You could sound the horn, too, that clarion note which really made people's hearts miss a beat if they weren't expecting it. And you could look out for the pretty women all along your route, and whistle at them as you went by. There were the girls who hitched up their skirts as they clambered aboard at a stop, and those who just missed tipping over when you jammed the brakes on, and those who travelled standing, close to the door, and chatted you up, and were good for a laugh. In the evening you'd have a drink, and go to bed tired out, and dream all night of that never-ending road. You'd know the route by heart, of course, you could drive it without tiring yourself, and the days passed quickly. You made your own private map of this small section of the world. You learnt all the important things about it— the bits where you had to keep a sharp look-out, the bits where there were always lots of people around, the deserted stretches where you could relax. You knew every fountain and signpost and built-up corner and crossroads and bridge and level-crossing. You had your own landmarks. You knew exactly where you were going. Several dozen miles of wealthy and thickly-populated countryside, where something—the same sort of thing—was always happening.

The bus drove on through the countryside. There were large numbers following the same route, bowling along in the sunshine, glossy as cockchafers, leaving a small trail of whitish exhaust-smoke behind them. They came in all shapes and sizes—long automobiles with high tail-fins, in various pastel colours; squat rounded mini-cars with rear-lights like small portholes, and engines that roared loudly going uphill; light vans and heavy haulage trucks, vehicles old and new, some all chromium plating and shiny enamel that you could see your face in, others with smashed headlights and dented bonnets and patches of red-lead undercoat everywhere. The men inside these steel carapaces were more or less invisible. You might just catch a glimpse of them—pale ghosts lolling back on the seat-cushions, half-hidden behind dirty windows. Every make of car was represented. Volkswagens, stuffy and claustrophobic, like tiny armoured vehicles. High-riding Chevrolets, low-slung Panhards. Mole-like Citroëns, Jaguars built to resemble smart slippers. Narrow Austins, fore-shortened Renaults; the Alfa-Romeo for women, the Mercedes Benz for men. Simcas looking like Prisunic toys, Skodas, NSU's, BMW's, Lancias. Fords straight from the hardware shop, funeral parlour Cadillacs. All were exactly the same in the last resort, fast, noisy, each with its load of feet and hands and heads, each like a railway carriage transporting its humble crowd of women in shawls and men with dark glasses, children, grandmothers, sleepy dogs. Life gleamed from their polished metal, diffused the smell of hot rubber. One day their journey would end in some vast scrap-iron dump, an old cars' cemetery outside the nearest town, where the rust, season by season, would slowly bind their immobilized bodywork into one solid mass.

The road was straight as a ruler now, running beside the sea to the right of the railway track, and the houses were thinning out. Fields stretched away to the hills beyond. There were fruit orchards, rock-gardens, ruined buildings, clumps of cacti. The sun was high over the sea, and the sea was a dazzling blue, with small crisp ripples ruffling its surface.

Besson decided this would be a good point to get off. He rang the bell, waited till the bus stopped, and found himself out on the road. When the bus started off again without him, he watched it pass; but the windows were opaque, and he could not recognize anyone. He began to walk along the shoulder of the road, in the same direction.

In this manner he covered several miles. The ground was soft and covered with a kind of short springy grass that crackled underfoot. The sea was now completely out of sight, and the earth was beginning to crack and split under the effect of the heat. Everywhere insects were buzzing in the undergrowth, and the air was loud with the dry chirp of locusts. The landscape was completely deserted. Across this rough stretch of open countryside the road carved a furrow of noise and movement. The houses, set between sloping fields and surrounded by clumps of umbrella pine wore an abandoned air. There was nothing to do here except go on walking and survey the scene around you.

The sun was beating down fiercely, and Besson had to take off his raincoat. For a moment or two he carried it over one arm, but this hampered his movements, so instead he left it on a sheltered spot close to the roadside. A little further on he abandoned his beach-bag too, hiding it behind a bush so that he could pick it up again later if he ever had need of it.

When he was tired of walking he stopped and sat down on a milestone to watch the cars go by. He could see them coming a long way off, wavering in the air when they hit a patch of heat-mirage. Then they came tearing past Besson at a tremendous lick, some of them sounding their horns as they came, and dwindled away to the horizon again, with a glitter of metal before they finally vanished for good.

Further on still, Besson passed a filling station. At the top of a sort of cement tower was a large sign on which was written the one word: AZUR. The garage itself, below the tower, was a sprawling, all-white edifice, as beautiful as a church. There were lots of signboards swinging in the wind, with red and blue stars on them. Pot-geraniums were much in evidence, and at the entrance to the workshop a wolf-hound lay asleep. Beneath a concrete roof four petrol pumps stood enthroned: square-cut, blue and red, each with its rubber hose neatly folded away, and a glass-fronted panel at the top for reading the figures on the dials, but not in use now, unattended. Not a soul was to be seen anywhere—man, woman, or child. The ground had been sluiced down with water, but the smell of petrol and oil still clung to it. The sun beat down fiercely on all exposed areas, white light striking white stucco.

Besson walked right through the service station. When he passed near the garage workshop, the wolf-hound pricked up its ears, still with its eyes closed, and growled. Besson retreated to the road.

A few yards further on, close to a stream which much resembled a blocked sewer, Besson found a beaten earth track, and turned off on it. He proceeded across country in this way, stumbling as he negotiated the old path, struggling up steep rises, catching his clothes on thorn-bushes, lizards scattering at his approach. The track led heaven knows where, between high thorn hedges, twisting, turning, meandering, sometimes even doubling back the way it had come. He had his back to the sea now. In front of him were the hills with their rough, arching backs. A few houses were scattered here and there among the trees, surrounded by vineyards and olive-groves and terraced slopes. Spirals of smoke curled up into the sky, and animals crowded into the shade behind half-demolished walls. Behind, the sun continued to climb towards its zenith, reaching a maximum intensity of heat and brightness. Light and shade were sharp and clear-cut, as though sliced out with a razor, and there were thorn-bushes everywhere. Grass covered the earth like a furry pelt, letting the heat smoulder damply beneath it. All odours were strong and acrid, clinging to

253

the ground like a second atmosphere. Little by little, as he strode along the track, feet crunching over prehistoric pebbles, Besson made a surprising discovery: *there were no men on earth*. The landscape was vast, indisputably *there*, its whole weight pressing down on the outer surface of the soil. It was a mask, a curious celluloid skin which had melted over the countryside's contours and could no longer be unstuck. He could see it quite clearly now. He examined it as though from the vantage-point of a dirigible balloon, observed mile upon square mile of solitude and brutishness spreading out to all four points of the compass. Towns, squared-off apartment blocks, streets, stations, cars, highways, airports, stadia—all these had suddenly vanished, absorbed by the soft-textured skin of the landscape, lost in those shades of brown, those reddish striations, that fine still graining. And the inhabitants had disappeared with them, had been swallowed up by the sand, reduced to dust once more, not wiped out of existence, simply turned into microscopic entities like any other. Trees, mushrooms, mosses, lichens; grasshoppers and millipedes; crocodiles, oxen, horses, even elephants—all were dissolved now, their substance thinned out in mud and alluvial deposits, written in the soil, brought low by this tyrannous and ghostly hand, tiny spiders in their grey webs, ridiculous parasites burrowing into the pink and bristly skin, and drinking, with their small repulsive mouths, two or three drops of all those millions of pints of blood!

Besson sat down on a large stone by the roadside. He was no longer so occupied by the scene around him. In the bright sunlight swarms of tiny insects began to dance on the spot, like mayflies: he could distinctly hear the beating of their wings, and see the bluish gleam from their backs. The air was still fresh, especially when the wind got up, but here and there the sun's rays struck home with burning intensity. It occurred to Besson that he would have enjoyed sitting here and smoking a cigarette. He would have smoked it unhurriedly, legs stretched out over the sandy soil, from time to time dropping a little ash on the ground. Then, when he had finished the cigarette, he would have stubbed it out with his heel, right beside the big stone he was now sitting on. In this way some record of his passing would have been left there, a tiny, scarcely visible black smear, topped by the eviscerated dog-end, with strands of yellow tobacco still escaping from it.

Every point in this landscape was worth stopping for. Each little patch of mud and bushy undergrowth was worth one's building a hut there, and staying for at least a day and a night. Here one could make vast and endless journeys, in stages of fifty yards or so, travelling from one stone to another, from tree to a well, from a ruined cottage to a thyme-bush. One could set off on one's adventures through the hills, living off the land, picking bramble-berries in the tangled thorn-bushes and wild strawberries from the arbutus trees, gathering windfall black olives. Here was a vast continent, scored by rivers a few inches long, with torrid deserts and sheer mountains and forests of knife-edged grass, through which there scuttled lithe and monstrous creatures all bristling with paws and antennae and mandibles. No doubt about it, the earth was limitless. There was no end to the process of exploration and reclamation and conquest. Every inch of these territories was guarded by vigilant creatures ready to fight for their own. They had authorized men to hack paths and roads here and there through the area. They had ceded them plots of land on which to build their houses and towns. But all the rest was well and truly *theirs*, and woe betide anyone who tried to take it from them. They would raise their savage armies, by the million, indeed by the billion, and commence hostilities on their own account. Night and day they would keep up the assault, wave after invincible wave, swarming over the houses, nibbling, destroying, endless winged battalions that darkened the sky from one horizon to the other, their minuscule bodies eclipsing the light of the sun. You could try anything you liked on them, fire, insecticides, bombing, it would all prove useless. They were sure to win in the end. They'd appear from every corner, marching over corpses, putting out fires, swimming across oceans, devouring, gnawing, stripping back to the bone. At all costs you had to avoid provoking them. At all costs you had to avoid arousing their anger.

Besson lay back in the grass and stared up at the sky. He could feel the densely-packed stems pricking his skin through his clothes. There were certain small protruding stones, too, shaped —or so it felt—like pyramids, which pressed hard against his body. Lying there close to the ground he could hear everything distinctly: all the strange and myriad noises of life vibrated in his ears, yet each remained clear-cut, individual, standing up like a separate twig in the brushwood. The rattle and whirr of insects, seed-pods bursting in the sunlight, the displacement of stones and sand, little crumbling and crackling noises—there were millions of such sounds, no one could ever count them all, however hard he listened. Existence was located here, at ground level: a mist, a kind of warm, milky cloud in constant motion.

Soon Besson found himself stretched out on the grass like a dozing giant who has been tied up, while asleep, by an army of little dwarfs. These Lilliputian creatures had driven pegs into the ground and then attached his hair to them with lengths of spider's thread. His clothes had been sewn down, his hands and feet were covered with a fine-meshed, almost invisible network of creepers. That was it, he had been made one with the grass he lay on, they had taken him by surprise, he was a prisoner of the stubble and brushwood. Above him the sky stretched, pale and unfathomable, so vast that it was as though it did not really exist. Far up in the empyraean light swarmed and dazzled, streaming out on the sun's right hand.

Little by little, Besson realized his position. He was pegged out as an offering on some high plateau, spreadeagled over the naked dome of the world in preparation for an incomprehensible sacrifice. Even from the depths of that tenderly pellucid sky the threat of death could materialize. There was no sure protection, nothing to cover him. Man's flesh was frail, a touch could shiver his bones, he was exposed to endless unknown dangers. Stars, dead planets, meteorites—at any moment one of these could slam through the violet barrier of the atmosphere into the earth's crust, digging a crater anything up to four hundred miles in diameter. Between him, Besson, and the freezing vertiginous nothingness of outer space, where suns exploded instantaneously, like bombs, what

protection was there save this curtain of tulle, this scanty phosphorescent veil, this thin and all-too-penetrable envelope which
did not even conceal him from view? A cold and comet-like
frisson seemed to flash down from the clouds, entering Besson's
body by way of his navel. In broad daylight—despite the sun and
the scent of pollen and these semi-reassuring noises—the cold
breath of eternity spread through Besson's guts as he lay there on
the ground.

Some time later a white bird began to wheel around, far overhead: Besson watched its movements, the tight circles it described in the boundless air, with scarcely a flicker of his own eyes.
The bird did not really use its wings at all, simply spread them
wide and sailed down in a long planing glide, banking on air-
currents, turning incessantly, round and round, so far up in the
sky that its movements seemed reduced to immobility. It revolved
about an invisible axis right over Besson's head, constantly
turning back on itself, following its previous track, dipping, rising,
pivoting in the calm and silent void. Sometimes—whether on
account of an air-pocket, or because it felt its balance in some way
disturbed—it would flap its great soft wings, for a moment or
two; but then it would set course once more, gliding, banking,
turning, as though coming down an invisible staircase with no
apparent bottom to it. Besson watched the bird with passionate
absorption: he felt that its flight should go on for ever. From
where he lay, on his patch of grass, he could not make out any
details of the creature's body: he could not isolate its head or its
talons or the brown patches (if there were any) on its feathers. It
could have been anything—seagull, sparrow-hawk, falcon,
buzzard. Or an eagle, perhaps, an eagle that had flown down from
the nearby mountains, and was now using those cruel eyes to spy
out the victim on which it would shortly drop like a stone. It was
impossible to tell which it was.

The bird continued to circle round, with a kind of stubborn
violence. But all one could see of it was the cross formed by its
body and outspread wings, poised aloft while the earth turned
slowly under it. A sign indeed, a living emblem hung in that white

257

abyss of sky, its progress stiffly majestic, rigid with hatred. The bird was the only image of activity throughout this whole enormous void: it was monarch of all it surveyed. As far as the eye could reach, on every side, nothing else existed. It hung there, supported by the density of the atmosphere, as one might imagine death—opening and shutting its snow-white calyx, or gathering its strength in preparation for the struggle against mankind. Its light, buoyant body exulted with joy, faint breezes ruffled its white plumage, and the light played over it from all sides, rendered it diaphanous, a mere drop of glass and vapour with blurring, crumbling outlines. It was flying, it would go on flying for ever. It belonged to the range of gaseous matter, and without the slightest doubt would never be able to return to earth. It would have to go on circling in the upper air, describing one circle after another, until the moment came when it reached exhaustion-point and gently evaporated into nothingness. It no longer breathed, it was in all likelihood no longer alive—or else had entered upon eternal life: volplaning, glittering in the azure void, forthright, concealing nothing, casting its terrible cruciform shadow on the ground, three yards from wing-tip to wing-tip, gliding in blank and solitary splendour, nothing now but the living, breathing spirit of flight, unable to give up. Intoxicated by its own perfect circles, hunger and fear all forgotten, having quit the world's heights and crevasses centuries since. Lost, dumb, a sacrifice to the horizontal infinite; airborne. Airborne.

When Besson could no longer see the bird, he got up and made his way back down the path. At the foot of the hills lay the sea, under a blanket of mist. The sun had almost reached its zenith, and the wind had fallen. The chill in the air slowly turned to heat, drying off the rocks and forming dust in every cranny. Cars came tearing full pelt along the highway; the roar of their engines set Besson's teeth on edge.

He set off along the shoulder of the road again, till he reached a clump of houses. The cars slowed down here, because of traffic lights. A little way off the highway Besson saw a square, with old men sitting on benches. In the middle of the square a jet-hose was spitting over a patch of green lawn, and pigeons swarmed everywhere. The sidewalks were also occupied by dogs, and cats with raw scabs on their backs, and sparrows. The houses were ugly and decrepit, with barred shutters. At a pinch, he thought, one could live here, too: marry, and have children, and call them names like André or Mireille. Twice a week the town hall was turned into a cinema: there were the posters on the walls—*The Plainsman*, *The Crook who Defied Scotland Yard*. The tobacconist's name was Giugi; the doctor was called Bonnard, and the local lady of easy virtue Marie de Cavalous. From time to time there was a robbery, or some other crime. The village idiot was the deputy mayor's illegitimate son. None of this mattered very much.

Everyone stared at Besson as he went by. He stopped at a bar and ordered a glass of lemonade over the counter, staring with great concentration at the yellow plastic surfaces and the chromium plating on the coffee-machine. At the far end of the room a juke-box started up: a raucous woman's voice, supported by chorus and rhythm group, singing a mutedly vibrant number that went:

> *C'est bien la plus la*
> *C'est bien la plus la*
> *C'est bien la plus belle*
> *Celle qu'on appelle la*
> *Celle qu'on appelle la*
> *Celle qu'on appelle la belle*
> *La belle Isabelle*

Besson drank his lemonade and paid for it. Then he stayed for a moment with his elbows on the counter, staring out at the street. Flies were busily sipping at the spilt water on the tables. Down the far end of the bar someone sneezed twice, and blew his nose.

Besson walked on out of the village. He had hardly seen anyone there.

Half a mile or so further on he went over a level-crossing and took a road that led down to the beach. The whole site was dotted with huts, shut up now, where they sold ice-cream, and peanuts during the summer. There were one or two notice-boards, too, which said things like CAMPING SITE or THIS WAY TO THE SEA or ALTITUDE ZERO or FIESTA BEACH. Besson stopped for a moment to look at the beach, and the headlands that enclosed it on either side of the horizon. The long stretch of shingle was deserted; incoming tides had forced it up into a high ridge. To the left, some way off, there was a concrete jetty, with groups of anglers dotted along it. To the right, in the distance again, there was what looked like a sewage dump. It was in this direction that Besson now proceeded, stumbling along over the warm shingle, breathing in the tangy smell of the sea. Everything had become white, grey, or pink, except the sea, which was so blue it hurt one's eyes to look at it. Occasional patches of crude oil glistened in the sunlight, and along the tide-mark, small heaps of vitreous blubber, lay a number of stranded jellyfish.

When Besson had got almost as far as the sewage dump, he sat down on the shingle for a breather. It was now decidedly hot, so hot that he had to remove his coat and shirt. He leaned back on his elbows, watching the waves roll gently in. Time dragged, and the second-hand of the watch on Besson's wrist moved forward in a series of tiny jerks, on and on. Eventually this irritated him so much that he unstrapped the watch, laid it on a flat stone, and then hammered it into tiny fragments with a sharp flint. Bits of spring and fragments of broken glass were scattered over the beach. He examined them with interest.

There was no longer a cloud in sight; they had all been absorbed into the azure expanse of the sky—all, that is, except the long white trail left by a jet aircraft flying at about 40,000 feet, though this too soon melted away. The bird had flown away, and there were no people around any more. Nothing remained except the sun, now at its zenith, beating down on land and sea as though through a burning-glass.

The last time he heard signs of human activity was when these two children passed close by him, talking in loud voices. The little boy was called Robert, and the little girl's name was Blanche. They strolled along slowly, stopping every two or three yards to discuss something. Without sitting up so that he could see them, Besson lay and listened to their conversation.

'Blanche! Blanche!' Robert called out. 'Come and look here!'

'Found a monk?' Blanche enquired.

'No. Come and see.'

'It's a candlestick,' Blanche said.

'Pretty, isn't it?'

'Not bad. That's one more you've got. What's your total now?'

'Three,' Robert said.

'I've got two candlesticks and about ten monks,' said Blanche.

'Yes,' Robert said, 'but one of them's no good: it hasn't got a stripe.'

'It *has* got a stripe! You can't see it very well, but it's got one.'

'Anyway,' Robert said, '*I've* got a candlestick with something written on it.'

'What sort of thing? Show me.'

'Wait a tick—it says Farge, or Farga, something like that.'

'Here, let me see,' Blanche said, and then, after a pause: 'It's Forge. That's what's written on it. Forge.'

'No it isn't, that's an A there, not an O. It's Farga.'

'Going to let me have it?'

'I found it, didn't I? Down there in the rubbish-dump.'

'If you give it me, I'll swop you half my monks.'

'Nothing doing. You can pick up monks anywhere.'

'Even one with three stripes?'

'If you want my candlestick, it's because it's worth more.'

'Oh keep your silly candlestick, then. Anyway, I've got two already.'

'Yes, but they haven't got anything written on them.'

'I don't care. Anyway, Farga doesn't *mean* anything. Hey, look, over there—another monk.'

'That's just what I was telling you, you can find monks anywhere.'

'Yes, but *you* don't.'

'Monks are just pebbles, anyway.'

'Well, so are candlesticks.'

261

'That's not true. Candlesticks are more like cement.'

'Well, it's the same thing, isn't it?'

'Anyway I prefer candlesticks. At least they're useful for something. Come on, let's have a look further on—'

The voices dwindled and faded. Silence closed in again, there was nothing but heat and brightness. Besson gradually began to perspire.

This moment had been a long time coming. Besson had been waiting for it for years, perhaps for centuries. Today the curtain of rain and cloud had suddenly been torn apart, to reveal the sky in all its nakedness, the blinding circle of the sun. The agonizing beauty of this hard landscape, all rough and stippled with cross-hatching, was so intense now as to be quite unbearable. The light had become a bright and burning abyss into which one had to plunge head first. The town, the highways, the noisy airfields, the blocked-out pattern of fields and woodland, the steep mountainsides, animals watchful or sleeping, women and children—all had led here, to the place and moment chosen by the gods for the expiatory sacrifice to be accomplished. Every line had been traced so as to converge on this one point, this beach of grey pebbles, this particular day and hour. He could not escape. He could not go back: time had stopped for this event, there was no possibility of either advance or retreat. It was there, and now. The things had to happen. Like a sequence of events the action of which progresses by its own impetus towards its first and final crux, so Besson's life (as he was well aware) had been orientated towards *this*. As though to avoid the moment of reckoning, he tried, briefly, to conjure up old memories. Faded snapshots flashed through his mind. Here was a picture of a child leaning against an iron balustrade, in a village the name of which had vanished beyond recall. Here was the seated figure of a mother, her hair braided up round her head, with a tiny bald grimacing doll held in the crook of her right arm. Other shapes and figures, absurd figments of his imagination, flickered across the blood-red screen of his closed eyelids: wolves with pointed ears, runaway horses, monsters wearing steel-rimmed spectacles. He was shut in the spider-haunted cupboard, the gleaming texture of a porcelain flower-bowl held and mesmerized him through the drowsy evening, while the voices went on talking, talking, in the flat exhausted accents of those who have nothing to say. He was back in the shut rooms of his childhood dreams, that fearful, hermetically sealed chamber in which the walls were at once so close and so remote.

Then there was that submarine abyss, the plummeting dive down, down, past a rampart high as a twenty-storey building, into the depths, down to squid-haunted grottoes and thick waving carpets of seaweed. The black hole expanded, became a volcano's maw, a cavern, the heart of a glowing cathedral of embers, where the bloated, half-eaten corpse went tumbling down, over and over, to the bottom.

*

Minutes passed. Hours passed. Days, years passed. All elements mingled and merged, interlocking, fused in an automatic sequence Nothing was left now save the immense misery of having survived. Nothing—not a single pattern, not one word written on actual solid paper—could palliate that fact. The days resembled a knife, a knife with a keen blade. Maps and dictionaries were appalling, because they could never be complete: there was always some elusive factor omitted. The tiny palpitating animal fled through the undergrowth, leaving no trace behind, not even a scent; yet everything had been enclosed within a smooth-walled sphere, without any opening, crazily reflecting each object back towards its centre.

Besson lay stretched out on the pebbles—they had begun to hurt him—and watched the stormy future approach him. Here, too, it was possible to forget what was going to happen in a few mintues. In a few hours, days, years. Old age would descend, one of these days, bringing its shameful peace. Features would wither, muscles lose their strength. Yet none of this mattered. Death would come like any other visitant, falling from roof or sky without warning. In the street, in a group of loafers. In some stinking bed, against a beslobbered pillow. In a wrecked car. Half way up a staircase, so that the silly lifeless body rolled down to the bottom again, bumping from tread to tread, skull knocking like a hollow calabash. Forty years old. Fifty-five. Sixty-eight. Seventy-seven, seventy-nine, eighty-one, eighty-four, ninety-two, a hundred and four, a hundred and five, a hundred and six. Which of these figures would turn out to be the right one? Which would be the fatal day? 22nd August 1999, or 4th May 1983? Or 13th December 2002? Or perhaps 1st April 2014? Which day would it be? And what time of day? Noon? Two in the afternoon? Nine-thirty p.m.? Or in the small hours of the morning, after an exhausting and nightmare-ridden sleep? What would give out first? Heart? Kidneys? Liver? Lungs? Spine? But none of this had very much importance. For the years, the years would continue to unfold in their serried ranks, no more distinguishable from one another than buffaloes at a watering-hole, and the years would become centuries, and the centuries would follow one another in turn, like great striations of marble. In the remote future, far beyond this place, this moment, time would still be thrusting out its branches, a growing tree. Languages would decline, arts gutter into oblivion. Ideas would glide smoothly on, small boats borne by the stream, never reaching any destination. There would be no end, just as there had been no beginning: simply night falling over the world's achievements, veiling them in light shadow. The invisible record would turn on its own axis, swiftly at the periphery, almost stationary towards the centre. And eternity would be there, not hidden but omnipresent; not an external pall, but permeating the inner heart of things, at the centre of time's central point.

Then, when Besson recognized this great beauty; when he understood that all had been in vain, and that the moment could not be sustained; when he acknowledged his defeat, and saw the proclamation of his destiny; when, at last, he turned his violence against himself: then he opened his eyes wide and stared at the sun. The blinding brightness entered his eyeballs and exploded there; the sudden pain was almost unbearable, and tears began to run down his cheeks. Besson turned his head away for a moment, trying to find some object that could stop him slipping away from the world: his eyes scanned the beach avidly, trying to find something, anything, that instant—a wasp, a wandering ant, a gnat. But there was nothing, nothing but shingle and pebbles with a vast bluish hole in the middle that shifted as he looked at it. Then his hand closed on a small pebble shaped like a snail, and picked it up. Besson lay back on the beach, and still clutching the little pebble, opened his eyes and looked into the sun again. This time he did not shut them.

Light pierced his skull as though he had never seen light before, a burning and lava-like flood, a cleansing influx that permeated the furthest recesses of his skull. A blank, white, monotonous sound invaded his body little by little and floated it off the ground. The ground receded, opened to form his unfathomable tomb, and the air parted asunder. This was the moment, *now*. Stiffening his will to the uttermost, Besson pitted his staring eyes against the sun, against fire and earth and water, never flinching, against men and beasts, against stones, against the air, against the vast and planet-swarming emptiness of outer space. He stood there in defiance of them all, racked by pain and loathing, and offered them the delicate shield of his twin eyes, from which the tears now flowed ceaselessly. These two globes, with their delicate irises and dark translucent pupils, he now surrendered to the world. To the sun's savage brightness he exposed the dark and secret surface of his retinas, so that by burning the memory of vengeance might be preserved, and never perish. Then, at last, he began a soft and agonized whimpering, the hoarse unhappy cry of a gibbon, screaming without rhyme or reason at the onset of darkness.

Chapter Thirteen

*Society at large—In a train—A little boy smokes his first cigarette—
The tourist bus—Mothers—The end of Anna's story—Echo of a
suicide*

ON the thirteenth, fourteenth, and fifteenth days, and all the days
that followed, there was no more day: only one black unbroken
night, that went on for ever. The town was rid of its incubus now,
and inside the houses, with their warm electric radiators, people
went on living just as they had always done. Angèle Basman, for
instance, a woman of forty-two, was busy deep-frying potatoes in
boiling oil, a red-flowered apron round her waist, tiny drops of hot
fat spitting out of the pan on to her bare arms as she stood over the
gas-stove. Or Michou, a tabby cat, who was fast asleep in the
sunny part of some suburban back garden, while the fleas tracked
through his thick fur, looking for the best place to bite him. Or
the thin young girl with washed-out complexion and cropped
black hair, who was wrapping a handful of bleeding lights up in
newspaper—having previously smeared her sheets with it to stop
her mother realizing she was pregnant.

On one clear pane of glass a tiny gnat was visible: it might have
been walking across the blue-grey sky. It advanced very slowly,
millimetre by millimetre, on several gossamer-fine pairs of legs.
Its body had a greenish tinge about it.

The newspapers carried their usual news items, with banner
headlines for earthquakes and revolutions, somewhat smaller
cross-heads for *crimes passionnels*, and so on down to ordinary
close-set type for such things as car accidents, thefts from parked
vehicles, or the exploits of bums and down-and-outs.

In various discreet corners the beggars were plying their trade.
Old women were scattering crumbs for the pigeons on their

window-sills, and in the restaurants couples were eating sauer-kraut. Wherever you went there was the same faint odour of garlic and grease and rusty metal, the gurgle of stopped-up sinks. A man was sitting in his car at an intersection, waiting for the red light to turn green, and picking his nose. Drunks were taking nips from their bottles of wine, and fat women were licking at chocolate ices.

Some people were reading novels in the dim light of their shuttered rooms, stories all more or less written according to the same formula as this sample: 'Once more my mouth tasted the joys of her soft, burning skin, and we rolled over on the quiet sand, muscles rigid with desire. When my hand, in the course of a wandering caress, found the zip of her swimsuit, down her back, she tried to struggle for a moment. But the satiny material parted, like a flower tremulously opening in the warm sunlight, to reveal the agonizing delights of her nakedness. But only for a brief instant did I feel her bare breasts soft and caressing against my chest, explore the roundness of her buttocks, feel her still childish stomach and long slender legs melting into mine; only for a brief instant did I savour that rare sensation of a body still freshly damp in patches from the sea, and tanned for long hours by the sun. For suddenly, supple and elusive, she slipped from my grasp and ran with a defiant air, still half-naked to the sun and wind. From a long way off came the faint hoot of the ferry-boat. With an enchanting lack of modesty she ran on, paying no attention to her unzipped swimsuit. The sun suddenly touched the horizon, turned blood-red, and flooded sea and beach with the glow of its magnificent demise ... She came back towards me, hair flying, a grenadine tinge colouring her pointed breasts and the curve of her belly. "Half past five!" she called out furiously. ...'

Others were painting gaudy pictures, in which the dominant colours were shocking pink and madder. Others again spent all afternoon playing the flute, or listening to jazz records. Any insect society has its organization. Throughout the town at this moment everything was perfectly flat, or perfectly square, or, at a pinch, perfectly round. On the doors of public toilets and bar-room

W.C.'s penknives had carved obscene words and incised porno-graphic figures; but these words and figures possessed a dignity almost amounting to virtuousness. On two identical notices, printed in red letters, appeared the words GENTLEMEN and LADIES. A train moved slowly along the coast from one stop to the next, twenty black carriages drawn by a steam locomotive belching smoke downwind. As it rattled along the track it emitted, with monotonous regularity, a deep *wooooooooooooo!* which shook the ground underfoot. It would plunge into tunnels, emerge again, steam round long curves, brake, whistle, labour up gradients and rattle down them the other side, trigger off signals and level-crossing alarm-bells. It wheels drummed along regularly over the rail-junctures, producing a cadenced *clack-clack, clack-clack* which formed its basic rhythm. Valves opened and shut, steam blew off. Occasionally the train passed over a set of points, and the rhythm of the wheels became confused, made noises like coughing and sneezing and spitting. In each compartment, with its worn felt seats, people sat smoking, chatting, eating, drinking, or just staring at one another, while the ground fled back beneath them. Their conversations were always the same:

'What time do we get there?'

'I'm not sure—if we're not running late, we ought to be in about eight o'clock.'

'They always run late.'

'Did you see how long we were held up last time?'

'Well, a train had been derailed further down the line.'

'That's no excuse.'

'After all, we've paid for our tickets . . .'

'Let me tell you, madam, when my son came out of the army, do you know what time he got home? At midnight, madam—*midnight!*'

'Just like my sister-in-law—she was on her way home from Italy—'

'And the time when our kid had the mumps—'

'What can you expect, eh? What can you expect. . . .'

A little boy stood leaning against the wall in a quiet back street, smoking his first cigarette. He had taken it from a brand-new packet with red and white stripes, labelled WINSTON. Then he put it in his mouth. He struck a match and lit it. Now he was inhaling the acrid, sweetish aroma of the smoke, and salivating.

Two young women in bikinis were strolling round the edge of a swimming-pool that smelt of disinfectant. The one on the right was a tall brunette; her costume had a pattern of small green and white squares. The one on the left was thinner, and wore a white bikini, all covered with little pearl shells. Both had on sunglasses with large circular lenses, and the white radiance blazed down on them like a searchlight's beam.

Everywhere civilization was established, and had set up its notices: no parking, no entry, no billsticking, private property.

In the middle of the countryside lay a large ham-shaped rock, quite motionless. The plane-trees grew imperceptibly, seeing nothing, hearing nothing, feeling nothing, simply thrusting back clods and granules of earth, stretching up their branchy fingers to the bright sky above them. This was the way it was.

A coachful of tourists spent some time threading its way through the streets of the town. Then it set off across the hills, and each time it stopped all the passengers turned their heads as one man to left, or right, in obedience to a voice which announced, in several languages:

'You can see on your right the ruins of an aqueduct built by the Romans. Lens aperture, f.1.5.'

'Vous apercevez sur votre droite les ruines de l'aqueduc construit par les Romains. Ouverture de l'objectif: 1.5.'

'Rechts können Sie die Ruinen der von den Römern gebauten Wasserleitung sehen. Offnung des Objektifs: 1.5'.

'U ziet nu op uw recht de ruinen van de romeinse waterleiding. Opening van de lens: 1.5.'

'U kan regts die ruiëne van die Waterleiding sien, wat deur die Romeins gebou was. Opening van die lens: 1.5.'

The construction team was still busily at work on their site in the middle of the river bed. Another month or two, and the bridge would be finished. The blind man sat on the beat he had bought and sold newspapers, listening to music from his transistor radio. Every night the *voyeur* prowled through the thickets up on the hill and every evening, at the same time, the woman whose face was so white that it might have been made of plaster would enter the church and sit staring straight in front of her, at a point just above the closed tabernacle.

Josette was driving through the streets in her new car, looking for somewhere to park. A young red-headed girl, accompanied by a small red-headed boy, could often be seen walking along the pavement. But these were not the only solitary women in town: there were many others, blonde, brunette, light brown, dyed or rinsed, grey and black. Each went her own separate way to her private domain, in a green or a blue dress, or sometimes in check pants, equipped with stockings and bra and briefs, or nylon tights; suffering from toothache, or migraine, or diarrhoea, constipation or a cold in the head; depressed or cheerful, jealous, in love; real people. Real people.

In the dining-room of a flat half-way up the dilapidated apartment block, a man sat smoking and reading the paper. A women was there too, darning socks. Her heavy face was weighed down by fatigue. Light and shadow flitted across it like puffs of air. She was *there*, a massive maternal presence, whose belly had opened and closed again, queening it all unawares over the world, at once triumphant and humble. There was nothing in her; yet she was immovable, solid as a marble statue, a weathered, polished block of quarried stone, and in her water and fire came together, in her, there in the folds of her inmost parts, the hollow seeds of past and future were already concealed. The tree, the green tree with its upthrusting, bursting shoots grew perennially from her belly. But of this she remained unaware.

It was for her, or against her, that everything had been created. Blood, bone, nails and hair, all belonged to her. Outrage her, fling her down and kill her, she would still emerge victorious. She would look up at you with those heavy, liquid eyes, and go on giving birth to you, without hate, without respite. Even in defeat her face would still wear an expression of victory, and her body would contain all the strength of a conqueror.

When those three drunks fought at night outside a bar, it was for her. They threw clumsy punches at each other, and rolled on the ground, and one of them lost his shoe. The other two stopped fighting, went down on hands and knees, recovered the shoe, and carefully put it back on its owner's bare foot. It was for her, too, that the sadist of Fontainebleau attacked his victims; for her that cars skidded off the highway and piled up in fields.

Century after century, women had given birth in joy and travail. Céline had borne Marguerite, Marguerite had borne Jeanne, Jeanne had borne Eléonore, Eléonore had borne Thérèse, Thérèse had borne Eugénie, Eugénie had borne Cécile, Cécile had borne Alice, Alice had borne Catherine, Catherine had borne Laura, Laura had borne Simone, Simone had borne Pauline, Pauline had borne Julie, Julie had borne Yvette, Yvette had borne Monique, Monique had borne Gabrielle, Gabrielle had borne Claudia, Claudia had borne Gioia.

In the deserted room the voice rose from the tape-recorder through the darkness. It spoke for the yellow walls with flashes of light playing over them, for the bed with red blankets, for the curtainless windows, for the empty ash-trays, for the moths asleep under the coverlets, for each thing in its place, including the creature like a bundle of old rags feeling its way blindly round the room. It said:

I'm going to record on the other side of the spool. I want you to know—Well, perhaps it's not all that important, after all. But I did want to tell you everything that I said that first time, ten days ago, was untrue. Honestly. I was lying the whole time. But I didn't know I was lying, and that's the reason—that's the reason I spoke to you the way I did. Afterwards I realized the truth. Oh, I didn't play the tape back—I hadn't the courage to listen to my own words, all I'd said about me and Paul and the rest of it, because if I had I'd never have summoned up enough courage to send it to you afterwards. It was just remembering what I'd said. I mean, when I told you all that stuff, it was all fairy stories, just plain lies. Well, obviously, everything I *said* to you, the facts I mean, was true enough—but it was all wrong to tell you. It was stupid, I—I thought one could talk to people in a straightforward way, tell them what one thought, or believed one thought. That's why I lied to you. I talked on and on, holding the microphone and watching the spools of tape unwind, and it was all pure drivel. An alibi, that's what it was, a way of hiding the truth from myself no less than from others. Just the same as when I was typing a story, just like it was when I did that thing on Albert the snail or the old woman with an obsession about her trolleybus. Now I know —I know what it was fundamentally in aid of: lying, concealing the truth, oh, everything—You know, it's an awful thing, not talking. It's an awful thing never lying, too. That's what I'd have liked to learn how to do. I don't know if I'll manage it. I'm going to try and carry it right through to the end, but it won't be easy. In any case, when you've heard the spool through, please do one thing for me: wipe off what I've recorded. Don't preserve any of it, not one word. Leave nothing but silence in its place. Do you understand? The thing is, I'm always being tempted to wander off from the point—anecdotes. Really, you know, there's only one thing I have to tell you. I—I don't know how to begin, though, because it's really very simple, and it's not easy to explain something simple without—well, without talking a lot of rubbish, and dressing it up and putting frills on it.

One thing that will make it easier for me is that I'm going to die. It's true. It's only a question of moments now. I've got very little time left. That tube of pink sleeping-pills belonging to my mother—well, I've taken the lot. I've still got the glass in my hand, I had to drink nearly a quart of water to get them all down. I'm beginning to have feelings of nausea already, and my head's spinning. I must act quickly now. I want to tell you everything I left out last time. I don't know where to begin, though. In a few moments everything will be over. I shall be dead. I hope it won't hurt. Anyway I know now this isn't just make-believe. What I'm experiencing is the truth, the whole truth and nothing but the truth. I don't run any risk of, well, of making a fuss about nothing. Not this time. I know what I'm doing is cowardly, but the thing is I couldn't stand being alone any longer. Loneliness is a horrible thing, you know—that, and knowing you're past all self-deception. Oh, words used to deceive me all right, well and truly, but that's finished now. Or will be in a moment or two. Words, words, an endless unnecessary stream of them, all the stuff they teach you and you dish up again thinking it's your own. And knowing you're not alone, too. That's the trouble. No longer being sure what's part of you and what isn't, can you understand that? Do what you like, play it flippant, try the couldn't-care-less line, it's no good, you're always screwed in the end. There's always someone who fixes you—so many people around, everywhere, nothing but people the world over, and things that hurt you, words that raise your hopes only to dash them down more abjectly, and all those emotions— it makes you dizzy thinking how many emotions there are around; love, the sort of love you get in picture magazines, and friendship, hatred, jealousy, rancour, pity, compassion, faith, pride, all that jazz, on and on, never any end to it. And each individual has his own special emotion, and my the trouble he takes over it, waters it like a tender seedling, listens to its complaints, nurses its crises, makes a full-time job of it. I mean, you've got to, after all, we're not animals, are we? Oh, it's too ridiculous for words. You know, when it comes to the crunch I'm sorry to be shot of all this nonsense. Oh, there were some things I really liked, that's true. Pity. But as for the rest—! Surely it wasn't worth all the effort of being born and growing up and struggling through illnesses and going to school—all that just to enjoy a succession of fine delicate emotions? When you're young, you fall in love. That lands you with problems, right? You fight to make

274

someone else love you. You want to get married, but your parents are against it. You have crises. Crises. Jealousy, too. It's all so complicated, such a tangle—I mean, civilization's brought problems to a fine art too, hasn't it? Well, in the end everything sorts itself out and you get married. Fine. Then there are children, and the problems of education. My son wets his bed at night, doctor, what should I do about it? Or my daughter now, she's three and a half, she's a little madam, won't let anyone order her around. I don't want to damage her psyche or give her a trauma. What's the answer? Oh yes, every age-group has its own problems. There's the midday demon, the menopause, the stepmother's role. And then old age. Old people are wise, that's well known. They've got their heads screwed on all right, they have their memories, they can't be really vicious. It's funny, just so funny . . .

You see, there's too much going on in the world for me, I can't take it, people doing all those things at once, that's what gets me down. I've tried to contract out and just be a spectator. But it's not possible. They come and search you out. You can hide where you like, it makes no difference, there's always friends or relatives or *somebody* after you. They button-hole you and discuss things with you, they're full of ideas and just bursting with good intentions. They smile a lot, on the street, in cafés, out of photographs in the papers. All right, I'll admit it, some of them—well, I find them quite touching, they're so *nice*, they roll up just like that, they haven't a clue. And that touches me and hurts me and I need all my will power to resist them, to avoid getting sucked in. That's what happened with *him*—Paul, I mean. That's how he managed to pull a fast one on me. That's what I wanted to tell you, too—Because I don't feel at all well now. I've got this nausea, I think—I think I'm going to throw up. It's so idiotic that one can't die more easily. I wish I could obliterate myself without any effort, just like that, peaceful annihilation. Maybe I'd have done better to put a bullet through my head, but I didn't happen to own a pistol. And with these pills

275

there's even a chance that—that I won't die, after all. They ought to knock me out, and at the moment I feel anything but sleepy. There's—there's just this awful feeling of nausea. You know, my mother tried to commit suicide once, when she was a young girl. She threw herself into the river, but someone fished her out again. She had no idea why she did it, but in any case it wasn't because she'd been jilted. Apparently she'd had a whitlow on her thumb, and had been in a depressed state after taking antibiotics. There are people who say that when you do something like that you're temporarily insane. But seriously, François, I do assure you I'm not mad. You can't conceive just how much I'm conscious of what I'm about. On my word of honour, I can see the whole thing very clearly, black and white, and in the most minute detail. It's as though, well, as though my body had had enough of living, as though it was absolutely exhausted, and had to sleep. I'm living in a desert, that's the long and short of it. There's nothing whatsoever to hold me back. It's weird, François—everything being such a desert, I mean. It's hard to imagine what it's like. You're in a sort of bubble, and everyone's deaf, they can't hear you screaming, and your voice bounces back at you like a ball, like—it's difficult for me to say this, François, but there ought to be a God. . . . When anyone's reached this point, how can you expect them to turn back? You can't turn the desert into—I mean, it would be mere illusion, and anyway you can't go on deceiving yourself all that long. There's no pleasure in anything any longer. I—I was right to take these pills, because I honestly believe I've come to the end of the road, whichever way you look at it. That was my basic motive. Maybe I should have just let myself starve to death. I'd given up, lost my belief in anything. So had my body, that I'm sure of. So—

I don't know if evening's coming on, or if it's the effect of the pills, but I feel everything's getting dark. There's a slight chill in my legs and hands, too. I don't feel I want to throw up any more now. But I'm getting stomach cramps—*ooh*, they hurt like hell—What was I saying? Yes, well, it's—that's how it is, and I'm going to be able to rest now. When the pain stops. What I ought to have had, when you really get down to it, is some sort of deformity—a leg withered by polio, or a club-foot, or a hunched back, some very obvious defect, a constant source of suffering. That would have given me something to hang on to. I once knew a girl who had one leg shorter than the other. She used to walk by under our apartment every day. She had an awful limp. But there was something about her face and bearing—a sort of pride, can you understand that? I'd have liked to be the way she was. Maybe then I'd have had the same courage and will-power— I realize that now, when I'm feeling so frightful—*a-ah-aah*, oh God, yes, that's what I needed. Blind! That's what I ought to have been. Too late now. I'm passing the secret on to you. It might even have saved me. Weakness, disability. With a white stick. Seeing nothing, seeing nothing—people would have moved aside to let me pass. There'd have been no need for me to say or do anything, just the struggle for survival. I'd have had, oh, big black glasses made out of plastic, and I'd have learnt to feel things out with my finger-tips. Warm colours, cold colours. . . . I'd have really listened, used my ears. The feel of blackness. Not seeing anything, ever again. . . . Blind! That's it, tossed like a parcel into areas of movement, feeling my way. Armed with a stick. The victim's weapon.—Too late now. . . . I've taken these pink pills. . .

You know, I nearly passed out then. I felt—I felt *it* was coming. I had to shake myself awake. Nearly dark now. . . . I feel fine, just fine—oh, but there was still something I wanted to tell you. . . . Yes, that was it. . . . The most important thing of all. . . . Look, I'm going to hold this glass in my hand so you can tell when, when *it* happens. I'm going to hold on to it as long as I can. . . . So when—when the moment comes, and I fall asleep, the glass will fall. . . . Fall on the floor, and you'll hear it. . . . And then you'll know it's all over. All right?

Aa-a-aah, another cramp. God, this one's going on and on

—*argggh*, how it hurts. . . . Anyway, I'm sure this will be the best thing I've ever written . . . even if the ending isn't all that brilliant. . . .

It's some consolation for all the meretricious rubbish I've churned out. . . .

Funny. If *this* is death, it wasn't worth while making up all those . . . those philosophical systems. . . . You know, once before I thought I was going to die. . . . I was thirteen, something like that. And I—I fell down on the ground, I felt all the blood had drained out of my head, leaving it quite empty. . . . I was falling . . . falling . . . Oh, it was awful . . . People gathered round me. . . .

It's as if . . . as if the Flood had happened . . . you understand? . . . and Noah was looking at those still waters. . . . He didn't realize that . . . [*long pause*] The earth was so teeming, so full of myriad life . . . and the sky . . . And the light is so diaphanous, especially—especially towards evening . . . I can still see it, through the window. . . . Translucent. . . . One day I believe it'll be possible to . . . lose oneself in it. . . . out there . . . How lovely it'd be . . . I think I've thrown up. . . . I felt something. . . . I can't be . . . a very pretty sight. . . . *Aa-aah*. . . . There goes the glass. . . . Listen. . . .

There was a sharp sound as the glass smashed, and then silence. Sound-waves distorted by electrical pulsations, the glass lying where it fell, scattered on the floor, tiny sharp-jagged fragments like claws, glittering in the gloom, bright, motionless, a granulation of salt-crystals.

*

Beyond the dividing barrier of darkness now. Death may be close at hand, that foul rain of destruction which will cover every object with its fine ashy film. Has this area so much as a name now? Do these places so much as exist on the face of the earth? In this harsh and frozen expanse nothing is missing, not one angle, not the tiniest surface scratch. The hospital's façade, the barrack walls, the high front of the S.P.A.D.A. building loom heavier, lean inwards; and within this closing vice, as though oblivious of their condition, their destiny, men and women alike are getting their lives over. Away and beyond, the negative geometry becomes more marked: white bridges arching across the highways, deserted asphalt squares. Low down on the walls, and so small that you have to stoop to see them, are a series of graffiti, proof that people have lived and loved here. The letters are spidery, scratched with something like a fingernail, a penknife maybe or the edge of a sharp stone. Along the coast the airfields stretch out, parallel to the sea, dead flat, with the same desert-like appearance. And across this whole great desolate expanse, amid the isolation and the enfolding sense of sleep, under rain or sun, by lamplight or day's bright reflections, the cars come and go, passing one another, tracing their insect-like tracks, a hum and susurrus over the ground, then dwindling out of sight over the horizon towards other man-surveyed domains.

Everything merges and deepens; sleep and torpor have their own sharp texture, which produces its own reality.

Now, at this moment, the abyss may be close. Rooms with yellow-painted walls harbour the smell of stale cigarette-smoke. Solitude closes in, a compact and indissoluble block, immobilizing arms, imprisoning torsos, pressing down on men's guts and private parts. People are cast-iron statues, heavy, solid, dull, mute, frozen into a posute suggestive of anger. The storm continues to discharge its fury, the sky is like a sheet of iron, and lightning-flashes advance slowly across it like cracks in the metal. François Besson, seated in his coffin, has ceased to exist. Crouched in a corner, back resting against the bed, he nevertheless no longer exists. He has no name, no face. He has come to a stop. Nor does he survive as memory, since no object or artifact or visible shape exists except as itself: it is what it is, and no more, rooted in the bedrock of actuality. It can never be liquid, never melt and drift, bearing down with its fresh current feelings of happiness and pleasure. He is denied the unbounded pleasure of *having lived—*

and quite by chance, because he finds himself shut in beside a window, facing the naked sky, because time itself has penetrated his room and traced every detail of it, in a caricature that can never be effaced.

What it means is suffering, continual and progressive suffering, an increasingly precise revelation of the life and beauty that have eluded him. I am rooted like a tree on a vast mountain plateau, in the heat of summer, hemmed all about with rock, unable to move, unable to escape anything, fixed, wide open to every hazard, like a pylon in a severe electric storm. Everything around me is dead—rock and glacis, dry scrub, sunken watercourses, dead, all dead, yet they never loosen their grip on me, and I can do nothing but count the slow minutes, number the very stones, while the clouds drift on over me. In the high rock-face a waterfall has scored its vertical channel. Flies cluster and buzz on my eyelids. An occasional reddish insect flies past, with great effort, as though dragged down by its own weight. Even here, surrounded by all this open space—it seems positively to invite movement—I can still do nothing. I am still the prisoner of those who belong *down there*; this upland is gradually turning back into the concrete-and-girder platitude of which I form a part. Scaffolding. Parking lights, traffic lights. The surface of the pavement at two o'clock in the morning. The ever-louder creak and clatter of the night-time roadsweepers, advancing from road to road, dragging their sprinklers behind them. There's no doubt about it, I'm a slave, reduced to mere dust. I can't break free. Danger stalks the earth's surface, you can feel its muted vibrations ripple through sewers and cellars. Danger, real danger. Hell is right under us, so close that you could knock a spyhole through to it. Hell is our memories, too, our sleepless memories, a little stiff and starchy, memories of the days when our eyes were opening—life as it used to be, tranquillity written across the lined pages of school exercise-books, sensitivity, egotism, happiness. Those pages are illegible today, yellow and spotted. It was as though one were fixed and static, stiff as a figurehead, while the strata of experience descended past one. The upward movement was illusory, the fiction of movement

280

amid stillness; and one day, after long contemplation of these passing chimeras, it turned out that the universe was not the same, that the metamorphosis lay there, and not in you. It was the universe that had ordered this stratification of elements, these strange and transient smoke-patterns. Slow erosion has reduced you to a skeleton, yet you yourself have always remained in the same spot, you have never budged. You are still the same, this Besson-like person, now sitting in his room—third floor, on the right—back against the bed, eyes fixed on the slits in the closed shutters, perspiring in summer, torpid in winter. Yes, you are this freak, this pop-eyed clown, these grey features striped and haloed with light, these closed lips, this decayed tooth throbbing hotly in the jawbone. What you are is Besson + X, your body has been extended by a dimension you never imagined—the weight of a mahogany table, for example, or the burn you get from holding a match too long, or the smell of some particular scent, or the rough, powdery feel of a sheet of fine sandpaper.

Just as you could never escape from the hell of your visible surroundings, just as you could never escape the tormenting presence of those countless million faces that hemmed you in on all sides, so likewise you will not be able to escape the revelation of your own existence. Your name will be inscribed on the wooden panels: BESSON. Your date will be set down at the foot of a memorandum: 22nd March 1963. Your life, your shrivelled-up existence, the life of a fusty, parchment-yellow creature now, plunging down the final slope of oblivion, will be known and recorded in detail. Your end will take on a cataclysmic magnitude; you will be devoured alive by your own powers, your energies will spend themselves on your own destruction. You are BESSON. You are alive. One day you will be a mere bundle of bones, dead meat, the pale gelatinous substance of a coffin-worm. One day you will lie on your back, as though on the beach, and become aware that the earth no longer supports your weight, that it's opening slowly under the pressure of your body, deeper, deeper, till it becomes the cushion of foul air contained within a sepulchre. Thicknesses of black marble still stand between you and that day, but each passing second gnaws a little more from your protective ramparts. Now, till the hours of sunshine and clarity return, the rain still falls, the gentle drifting rain, all-imbibing, falling noiselessly on my face in the street, a few yards from the intersection, moistening my eyes, leaving my shirt heavy and sodden. It is just such peace and harmony that produce yet another hell: calm and tranquillity become remorse, grinding me down into powder. Water trickles through the excavations, and I know this water is bearing me away with it, bit by bit, is stripping me of my secrets.

Behind the rampart of mist and ruin, I know, paradise lies concealed. But this paradise is one that needs must remain lost to us, since no road to its attainment exists. Such are harmony and beauty. Everything was swift, logical, well-defined. This was the time of that mystery that I bore within myself all unawares, and which bound all things together one with another. It was neither faith nor passion, but a delicate subtle joy, the perfect virtue of a shadow hermetically sealed in a box, cohesion in thought and deed, a reunited family about to sit down to table. And all this was irremediably destroyed by the acuteness of a pair of eyes, the agony of two retinas, the exacerbated functioning of nerves and cells.

The landscape, the scenery, has passed beyond whiteness now to a dazzling radiance. Lines have become razor-edged, colours stick like glue. Each sound is magnified into a vast uproar, and silk-smooth coverlets suddenly harden, become great rough-surfaced blocks against which—as though after falling twelve storeys or so—the flesh smashes with squelching impact.

Language has resumed its crazy ballet: words pass, join up, divide, streaking across the night like so many fireworks, without rhyme or reason, an endless, repetitive sequence, always tracing the same image. The mind of this man is exactly like a long sentence: you think, every moment, that you're about to reach the end of it, yet you're confronted by one extension after another, interminably, all linked up by connecting particles, prepositions, adverbs or whatever, while the movement and articulation of the sentence as a whole gets progressively faster and faster. There is an invisible hand engraving it on some imaginary wall, word by word, phrase by phrase, drawing it out with clause after modifying clause, each letter adding a fresh nuance to the whole, each syllable imperceptibly altering the overall tone, just as one can spoil a room's colour-scheme by the slightest rearrangement of its contents—masking the orange-tinted surfaces, grouping a lot of shiny reds and blues in the corners, cluttering up the line of the skirting-boards with baroque pieces that are all glittering reflection and dark shadow—and so the sentence continues, swells to colossal dimensions, until it reaches that precise point—a tenth of a second will turn the scale—where the mind is no longer capable of grasping its meaning, whereupon the whole ill-balanced structure explodes into a thousand pieces, plunges down the void, tumbles into madness and night, the fierce, echoing vortex of the abyss.

Yet this Besson, Besson I as it were, is still alive behind all his sufferings. Once in the past he was alone, caught in the ant-heap, shoved and jostled by the surging crowds. In the evening, he used to walk up and down the street near the gates of a factory, or outside cinemas, unknown and unnoticed, hands thrust into the pockets of his Bedford cord trousers, wearing an old out-at-elbow jacket. Neon signs flooded him with their dull yet intense glare; raindrops, descending magnificently from the furthest reaches of a black and hole-like sky, beat down on his head and hands and the glass of his wrist-watch, spotting the toe-caps of his suede shoes, zig-zagging invisibly before his eyes. He was well and truly planted, yes indeed he was, in the centre of this town, he really belonged to this century, this year, day, and hour, recoverable in perpetuity; a Lartigue, a Benoît, a Schultz, a Rivière. Cars swept silently past him as he walked the pavements. A bus, every light ablaze, stood waiting by its metal stop-sign, shuddering in triple-time rhythm, *rak-a-dak, dak, dak, rak-a-dak, dak, dak*. A man in ragged brown clothing lurched along past the shop-windows. Dim figures were making love unconcernedly in doorways. And there were voices that kept calling out, hoarse voices, and these hoarse, human voices mingled with one another, perhaps they rose out of the ground, something else to add to the smells of tar and petrol, and the voices rose and the stink of sulphur grew and spread, in a general atmosphere of power and intoxication and chaos, suggesting confusion and death indeed, but also hinting at resurrection: 'Now then, now then! . . . Sorry . . . Henri's going to . . . You just look out or I'll wring your bloody neck . . . What did I tell you [*slash*] . . . Bit of friction there. . . .'

Most of the men are wearing glasses. Their features look quite monstrous, distended by sudden appetites which only puff out their lips and cheeks. The way they walk is sheer torture, each movement harsh and abrupt. In the half-light one can see the swarm to which they belong grouping itself in accordance with some unknown structure: to the left, to the left, left yet again, one more to the left. Right. Left. Right; right; right. Right; left; right. Sounds stab the atmosphere like buzzing flies; then, caught between those pitiless jaws, they imprint themselves on the surface of vapours and clouds, incised reminders of the objects they have left behind. On the roofs of houses we find outlined, in reverse, the confused mythological figures that watch over men's lives: the dangerous bestiary, those maleficent points in space that one links together almost without intending it, greedy suckers, sharpened claws, vertebrae eaten away with tetanus, teeth hollowed out by necrobioses, chapped and wrinkled lips, blood dripping from the secret folds of the belly, and eyes, eyes, eyes— huge, glowing, full of fragmentated gallows-imagery, eyes with seized-up muscles, eyes with glaucous humours, eyes with constantly weeping tear ducts, a flood, a rain, water streaming over the flat roofs of the apartment buildings, water striping the air, a grim and deadly liquid that in all likelihood, one day soon, will disintegrate the unique existence of mankind, and leave them sinking in the mud, half dressed and half asleep still, like so many iron crosses, still protesting their eternal fidelity to that hellish oath—ignoble mindlessness, after the deluge, abomination and suffering, suffering, *fear*.

Silence is creeping over the town, and the street-lamps are humming again. It is nearly dark now. Here, on the smooth level surface of this concrete bridge, is this person, this individual, turning hesitantly, like a metal top dropped spinning into an ashtray. The rotations of his body are accelerating *ad infinitum*, his fury is caught and held in a series of metallic reflections, vibrates on his spinning centre, drills through glass, mingles with the blurred strata of the air. A tiny breeze blows over the ground, scattering the dust before it can come to rest. This is the song— hard and chill as a blade-edge—that has taken root here. Its words are barely audible, they are mere inarticulate sounds, the words make and unmake themselves in vertiginous sequence, in impotence and hatred. Bright flashes of light, exploding at irregular intervals, black lightning, powdery branches.

I no longer believe in god
I no longer believe in god
I no longer believe in god
I no longer believe in god

A giant hand presses down on Besson, bending him double, forcing him to embrace the earth. Slowly he crawls beneath it. The top still revolves on its glass plate. All round him—it—the indispensable crowd of people wearing glasses. The sound of footsteps approaches, dwindles, returns. No more portraits. What is this enormous Café that's suddenly sprung up on the right? No more books. The sum and totality of every flash of light is there, a blurred spectrum in which every element has to be absorbed simultaneously, blood-red, blue, ultramarine, black, white, the pure and terrible whiteness of snow. A workman with a negroid face trudges through the streets carrying a beam on his shoulder. It jogs as he moves. Suddenly the windows are counted, just like that—854, there are 854 of them. Tiny flames rise trembling from match-heads. Look, the world is breaking up. *Look, I am going to die.* That's the alarm going off. Or clockwork toys, that some hidden hand wound up while I slept, underneath my worn and rumpled pillow. In the scars left by biting teeth, in yellow patches of mucus. Besson turns on himself, without turning.

Today,

he alone remains; his features have shrunk all round, symmetrically, his cheeks have sunk below the inner angle of the eye. His drowned hair lies at rest now, rain and air rest sprawling over him. He has given up. Two things have happened. The barrier of his will no longer exists. He wanted dissolution, and now this dissolution is coming about without him. Houses collapse in the roadway with the most grotesque sound—the noise you hear in a hollow rock cavern when the tide, surging forward with that to-and-fro motion, pours through for a moment, swells, rises, is cut hollow rock cavern when the tide, surging forward with that to-off, fills with internal eddies, becomes rock, then—in another brief moment—streams back out of the dark abyss, hard, glassy, utterly different now, sucked out by the ebbing current, flowing down below the surface in foam-streaked tumult, leaving trails of bubbles behind.

As though a moon had suddenly appeared, a parasitical heavenly body within the vault of the firmament, as though another planet were in existence, rounded, spherical, a pale refulgent globe, charged with the magnetic powers of iron, of the mineral world frost reflecting naked sunlight, the motion of the sea has communicated itself to the world ashore. In the part of the town immediately around Besson, say a square mile or so, the tide ebbs and flows continually; magnetic fusion has thrown gravity askew. The mass, the volume of objects becomes elongated, things possess skin-like surfaces. Ramparts erect themselves, stratifications appear. One layer, then another. Men merge and mingle, the undertow sucks them in, spews them out, sucks them in once more. The misty air is alive with waving hands and a thrash of limbs. The sounds of voices meet, cross, low-level sound-waves interweaving. They leave a warm yet impalpable ball in the hollow of the ear, a liquid globule quivering a hair's breadth from the tympanum. The head grows heavier moment by moment, balanced painfully on its supporting neck, the cervical vertebrae cracking in protest, preparing, no doubt, for the moment of final crushing annihilation, the tiny spark-cluster of the death-agony. Into this head the square mile of the town now passes—not direct, but obliquely, as though by way of a mirror. Pat on its cue the void moves into action, drilling its bottomless well through the brain. The gulf that was his skull and the gulf opening beneath his feet are isolated from each other, cut off. Little by little objects leave the earth and enter his body, one after the other, with cries of pain, mute vibration of vocal cords. Like a fish with dilated gills, he embarks on this process of deglutition, swallowing, devouring. Houses pass into him, slowly, like huge mouthfuls of stale bread. Railroad tracks twist up their hideous rails into his mouth, two by two, roads hump themselves towards him. Then come waves of colour, special colours. Orange orange. Violet. Grey. Green green green green. Grey. Pink. Pink. Black. Pink. Emerald emerald. Black black black black black black black. Yellowish. Locomotives, boiling hot engines sweating oil drop by drop. Blocks of ferro-concrete, still humming with sound, lift-shafts with closed lifts going up in them. Grey, grey, grey. Black pink green blue black white WHITE. Floors of rooms covered with a thin film of dust. Cigarettes, lit or stubbed out. The sound of a peal of bells, a drunk cursing, the flatulent bumbling of a television station. These vast sloping roofs, where birds cluster to watch the sun go down. The East Side pylon with a few insulators missing. Electrocution. Danger, no entry, high voltage, death. A small hut into which one could slip without a qualm, teetering as though half-anaesthetized, both hands turning cold already, already encased in a strange blackish skin, feeling their way towards that complex centre where thousands of blue-steel wires hum on their red bobbins; then a soft, furtive scraping sound, and the blinding shock, like a door being flung open to let in pure fresh air.

Then a sudden flood of men sweeps him from his vertical position, a maelstrom that seems as though it was never born, and can never die, from everlasting to everlasting: a stream of black ants, gently bearing away the empty husk of a huge grasshopper.

Not at another time, for there was only the one time, day and night mingled together, vast and indifferent: with rain still falling from the sky and cascading down the steps of the town, the noise and the terror reached their climax. Letters and words began to play general post; thoughts, as replaceable elements, underwent various permutations. The messages no longer reached anyone. Strange passwords made a road for themselves through the tumult, cries to which no individual could have laid claim: CHRIST, SALUT, OLLA, LE GA. Letters were dispatched in white enevlopes with the flaps stuck down. In the top right-hand corner of each was a stamp carrying within its serrated edges some little picture—a woman's head, a cook, or a landscape drawn in fine minuscule outline. Wherever you looked there were millions of written messages; their power still survived when they lay abandoned in garbage-cans or at the bottom of drawers, exposed to every insult. Pages of unknown bibles retracing people's private, insignificant histories:

My dear Jean:
  Thanks for your letter. I've fixed up the insurance and all that jazz, though because of the fine they made me cough up an extra £4.10.0d. The worst thing of the lot is that I lent the motor-bike to John James, who took off with Anna on the pillion. All of which means that we're still not in the clear; this infernal bike is beginning to cost me a pretty penny.
  I've paid £20 for it—hope that's the price you had in mind. I've handed the money over to Libby, and you ought to get it fairly soon.
  France and Eric agreed to take the guitar back to Paris for me—I expect you'll know who they are? Anyway they've left it with some friends of theirs, and Libby's given your brother the address, so I suppose he'll have picked it up by now.
  See you one of these days.
  Yours ever,
              Nick.

'You are young, you want to study, and have fun, and live.
BUT

Do you realize that every year the world spends 60 billion
francs (old currency) on weapons of destruction?

Do you realize that 100 million men and 70 per cent of the
world's scientists are employed on war production?

Do you realize that 60 tons of T.N.T. per human being
could at any time reduce the entire globe to a cinder?

Do you realize, lastly, that if nuclear war broke out it
would kill 300 million people in a matter of minutes?

THREE HUNDRED MILLION CORPSES: THAT IS YOUR FUTURE
But it is not inevitable. You can and must exorcize this
bogey. Of course you are against war. But that is not enough:
you must SAY SO. You think it's pointless, that it's none of
your business—
YOU'RE WRONG, IT IS NOT POINTLESS, AND IT IS VERY MUCH
YOUR BUSINESS
BECAUSE YOU HAVE THE RIGHT TO LIVE
If you are on your own, no one will hear you. BUT YOU ARE
NOT ON YOUR OWN.'
'Jessie James: Hopeless Blues'

There are other words, more secret and terrible still. What hand
—adult's or teen-ager's—carved them with a penknife in the
wood of the table? They're nothing much in themselves, it's true,
and ever since the moment when hand and knife came together in
this Café, they have been overlaid by a constant stream of bottles,
glasses, cups, other hands, other words; an endless battering
assault, a silent act of restraint made endemic by events, a paralyser
of time, skewering the hours like a long steel engraver's point.
And yet they continue to proclaim, for all time, this message of
happiness and torment; they still eternally relate, in time's unmoving sphere, that exodus of God's people through war-torn
lands and the swamps of good fortune.

Drum
Molotov

Lollypop
Shrimp
Elite
Key
Foot
Sékou Touré
Passion Flowers
Bourbon
Honey-bee

In this rough sketch, so sharply outlined that it is as though one saw it from a third-floor window, the distant houses repeat their pattern of solid cubes, and a layer of pink gently spreads over the walls, frittering out towards the roof-tops like a shock of hair. At the centre of the sky are deployed all these signs and traces of superhuman life: each knot, each concentric circle to be found below is traced on its wide and ashen surface. The black broken lines and anthracite gleam of cars' bodywork flicker aloft there, with an imperceptible and tireless motion. From the human city there goes up a multitude of voices, a hubbub of activity, and this monotonous clamour reconstitutes itself among the clouds. Twentieth-century awareness. And speed overtakes innumerable objects, projects itself in a near-scientific illusion, as here with slate tiles, for instance, or the flesh of women and children, or some dark-coloured metal of unknown composition. The eye must penetrate to the very heart of matter, cutting a path with agony and fever and palpitations of the heart—through millions of molecules. Deeper still then, at the core of cloud and vapour, the eye must become number, must pierce further, while molecules separate and matter divides, till it reaches the unchartable point of mathematical bewilderment, that point x of anguish and despair where all physical matter ends and nothing remains beyond it but the empty void.

The landscape has suddenly become, at one and the same time, so vast and yet so restricted: a cone, a genuine cone, its apex non-existent, its base always stretching further than one can see.

Cohesion has not totally vanished: some element of being still remains, a vague blurred light, as still as a letter of the alphabet, amid this vast void which is illuminated by its presence. And yet an order has been broken: some process of acceleration, some electrical charge, perhaps—who knows?—has split the atoms apart at a point near the surface, breaking away small masses of energy which are liable to shoot off on a dangerous course of their own. Gamma rays. But this process of dissociation is not unlimited as far as the eye *qua* number can see, objective existence still survives, its presence theoretical but certain, like that of a nebula. Sources of energy have their own appointed place: behold them now, like stars, gleaming alone in the night's immensity. They are words, they are symbols, they stand inscribed in the turn of a formula on the blackboard, and from them spring truth and abundance. Each fragment of granite mingled with tar that makes up the pavement, every gleaming piece of enamel, each square yard of the sea's surface, each plane-tree, every patch of living skin—all have been destroyed utterly, yet still remain alive. The world has an infinite capacity for breaking down and rebuilding its elements: everything is subsumed in that apotheosis of letters and numbers, Xi Zero–Anti Xi Zero. And then, by way of counter-current, and springing from the hard central core of this certainty, there rises a kind of damnable hope, a kind of hope like the onset of a cyclone. The will projected by these centuries of energy. Little by little tables and chairs assume solid form, gradually harden into existence beneath these blind fingers, arrange themselves architecturally within the four walls of a room. Corpuscles agglomerate, wooden feet thrust out, colours vibrate like sounds. Red, red. Black, red. Ochre, red. White, white, red, Red, black, red. Cohesion begins again, the slack assembly of nails and dadoes. The floor shakes back into its pattern of squared lines and purplish tiles. Dust lays its film over the cracks again, time puts on its make-up. A second. Dust. A second. Dust. A second. Dust A second. Dust. Everywhere homes become ready, one after the other, solid and durable; everywhere, without one realizing it, flesh quivers into life, veins distend as the rhythmic flow passes through them. Here is a woman. Here is a man. There is a child. A dog. A winged ant. Here is another woman. In one corner of the kitchen, near the cubic yard or so of air impregnated by the odours from two overflowing garbage-cans, a cockroach rustles as it moves under the sole of a slipper. Against a wall down near the beach a tree (impossible to describe it) stands stifling in its own washed-out halo. Rain trickles over its outspread branches a deep drain eats it away at root-level.

So everything is ready: ready for the journey to Purgatory, the journey to the land of black and white. The whole town glows ruddily with matter, with solid substances. In twenty seconds, perhaps even sooner, the crisis may return, and the whole process begin all over again. Things will pass into themselves, like devouring serpents that greedily consume their own bodies. Life will plan itself unaided, and at random, on the first coarse and yellowing sheet of paper that comes to hand. The plan will grow and grow, bursting and pullulating with details, like a kind of lengthy narrative, its handwritten words gradually nibbling away what free space remains. The point of the ballpoint pen moves forward, on and on, very fast and in a small neat hand, tracing a wriggling, broken blue line, from left to right, next line down, left to right, next line down, and so on. When the whole surface of the paper is covered with this scribbling, the tip of the ballpoint still goes on searching. It finds blank spaces between the lines or down the margins. It fills them all. The words on the page now run in every direction. But the ballpoint still goes on searching inde-fatigably. It overscores what it has previously written, it crams every cranny, first making fine scratches like tufts of hair, then a whole fuzzy topknot, and finally a large sooty cloud. There are still words, more and more of them, interminable adverbs; the crosses on the t's trace a kind of straight line from one side of the paper to the other. Too much overwriting has produced the occasional hole. About six inches from the top there is an acciden-tal and quite unbearable row of looping o's. But the words keep flowing back, and suddenly, after using up several thousandths of an ounce of dark blue ink, after hours on the job, after working through three ballpoint pens, as though a million spiders had wandered over the page, at nightfall only one empty space remains— a tiny star-shaped patch at the bottom left-hand corner, preserved by the slapdash loop of an l, in some word now otherwise obliterated—'Iliad', maybe, or 'calamity', or 'Lilliputian'. Then the hand grips the ballpoint pen, all slippery with sweat now, and closes the loop of the l. During the accomplishment of this act, in silence and fear, something akin to darkness, a sense of solemn peace, like the deepest night, spreads over the paper. The last remaining area of imperfection seems to disappear; and nothing is left now, beneath that bent forehead, before those weary, burning eyes, except this vast page of writing, in which all the words and letters have melted into one another, the perfect work of not-being, a beautiful poem, monochrome and illegible.

*

Looking out of the window, or down in the stair-well, head squeezed between the banisters, or lost among the mirrors of a cinema foyer, or—more simply—just stubbed out at the bottom of a jam-pot doing duty as an ashtray. Tobacco coming out of the body, thrusting through the skin, sticking to the glass sides of the jar. Head still burning, a mass of close-packed embers, but guttering down to extinction, giving off carbonic gas. Occasional tiny explosions from glowing fragments of wood, and that sickening smell given off by the dead cinders, rising gradually towards the ceiling, the acrid stink of cooling ash. On every part of the street, on every house, over the whole town, Besson descends and settles: like a fly circling round some imaginary lamp, moving in a random course across level or uneven surfaces, leaving its trail of excrement and microbes behind it.

These white houses, that square you can see, these still, tranquil streets are the areas in which he deposits his eggs. This neighbourhood is his domain: here he hunts, sleeps, lives, and perhaps reproduces in season. In front and on all sides of him cars speed to and fro, passing, repassing. The continual snarl of their engines forms a harsh, metallic song: the rhythmic pulsing of valves and pistons, vibrating bodywork, the silent whirr of the fan, and so on and so on, all that blurred mass of minuscule sounds, endlessly affirming the existence, as a construct, of the internal combustion engine, in all its beauty, power, novelty, warmth and regularity. A view from a telegraph pole. Or even, if you prefer it, arched over the road like a bridge, body curving slightly, set on pillar-firm limbs, back supporting the passage of all those swarming creatures known collectively as 'mankind'. This sudden joy that comes over you, this manic passion for bright metals and translucent inflammable liquids, the sense of roundedness, the smooth enamelled skin you've acquired, which turns you into an *object*, and the delight, the indescribable sense of optimism that hits you, yes, *there*, between the radiator cap and the rubber lining of the windshield, the joy of being made out of sheet-metal, thirty-six B.H.P. with direct injection, and kindling, down under those steel cylinder-heads, the explosive spark that irradiates out on combustion like the spokes of a wheel. Opel Olympia. Ford V.8. Man-into-car enclosed within this room with its four unyielding walls. The insect is flying round the table. It came down from the ceiling during the night, Through the open window drift the sounds of falling rain. The insect is a gnat, a square millimetre of black body and wings, its flight sustained by some invisible plane surface, as though the horizon that suddenly tilted its plexiglass sheet and left no sign of any living presence on it save this one solitary creature. Inside the room atmospheric waves eddy and multiply. Bodies of gas move from one corner to the other, knocking against the bed, the skirting-boards, the door, the two open windows. This undulatory movement intensifies, becomes more precise. The gnat, crushed between two layers of oxygen, lies there on the table, asphyxiated, delicate legs just quivering their last, one wing half torn off and adhering to the creamy matter discharged from its abdomen. But the air in the room has suddenly changed to water, and the to-and-fro movement passes through this new body, braiding its texture, tying slip-knots into it. In the aquarium objects smoke through the water, sometimes leaving a trail of bubbles behind them. Strange noises, rumblings as of an

294

earthquake, the motive force behind heavy vehicles, now make themselves heard: the S.P.A.D.A. trucks, enabled thus to pass through the walls of the room, arrive loaded with transistor radios, barrels of olive oil, refrigerators. The oscillatory motion of this matter steadily increases, reaches a high peak of intensity, a regular rhythm which nothing can disrupt. With effort certain obstacles at the back of the mind are removed—things such as human flesh, the breasts and bellies and buttocks of women, perhaps even a face, the face of a young goddess, with fine features and a Byzantine profile; deep sad eyes, set at a curious and touching angle to the line of the nose; the expression of a statue, all statues, eyes looking gently upward from the inclined head, revealing a sclerotic pattern of unhappiness and yearning regret, endlessly repeated; a tiny mouth, set in a firm line above the chin, and that lone pale, almost translucent body, draped in blue material. Near her, a man lying on a divan stretches out one hand in token of command, and calls, like Orsino Duke of Illyria, for music.

But nothing here is real: these eyes and hands have no existence, the guitar, the mist-shrouded landscape, all are illusory. The oscillatory motion reaches down to the deeper points at the back of the mind, dredges up young untroubled voices, afternoons spent leafing through the dictionary, sitting in the pleasant slate-grey common-room, with its leather armchairs and cake at tea-time and bells ringing the Angelus. Noises dwindle away, giving place to a kind of magical silence: soundlessness such as exists under a glass bell, or in telephone booths that let through nothing, almost, except the vibrations immediately beneath them, a hair-fine thread floating on the air that alone serves to remind us of that other world outside. Then, after a little more time, a little more suffering, one finds oneself enclosed by four walls, a floor, a ceiling; a closed door, two open windows. Continual restriction. Hollow, hollow. Equilateral.

For the last time during this immense day-and-night there appears that supreme synthesis, that stunning of the senses, that conscious abrogation of mind which is known as hatred.

Besson stands outside the building now, hidden in the shadow of the arcade, eyes devouring the whole sweep of the scene before him. Hands thrust in his pockets, right shoulder resting against a pillar, he feels an inexplicable stiffness spreading through him, centred somewhere in the back of his neck, but makes no resistance to it. The sun is rising, or setting: it makes no difference which. Buses come and go, brake to a jerky halt along the kerbside. From time to time a green wall of metal interposes itself between those staring eyes and the middle distance, and sits there, shuddering in time with its engine. There is a smell of exhaust gases everywhere; nothing can disperse them, not even the upward-moving air-current that rises skyward with the force of a plane on vertical take-off.

Millions of tiny holes in the tarred macadam, all made by women's stiletto heels.

In a trash-can attached to the bus-stop sign lies a half-eaten tangerine, exuding acidity. Memories of plums brush lightly across the cornea of the eye, with just enough friction to start a tear, a fleeting pain much like grazing one's skin against the rough surface of a wall, the small pleasures afforded by something utterly insignificant, the sharp impact of a cigarette-butt lying on an ashtray's edge, smoke curling up from it—everything is there, really everything, nothing has been forgotten. The whole pattern comes together at this moment before his eyes, there between the two pillars, presenting a panoramic spectacle from which not a single element is missing.

The picture is complete now. If there are still a few movements down in its bottom left-hand corner, they are caused by nothing more than streaks of colour gliding along their set tracks, masses of black metal (or grey, or green), the shadows of human figures walking. It is as if a sudden breeze had got up, blowing away their mists; as though the latent power inherent in matter, cube upon cube of electric energy, had slowly invaded the air and all open spaces. At an angle of 24°, behind the public lavatory, stand the stark trees and the wrought-iron palisade dominating the harbour. Cast metal, wherever you look you see cast metal. The landscape is naked in the half-light. The street-lamps have just been lit—or are about to be turned off. You can see this by the glow of that neon-blue star that flashes on at each cardinal point of the compass: NORTH, flash, WEST, flash, SOUTH, flash, EAST, flash. Each object is lightning-struck in turn: the surface of the street, first, where all noises sound like the screech of brakes. Is it a fierce heat, come from God knows where, a kind of sun blazing out through the windows? Or is it a Polar freeze-up, with blue iceberg reflections, a pale and whirling whiteness, misty, vapour-shrouded? Perhaps it could even be a mixture of the two, the weird result of setting a fiery furnace at the very heart of the ice? Two extremes in conflict, penetrating each other's defences, in a tearing orgy of mutual annihilation. As though a giant hand, a hand without any body attached to it, not a god's, rather the crude fist of a worker, its joints all muscle-bound, as though this human hand had seized both of them, ice and fire, and crushed them together in its palm, while away on the periphery of things, beyond reach of the hand, the two bodies thrashed and reared amid drifting clouds of steam and vapour.

Then each vortex returns to its own sanctuary at the earth's centre, close to the liquid core of the planet. But where the hand holds them fast, there remains two colourless, shrunken cords, hardened by intense agony into spirals of twisted glass.

Phenomena are now transformed into states of being. The void has struck at the very heart of this big square between the surrounding apartment blocks, bringing all movement to a halt: the man who was running towards the steps of the church, that other one getting off the bus, the helicopter passing over the river, the child playing hopscotch in the arcade, the hundreds of flies blazing invisible trails everywhere, between the wheels of that coach, or towards this garbage-pail, or in the vicinity of that sixty-five-year-old woman. The movement of an American car, an Oldsmobile by the look of it, has been brought to a halt in this square by the mere existence of four or five reflections glinting on its beige bodywork. There is no more movement now, no more action. Even the normal swarming dazzle in the sky—that misty agglomeration of countless million tiny points, black, grey, white, blue, red or green, which formerly kept up a ceaseless dance, soaring upward heavenwards or sinking slowly back towards the ground—has entirely ceased to function.

The sky is as spacious as ever, but with that stipple of black dots gone dead, nothing remains but a half-tone screen photograph, newspaper style, blown up to enormous dimensions, and embracing the entire visible landscape. The still points coagulate, become a more intense black, increase in number—and there is a pigeon. They space themselves out, become almost imperceptible —and there is the sunlight reflected on a young girl's face. Eyes become dark hollows, noses are accentuated, mouths tend to be optional. This fierce and incessant rain of dots leaves both people and inanimate objects looking calm but cheerless, as the colour drains slowly out of them. The process is a very simple one, and one gets the impression that as these impalpable surface layers peel away, angles become sharper and cleaner, the framework stands out, ridges are stripped bare to the bone. The plane-tree has been drastically reduced to a mere black skeleton of its former self. The modern apartment block has crumbled away and is now floating up in the blue empyraean like a cloud. Men's faces have been replaced by a strange inhuman mask, dead white, hollow, with great empty eye-sockets and a bird-like beak. In an old worm-eaten foreign tome, dated 1683, and entitled *The Visions of Dom Francisco de Quevedo Villegas, Knight of the Order of St James*, the following passage is to be found:

Howsoever ye others know not what Death may be: it is ye yourselves who are your own proper Death: Death beareth the features of each several one of you, be ye never so mighty, ye are your own deaths. Your skull is Death; and your features are Death; that which ye term dying is the conclusion of life, and that which ye term birth is the beginning of death: in like fashion, that which ye term living is but dying in the midst of life: and bones are but what death leaves of your kind, and what remaineth behind in the sepulture. If ye were well apprised of this, then each would have a mirror of

Death within himself all the days of his life; and then would ye see divers truths, as that all your houses are full of dead men, that there are as many dead persons as living, that though ye hear not Death, natheless ye walk beside him all the days of your life. Think ye that Death is but bones, and a carcase, and that Death cometh not unto your person ere ye behold a Skeleton that holdeth a Scythe? Thus do ye deceive yourselves in heinous wise, for ye shall be bones, carcase and skeleton sooner than ye may conceive.

And further off, away beyond the square where everything has come to a stop, the whole town lies spread out between the sea and the mountains, quite motionless, like a great sombre pool. This battered skin, with so many countless wrinkled contours, this purple-tinged coverlet of fine interwoven thread, is in fact the town's upper surface; and blackness has flowed into every hollow of it, silently, as though filling a mould. Here is the photographic representation of death; and above and below it the tragic twilight raises a long and voiceless chant, unfurling its purple ribbons across the horizon, whole spools of purple ribbon, bright crimson streamers, bloodstained dressings, shot-torn tattered ensigns, lightning by the barrelful, lurid orange storm-clouds, bombs bursting to reveal vermilion craters, the whole majestic airy procession that forms a refuge for the last outpourings of passion, torture and war. There: now all is poised in ardent stillness.

As the sun retreats, or the street-lamps are extinguished, the world grows steadily darker, with inceasing calmness and serenity to match the broad swathes of crepuscular twilight now drawn across it. The sea's glinting surface has burnt out. Ships lying at anchor send up columns of black smoke to mingle with these violent reds and golds. Here too colours have become so elongated, so extended, that they might as well not be colours at all: it would make no odds if they were transposed into smells, or phrases of music. The humble, hackneyed odour of a *brioche*, lard and butter mingled, all interwoven from an off-yellow colour and the taste of vanilla, insipid, too insipid, then, suddenly piercing it, the tart flavour, pencil-sharp, of one dried raisin.

Or look at this man, riven by the white lightning-flash that struck down on the tree. The rescue party makes its way back down the mountainside in the rain, gently bearing the blackened body on the stretcher, taking it back to the widow, who will lose her wits. Rising through light like the length of a drawn sword, passing joyfully into that agonizing effulgence, he vanishes from sight as the boiling, turbulent mass closes over him; moves on with it now, up, up, to the topmost peaks of the world, plunged naked into the volcano's maw, carried up to that field of black azure that lies beyond all human values. Made light. Purified.

Or else, again, the dull thunder and murmurous confusion rising far out in some kind of sea, those glaucous, malleable rhythms—and then, hundreds of yards, perhaps miles away, so far off that it seems to lag behind the rest, the sound of a warning siren, the reverberations of war: like a cat miaowing, exactly the same as a cat miaowing, all alone on a vast and dreary expanse of tin roof.